The Kiss & Tell Tr

DESIRE
DRENCHED
DAYS

Kitty N. Pawell

Desire Drenched Days
The Kiss & Tell Trilogy: Book Two
Kitty N. Pawell

Kitty's Creative Emporium

Blurb

You're always warned to never fall for the playboy, but not once was I warned against the playgirl.

I lived a no-risk lifestyle. That was until I met Rose Thorne. The woman who literally wants for nothing, who has men and women hanging off of her every word, and whose kiss could melt an iceberg. I've tried not to, but I've fallen — hard. If I'm being honest I never stood a chance. She's the full package: intelligent, strong-willed, beautiful, caring, generous, fierce, and gentle.

Yet even with all that perfection, there are still two issues. Issue one: Rose has been abundantly clear about where she stands when it comes to relationships, and even with that information I still can't help but hope something about me will change her mind. Issue two: She's hiding something, and I have this strong urge to know what it is. I should mind my business and drop it, but I just can't seem to help myself. I don't care what I have to do. One way or another, I will convince her to tell me. Then, I'll focus on getting her to fall for me, too.

Wish me luck!

Dedication

For those who just want to be fucked in the best way possible.
For those who just want to scream until they're hoarse.
For those who just want to make a fucking mess.
I see you lil' brat. Be good and cum for me.

Trigger Warnings

This book contains content that may be triggering for some readers, including physical violence, explicit language, and sexual content.

Desire Drenched Days mentions but does not depict memories of prior sexual assault, child abuse, and hit for hire. Does depict murder.

Tropes include "Why Choose," strong FMC, Domme, Switch, bisexuality representation, diverse cast, toys, hand necklaces, open-door spice, Lil' Brat and Good Girl vibes, FFF, FF, and FM; no strings attached, comedic relief, witty banter, BDSM, duel POV, and dark pasts.

Be Good

Dear lil' brat,
    This is the only warning you will receive. Book one was spicy. Book two is spicier. Before you crack her spine, I suggest you prepare your significant other for nighttime fun, charge all your battery-operated friends, or be able to perform one-handed reading!

    This book is not for the faint of heart and will put you in the neediest of moods. So, heed my warning and enjoy the mess you create. I hope your toes curl and your lip grows sore as you repeatedly bite it.

    Did you take a moment to do as I asked? Good girl! Enjoy all that Desire Drenched Days has to offer. May you cum repeatedly and drench your sheets.

Contents

I

Melanie

E ver have someone tell you not to fall for the *playboy* type? Well, what do you do when you fall for the *playgirl*?

Seven days. It had been seven days since *that night*, and Rose was making it damn near impossible not to do just that. Night after night, we cuddled in her bed. Every morning, she woke me up with breakfast and the best sex I'd ever experienced.

Oh my God! How could I not fall for her?

I knew she was doing all of that to keep my mind off of King, and so far, she'd been successful. But she hadn't opened up about the nightmares at all, and she wasn't sleeping, either. Each time I tried to bring them up, she brushed me off with a heated kiss or danced her fingers between my legs. And every single time, I forgot my damn questions.

Honestly, it's not my fault she distracted me so easily. The depths she could reach when she was inside of me were mind-numbing.

OK, thinking about that isn't helping me stay focused on the point at hand: Rose's lack of sleep. Yeah, that's what I was talking about. Let me get back to that.

I didn't necessarily want to go back home, but I thought it would be a good idea. She was never going to get a full night of rest until she was alone, so that meant I needed to leave.

It would've been nice if I could've just stayed in the guestroom, but sleeping in her arms every night had ruined me. I wouldn't have been able to stay in the same house with her and fight the urge to not crawl into bed with her. I just needed to figure out how to tell her.

Who was I kidding, right? She wasn't going to care if I wanted to go home. If anything, she'd probably drive me there. I was only hesitating because deep down, I wanted her to tell me to stay, even though I knew she wouldn't.

That's the other reason I needed to go home. When there was separation between us, I could better control the feelings I have for her. Being so close was starting to blur the lines for me. Plus, there was other shit I needed to deal with.

The police had been in contact every day to go over the next steps of the case against King, but I'd ignored their calls, not really wanting to deal. That had to stop, too. I needed to see this through or I'd never be able to move on from him and his bullshit.

The morning after the incident, Xavier and another man named Elijah came over to the house.

They were kind enough to ask me if I was okay, but it was obvious they were more concerned about Rose. That didn't bother me in the slightest. If the roles were reversed, I would've been more worried about her than me too.

"I know you're a badass, Red, but did you really have to take on a lunatic by yourself?" Xavier asked seconds after Rose opened the door.

"Zey, don't start with me, 'ight. I was fine then, and I'm fine now. Stop worrying. By the way, what the fuck are you even doing here?"

"We were in a meeting when you called, Thorne. What was I supposed to say when you asked for legal advice? I couldn't very well just abruptly leave without explaining where I was going," Elijah responded, rolling his eyes.

"Oh, what type of business were you two discussing?"

"Don't change the subject, Red. What happened? Full details. *Now.*"

Xavier had a look in his eyes that clearly conveyed *no more games*, but true to her nature, Rose joked around a bit more before giving them the rundown. Elijah advised me to stop ignoring the cops because that was the same as not pressing charges, and there was no way King was going to get away with this.

He said the more I cooperated with the cops, the better the chances were of King going away. I agreed to call the detective back the next morning, and that satisfied him. After they both annoyed Rose with their worrying, they finally left. I called the next day like I'd promised, and the detective requested I come in to complete my statement.

Elijah and Rose went with me, which I was grateful for because I really didn't want to do it alone. The detective asked me several of the same questions I'd been asked the night of the incident as if

3

my answers might've changed. Elijah said it was standard practice, so I shouldn't be put off by having to repeat myself. The detective said there should be enough for a quick trial. I didn't really like the idea of a trial, but that was the procedure, I guess.

Alright, enough about that loser. Back to figuring out how to tell Rose I was going home.

I was probably thinking way too hard about this and just needed to rip the *Band-Aid* off and tell her. Climbing out of bed, I went to look for her. There were only so many places she could be. I guessed she might be in her library, which is where I found her, reading in her chair.

Even when doing something as simple as relaxing with a book, she stole my breath. A small smile spread across her face, letting me know she'd caught me staring.

"You just gonna stand there, or you gonna come sit down?"

"I didn't want to disturb you."

"Mhm, isn't that the very reason you came and sought me out?"

"Well... I mean, technically, yes."

Rose smiled again before placing her book on the side table. She leaned back and hooked her finger toward herself. Making my way to her, I climbed into her lap. Once I was settled she began to twist a curl of my hair between her fingers.

Moments like these were the ones that made it hard to leave, but as I looked at the dark circles under her eyes, I knew I was making the right decision.

"So, you goin' home today, huh?"

"Ye... Wait, how did you know?"

"I've seen the worry in your eyes. You think leaving will help me sleep better."

I leaned in and touched my lips to hers. "You *will* sleep better when I leave. You can't continue to stay up every night. You're exhausted," I answered before I kissed her again.

"Mhm. I don't think it's my fault that I've been up late every night. *Someone's* been very distracting." Rose picked me up, stood, and placed me in the chair.

"Don't blame me. I repeatedly begged you to go to bed."

Leaning in, she kissed my neck, making me whimper.

"Mmm... I do remember you begging. I even remember you saying *stop*, but if I recall correctly, there was a *don't* in front of it."

"I'm serious, Rose."

"As am I," she responded as she circled my hardened nipple through my shirt.

It was getting more and more difficult to focus on the conversation as she probed. I was about to point that out when she lifted my shirt, baring my lower body to the air.

"I-If you keep doing that, I'll get your chair wet."

Undeterred, Rose pushed my shirt above my breasts and spread my legs, giving her a clear view of everything she wanted.

"Good thing it's easy to clean then, huh? Plus, I like it when you're wet." She dragged her finger along my slit.

A moan flew from my lips as my legs instinctively opened wider, granting her better access.

5

"Look how your body reacts to me, Mel. Your pussy is dripping after one lil' touch."

I couldn't focus on anything other than her breath tickling my seam. She was too close, and my brain couldn't function.

"What do you want, Mel? Want me to stop, or..."

Her tongue darted out, mere inches from my core. Whatever part of me that had been resisting disappeared, slapped out of the way by the unadulterated need for her tongue to be deep inside me.

"Don't stop," I commanded.

"There it is again. Are you sure?"

"Yes. Yes! *Don't* stop..."

Rose pressed her mouth to my slit, making me gasp before she pulled back. My eyelids were heavy, but I still managed to send an annoyed look her way. She wasn't affected one bit as she smiled and licked her lips clean of my juices. As she'd said, I was dripping already, but watching her savor my taste had me drenched.

"You know what I want, Mel."

"Fuck. Please, *please*... Don't stop."

"You know I love it when you beg," she teased before dragging her tongue through my seam.

Lust-filled shivers sailed through my body, and my fingers quickly found themselves twined in her dreads. Grabbing my hips, Rose pulled me to the edge of the chair and put my legs over her shoulders before she ravaged me.

Her name filled the room, but when I felt her fingers enter me, it was quickly replaced by a gasp. She synced her tongue with her finger strokes until I came down her throat. Even as my tremors slowed, she continued tasting me.

Stars danced across my vision. She kept one of her hands inside of me while the other roamed up my body and grasped my nipple.

Rose gave me no time to calm down as she twisted my aching peak and toyed with my clit. My second climax was harder than the first. As soon as I stopped trembling, I pushed Rose down and climbed on top of her.

I licked around the outline of her mouth. My nectar danced over my taste buds. The lust running through my veins was overwhelming, and she was wearing far too much clothing.

"Why attack me when you're fully dressed? It's evil to tease me like that."

"It's not my fault. I didn't plan to fuck you, but you came in wearing nothing but my T-shirt. I couldn't resist."

"I want you in *nothing*," I whispered against her mouth.

"Oh, really?"

"Mhm."

"If you want it, *take it*," she ordered.

The desire her tone made me feel was truly mind-blowing. That was a challenge. No doubt about it. Before Rose, I would've shied away from it, but now I wanted to match her energy every chance I got. My eyes roved over her heaving chest, snagging on her ripped collar.

Grabbing each side, I tore her shirt open, allowing me to view her breasts. They were hidden by a sports bra. I wished I was strong enough to rip it, too, but I wasn't, so I pushed it up to free them instead.

Her nipples hardened as soon as the air caressed them. The sight made my mouth water. Leaning down, I sucked one into my mouth and rolled it between my teeth. Rose moaned softly and trailed her fingers down my spine.

Moving from one breast to the next, I rolled my tongue and nipped her. She bucked her hips and pressed her legs together. I forced my knee between them, making sure she had no reprieve.

"So, it's gonna be like that, huh?" Rose laughed.

"You told me to take it. That means I control your release."

"Does it?"

"Yes," I answered before I undid her jeans.

As I tugged her pants down her hips, I realized she wore nothing underneath, and that was exciting because it meant I could get to what I wanted faster. I ran my fingers through her swollen slit, enjoying the small whimpers she made for me.

I circled my desire-drenched fingers around her nipples before I pushed her breasts together, licking them clean of her nectar. Rose's whimpers grew into cries, urging me on.

"Mmm... This feels good, but is that the best you got, Mel?"

There was that tone again. I wasn't just going to accept her challenge. I was going to crush it.

"Sit up," I instructed.

"What?"

"You heard me."

Rose stared at me for a moment before smirking. As she sat up, I grabbed the pillow from the chair, placed it behind her, and pushed her down onto it. There was curiosity in her eyes, and I wanted to capitalize on it, hoping no one else had done this to her before.

Sitting back on my knees, I pulled her pussy up to my face and slung her legs over my shoulders.

"Woah, woah, woah! What are you do — Ooh!"

Her eyes rolled back as soon as my tongue slid through her slit. Every time I tasted her, a wave of hunger shot through my body, and this was no exception.

"Keep yourself up. With all the strength you have, I'm sure you can manage that."

"Mhm."

"Keep your eyes on me. Watch my tongue as I lap up every drop."

"Oh, fuck."

Once her hands were in place, I slowly dragged my nails down her legs and over her ass. From this angle, I could see her nipples harden as she shivered.

Dragging my tongue up one lip and down the other, I took my time, licking everywhere but where she ached for me to touch. Her lids were heavy, but she kept her eyes focused on me. Her excitement dripped down my chin, and I almost went in for the prize, but I restrained myself. The groans and cries that escaped her lips were far too intoxicating to give in.

"Are you having fun, Mel?"

"Maybe."

"Well, you're driving me crazy."

"I know."

"Lil' brat. What do you want?"

Deviously, I bit my lip. "For you to beg."

"That so?" Rose asked with a roll of her eyes.

Her earlier words floated through my mind. If I wanted her to beg, I'd have to make her do it. Using two fingers to spread her lips, I licked a path from her entrance up toward her clit.

"Fuck! Mel, please... *Please*."

"See! That wasn't so hard," I taunted, then I sucked her clit into my mouth.

Rose shook so hard, I had to place both arms under her back to keep her steady. My name became a chant, repeatedly falling from her lips until she screamed it in her climax. We kept eye contact the entire time, just as I had requested, and she watched me as I lapped up every delicious drop.

II

Rose

Mel was right. I wasn't sleeping enough. The nightmares were always worse during the summer. But it was nothing I hadn't dealt with before. I would be fine. Eventually.

I truly had no intention of fucking her that morning, but I was serious when I said the way she looked in my T-shirt was too good to resist. The more time we spent together, the more she continued to surprise me. That move was something I would have to add to my arsenal.

After she came up for air, we made our way down to the playroom. I strapped up and dicked her down ruthlessly. Watching her cum was quickly becoming one of my favorite things.

The rest of the morning went smoothly. We had a late breakfast before she gathered her stuff. Tsuki and Yuki were distraught when Mel put Kuro in his crate. They both continuously circled it and meowed in their displeasure. They even went so far as to lay in front of the door when we were getting ready to head out. I had to *lovingly* toss them into their room so we could leave. The attachment they displayed after one week was a bit concerning, but if I was being honest, I understood the feeling. However, I was not ready to consider how deep my attachment to Mel was becoming. At least, not yet.

The drive to her place was filled with silence like it had been the night of the incident, but thankfully, this time was different. Less tense.

That night, the silence had been pregnant with fear, disbelief, uncertainty, and rage. This time, there was still trepidation, but there was also a gentle peace mixed in, as if she knew no matter what, King would never do that to her again.

That peace was something I'd make sure she always felt. I couldn't wait until his trial was over and he was locked up for good, being passed around as the new *bitch* of D-block.

"Are you OK?" Mel asked, bringing me back to the present.

I glanced over at her and noticed she was studying my hands on the steering wheel. I loosened my grip and gave her a small smile.

"Yeah, I'm fine. Just got lost in thought for a second there."

"What was going through your head just now that pissed you off?"

"Nothing major. Just thinking. Don't worry about it," I answered as I pulled into the lot and parked.

The silence returned. I leaned back in the seat, looked over at her, and waited. Mel didn't notice. She was too busy staring at the path that led to her condo. I didn't want to rush her, so I opted to go for some gentle encouragement.

"We can go back to my place. This can wait. I like you warming my bed."

Mel smiled and took a deep breath before opening the car door. It was like she'd come to an internal decision. She held her head high and kept her shoulders straight. I wasn't going to get in the way of her determination by talking her into coming home with me.

I couldn't help but think the walk toward her condo was starkly different than when I had been here last. My heart was pounding out of my chest. The *Grubhub* driver had been a complete idiot, and then there was King...

As we approached the corner by Mel's place, I heard her suck her teeth, and that pulled me from my darker thoughts.

"Ugh," Mel groused. "You'd think I'd be ready for the clean-up I need to do, but I'm not. I wish I lived in a world where magic existed, and all I had to do was snap my fingers, then boom! No more mess."

Inside, I smiled, glad I hadn't second-guessed my decision to fix her place up for her while she'd stayed with me.

When we reached the door to her condo, Mel hesitated. "That's weird."

"Hm?"

"Well, I didn't get a call from the HOA about having the door replaced. Now, I need to go to the front office to grab the new keys."

"Ah. We're good. I have the key," I told her as I pulled it out of my pocket and unlocked the door.

"You have the key..." Mel's voice trailed off as we walked in and she took in her condo.

She dropped her bag as her eyes roved over her condo, from the repaired hole in the wall where King had pushed her into it to the fixed bathroom door he'd kicked in. I even made sure to have the furniture and floor cleaned for her.

Setting Kuro down, I unlocked his crate and closed the door behind me. As soon as the door clicked shut, Mel pushed me up against it and kissed me.

"I don't know how you did this," she said between kisses, "but thank you. Thank you so much!"

"You're welcome, love," I replied with a smile. "There was no reason for you to have to deal with more bullshit."

Mel kissed me once more before she left to check on everything. Kuro came out of his crate a few moments later and rubbed himself against my ankles. He yowled until I picked him up and scratched behind his ears.

"You even made sure my plants didn't die!"

"What? Oh, no. I use my thumbs to toggle analog sticks and clits, not dead-heading. I had Shelly water them while you were gone."

Mel laughed and shook her head. "See, you're trying to convince me you don't have a green thumb, but you know what *dead-heading* is."

Kuro jumped out of my arms and made his way up the stairs. Mel stared at me, waiting for an answer.

"Are we playing twenty questions, Mel?"

"Ooo, can we? I have a boatload of questions for you," she said as she made her way to me and wrapped her arms around my waist.

I rolled my eyes. *I walked right into that.* Lifting her chin, I kissed along her jawline. Mel gripped me tighter and whimpered.

"Both my mother and grandmother love their gardens. I help when they need me to. Hence, my knowing the word *dead-heading*, or pruning for the plebs. I will not open the door by saying, *any more questions*, so let's get you unpacked."

Mel grumbled before she stepped back and crossed her arms. "Fine. I concede for now, but I will get my answers from you one day, Ms. Thorne."

"Mhm. Perhaps, one day you will, Ms. Thompson."

Mel smiled, grabbed her bag, and walked into a room near her bathroom. I followed after and hung in the doorway. What I had thought was a laundry room was actually a walk-in closet.

"You know, there's something that's been bothering me about your place."

"Oh?" she asked as she put her clothes away. "What's that?"

"You've got all that space in your loft, but everything, excluding your bed, a nightstand, a wardrobe, and a reading chair is all down here. It just seems like the loft was an afterthought."

Mel came out of the closet and kissed me with a giggle before heading for the steps.

"That's how I got such a great deal on it. All of the condos in this complex were like this at first, then new management came in and turned them into two-floor 'condominiums' with more bathrooms and bedrooms.

"I was already doing a rent-to-own on this place, but there was no way I could've afforded it after the changeover. Thankfully, the old manager was sweet on me, and I was able to keep my same deal. In twelve months, this place will be mine for good."

Mel fell into her bed and smiled up at me before hooking her finger. I climbed into the bed beside her and kissed a path up her chest to her lips.

"I can understand him being sweet on you. I, for one, am extremely enamored," I teased.

"Is that so?"

Here we go again, walking right into questions I know she wants answers to. Rolling onto my side, I wrapped her up in my arms, and grumbled a quick, *Mhm.*

"I'm almost positive you and Shelly got drunk one night and performed an infatuation spell on me. I just haven't found the proof yet," I added.

Mel looked over at me before she burst into laughter. "First off, I don't drink. Second, I would never be *that* bored. And third, I don't need magic to put you under my spell."

"I admit to nothing," I joked as she giggled.

Mel rested her head on my chest and drew circles on my stomach. I mirrored the movement on her lower back as that peaceful silence fell over us once again. I didn't want to bring up bad memories for her, but I felt this question needed to be asked.

"Do you think you'll be OK tonight... Without me?"

Her fingers stilled, and she sighed deeply. Immediately, I wanted to kick my own ass for upsetting her. Mel shifted to look up at me with a beautiful smile curving her lips.

"I'm a big girl. I'll be fine. Plus, I know traffic laws wouldn't stop you if I needed you."

I gave her a small reassuring smile before capturing her lips. She was right. Even if I ended up in a police chase, nothing would stop me from getting to her. I probably needed to dissect that line of thought but not yet.

Right now, Mel had her head on my chest. We were snuggled up, and she was resting. This moment was worth savoring, and it was the only thing I planned to think about.

For now.

III

Melanie

Rose tried to convince me to let her stay the night, but I stood my ground against every one of her salacious tricks. The whole point of coming home, besides getting back to reality, was so she could get some real sleep.

All that would have been for naught if I'd let her stay, even though I really, really wanted her to. Although it was difficult, I resisted. Eventually, I climbed into bed alone and tried to settle down.

It was difficult to fall asleep at first. Every little noise that had never bothered me before set me off, making it sound like someone was inside.

When Kuro jumped on the bed, I nearly punted him by accident. Thankfully, he meowed after he landed, like he was saying, *'It's me, bitch. Don't kick me.'* My nerves were fried, and I spent an hour ping-ponging the idea of calling Rose and asking her to come over.

Just as I made the decision to stop being a baby and go to sleep, my phone rang.

"Have you slept at all?"

"A little... Not really," I answered, settling into my covers. Her voice immediately comforted me.

"You should have let me stay."

"You wouldn't have slept if I did."

"Maybe not, but then we could have been up together instead of apart."

"That's true," I sighed.

On the other end of the line, the blankets rustled, followed by two small meows. Obviously Tsuki, Yuki, and Kuro all had the same plan in mind: Annoy the shit out of their humans until they got to see each other again.

"Are the girls still fussing?"

"Yes! These lil' hoes won't quit fucking whining about you and Kuro."

"Aw, I miss them, too, but don't worry, they'll forget me soon enough."

Rose was quiet for so long that I thought she'd fallen asleep until she whispered, "I highly doubt that. You're far too hard to forget."

We continued to talk on the phone until at some point, I fell asleep. When I woke up the next morning, she was still on the line, and she sounded exhausted. I felt terrible for keeping her up, but she assured me she'd slept and had just woken up before me.

I didn't really believe that, but I had no time to argue. My mental health break was over, and I had to get to class.

I was on my way out when I opened the door to Shelly, holding two coffee to-go cups. She placed the drinks down on my side table and pulled me into a hug.

"I'm so glad you're OK," Shelly whispered as she hugged me tighter.

"Me too," I told her, stepping back. "I didn't know you were coming over this morning."

"It wouldn't be a surprise coffee date if you did, now would it?"

"I guess not," I said with a smile. "Wait, don't you have class?"

"Meh, I skipped," she answered with a shrug.

"I guess maintaining an A+ average allows for one skip day, huh?"

"Exactly! Plus, I haven't seen you in a week, and I was going through bestie withdrawals."

I rolled my eyes, grabbed the cup plugged with a stir stick, and raised an eyebrow in question.

"Yes, that's yours. Btw, you know adding that much cream, sugar, and cinnamon masks the taste of the tea, right?"

"Mhm," I said as I sipped. "That's what makes it good. I could kiss you. This tastes like heaven."

"I would take you up on that, but I don't think Rose would want me to kiss her girl. She seems like the territorial type."

"First off, I'm not Rose's girl. She doesn't do relationships, re-member?"

"Mhm."

"And second... Hmm, well I don't have a second. I don't wanna be late, so let's go."

The first half of the day went fast, and all of my classes ran smoothly. Even though I'd missed a week, I wasn't behind because of Shelly. She'd made it a point to send me my classwork while I was gone. I really needed to do something nice for her.

Shelly truly was the bestest friend a girl could ask for. She and Rose told everyone I was sick to explain my absence. So, when I walked into the classrooms, all of my professors asked if I was feeling better. I gave generic answers.

Since I had never missed a class, or work for that matter, illness was a believable story. Work, thankfully, was uneventful. Michelle and Stephanie (my assistant) both asked me how I was feeling, too.

I knew they meant well, but I was really starting to get tired of hearing that question. Although, the alternative line of questioning was something I didn't even want to think about.

Shelly *told* me she was coming over for a sleepover tonight so we could catch up. I clearly had no choice in it, but honestly, I was all for it. It would be nice to have some girl time with her, and it would be the perfect chance to do something special to thank her for all she'd done.

After work, I ran some errands, making stops at the grocery store, craft store, and bookstore. Once I made it home, I took care of my usual chores and got to work. Shelly loved breakfast food at any time of the day, so that was my plan for dinner.

I cooked up eggs, bacon, and pancakes, then I topped them with homemade whipped cream and strawberries. After the food was ready, I put together a bouquet of some books from her favorite authors.

Shelly strolled in a couple of minutes after I'd changed into comfy clothes. If it was anyone else, I'd have been pissed they had just walked into my place, but a bestie is allowed to cross certain boundaries.

She was carrying a bag, but she stopped inside the door after she saw the food on the table.

"Did you double-book your night with me?"

"Huh?"

"This looks like a date," she said as she put the bag down on the side table and closed the door. "Is Rose coming over, too?"

I laughed and rolled my eyes. "No, you dork. I did this for you. If it looks like a date, then we'll call it a 'bestie date.' "

"For me?"

"Mhm," I said and nodded toward the bag on the table.

Shelly smiled, picked it up, walked over to the kitchen island, and dumped it out. A smorgasbord of snacks tumbled out. There were chips with salsa, enough candy to cause a toothache, and four different cheesecake flavors.

"Um... you know there's only two of us, right? This is a whole lot of food. Did *you* invite someone over?"

"No," she giggled. "It's a girls' night. We deserve to pig out every once in a while. I brought some stuff for pampering, too. But first, I need to dig into this dinner. I wouldn't want all of your hard work to go to waste."

Shelly grabbed a plate and piled on the food. She was so excited that she did a little happy dance when she spooned another dollop of whipped cream onto her pancakes.

"Please tell me this is your homemade whip. It tastes so much better than store-bought."

"It is. I knew you would want it," I answered as I filled my plate then sat down.

Shelly caught me up on all of the current events at school, including the newest gossip, hookups, and scandals. I don't know why any of these topics even mattered to her, but she found them fascinating, so I just sat and listened, humoring her.

Once she finished telling me about who was fucking who, she grew quiet for a moment, and I thought she'd run out of stories to tell. When I looked over at her, I noticed she was staring at her plate.

Clearly, something was on her mind, but she either didn't know how to broach the topic or it was going to upset me. I guessed the latter. She probably wanted to ask about the King situation but didn't want to stir up any negative feelings.

"So, can I play devil's advocate and ask you a question?"

"We both know you're gonna ask even if I say no," I said, bracing myself.

"True. Well, alright. Let's just rip off the Band-Aid. How do you *really* feel about Rose?"

I was taking a sip when she asked and began to choke. Out of all the questions I was prepared for her to ask, that had not been one of them. At all.

Shelly leaned over and patted my back.

It took me a moment to compose myself before I could attempt a response. Once I was able, I sucked in a deep breath and looked up. Shelly was still waiting for an answer, but I still wasn't ready for the question.

"Where the fuck did that come from?"

"Don't answer my question with a question. Just answer it."

"I— I... Why are you asking me that?"

Shelly sighed and rolled her eyes. "Because. I've seen the way you look at her and hear the way you talk about her. You guys have to be more than just sex partners, but what you said earlier threw me off."

I searched my brain for what she could be talking about until it dawned on me that she meant my relationship comment.

"You mean, how Rose doesn't do relationships?"

"Yes," she said exasperated. "I know you told me that before, and honestly I forgot, but that begs the question: How does a girl who did all of this for you not claim you as her girlfriend?"

"I never asked her to claim me?"

"But why not? You love her, don't you?"

"No. I mean... Wait, wait. I..." I stumbled over my words. These questions were becoming too much.

"No, there was hesitation in that answer. I'm right, aren't I? You love her?"

The expression on her face was confusing. There was excitement, but there was also what looked like sadness.

"Why do you look sad? I haven't even said yes yet?"

"See, that's the problem. That *yet* is not good."

"OK. OK. Maybe I'm missing something here. How is it bad to be in love with someone?" I asked, trying to swallow my irritation.

"Lane, you being in love with someone will never be a problem. You being in love with someone who doesn't love you back is. Also, how can you be in love with someone you don't even know?"

"I do know her, and who said she doesn't love me back? According to you, everything she did for me grants me girlfriend status."

"Yeah, I did say that, and I thought that until you reminded me she doesn't do relationships. But don't change the subject. What do you know about her?"

"I know she's a successful author. She has two cats and three cars. She went to our school and took Professor Lynn's class, and she's bi-sexual."

I wanted to keep going, but the look on Shelly's face called me out on my bullshit. I sighed and slumped in my chair. She was right. My feelings were dangerous because they'd lead to heartbreak, but I couldn't stop myself from feeling them.

"How am I falling for a woman I don't even fully know?" I whispered.

"Oh, sweetheart. That's simple. Everything she's shown you up 'til now has been worth falling in love over. Before you freak out and spiral, why don't we turn the tables."

A mischievous smile broke out across her face, and I couldn't help but think whatever she had up her sleeve was going to get me into trouble.

"What does your twisted mind have brewing?"

"So glad you asked," she answered as she rubbed her hands together. "OK, we've established you don't really know Rose and that every time you two get together, you're easily distracted. What if you played twenty questions with a twist?"

"What kind of twist?" I asked, curious.

"A sexual one, of course," Shelly said as she dipped her finger into the whipped cream.

"Ah, let me get this right. You want me to tease her into telling me about herself?"

"Why not? You're going to have sex. We both know that. At least, you'll get some answers before you do."

"Mhm. And, um, what does the whipped cream have to do with this twisted game of yours?"

"Well," she smiled and licked the whipped cream off of her finger. "You have to make it fun for her."

"Fair enough."

"So, you'll do it?"

"Don't get too excited. I'll consider it."

Shelly rolled her eyes and shook her head. "Think of it this way, Lane. Do you really want to keep falling for a stranger? The more you learn, the more you two share, the harder it will be for her not to fall for you, too."

I didn't want to admit it, but this twisted game of hers actually sounded like a good idea. I wanted to know more about Rose, but I could never focus after we kissed.

It was time that I leveled the playing field and got some answers. I couldn't help my excitement as a plan slowly formed in my mind.

"From the look on your face, you don't just like my idea — you have a plan already. I'd love to hear it, but tonight is not about your love life. This is bestie time. So, for the next twelve hours, put Rose outta yo' mind, and let's have some fun."

All I could do was laugh. My plan was coming together beautifully, but Shelly was right. This was bestie time. To show just how focused I was on the two of us having fun, I dipped my spoon into the whipped cream and flung it at her face.

"Oh. This means war!"

"Bring it!"

IV

Rose

I was in the middle of a workout when I heard Eli's ringtone. I thought he was calling to update me on King's case, so I picked up immediately.

"Sup, Eli? What's going on with the case?"

"That's not what I was calling about, but we do have a court date set for next Friday."

"That's good. I'll tell Mel. Now, what did you *really* call for?"

"I want to see you."

"Oh?" I bit my lip in excitement. "You coming through tonight?"

"No. You're coming to my place."

"Eli, you know how I feel about th—"

"I'm not asking, Thorne. I'm telling. That ass will be at my place tonight at eight. The front desk will let you up."

Click.

The mother fucker hung up on me! He demanded that I come over and then hung up the phone? I was... horny. Pissed off, but horny. My wild side was already wondering how long the wait would be.

I checked the time. It was four o'clock. I had to wait *four fucking hours*. That knowledge only added to my ire. I needed to kill time somehow or else I would end up at his place within the next sixty minutes.

I didn't know if father time was always an asshole or if that day was just special. Time went so fucking slow, and I was losing my mind. I tried to read, but none of the books I picked up were hot enough to elicit a one-handed experience.

Then, I tried to write, but all I could focus on was fucking, and all that did was make me hornier. Next, I moved on to video games. Five boss rooms later, I still had ninety minutes to go.

I'd exhausted all of my other options, so I finally just said 'fuck it' and played with myself. It didn't really cut down my wait by much, but it did help me mellow out.

After a soothing shower, I tugged on a black, skin-tight maxi dress, slipped on my favorite loafers, and drove over to Eli's Highrise. When I pulled into the parking garage, I took a moment and sat.

The word *Highrise* was a fucking understatement. This building was so tall, it had to contain at least 50 floors. I don't know what I was expecting from Eli. I knew he was a prosecutor, but I didn't think he could afford a place like this. Obviously, I had been dead wrong.

The front desk gave me the pin for Eli's *floor*. Not his door — his fucking *floor*. If I had the patience for the political bullshit being a lawyer entailed, I would've thought about a career change.

I entered the pin on the elevator keypad and rode it up to the twenty-fifth floor. As soon as the doors opened, I was met with a breathtaking view. The first thing I saw was a wall of glass, giving way to the cityscape surrounded by sunset hues.

The ding of the elevator snapped me out of my reverie and got me moving. I was able to stop the doors before they closed and stepped into the space. My initial focus on the view shifted to the apartment itself.

Eli's place was surgically clean and a bit cold, which was a complete contrast to his personality. Even when he annoyed me, he did it with passion. That same energy I associated with him was absent here. The apartment was an open space filled with expensive pieces that seemed brand new. The whole place consisted of dark woods, black trim, and gold accents. The wall of glass I'd seen held a door that led to a terrace I was itching to step out on.

It was pin-dropping quiet, and I had a small craving to snoop. I let the impulse pass because it was far too cliche, and I knew I would probably get caught.

I was heading for the terrace door when the elevator dinged behind me. I turned just as the doors opened and caught a glimpse of a view that was almost as good as the cityscape.

Eli was wrapped in a tailored royal blue three-piece suit. It fit him to a tee. He'd pulled his dreads back into a ponytail. His beard had grown, but it was still trimmed, and he had his glasses on.

He looked like sex on a stick, and my mouth watered for every inch of him. When his eyes focused on me, they became even darker than his suit. That look and the way he stalked toward me had my pussy clenching with need.

I couldn't get a word out before his lips wrapped around mine and his tongue slid down my throat. As I stood there, my toes curled in my shoes. I had no idea where that kiss came from, but I *needed* a great deal more of them.

Eli moved his hands down my body, gripped my ass, and picked me up. My arms and legs wrapped around him tightly, pulling him closer. The heat I felt from his body was driving me crazy, and my wild half was pissed that the two of us were still clothed.

Sitting me on the back of the couch, he pushed my dress up over my hips. We both heard how wet I was when his fingertips ran through me. Breaking the kiss, Eli groaned before pulling his fingers from my slit.

"Fuck! I can't wait to have this soaking wet pussy swallow my dick."

Shivers raced down my spine so fast, I had to bite my lip to keep in the moan. He was wearing far too much clothing for me. That needed to change immediately. I reached up and pulled his ponytail loose. Once his dreads were free, I tugged at his tie to loosen it and started unbuttoning his suit jacket.

"Whatcha' waitin' for? All you need to do is get rid of some layers and slide in."

"Mmm... True, but not yet," Eli responded as he stepped away from me, took off his glasses, and undid the rest of the buttons.

"The fuck? Why not?"

Eli pulled off his suit jacket and vest, laying them across the back of the couch. Then, he undid his tie and shirt. The whole time, my eyes were glued to his chest and abs.

"I had one hell of a day, and although I want to fuck your brains out, I don't wanna rush. Plus, this is your first time here, and I wanna make it memorable."

My curiosity had been piqued since his abrupt call that afternoon. Now that I was going to find out what he had planned, I could barely contain myself.

"What did you have in mind?"

He tied his tie around my neck like a leash and pulled, forcing me to lean forward. Our lips hovered mere inches apart. The tug aroused me in more ways than one. I whimpered against his mouth.

"First, I want you on your knees so I can fill your throat. Then, I have a surprise for you," Eli told me as he pulled on the tie again, forcing me to slide off the couch and stand up.

"I'm not big on surprises," I said as I slid my dress down my body.

Eli watched it fall before wrapping the tie tighter in his hand and yanking. I fell to my knees and looked up at him. The view sent lust flooding through my veins. Eli smiled down at me, flexing his chest. The fabric of his pants was so tight, his dick looked like they were choking it.

"I'm aware," Eli said as he unzipped his trousers. "But this one, you'll like. Now, be good and do what you're told."

My eyes narrowed to slits. I was severely turned on by the way he was talking to me and treating me, but it's just not in my nature to be docile. Freeing his dick from his pants, I gripped it tightly and licked my lips.

"You prolly shouldn't oversell. I wouldn't want to be dissapo—"

"Do me a favor, Thorne. Open your mouth and shut the fuck up," he growled, cutting me off as he fisted my dreads.

My mouth fell open in shock, and Eli took full advantage of my reaction, forcing his dick down my throat. I wasn't ready, so I gagged before I adjusted to his size. Tears sprang to my eyes, but the slight pain quickly turned to pleasure.

His taste overwhelmed me so fast that I couldn't stop my wild half from taking over if I wanted to. I tightened my lips around him and circled his shaft with my tongue. Eli's groans became moans the harder I sucked.

He pumped his dick in and out of my mouth, forcing it deeper with each stroke. I happily let him use me however he wanted because it allowed my hands to roam freely.

One of my hands stroked my clit while the other twisted my left nipple. Eli grew louder and picked up speed for a few moments before his warmth flowed down my throat.

"Fuck, you're mouth can be so sweet when it's full of my cum."

I smiled as I licked my lips clean and swallowed. His fucking mouth was getting reckless, but it also stirred me up in the *best* way. Rolling my eyes, I shook my head. Now that his dick was out of my mouth, I was back in control.

"I hope I didn't break you. I'm actually kinda looking forward to that surprise," I taunted.

Eli dropped the end of the tie, grabbed the collar, and yanked me up onto my feet. In an instant, he turned me away from him and slapped my ass. His breath caressed my ear as he leaned in and whispered, "Bedroom is straight back. I want you on the bed, ass up, face down, with your arms behind you."

He stepped away, and the chill of the air hit my body in full force. I took one step then stopped, realizing how obedient I was being. I glanced back over my shoulder and bit my lip. Eli had already pulled off his shirt and was working on his pants.

"So, I can suck you off, but I can't get a tour? Way to make me feel like a whore."

He rolled his eyes and snatched my hair again. The return of his body heat against my skin sent excitement soaring through my veins.

"There are so many words I would use to describe you, Thorne," he growled, "but *whore* would never cross my mind. You can either walk to the bedroom or," he paused and tugged on the tie around my neck, "*crawl*. Your choice."

That got me moving. Quickly, I walked to the bedroom, climbed onto the bed, and put my arms behind my back as he'd demanded. Seconds later, Eli came in behind me and moved over to a nightstand. He opened a drawer and pulled out what looked like a vibrator and fur-lined cuffs.

"Oooh, are those my surprises? Is that it? I got all excited for this," I taunted with a smirk.

Climbing onto the bed, Eli shook his head. "You simply just can't help yourself, can you?" he asked as he cuffed my wrists, then pushed my face into the pillows. "No more bitching," he instructed. "All I wanna hear are your moans, screams, and my name."

He gave me no chance to respond before he slid into me roughly. Instinctively, I moaned and arched my back. The strokes started out slow but quickly picked up pace as he pounded deeper and deeper.

I couldn't have bitched if I'd wanted to. Every thrust felt so amazing that all I could get out were screams and moans. I'd forgotten about the tie until Eli yanked my neck up with it. The depths he reached had my knees weak, but I couldn't fall because of his hold.

"Does it feel good, Thorne?"

"Yes. Yes. Yes!"

"Are you ready for more?"

"Oh, God! There's more?"

"Mhm, but there ain't nothing holy about the sounds you're about to make. I want to hear my name, not God's. Open your hand and hold onto the tie. If you let it go, I'll stop."

Eli placed the tie in my hand before he snatched the chain connecting the cuffs and slammed into me, over and over again. I didn't think he could go any deeper than he already had been, but I was so happy to be proven wrong.

"Eli. Eli. Eli! Fuck!"

"Screaming my name already? We haven't even gotten to the best part yet."

It was then I remembered the vibrator. He placed it on my clit and turned it on. I *shrieked*. Fucking shrieked! Eli was clearly in the mood for payback because he pulled the toy away from my clit. I was so fucking close that I growled.

"You want to cum, Thorne?"

"Desperately..." I whimpered.

Again, he pressed the toy against my clit for a moment before taking it away once more. "Stop fucking playing games, and give me what I want, Thorne," he demanded.

"FUCK! Eli, please. *Please*!"

Eli turned the vibrating power up and slid it inside of me. I have no fucking idea how it fit when he was already there, but that was the last thing on my mind. I felt so full, so mind-blowingly good. My eyes rolled back so far in my head, I couldn't see anything.

"Cum for me," he ordered. "Cover my dick with it so you can lick it clean."

I came so forcefully, I couldn't keep my hold on the tie. Every nerve in my body ignited. I fell onto the pillows, attempting to catch my breath. Eli unlocked the cuffs and slid out of me.

Flipping my body so that I was facing him, he moved down until his mouth was inches from my pussy.

"Tired, Thorne?" he asked.

"Mhm."

"Too bad. I told you, you have some sucking to do. You can sleep after," he said before rolling his tongue around my clit.

My entire body was sore, but that one lick had me starving for more. Eli flicked his tongue repeatedly, building up my pleasure. I was still sensitive from the toy, but that didn't deter Eli one bit. He picked up his pace and had my body soaring seconds later.

"Great. That should've given you enough energy to do as I asked," Eli said with a smile.

"Mmm. Nope, but you doing that with your tongue one more time just might."

Eli smirked and leaned back down.

"Fine."

V

Melanie

Rose sent me a text this morning about the arraignment hearing having been set for this Friday. It almost ruined my day, but then I remembered Shelly's idea.

Instead of letting it get to me, I asked Rose if she would come over tonight, and she agreed. That put a smile right back on my face. School and work both went by in a blur, and I don't remember any of it.

I was too excited for tonight to care. I ran some errands, picked up some things I would need, and headed home. As soon as I walked through the door, Kuro began to whine for food.

"You have an automatic feeder, boy. Why are you acting like you're starving?"

Kuro circled my legs, letting out high-pitched meows until I stepped into the kitchen. I guess he thought I was going to feed him soft food. I wasn't. Ignoring him, I made a new bowl of whipped cream and put it in the fridge.

Then, I went upstairs, changed into a red lace lingerie set, and attached the new cuffs I'd bought to my bed. Everything was set. Now, all I needed was Rose, and my game could begin.

Rose was supposed to be here in an hour. I spent every minute of it thinking my plan wasn't going to work and she wouldn't tell me anything. My negative thoughts continued to spiral until my doorbell interrupted them.

Before I opened the door, I drew in a calming breath. I leaned against the frame and smiled as Rose took me in. Her jaw dropped. For a moment, her eyes burned bright with lust. Then, she stepped inside and captured my lips.

All of my thoughts immediately scattered as her hands roamed my body and lifted me up. My back ended up against my closet door, and that brought back the memory of our first kiss.

"You look good enough to eat, Mel. I don't think we'll make it to your bed before I devour you."

If she laid me on that table, everything I had planned was going to come undone. I needed to focus and do it quickly. Leaning back against the wall, I gripped her shoulders to steady myself.

"No eating tonight," I told her. "I have plans for us, and if your tongue gets anywhere near me, they won't happen."

"Oh," she whispered against my neck. "Is that so?"

"Yes. Yes, it's so. Now, put me down, please."

"Fine."

As soon as my feet touched the floor, I grabbed her wrist and dragged her up the stairs. Thankfully, Rose didn't try anything else to distract me, and I was grateful.

"OK! Tonight, you're going to play a round of twenty questions with me."

"Mel, I..."

I leaned in and kissed her to cut her off. Her arms wrapped around my back and pulled me in closer. I nibbled her bottom lip before I stepped out of her embrace and put some distance between us.

"I'm not going to ask about *that*. Although I really want to, I will save it for another time. You've fucked me until my legs were weak and my brain was numb, but it's been brought to my attention that I don't really know you. So, that's what tonight is about. But don't think you'll get nothing out of it. I'll make it worth your while."

Rose raised her brow and smiled at me, interest piqued. "Go on."

"Well, first I need you to strip for me. Then, I need you to lay on the bed," I instructed.

"I think I can manage that," she said as she tugged off her clothes until she was naked. Watching me, she climbed onto the mattress.

I didn't realize I was staring until I heard Rose clear her throat. I hadn't meant to. It was an accident, but she had such an incredible body. My eyes moved up and landed on her dazzling smile.

Rose sat on the bed, watching me, and I didn't want to take too long and end up second guessing myself. So, I climbed onto the bed beside her and reached for the cuffs. I could feel her eyes on me as I snapped them around her wrists, but I focused on my task, just in case looking directly at her made me lose my nerve.

Once she was secured, I went downstairs to grab the whipped cream. Before heading back upstairs, I sucked in a breath.

"Oh, you were really serious about making this interesting, huh?" she asked when she noticed what I'd brought back with me.

"Yes, I was," I answered with a smirk. "So, here's how it's gonna go: For every question you answer, I will put whipped cream somewhere on your body and lick it off. You game?"

"Yeah, I'm game. Honestly, I think you went too easy on your rules, but it's too late to change them now. Ask your questions," Rose challenged.

"OK," I began. "Is your real name Rose Thorne, or is that just a pen name?"

"Just so you know, that's two questions. So, you have eighteen left. And no, that's not my real name. Yes, it's just a pen name," Rose answered with a wicked grin.

"Wait, that's not fair."

"It doesn't have to be fair. You didn't say two-part questions counted as one in your rules."

Her earlier comment suddenly made sense. I *should've* thought my rules through better, but like she'd said, it was too late to change them now. Dipping my finger in the whipped cream, I placed a dollop on her lips before gently licking it off.

"Mmm, that's good. What store did you get this from?"

"My store," I said with a wink. "It's homemade."

The genuine surprise on her face made me blush. I knew it tasted good because Shelly always told me it did, but seeing Rose's reaction made it more special somehow.

"Thank you. Next question," I continued. "What's your real name?"

"Rosalina Thornton."

"Oh, that's really pretty. Why the pen name?" I asked.

"I just liked shortening my name, I guess," she said with a shrug. "You owe me three licks now."

I rolled my eyes. I wasn't really satisfied with that answer, but it was an answer nonetheless. So, I placed whipped cream on both sides of her neck and on her chest before cleaning it off with my tongue.

"Happy now?"

"Does that count as one of your questions?" she asked with a smirk.

"Fuck! No. It was rhetorical and does not count."

"Hmm, fine. I'll let it slide. You got sixteen left."

This game was trickier than I'd expected. I took a moment to collect my thoughts. I needed to make sure I asked my questions correctly and didn't run through them too quickly without getting the information I wanted.

"Alright, do you have a good relationship with your parents?"

"Wow, we're going for serious information now, huh?" Rose laughed. "Yes, I have a great relationship with my parents. I text with my mom every day, and I visit them every other week."

A small dollop of the whip and a twirl of my tongue around her nipple drew a small whimper from Rose's lips. The taste of the cream and her skin danced over my tongue making it damn near impossible not to go back for more.

"You have nicknames for everyone, including me. So, can I call you Lina?"

"Yes, and that most definitely counts, so get to licking, Mel."

That one was my fault. I should've waited until after the game to ask. Flustered, I licked the cream off of her other nipple, then nipped it. Lina moaned and smiled down at me.

"Thirteen left."

"Why don't you have an author picture in any of your books?"

"Your friend asked me that the day I did the reading for your class. Now, I *know* you weren't paying attention." Lina chuckled. "Ask something else. I won't count that one against you."

"How generous of you," I retorted, rolling my eyes.

"I know, right?"

The next few questions were rather general in nature. How long had she been writing? What were her favorite foods and favorite colors? Did she have any siblings? Favorite movies? Favorite books? Games? TV shows? What was she like in high school?

By the time I was finished with these, I'd licked everywhere but one place. That, I was saving for my last few questions since they were sexual. I made a trail of whipped cream from her neck down to her pussy.

"Favorite position?" I asked.

"Doggy, of course."

"Oh, of course," I agreed, licking my way down to her stomach.

"Have you ever done a sixty-nine?"

"Yes," she panted as I dragged my tongue down to her pussy.

"Who do you like fucking more, guys or girls?"

"Um... You're gonna need to move your tongue if you want me to focus enough to answer your question."

Pleased with her response, I flicked my tongue against her clit before leaning back to allow her to focus. She shivered and sucked in a breath before leveling her heated gaze on me.

"Don't get me wrong, I love dick, but there's just something about strapping up and pounding into a woman that's so intoxicating."

Sucking her clit into my mouth, I rolled it between my teeth before I cleaned away the rest of the whipped cream. Lina let out a small moan and rolled her hips, grinding her pussy against my face.

I knew what she wanted, but since she'd decided to be such a brat during the game, she wasn't going to get it. Instead, I kissed her clit, then moved away and reached up to undo her cuffs.

"Even though you were a brat about it, thanks for playing my game."

"Mhm," she said as she shoved me down and climbed on top of me. "All those questions and all that licking made me parched, so Ima go grab some water. But when I get back, we're gonna play a different game."

"Looking forward to it." I laughed and watched her ass as she descended the stairs.

While she was gone, her phone began to ring.

"Go ahead and answer that, please. She'll keep calling if you don't," Rose shouted up to me.

Her clothes were still lying in the middle of the floor, so I had to rifle through them to grab her cell. Finally, I managed to dig it out of her pocket. I almost dropped the phone when I saw the contact photo.

The caller was a very naked woman with a stunning body. In the photo, her eyes were closed, but she wore a beautiful smile on her full lips. She had long blue dreads that covered her breasts and a man between her legs. As for what they were doing, the picture left nothing to the imagination.

The phone was still ringing. I didn't want Lina to be annoyed if I missed it and the person called back, so I let go of my shock and answered. I'd been so thrown off by the contact photo that I didn't realize the call was actually a video chat.

The picture didn't do the woman one bit of justice. Seeing all her beauty live instead of captured in a moment was over-whelming. It wasn't logical to be jealous, but I had no idea who this woman was, and she was fucking gorgeous.

"Ooh, no wonder you're her kryptonite," the woman said without introduction.

"Um... Excuse me?"

"Rosey has a real hard-on for those blessed with beautiful eyes, and you, sweet Melanie, have quite the set."

"Um... T-thank you. I'm sorry. I don't mean to be rude. You seem to know my name, but I don't know yours."

The woman poked out her bottom lip, pouting for a moment before a breathtaking smile broke out across her face.

"So fucking rude of her to not mention me. I'm Hazel, Rosey's wife. It's nice to finally meet you."

Both my jaw and the phone dropped at the same time. Out of all the information I'd expected to learn tonight, I didn't think I would find out Lina was married. Too many questions flew through my mind, but Hazel's voice broke through and pulled me back to the conversation.

My questions came out like word vomit as I snatched up the phone. I'm sure I sounded like a crazy person, but I was just too stunned about the wife thing to think clearly.

"Wife! She has a wife? You're her wife? W-Who's the man... Um?"

"Oh! You mean the one deep-diving between my legs in my contact pic?" Hazel responded with a smirk.

I nodded my head vigorously, trying to follow the conversation.

"I was too adventurous one night and got caught with him. Rosey took that pic to make sure I never forgot how much I'd hurt her."

My mouth opened and closed, but no sound came out.

"Close your mouth, Mel, before I put somethin' in it," Lina ordered as she reached the top step.

"B-but... She... She said... She said she was your—"

"Really, love?" Lina rolled her eyes. "You think I have a wife? Me?"

"So, you just gonna deny me like that? Really, Rosey? I'm hurt."

"Enough, Hazel. She's two seconds from a heart attack."

Glancing between Hazel and Lina, I waited for someone to explain what the hell was happening. Hazel broke the silence first, filling it with her laughter.

"Alright. This is gonna sound rude, but I don't really care," I began. "Can one of you please explain what the fuck is going on?"

"Ooh! You're sassy. I knew I would like you," Hazel answered with a giggle.

"She's fuckin' with you, Mel. That's my best friend, not my wife. The man tongue-diving in the pic is her *husband*. She took it a couple of years ago and sent it to me, hoping to rile me up. So, I sent her a quick vid of a girl cumming on my dick. I'm sure you can guess who won her stupid lil' game."

Again, I found myself staring at Lina as she explained. That is until I noticed Hazel had a huge grin on her face.

"I still have that video," she added. "The noises that girl made were fucking delicious. What size was she taking, again?"

"Ten inches."

"Oh, fuck! I really need to pick one of those up."

"What? Zeke's not big enough for you anymore?" Lina asked as she climbed back onto the bed and crawled toward me."

"Oh, he's plenty. Hits all the right spots. Doesn't mean I'm not curious."

"Mhm," Lina said as she leaned in and dragged her nose along the crook of my neck.

I was frozen. I knew Lina had said Hazel was her best friend, but she was still butt-ass naked and openly doing something sexual to me. I'm sure the panic was evident on my face, but neither girl was fazed.

"If you guys are about to fuck, can I watch?"

Lina chuckled darkly before taking the phone from me. She held her arm out to show Hazel she was the only one naked. Hazel didn't attempt to cover up the fact that she was admiring Lina's body. The same jealousy from earlier began to burn through my veins once more.

"Did you want something, or did you call just to bother me?" Rose asked, snapping me out of my unnecessary thoughts.

"Mostly to bother you, but I need to know what you want for your birthday." Hazel grinned.

"The same thing I want every year."

Lina's friend rolled her eyes. "You always say *nothing*. Every year."

"Then, you already know what I want. Which brings me back to you just calling to bother me."

"Mayyybee!"

"Yeah, I figured. Well, as you can see, I have quite the meal next to me. So, if you don't mind, I'm hanging up now."

"Wait, wait, wait. If I can't watch, can I at least get a video?" Hazel whined.

"Bye, Hazel," Lina said as she ended the call. She turned and smiled at me.

"And here I thought Shelly had no boundaries," I commented.

"You've got no idea, Love," Lina said as she leaned in to kiss me.

Something Hazel had said stuck with me. I dodged her. "Wait, hold on. When is your birthday?"

"We ain't playing twenty questions anymore, Mel."

"Fine. Give me your phone. I'll just have Hazel tell me," I said, reaching for her cell.

Lina snatched my wrist and kissed a trail up my arm until she reached my neck. The light touches caused a thousand shivers to rush down my spine.

"August twenty-seventh."

"That's in three months!"

"Is it? Wow, I had no idea."

Annoyed by her sarcasm, I sat up and bit her neck, eliciting a loud moan from her.

"Let me see your phone," I repeated.

"Why?"

"I wanna pick Hazel's brain about birthday gifts."

Lina rolled her eyes, but she handed me her cell, anyway. "Didn't you just hear me tell Hazel I don't want anything?"

"Mhm," I nodded as I took it from her.

I was lying. I wasn't planning to text Hazel. Or at least, I wasn't going to text her right now. I ran through Lina's contacts, found all the fuckables, and sent all of their numbers, as well as Hazel's, to my phone.

A plan was forming in my mind, but for now, I needed to put it on the back burner. I didn't want Lina to figure out what I was doing. After the text went through, I deleted it and handed her phone back.

"That was a short conversation," she commented.

"I sent her number to my phone so I could talk to her later. Didn't want you to get jealous that I was giving your bestie all my attention."

Lina smiled at me before she lifted my arms and cuffed them to the bed where hers had been.

"Yeah, we wouldn't want to make me jealous," she retorted, rolling her eyes. "Now that you've done what you wanted and gathered your information, it's time to play my game."

"And which game would that be?" I asked.

"The game where I make you scream until you're hoarse."

I licked my lips and rubbed my toes over her leg. Lina dipped her fingers into the whipped cream and drew small circles on my chest.

"That's my favorite game," I told her between quick breaths.

"Mine too."

VI

Rose

The boss I was fighting was really pissing me off. It was a humanoid enemy with quick short-range and long-range attacks. What made the situation even better was that her hit-box was the size of a fucking penny. So it took for-fucking-ever to get my attacks to connect.

My phone vibrated and distracted me. I only looked away for a second, but it cost me. As soon as my eyes switched back to the screen, the boss bitch-slapped me with a sword made of her blood.

Half my health was gone, and so far, I'd only managed to hack off a quarter of hers. My phone went off twice more, but I ignored it. I was dedicated. This bitch needed to die.

Three more buzzes sounded, and I lost my patience with whoever the fuck was texting me. I moved my character to the corner of the room, as far away from the boss as possible, before looking at my phone.

I expected it to be Mel, or if I'm being honest, maybe Eli. To my surprise, it was Zey blowing up my phone. Out of all of the fuckables, he was the most laid back, so this was new.

The controller vibrated in my hands, letting me know I had gotten owned when I was looking away. That was annoying, but it was whatever. I'd just have to do it over. I was more curious about what Zey wanted.

Zey: Hey

Zey: Yo

Zey: Red

Zey: R

Zey: E

Zey: D

Me: What?

Zey: Where are you?

Me: Home y?

Zey: I'll be there soon.

Me: What if someone's already here.

Zey: They can either join in or leave. I don't give a fuck either way.

Me: Even if it's one of the guys?

Zey: I said what I said. Let me in.

Me: I'll keep that in mind. It's unlocked.

"Where the fuck are you?" he bellowed as he came inside.

"Media room," I yelled back at him.

Booming footsteps reached my ears as I walked back into the boss room again. I didn't know what Zey's issue was, but he needed to chill the fuck out.

He stormed into the media room a few moments later, snatched my controller out of my hands, tossed it, and fell to his knees.

"Bro, what the fuck is your problem?" I snapped, glancing between him and the screen.

The boss was having a grand ol' time kicking my ass in the now one-sided battle. I was one slap away from death if I didn't get back in there, but Zey clearly had other things on his mind.

As I scrambled for the controller, he grabbed my ankles and pulled me toward him. The nightshirt I wore rode up, baring my body to his heated gaze. His hands snaked up to the back of my knees and forced my legs toward my chest.

Immediately, Zey lowered his face to my pussy and rolled his tongue over my clit, forcing a moan from my lips. My fingers wrapped themselves in his hair.

The way he devoured me defied the very laws of cunnilingus. I don't know if I was just lost in my pleasure, but it felt like his tongue was somehow reaching every deep spot inside of me. The need for his touch in other places was palpable. I pulled my fingers from his hair and slid them up my body.

They made it up to my breasts before Zey snatched my wrists and pinned my arms down.

"Hold your legs up. I'm not in the mood to be choked out today."

"If I'm holding my legs, what are you gonna—"

"Shut the fuck up, Red. Not in the mood for your lip, either. Just your screams," he growled, cutting me off.

"What is your pro—"

He cut me off again as he twisted my nipples and flicked his tongue. The scream he wanted flew out of my mouth, followed by a few more before I let out a final gasp in my climax.

"Perfect," he sighed. "Just what I needed."

"Glad I could help," I said, both satisfied and annoyed. "Wanna tell me what your damage is now?"

Zey ignored my question, picked me up like a bride, and walked us into the playroom. He sat me on the nearest dresser and kissed me. The taste of his lips covered in my cum was exquisite.

Each kiss stole more and more of my breath until I was high on bliss. I needed him inside of me, but for whatever reason, he was still fully clothed.

"Can you do a backbend, Red?"

"That was random as fuck. I like how you ignored my question but expect me to answer yours. Why you wanna know?"

"Can you do it?"

"Why?"

"Red!"

"Zey! Tell me why."

He rubbed his thumb over my bottom lip as his eyes roved over my face. The heated look he gave me made my throat run dry. There was irritation underneath the lust that had a tight grip on my tongue.

"I want to be deep enough inside of you that I can stroke your taste buds as I fuck you. Now, can you do it or not?"

"I— I haven't done one in years."

"That's a shame," he whispered.

"Maybe not," I said with a quick smile.

Zey raised a brow and studied me as I pushed him back and climbed off of the dresser. I could feel his eyes on me as I pushed open the doors to the closet and showed him the swing.

"If that's what you want, then this is the best way to get it."

Zey stepped into the wardrobe and admired the swing.

"How is this going to..."

His voice trailed off as that panty-drenching smile broke out across his face. His eyes were focused on the pulley system, so I guessed he'd answered his own question. Zey dragged his fingers up and down the chains connected to the swing before turning to me.

"How does it work?"

With a small smile curving my lips, I walked over to the dresser, grabbed the remote to the swing, and waved it at him. Zey stepped toward me with his palm held out, but I pulled my hand back.

"Who said you get the control?"

Zey moved quicker than I could react. He grabbed the wrist attached to the hand holding the remote, twisted my arm behind my back, and bent me over the dresser. His other arm snaked up my spine, and he wrapped his fingers in my dreads.

My desire fueled a lust-filled heat, sending it through my veins. They burned hotter the closer he came to me. When his breath tickled my ear, my knees weakened. If I hadn't been leaning over the dresser, things would have gotten quite embarrassing.

"I usually enjoy your stubbornness. It's cute most of the time. Irritating the rest of the time. Today, it's just aggravating. I told you I was in no mood for your bullshit."

I tried to pull my wrist free, but he tightened his grip, forcing me to stop. Since I was locked in this position, I needed to at least make it fun. Pressing myself against him, I ground my ass against his pants, enjoying the hiss that left his lips.

"So, what *are* you in the mood for, Zey?" I challenged.

"To blow your fucking back out," he whispered in my ear as he pulled my head toward him. "Now, give me that fucking remote and drop the shirt before I rip you out of it."

Excitement raced down my spine as my thoughts scattered. Any 'bullshit' plans I had no longer mattered. All I could focus on were the words he'd whispered in my ear and the pleasure they would bring.

Zey released me and stepped back, giving me space to turn around. As we locked eyes, I opened my hand and held the remote out to him. He snatched it quickly from my palm, probably assuming I was going to play around and change my mind.

Well played.

Smiling at me with a raised brow, he waited for me to take off my shirt as he'd commanded. Inch by inch, I pulled it over my stomach and chest, watching Zey fidget with impatience.

It was like a starting pistol went off as soon as my shirt hit the floor. Zey picked me up, placed me in the swing, and wrapped his lips around my nipple. Thrilled, I leaned back to give him better access.

The need for his tongue to trace every inch of me had me thoroughly distracted. Before I knew it, he'd tied my wrists and ankles to the swing. I had no idea how he managed that as he rolled my nipple between his teeth.

The man truly had skill.

Zey released my breast and stepped back to admire the remote. Although I was overly excited about what was about to happen, I just couldn't resist being difficult, so I didn't tell him which buttons controlled which ties.

At first, my arms went up as my legs went down, making me giggle. He was clearly unamused, but he didn't ask for assistance, and I didn't offer. After a few more 'adjustments,' he finally figured out how to work the swing.

He started by raising up my entire body until I was in line with his waist then lowered my arms and upper back. Once he was satisfied, I ended up in a similar position to the one I'd put Wynter in a few months ago, but the arch in my back was a lot deeper than hers had been.

As soon as that realization struck, I began to pant like a dog in heat. My sane and wild halves were in sync for the first time in my life. Only one thought took precedence in my mind.

He's about to wreck me... and I'm gonna love every fucking second of it.

Zey pulled his shirt and pants off at an excruciatingly slow pace. That treacherous smile stayed on his lips as I failed to contain my reactions to his glorious body.

"I'm going to fuck you, Red. It's going to be rough, and I'm not going to stop. Beg, cry, or scream all you want. I'll devour every sound you make until I leave you breathless and spent."

I couldn't process the pleasure he was prepared to deliver to my body. The more I attempted to contemplate it, the more possibilities my mind conjured.

I was so lost in thought that I forgot to respond before I felt his tip slowly parting my lips. I was so wet, he slid in without resistance, but it was always a tight fit with him. Zey was so thick and long, and it was absolute torture that he took his time, sliding each inch inside of me so fucking slowly.

Gripping my thighs tightly, Zey slid out of me, leaving only the tip. My lips trembled in anticipation. Our eyes met, and we stared at each other for a moment, waiting for the other to make a move.

It became *too* quiet.

He was *too* still.

I was *too* excited.

His tongue darted out and wet his lips. My eyes tracked every movement until it disappeared back into his mouth. Again, I found myself panting for what was to come.

How he could manage to undo my very being with only one simple thrust was mind-boggling. I couldn't take it anymore. The wait was *too* much, and I just needed whatever he was planning to do to happen at once.

"Ready or not, Red. Here. It. Comes," Zey whispered a split-second before he viciously impaled me.

A loud scream tore out of me before the shock of being filled so quickly cut it off. He was balls deep inside of me. My eyes rolled back into my skull. My fingers and toes began to tingle with each long and deep stroke he made.

Even though he'd given me fair warning, I still wasn't quite ready for the brutality of his pace. But I didn't dare complain. He told me he wouldn't, but I knew if I genuinely asked him to, he would stop.

That's just the type of man he is, but there was no way in hell I'd ever ask him to. The way his dick rubbed every delicious spot inside of me was something I had no intention of ever ending.

Zey's hands moved over to my breasts. The rough texture of his callouses rolling over my aching nipples drove me mad, but I lost every one of my marbles when he started twisting them and increased his pace.

The orchestra of my screams, cries, and moans he conducted was the most beautiful piece of music I'd ever had the pleasure of hearing. My orgasm sailed through me so fast, it made my head spin.

My mind searched for something snarky to say, but the only thing I could manage was to chant '*Oh my God*' over and over. The smile on his face was filled to the brim with mischief.

"There ain't no church in sight right now, Red. He hasn't earned your praise. This body is *my* domain. Your orgasms are under *my* rule. Your moans are your fealty to *me* and me alone. You're *mine* tonight, and I refuse to share your worship with anyone. Not even *God*."

I'd had trouble forming a sentence before. Now, I completely forgot how to speak. This possessive energy he displayed was turning me on in ways I couldn't even begin to describe.

Although I was still trying to form a response, Zey gave me no reprieve, wrapping his fingers tightly around my throat. My body was overheating, and I'm sure he could feel my pulse thrumming wildly against his thumb.

He pounded into me, reaching deeper and deeper with each thrust. His possessive words played on a loop in my head. Both his declarations and his movements were all-consuming.

All I could focus on were the mere seconds away I was from having another mind-shattering climax. But Zey apparently had other plans for me. He flicked my nipple, effectively pulling my focus off of that wonderful pending orgasm.

"What the fuck was that?" I complained.

Usually, I would just convert the pain into pleasure, but it was so sudden that it threw me off.

"What did I say about your orgasms being under my rule?" he asked, rolling the offended flesh between his fingers. "You've already cum without permission. You won't be allowed another one."

With a roll of my eyes, I gave him a subdued smile. There was no need to wait for his permission. All I had to do was...

"Oh," he breathed. "Nice trick. I really need to stop forgetting you like to cheat."

My smile grew bolder as I continued to squeeze my walls and sucked him in farther. All it would take was a few more squeezes, and then I would be off to the races. But again, Zey didn't want to concede this battle of power, so he abruptly pulled out of me.

Before I could unleash my rage on him, he slapped my pussy with his dick. Once more, I lost my focus. That was new, a sensation I'd had yet to experience. I was torn between liking it and being annoyed by it.

Zey rubbed his tip over my clit a few times before lowering it to tease my entrance. I don't know how he thought doing this would keep me from cumming, but I wasn't gonna point that out.

"Open your mouth, Red," he ordered.

So many questions flew through my mind, but he gave me that 'do what I say' look. Figuring it would get me to my orgasm faster, I obeyed. As soon as my lips parted, he pushed his middle finger between them.

The taste of his salty sweat was sharp. I didn't know the plan, but if he wanted to shove things in my mouth, I was going to play with them. I sucked it in deeper and rolled my tongue over it.

His eyelids were heavy over his eyes, and I knew he was probably wishing I was sucking his dick instead. I bet he regretted putting me in this position since head would be damn near impossible.

"Are you ready to cum now, Red?" Zey asked.

He must have forgotten my mouth was full. Raising a brow, I bit his finger. Zey chuckled darkly when he pulled it from between my teeth. He trailed a wet path down my body before slipping it inside of me.

"Answer the question," he commanded.

"Don't put things in my mouth if you want me to talk," I shot back.

Zey lined his tip up with my entrance, and for a moment, I thought he was going to do the same thing Eli did to me back at his apartment. But I was *so* wrong. Instead, he removed his finger (which I'll admit made me a little sad) and stared at me.

"Oh my god!" I complained. "Yes! I'm ready to c—" Simultaneously, his finger entered my ass and his dick slid into my pussy. My words became a garbled mess, and it felt like all the oxygen in my lungs dissipated. He synced the stroke of his finger with the relentless thrusts of his dick.

There was no adjustment period. As soon as he got into a rhythm, his pace increased. Nothing that came out of my mouth could be considered English anymore, so I couldn't even attempt to tell you what I said.

I had an iron grip on the straps holding my wrists, and my legs bucked against the restraints around my ankles. If he wanted me to wait for permission to cum, he was quickly running out of time.

I was far too close to wait any longer. Thankfully, Zey knew my body well and gave me exactly what I needed.

"Cum for me, Red. You have my permission," he said as he removed his other hand from my neck and dropped it down between my legs, rolling my clit between his fingers.

My body was overwhelmed with too many sensations to even attempt a snarky remark. I was far too busy screaming his name as I came.

As soon as I came down, I realized my limbs were so fucking sore, and so was my ass, but I gave no fucks. Every second of this was fucking worth it. Even through all the muscle tightness, I couldn't stop one single thought from repeating in my mind.

I. Fucking. Want. More.

Zey's chuckle pulled me out of my thoughts, and I realized he'd already undone the ties. I stretched out my limbs to cut down on the discomfort while waiting for him to tell me what was so funny.

"You looked like you were about to fall asleep right after you came, but not even five seconds later, the heat was right back in your eyes. You actually want to go again, don't you?"

"You've fucked me long enough to know the answer to that. I just need ice. Some head would be great, and then a whole lot more dick," I answered with the full force of my wolfish grin.

A smile just as devious as my own spread across his lips as he glanced over to the cuffs attached to the wall.

"I think I can manage that," he said. "There was something else I wanted to do to you."

"Oh?" I teased. "Hope you're not expecting me to stand. My legs are too weak right now."

"Don't worry. Mine aren't, and I'm strong enough to hold us both up."

"In that case, sign me up for round two, please. But don't forget about the head part."

"I wouldn't dare."

VII

Rose

Being surrounded by heat always made me irritable, which was a minor reason why I didn't really cuddle. Half-asleep, I struggled to remember what had happened before I passed out. But when I was pulled up against a broad chest, my mind played cruel tricks on me, and I freaked out.

I threw his arm off of me and scrambled out of the bed. A strong hand gripped my wrist, and all of my training flew out the window. Caught off-guard, I did the most idiotic thing I'd ever done in my life: I screamed.

The tight grip on my wrist disappeared, and I took off. I was already out of the room and heading straight for the stairs by the time I heard it.

Red.

Red? Only one person calls me Red.

The haze of my nightmares receded, and I glanced back toward the playroom. Zey stood in the doorway, very naked and at *attention*. This was an interesting situation to be in. One I hadn't anticipated. I had just freaked out in front of him because of who I *thought* he was.

Shit.

There had to be a way to make this whole thing seem frivolous. At the moment, the only thing I could think to do to fix the situation was something sexual, so that's what I fell back on. Leaning against the wall, I crossed my arms and smiled, as though everything was perfectly fine.

"Well, now," I teased. "Someone's quite happy to see me, huh?"

"Don't do that," he said, rolling his eyes. "What the fuck just happened back there?"

Avoiding his question, I said, "I don't know what you're talking about. Wanna tell me why we were cuddling in the playroom?"

Zey stalked toward me and crowded me against the wall. He placed his arms above me, framing me in and slowly dousing the small flame of hope that I could get him to drop this.

"I'm usually very accepting of you treating me like a piece of meat, but I'm not gonna let this go. You've never screamed like that, even when I've gripped your wrist too tight when we spared. Now, explain."

"It doesn't even matter. Just let it go," I tried. "Our relationship is physical, not emotional. Let's just ke—"

"Damn it, Rose! Answer my fucking question!" he growled.

"Oh! Are we using real names now, *Xavier*?"

Zey leaned his forehead against mine and sighed. It had been a long shot to hope he'd let it go, but it was also too much for me emotionally to actually tell him the truth.

"Please," he whispered.

That 'please' was the weakest I'd ever heard him sound, and it rubbed something deep in my heart. The conversation we'd had in my gym a couple months ago came flooding back to me.

You may not like the emotional part of these relationships, but you bring an abundance of excitement to our lives. I'd bet my whole business they all have strong emotions for you, but some of us are far better at controlling them than others.

There was so much truth in his words that I never wanted to admit to, but the reality was that I'd held on to this group of fuckables around the longest. So many of my rules had been broken by one or another, and instead of swapping them out like I usually would, I'd kept every single one of them.

Whether I was ready to admit it out loud or not, I trusted and cared about them to a certain point. My heart and fears weren't really ready for that to be true, but I guess I had to get ready because I didn't have any plans for new fuckables in my future.

I was willing to tell him I had nightmares, but I wasn't going to discuss the subject. He'd just have to settle for the partial truth for now. We both knew how stubborn I am. If he insisted on more, then I would have had to make a change to the roster.

Sucking in a deep breath, I braced myself.

"Ugh, fine," I relented. "I had a nightmare. I haven't actually *slept* with a man in a very long time, so when you pulled me up against you, it took me back to a dark place." I chose my next words carefully. "Sooo, instead of kicking your ass like the badass I am, I wimped out and ran. That's all I'm willing to say. Please don't ask for more."

Zey was quiet for a moment. I could see the gears turning in his head. He was having a vicious debate about whether to push the issue. When he finally opened his mouth, my whole body went into flight mode.

He wrapped his arms around me and hugged me before I could run off again. That was unexpected, but I was still tense because I had no idea what he was going to say.

"I'm sorry something happened to you that causes you such fear. I won't ask any more for now, but I hope that one day, you will feel comfortable enough to tell me."

My knees gave out as relief surged through me, but Zey caught me and picked me up. Calmly, he walked us back to the bedroom and sat me down on the bed. I hadn't realized how much weight had been on my shoulders until he'd said I didn't have to go into more detail about it.

I hadn't told a man about my nightmares in almost a decade, and the last one I did tell handled it terribly. I knew Zey had an idea as to what happened to me, but for him to not insist I tell him... It was just so... refreshing.

The last time I'd had this discussion, when it was all said and done, the one I told temporarily lost his mind. That scenario plagued me any time I thought about going to sleep next to a man. Then, there was the issue that they would see me as damaged if they found out, so that kept my lips permanently shut.

That's where the *no cuddle* rule really came from. The women I slept with didn't really like that rule at first, but I usually didn't keep them around long enough to care. Mel was still the first woman I'd ever cuddled with, and now, she and Zey both knew about my nightmares.

What the fuck is going on with me? When did I become such an open fucking book?

"Will you tell me why we were cuddling?" I asked. "And in my playroom, at that?"

"You really don't remember what happened?"

"My body sure as hell does, but my mind is a little fuzzy."

Zey chuckled and stretched out on the bed next to me. His dick and I were having a staring contest until he snapped his fingers, and I looked up to see him smiling.

"You don't remember how I fucked you last night, but you want me to fuck you again right now?"

"I meannnn... Perhaps, it would help me remember better."

"Mhm. Maybe later," Zey responded "After I fucked you in your swing, we moved over to the wall. I tied you to said wall, and you told me to grab a toy from the top drawer. Any of this ringing a bell yet?"

Several images of last night played in my mind as he spoke, and they were all delicious. Now, I was in the mood to repeat them, but sadly, my body was still too sore. So, I shifted my focus back to my original question.

"Actually, I remember now, and I'd love a repeat, but that still doesn't explain how we ended up cuddling."

"Ah, well, that. Um... You see... I kinda took advantage of the opening, and after the whole nightmare thing, I feel like a complete ass for doing it. But before you jump to wild conclusions, please let me explain," he said nervously.

I was mere seconds from going off on him, but I managed to calm down and listen. I knew he would never do anything to hurt me, but the phrase *took advantage* will always rub me the wrong way.

"Just remember that your balls are mere inches away from my hand," I warned him. "And if I don't like what you have to say, I will crush them."

"Noted. After I wrung three more orgasms out of you, you passed out. And I mean *out like a light*. I called your name several times, and you didn't even stir. This bed was the nearest one, so once I cleaned us both up — which was no fun by the way — I tucked you in."

"Uh-huh."

"I knew you would bitch, and I was set to make my way to the guest room, but I'd never seen you asleep before. I've always kept you up for the next round. This was the first time, and you looked so..." He hesitated. "So... cute."

"Did you really just call my unconscious form cute?"

"Yeah, yeah. Go ahead and crush my nuts if you want to. I don't care. You just looked so peaceful that I found myself lying next to you and fell asleep. After work yesterday, that was just what I needed. To fuck your brains out and get a little peace."

Well, that was interesting to hear. I'd never considered myself a bringer of peace, but for him, I guess I was. The thought was actually pretty nice, I guess. Still, he really needed to choose his words better because as far I was concerned, that wasn't really taking advantage of me.

Zey watched me, waiting to see if I would follow through with my threat. Just to show him I meant it, I lightly hit his balls, making him hiss and swear. His reaction brought me a great deal of satisfaction and put a smile on my face.

"You're gonna pay for that, Red," he growled as he rolled on top of me and bit my neck.

"Oh, no! I'm so scared," I taunted. "Anyway, why were you pissed yesterday?"

Distracted, Zey rolled off of me again and stared up at the ceiling. I wasn't born with a high level of patience to begin with, but as I got older, that level decreased and decreased.

It probably would've been the mature thing to just wait for him to get it out, but I'm just not set up that way. Instead, I climbed on top of him, straddled his stomach, and stared down at him.

The silence stretched, and I got annoyed, so I poked him in the sides with my fingers. The way he jumped was hilarious, but he grabbed my wrists before I could get another jab in.

"Really? You're gonna poke me until I tell you?"

"That was the plan. Speak, man," I demanded.

"I don't wanna talk about it."

I tried to pull my wrists free, but he tightened his grip on them, so I abandoned that tactic and used my knee to dig into his side. If he thought that he was going to get away with not sharing after making me spill, he'd lost his mind.

"You don't get to keep secrets after you practically forced me to tell you about my nightmares."

"I did *not* force you. And what happened to 'our relationship isn't emotional?' "

"That was before you forced me to tell you about the dreams."

"Ugh, I did not... Stop saying that word."

"What word? Oh, you mean... *forced*?" I asked as I giggled.

Zey tugged my arms, placed my hands on his chest, and went back to staring at the ceiling again. I was growing restless, so I opened my mouth to bug him, but he cut me off.

"You remember last week when Eli and I came over dressed up?"

"Mmm... Do I ever. You should really wear suits more often. It gives me a ton of delicious ideas.

"Does it now? Do tell."

"Don't distract me with sex when I'm trying to get you to talk to me. Spit it out."

"Fine," he sighed. "We came from a meeting with a guy who is selling a space I want to convert into a gym. If we can strike a deal, I'll be able to open a second location."

"Congrats. That's awesome, Zey. So, what's the issue?"

"Well, the greedy fucker changed the selling price, and since there was nothing signed yet, he can legally get away with it."

I traced the tattoos on his chest as he talked, hearing the disappointment in his voice. It was disheartening.

"As if that wasn't bad enough, he says he has another buyer willing to pay the new price and is only giving me a week before he takes the other offer."

I surprised us both with my next question, but I asked it without any hesitation.

"How much do you need?"

Zey studied me. "I didn't tell you about it to get you to cover it for me, Red. I told you because you f..."

"Did you almost say *forced*?" I asked before I broke out in a fit of giggles.

Zey narrowed his eyes at me. "I will admit nothing."

"Mhm. Anyway, that wasn't my question. I'll ask again. How much do you need?"

"Red, I..."

This time, I cut him off with a heated kiss. I didn't want to keep going back and forth. He was just as stubborn as I was, and we'd be at it all day if I didn't get him to give in. So, I took a page out of his playbook.

"Just let me help you..." I offered. "Please."

He was silent for so long, I thought he wasn't going to accept the help. Then, he let out an extremely deep sigh and whispered the amount.

"You don't whisper when you tell me to suck your dick. Don't start whispering now."

Zey wrapped his arms around me, rolled us over so that he was on top, and then kissed me.

"You drive me crazy," he groaned. "Twenty-five grand."

"Meh, you say that, and yet you can't get enough of me. I'll write a check before you leave. Now, all we need to do is work out a repayment plan."

"Don't worry. I'll pay you back within two months."

"Oh." I blinked at him. "Yeah, that's cool. I don't really give a fuck about that." Zey raised a brow in question. "I had something else in mind."

My favorite smile spread across his face as he realized what I wanted. Climbing off the bed, he picked me up and walked us to the closet, then secured my wrists to the wall and grabbed a toy out of the drawer.

"You ready for your repeat?" he asked.

"Fuck, yes!"

Without hesitation, Zey turned on the toy and rubbed it over my lips.

"Open your mouth, Red," he instructed.

VIII

Rose

Days like this always sucked ass. Terribly. I was trying to work on a new chapter, but I had no inspiration. The few sentences I managed to type out were mediocre at best.

The blinking cursor and empty white page teased me relentlessly until I slammed my laptop shut. At this point, I was in 'fuck it' mode. Staring at the screen wasn't helping, so it was time to do something else.

I was already heading out of my library when my phone rang. It was My. That was weird because she never called me. Not that I was complaining. I was in need of a sexy distraction, and she fit that bill to a tee.

Now, don't get me wrong. She could call me if she wanted, but she always stuck to texting. So honestly, I thought maybe something was wrong.

"Hey, My. Are you OK?"

"Yes, yes. I'm fine. I'm sorry for calling, but you were the only person I could think of who might be able to help me."

"First off, you don't have to apologize for calling me. You can call me whenever. Second, what can I help you with?" I asked as I hit the speaker button and laid out on my couch.

"Oh. O-OK. Well... Um..."

God bless her soul. My was so sweet and precious, but sometimes, I wished she would just be more self-assured. I let her stumble over her words for a few more minutes before I lost my patience.

Look, we've discussed that I'm not all that patient, but I do try.

"My. Please take a breath so you can get it out, and don't apologize."

"I'm so—" She cut herself off and cleared her throat. "A gallery saw some of my paintings at a pop-up and offered to give me an opportunity. They commissioned a collection to feature at their newest location."

"Yo, that's fucking amazing, My! Congratulations! But, uh... Well, how do I fit into all this?"

"T-thank you! I-I... Well, I... Um..."

Just breathe in through your nose and out through your mouth, Rose. This is a big deal for her, so you can't get annoyed that she's nervous. Well, I mean you can, but you're working on not being such a dick, remember? I reminded myself.

"Ro?"

"Yes, sorry. I'm here," I rushed out quickly, ending my internal monologue. Now, I felt even more like a dick because she was going to have to repeat her question.

"I have a really sensual idea, and I wanted you to be my model. Would you... Please?"

I don't think in all the years we've known each other, I've ever heard her speak that fast. Actually, let me edit that. She squeaked it more than said it, but I heard it, and that's what counted.

Of course, I was down to help her. No problem. But we've talked about me being an asshole in the past, right? Naturally, I had to tease her just a little.

"I don't know, My. What do I get out of this impromptu modeling job?" I asked.

"Oh! Um... I'm more than happy to compensate you for your time."

I think I rolled my eyes so hard, they got stuck in my head for a full five seconds. This was my fault. I should've just waited to tease her in person because doing it over the phone was failing epically.

"It was a joke, My. Of course, I'll be your model. For *free*," I emphasized. "Just tell me what you need me to do and when."

"Do you have time now?"

Today was starting to look up. I'd already wasted the entire morning trying to eke out a decent word, and that plan didn't sound enticing for the afternoon. However, spending the afternoon with My meant I would get a shit ton of inspiration, and that sounded marvelous.

"I sure do! Where are we meeting?"

"Ah... So, that's the other thing. Um, my art studio is also my home, and I know how you feel about coming over, but I—"

"That's cool, just text me the addy, and I'll be there soon."

The line fell silent. I knew My was convincing herself that I was joking again, and given how I was about going over to their houses, I understood her confusion. If I let her continue to mull it over, she would freak out and try to find a different space to do this.

"Yes, I said that's OK. Yes, I'm sure," I answered for her. "If you want me there, the only way that happens is if you send me the address. See ya."

Click.

My's text came a few seconds later, and I smiled. Nervous or not, she put her art ahead of her anxiety, and that made me ecstatic.

Myra had dreamed of being featured in a gallery since before I'd met her, and there was no way in hell I wasn't going to do everything in my power to help her achieve her goal.

By that point, I'd been to everyone's place but Wynter's, Xavier's, and hers, anyway. So, maybe it was time to reevaluate that rule. It was something to consider but not my primary focus right then.

My hadn't really given me any instructions on what to wear, and I guessed I wouldn't be painting, but just in case, I wore some old clothes that I didn't really care about.

Once I was dressed, I headed straight for her place. It was a really cool area because it was in an old warehouse district. Around ten years ago, a new developer bought it all and turned it into residential housing. Smart move on their part since it was abandoned for quite a while, so I'm sure when it was all said it done, they got the neighborhood for a fraction of the asking price.

After I parked and found the right entrance, I went inside. I had to take a really retro-looking lift up in order to get to My's floor.

It was kinda unique and cool. As I rode it, I pretended I was a secret agent in a movie on her way to a safe house or something like that.

Hmm... That sounds like it could be a good story for another book. Gotta keep that one in mind.

Anyway, I went up to her floor and walked down to the end of the hall. Her door was huge like the ones you'd see outside of a scrap yard. I knew it was hers without checking the address because she'd painted a breathtaking blue water dragon on it.

After a few knocks, the lock clicked and the door slid open, revealing My looking absolutely... adorable.

Whenever we'd met before, whether it was out or at my house, she was always dressed to impress with her hair flowing down her back. Today, she had her hair up in a bun, using paint brushes to pin it in place instead of hairpins. She wore tight black shorts and a blue sports bra. There were paint smudges all over her body.

The look on her face was by far the best part. Even though I told her I would come and she sent me the address, she was still surprised I was standing outside her apartment.

We'd have never gotten anything done if I hadn't moved things along, so I leaned down and kissed her before stepping into the loft. And when I say loft, I mean it. Unlike Mel's condo, this place was the very definition of it.

My's apartment had an open floor plan and only one big-ass room. It was separated into very distinct sections, like a living room, a dining room, and a kitchen, each area filled with corresponding furniture. But there was also a full-on art studio with easels, carts full of paints, and canvases strewn about everywhere.

One section caught my eye because it was up on a platform and curtained off. I guessed it was the bedroom, and I really wanted to visit that section the most, but I'd have to wait since I came here to help first.

The other thing I loved about this place was that her art was all over, and I mean all over. My's loft was an art explosion, but I suppose if I had the talent she did, I'd display my art everywhere, too.

"So, what do I do? Am I supposed to pose, or lay down, or strip?" I prompted.

She'd been fidgeting with her easel while I was talking, but her head popped up as soon as I said *strip*. I knew she'd said the collection was going to be sensual, but now, I had to wonder just *how sensual* this experience was going to get.

My ignored my question and went back to what she was doing. That was boring, and we all know how I feel about anything dull.

Since I had no idea where she wanted anything, I let her do her setup. She drug a chair over from the dining room area, placed it against the wall, and stood her easel up in front of it. When it looked like she was done, I snuck up behind her, wrapped my arms around her waist, and pulled her into me.

The scent of paint and lotuses overwhelmed my senses. You wouldn't think it would make for a good combination, but on her, it was actually... lovely. Deliberately, I kissed her cheek and neck in all the paint-free spots.

It actually became a little bit of a game for me, finding all the clean places to kiss. I fully enjoyed the noises she made after each one. Of course, this was distracting us both from the task at hand, but I couldn't help myself.

Just being there and touching her was already overloading my mind, filling it with all the inspiration I had been searching for earlier. And all the ideas it gave me made my hands itch with the need to test them out.

My finally found her voice again as I pulled the straps of her bra down. She spoke up.

"R-Ro! We're supposed to be working."

"Mhm..." I groaned. "I am working. Tryna work these clothes off of you."

My gave me a smug look. "You can... after I get the sketches done. First, I need you out of your clothes."

"Heh, so you *do* want me to strip!" I raised a brow at her.

Pulling away from me, My grabbed a black robe covered in red Kanji symbols off the back of the couch. She held it out to me.

"Yes, I need you naked," she said, "but I want you in this, too. I need a few poses from you and some different positions, as well. Once all the initial sketches are done, *then* and *only then* can you work me out of my clothes. K?"

I couldn't help but grin at her. That was the bossiest she'd ever been with me, and it was fucking hot. I don't know where My's nerves went, but I didn't give a fuck. The longer those little bitches stayed away, the more fun we'd have.

"My bathroom is to the left of the bedroom if you want to go get changed there," she said as I took the robe.

With the biggest smile on my face, I laid the silky fabric on the back of the chair and started to strip, making sure to keep eye contact with her the entire time. The blush that bloomed on her cheeks only made me smile wider.

I don't know what she'd expected. I've never been the shy type of chick. If I have the choice of stripping down in front of her to rile her up or changing in the bathroom, we all know what I'm going to choose. She should have known it was coming.

Once I was done stripping, I slipped into the robe, leaving it open, and sat on the chair, spreading my legs wide.

"Oh! That's actually perfect!" My exclaimed. "Lean back in the chair and put your arm over the backrest, please. Doesn't matter which one," she instructed without so much as a blink.

OK, this is going to be even more fun than I was hoping.

I followed her instructions, and she began her sketching. To avoid getting bored and fidgety, I started to imagine all the things I was going to do to her when we were done.

Two hours and at least fifteen poses later, My was finally finished with all her sketches. There was no way to tell if she would get nervous again, so while she was still in 'boss mode,' I made my move.

Over in her studio, Myra had her back to me as she put her art supplies away. Seizing the opportunity, I grabbed the chair I'd posed in, dragged it over to her, and pushed her into it. I'd taken her by surprise, but there was a delicious heat in her eyes, one I wanted to capitalize on. So, I tugged the paintbrushes from her hair and let it fall free.

My closed her eyes as I ran the thickest of the brushes down her body. When I reached her stomach, her legs snapped open without me even having to ask. I absolutely loved it when my girls' bodies responded to me without my having to command them.

Pressing the brush between her slit, I rubbed it up and down. Her head fell back, and a whisper of a moan left her lips. With my free hand, I pulled up her bra and latched onto her nipple as soon as it was visible.

The taste of her skin was electrifying and made my mouth water. I synced the rolling of my tongue on her nipple with the stroking of the brush over her clit through her shorts. Her moans increased in tempo, but they turned into delicious cries when I moved the brush down to tease her entrance.

I wanted to keep teasing her through clothes, but My obviously didn't care for my plan. Scooting the chair back, she stood up and stripped. Should I be annoyed that she foiled my plans? Maybe. Was I more focused on her naked and gorgeous body? Fuck, yes!

Excitement completely outweighed the annoyance as I pushed her back down into the seat. Now that she was naked, I could have more fun, anyway.

So, I dropped the brush, fell to my knees, and ravaged her. Her cries, moans, and screams — I devoured every last one of them until her cum spilled down my throat. As soon as she regained control, Myra grabbed the robe and pulled me up until she could reach my lips.

The way her tongue thoroughly dove into my mouth made me think she was trying to lick up the cum I'd just swallowed. It was one hell of a kiss, and I was intoxicated by it.

She grabbed my hand and pulled me toward the bed, but I stopped to pluck something out of her art supplies. A long, round-handled brush had caught my eye while she was doing her sketches.

I had no idea what you could paint with it, but I had other plans. The images that flooded my mind, of fucking her with that brush, had almost driven me crazy while she worked. It took a shit ton of patience (that I didn't really think I had) not to abandon the task and fuck her with it earlier, but I dug down deep and somehow checked the impulse.

Now, I was going to fully enjoy my reward for being so good.

"Um... What do you plan on doing with that?" My asked.

"Thought that would be obvious, actually," I told her. "I'm going to fuck you so hard with it that every time you look at it, you'll instantly cum."

I didn't give her much time to react before I threw her over my shoulder and headed for the bed. All of my patience was used up, and it was time to get to work. I tossed her on the bed, pulled the robe off, and descended upon her.

Our mouths melded together as her fingers dipped between my legs and found my clit. Her rubbing started out slow and gentle but quickly became fervent. Her pace was so fucking intense that I couldn't even focus on my plans.

She pushed me down onto the mattress, shifting positions, and resumed her rubbing once again. Her fingers were so fast that I came quickly and fiercely. It was fucking amazing! Since I'd mentally turned this into a game, by my count, we were tied. Which meant I had to make her cum again and again if I wanted to win. And I did.

I'd accidentally dropped the brush in my earlier haste, but it didn't take long to find it. While I grabbed it, My pulled out a bottle of lube from her nightstand and handed it to me.

Incredible.

When I'd first told her I was gonna use it, she'd looked at me like I was crazy. But now, after one orgasm, she was all for it.

She even laid back and spread her pussy for me while I lubed up the brush. I was so damn excited. So far, the scenes in my head were playing out in front of my eyes, and they were amazing. Exactly what I wanted.

The next part, I hoped, would be even better than I'd imagined. Once the brush was lubed, I rolled it over her clit. Her body reacted beautifully.

The shivers that raced through her had me salivating for her next orgasm because I could already tell it was going to be *mind-blowing*. I moved the brush down to her entrance and slowly began to push it in.

"Fuck! It's so fucking thick," My gasped.

I really wanted to move faster, but I needed her to adjust first or I could've possibly hurt her. Yet, she wasn't making the choice to go slow easy because she kept rolling her hips as I pushed it in deeper.

"I'm gonna run out of length soon. Your pussy is so fucking greedy," I told her, pushing the thickest part of the brush inside of her.

"Ro! Oh my God. Please, *please* fuck me," she begged.

Finally.

The adjustment period was over, and she was ready. I gripped the brush as tightly as I could and started thrusting it in and out of her at a rapid pace. My began to buck and ride the brush, all while screaming my name.

What I was seeing was so much fucking better than I'd imagined, and it was about to get even hotter. Positioning myself, so I wouldn't lose any momentum, I attacked her clit with my tongue.

My's fingers twined themselves into my hair as she rode the brush and my face. Those earlier shivers became full-blown tremors that made her body dance with pleasure.

The only fucking downside to this position was that I had to use my free hand to hold myself up or I would have twisted her nipples, too. Not even five seconds later, My started twisting them herself, causing her screams to grow even louder.

When she came, her orgasm shook the entire platform and almost broke the damn brush. Immediately, I pulled it out of her to avoid any possible splinters. I didn't put in all that effort for her to end up in the fucking hospital.

My's breathing was ragged, but the heat in her eyes hadn't dimmed one bit. She wanted more, and so did I, but I wasn't going to risk using the brush again.

"Sorry, My. It almost broke inside of you," I said as I tossed the brush onto the mattress. "So, no more of that, but my hands still work."

A small smile spread across her features before she rolled and leaned over the side of the bed. I had no clue what she was doing, but the view of her ass was great, so I had no complaints.

A few minutes passed, and she leaned back up, laying a very long and thick dildo in front of me.

"Or, we could just use this," she said with a smirk.

I really, really need to stop assuming I'm the only one with toys at home.

Impressed, I picked up the dildo and admired it for a moment. I hadn't imagined this, but it was going to make for fantastic inspiration. When I looked over at Myra, she opened her mouth, anticipating exactly what I craved.

I've said it before, and I'll say it again. I just fucking *loved* when my girls listened without my even having to say a word.

IX

Rose

Not that I'm not completely flattered you wanted me to be your model and everything, but why didn't you ask Wyn? She would've made an amazing muse for your paintings."

Naked, Myra stood in her bathroom and rubbed her towel down her body, fully tempting me to take her right back to bed.

"She's been ghosting me for a couple of days, so I figured she wanted to be left alone," My answered, bringing my focus back to my question. She stopped drying off and turned to look at me.

Worry was evident on her face. She could never hide her emotions from me. That's one of the things I adored about her.

"What's wrong?"

My began to fidget so damn much that I thought I was going to have to force it out of her.

"I think she might be having more family troubles?" she suggested.

"Whatcha mean?"

"I won't get too much into it because it's not my story to tell, but her dad is a real piece of work."

"OK," I said. I leaned against the door jamb and crossed my arms. "Let me guess, he's even more of a bully when he imbibes?"

My nodded pitifully before she went back to drying. I could tell she felt guilty about telling me Wyn's business, which was sweet. But I couldn't help unless I knew what was happening.

"I need you to tell me what's going on, but I'll make sure she doesn't find out you told me. I promise."

My hung up her towel and walked out of the bathroom. I followed close behind, trying to gently nudge her to open up. She sat on the couch and hung her head in her hands.

Based on the way she was acting, I was starting to get worried. My thoughts leaned to the disastrous side of possibilities, and if she didn't open her mouth and tell me what the hell was up, I was about to explode.

"Long story short, Wynter's dad was abusive to her mother, so her mom left. That was great for the mom because she got away from the situation, but she left Wynter behind with him.

"Wynter favors her mother, so when he's sober, he's a nice and doting father, but when he's drunk, which is more often than he's sober, he's cruel and vile to her."

"Does he hit her?" I pressed.

"I-I... I don't..."

"Simple question, My. Yes or no?"

"I don't know, but I think he has before."

"Explain."

"Well, I think one of the things he does when he's drunk is take all of her money. Sometimes, she'll call off for about a week, and at the same time, she'll ask me to borrow money for bills.

"At first, it was a bit confusing because my thinking was that if she needed the money for bills, why call off for a week and forfeit a check? But that's also why I think he may have hit her before. She might have refused to give it to him and used the time off to heal enough so she could cover her bruises with makeup."

If that's true, I'll fuck him up.

"I'll go check on her. What's her address?"

"The eighth floor."

I frowned. "Of this building?"

"Yeah," she nodded. "We realized we lived in the same building after we became friends. It was a happy coincidence."

"Oh! I'm sure that made sex a lot more convenient," I joked, trying to brighten My's mood.

Myra giggled, then looked at me and shook her head. "You're the first and only person we've both slept with simultaneously, Ro."

I swear, there are just some things my possessive traits don't need to know, and that was most definitely one of them. Shaking my head to clear it, I walked over to My and kissed her forehead.

"Which apartment is hers?" I asked.

"It's two doors down from the elevator to the left. There's a huge waterfall painted on it."

"You guys are making me jealous. I want a door painted with your art, too," I said, pretending to pout.

My rolled her eyes and gave me a mystifying smile. The tension in her beautiful face had finally dissipated. I was glad I'd accomplished my goal because I didn't want to leave without making sure she wasn't worried.

"Well, Ima go bother her, and I'll text you after, K?"

"K."

Wyn's door was easy to find because of the painted waterfall, and what a painting it was. It was so well done that I felt like I could actually hear the crash of the water against the rocks.

When I'd said I was jealous of their doors, I'd meant it as a joke, but now, I really was. My's art was so fucking awesome. I needed to find a door she could paint at my house, ASAP.

I didn't realize how long I'd been standing there staring until another resident came out of her apartment to walk her dog and asked me if I was OK. I played it off and knocked on Wyn's door.

For a minute, I was a little worried she wasn't home since she wasn't answering, but then a sudden bellow of rage rang out from the apartment.

That freaked me out, so I started to literally beat on her door as if I were the police and call her name. After three hard pounds, she finally snatched it open.

I rushed inside and looked around, trying to see if her father was there. Her apartment was the mirror image of My's as far as layout, but instead of art, there were electronics everywhere.

"What the hell? You can't just bum rush your way into my house like that!" Wyn bitched.

"You must be joking. You got hella nerve telling me about busting into a place, fam," I retorted, spinning to face her.

That was when I noticed her bruised cheek and busted lip. She must have realized where my eyes were because she placed her hand on her face and turned away.

"I'm not in the mood to entertain today, Rose. You can leave."

"After you tell me what's going on."

"Please. Just go," she pleaded.

"Not until you tell me why your face has two bruises on it. That sweet voice isn't going to get me to do what you want this time. Who did that to you?"

Wynter glared at me, and I glared right back. I was wearing comfortable shoes. I could've stood like that all damn night if I needed to. Clearly, Wyn came to that understanding because she slammed the door closed and walked past me. Ignoring me, she sat in her gamer chair and spun it around to face her monitors.

The setup was legendary. She had six screens all going, an LED keyboard and mouse, and a desk full of anime and *Funko* characters.

The computer in the corner of the desk was DIY'd, and it was fucking badass. I knew she wanted to be a video game developer, but I hadn't known she was that into tech.

Funny, the things you learn about people when you go to their houses.

"So, we've established that I'm not leaving. Wanna tell me what's going on?"

The only answer I received was the clicking of keys. That was aggravating, but I was patient because I don't like when people get into my business, either.

While I fully understood her hesitation, I don't really deal well with anyone hurting my friends. Several minutes passed, and the sands in my hourglass of patience continued to trickle down, running low.

"We both know I'll just keep bothering you until you tell me, Wyn," I reminded her.

Still, silence was the only answer she offered. My hourglass was empty now. I walked over to her chair, spun it to face me, and leaned down until we were eye to eye.

"Who? Did? This? To? You?"

"Why are you acting like you fucking care? We fuck. That's all! We don't ask personal questions. We don't get involved in each other's lives," she spat. Then, she looked me up and down. "Oh, wait. I know what you're here for," she said with a slick smile, trailing her fingers down her chest.

I'd been so damn focused on her face, I hadn't realized she was only wearing a long tank top. She dragged her fingers through her cleavage, trying to make me focus on that instead of my questions.

It was like I was questioning myself. A huge part of me never wanted to open up to people because there was a possibility I could get hurt, and I'd been hurt enough in the past. So, I kept my secrets close to my chest at all times. That's why I gave Wyn such a huge break when she got on my nerves. She and I were so damn similar in attitude, it was humbling.

But there was a smaller part of me that just wanted someone who cared to ask me until I opened up. Was that the right way to go about it? Maybe not, but sometimes when you have walls so thick built up, it's hard to tear them down by yourself.

Hazel had always been the person who did that for me. I knew each of the fuckables would ask if I let them, too. Mel and Zey had already proven as much. So, although Wyn wasn't going to like it, I was going to ask and ask until she told me.

Even as she reached to pull up my shirt, both my wild and sane halves were in sync. There would be no fucking. At least, not right now. This time, I'd get answers. If she wanted to fuck *after* we talked, I'd more than likely take her up on it.

Grabbing her wrists, I pulled her hands off of my shirt. She tried to tear her wrists free, but I tightened my grip before kneeling down in front of her.

"If you want me to fuck you, you know I'll do that without any hesitation," I told her. "But right now, I want to help you. Yes, we fuck, but you're my friend too, and I don't like seeing my friends hurt."

A solitary tear rolled down her bruised cheek and almost set off my anger, but I swallowed it down. She didn't need my rage on her behalf. She needed comfort, so that's what I would give her.

Standing up, I pulled her out of the chair and wrapped my arms around her waist. As soon as I had her in my embrace, she began to shake and cry. I drew small circles on her back, letting her get it all out.

After a few more minutes, she pulled back and rubbed her eyes. "I'm ruining your shirt."

Well, that's fucking adorable.

"You know, the great thing about Amazon is I can just buy another one."

She rolled her eyes and gave me a small smile. "Ugh, I'm sure I look horrible right now."

"Nope! You're still fuckable. Snot and all," I said as I lifted her chin and stroked her cheek.

She gasped and covered her nose and mouth before running off to what I assumed was the bathroom. I heard running water as I followed after her and leaned against the door jamb, just as I had with My.

Well, this sure feels familiar.

Wynter was bent over her sink, washing her face. Her tank top rode up over her ass. It took strength I didn't know I had to keep my eyes from landing there. After she was done, she stood up and patted her face dry.

Thank you for saving me from my horny self.

Wyn leaned against the vanity and stared at me. Her eyes were unfocused, so I knew it wasn't really me she was looking at. I'd been there before. At that moment, she was deciding whether or not to take some bricks out of that wall of hers.

"You ruined my shirt, so you have no choice but to tell me now," I said with a smile.

Wyn smiled back before she rolled her eyes and sighed. "My parents should have never been together," she admitted, "but as if that disaster of a decision wasn't bad enough, they decided to have me and bring me into their world of misery.

"I had a typical, dysfunctional childhood filled with daily arguments and fights 'til about high school when mommy dearest had finally had enough and left. One issue: She forgot to take me with her."

My heart broke as I listened to her story. Parents are supposed to protect their children, whether they like each other or not. The child should always come first.

Wyn's childhood made me appreciate my parents even more because they argued every once in a while, but my brother and I mattered more than anything else. Always. That wasn't the case for Wyn. When she finished talking, she slid down the vanity until she was sitting on the floor and hugged herself.

I stepped into the bathroom, sat in front of her, and rubbed her arms. This moment was crucial because so far what she'd told me was mild, and two things could've happened next.

She would either withdraw or she would continue. So, I gave her a small, extra nudge to make the difference.

"You've already started talking. Might as well keep going."

"I'd always favored my mother more than my father, and it used to be a good thing. He was an ass when he drank, but he was bearable. After mom left, he lost it. My looks pissed him off whenever he was drunk, and that was all the fucking time.

"As soon as I was eighteen, I left, but he was my dad, so I foolishly kept in contact with him. He would randomly ask for money, and I gave it to him every time. At first, that arrangement was fine, but then he started to ask for money more frequently and for larger amounts."

The longer she talked, the harder she shook. Internally, I was shaking, as well. I really hoped I could meet this piece of shit in the near future and help him reevaluate his life choices.

My imagination ran wild with all the painful things I wanted to do to her father. I got sucked into my thoughts, but before I knew it, Wyn grew quiet. That helped me focus back on the conversation.

"What happened here?" I asked as I lightly brushed her bruised cheek.

"I gave him the work number for emergencies only. He called up there looking for me on my day off, and some new bimbo waitress gave him my home address.

"So yesterday, he came banging on my door, screaming for me to give him money. I'd already told him I wasn't going to give him any more, but he refused to leave. I'd had enough, so I opened the door and threw two hundred dollar bills at him. I threatened to call the cops if he didn't go. He finally did leave, but not before backhanding me and calling me a selfish bitch."

"Wow, that's a shitty story, love. But I do have one question. Well, actually, two questions."

"Oook, what do you want to know?"

"One: Why was calling the cops just a threat? And two, where can I find him?"

"He's my father, Rose. I don't actually want to call the cops on him, and I'm not going to answer the second question."

"Sweetheart, that man has only reached the level of a sperm donor; he never received the honor of being a father." Wyn nodded, so I continued. "And why not? I'm not gonna do anything... too bad," I said with a chuckle.

For the first time since I rushed into her apartment, she offered me a genuine smile that lit up her face. I still wanted her to give me his address, but for now, I was satisfied that she was at least feeling a bit better.

I was about to ask for the address again when a barrage of furious banging on the front door cut me off. Turns out, I didn't need his address after all. The look of fear in Wyn's eyes let me know I was about to meet the *father of the year.*

Oh, that was easy.

I was already on my feet and making my way toward the front door when Wyn grabbed my arm.

"Don't," she whispered, shaking like a leaf.

"Wyn, you're terrified of him, and you want me to do what exactly? Nothing? That's not going to work for me, and you know it. You were smart for not letting him know where you lived, but now that he knows, he's not gonna stop coming unless you make him."

"B-but, he's... he's my f—"

"If you say father one more damn time, Ima lose my shit. FATHER'S DON'T HIT THEIR DAUGHTERS!"

I hadn't meant to yell, but my anger was starting to rise to a level that was difficult to control. Her *father* had yet to stop banging, and he was screaming and calling her all types of disgusting names.

Likewise, Wyn had yet to stop shaking, and she'd begun to cry. I knew this was going to get out of hand and one of her neighbors, if they were home, would call the cops, anyway.

That's when I had an idea. Now, before you judge me for manipulating the situation like this, know that I did it for the Wynter's betterment.

"Hey, you know if he's left out there, one of your neighbors is gonna call the cops on him, right?"

"Oh my God! You're right," she said, quickly letting my arm go and rushing over to the front door. "Do not attack him," she pleaded before opening it.

Without hesitation, her father barreled into the apartment, raised an eyebrow at me, and then shifted all of his attention to Wynter.

"What the fuck took you so damn long to answer the fucking door? I know you heard me calling you," he snarled.

"Since my name isn't bitch, slut, or whore, I actually *didn't* hear you calling my name," Wyn answered. "But as you can see, I have company over, so could you just leave?"

"I ain't goin' nowhere until you give me my money."

"Funny. I don't remember *you* working for it. I'm not giving you anymore of *my* money, so go."

Her father took a step toward her as if he was about to hit her, but then I guess he remembered I was there because he glanced back at me. Apart from his eyes, the man looked nothing like his daughter.

He was tall with lanky limbs, had stringy, oily hair he probably never washed, and his beard was overgrown and unkempt. It looked like the majority of his weight came straight from his huge beer belly.

My only thought as we glared at each other was that I wished I had gone down to my car and grabbed my baton before I came to check on Wynter. Guess it was time to improvise.

"Stop trying to act tough in front of your lil' girlfriend, and give me my fucking money," he hissed, focusing on Wyn again.

"I'm not giving you anymore fucking money. Just leave my fucking house!"

While he berated his daughter, I inched over to Wyn's desk, looking for something heavy. In a minute, he was going to stop caring that there was a witness, and I'd be damned if he was going to hit her in my presence.

The keyboard was the heaviest-looking item, but unfortunately, the damn thing was corded. Though they were still arguing, I was sure I was running out of time. Spotting a pair of scissors, I picked them up and cut the keyboard's cord just in the nick of time.

Her father had begun to stalk toward her with his hand raised to strike.

"Hey, Wynter!" I shouted. "I'll replace this, OK?" As hard as I could, I swung the tech across the side of his head, effectively breaking it in half.

"I asked you NOT to attack him!"

"Technically, I didn't. Your keyboard did."

"ROSE!"

"WYNTER! I wasn't just going to let him hit you, so quit it. He's not dead... Unfortunately. Now, call the cops, or I will!"

She looked as if she wanted to keep arguing but realized it was pointless. Wyn grabbed her phone and made the call. While she did, I gathered some miscellaneous cords from her desk and hog-tied her father.

Wynter sat in her chair and stared at the man. He had begun to thrash as he came to.

"Am I terrible because I still see him as my father?"

"Nope. You're just human," I assured her.

Soon enough, the cops came and took him away. Wynter had to decide on her own if she was going to press charges or not. Of course, I wanted her to, but I couldn't force her. She looked at me with a pleading expression, but I shook my head.

"Don't shoot those eyes my way. You have to make the choice for yourself."

Her shoulders sagged, but it seemed like she had come to a decision.

"Officer, I'd like to press charges," Wyn told him.

I wrapped my arm around her waist and kissed her cheek. "Good girl."

The cops took her initial statement and left, saying they would be in touch. I helped Wyn pick up the scattered keys from the broken keyboard, and we both crashed on the couch after everything was said and done.

"Well, this was quite an eventful first visit," I said, turning my head to look at her.

Wyn burst into giggles and pushed me. "You're ridiculous. *I'm not attacking him. Your keyboard is.* Really?"

"Not sure what you want me to say to that." I shrugged. "Technically, that's what happened."

Wyn shook her head. "Thank you," she whispered.

"Mmm... It wasn't really anything special, but you're welcome."

"Soo," she said, with a seductive smile. "What do you want to do now that all my family drama is over?"

"Hmm," I said as I tapped my finger against my lip. "Well, you did mention something about sex earlier. Did you not?"

She licked her lips as her smile widened. "That I did. I'm most definitely up for it if you didn't use all your energy taking down my dad."

"Oh, no! That didn't take much effort at all. I have plenty of energy left to make you scream and beg."

"Oh, really?" she said as she laid back on the couch and pulled me on top of her.

"Really!"

"Well, I'm sure you could already guess, but these last few days have been quite stressful for me, so I need a major destress session. Think you have enough energy to make me scream the whole night?"

"Oh, sweetheart," I purred. "Not only do I accept your challenge, but Ima fucking crush it!"

Reaching between us, Wynter tugged up her shirt, granting me a view of her glorious body.

"Please do."

X

Melanie

The first half of my work day went great. The author I was working with was happy with the developmental edits I'd sent over, and she was going to get back to me after she implemented them.

That left me some time to finish up the line edits for the other two authors I was working with. By lunchtime, I was a quarter of the way through one of the assignments. I tried to keep my mind busy, but even so, I couldn't keep my thoughts from straying to the text Lina sent me earlier.

> **Lina:** Did you go to work sans panties this morning like I asked?

> **Me:** Yes! For whatever crazy fucking reason, I did.

> **Me:** Now, will you please explain to me why you wanted me to come to work without panties in the first place?

> **Lina:** You'll see.

That was it — her last text. I wasn't fully sure what she meant, but I assumed she was planning to stop by for my lunch hour so we could fuck. That was a lunch date I could really sink my teeth into. The prospect was exciting, but where could she take me that would allow us time for our fun and for her to get me back before the end of my break?

As soon as I'd finished the thought, I realized I didn't actually give a fuck if I was late coming back. I'd never been late in all the time I'd worked here, so if it happened one time, I didn't think Michelle would mind too much. If she did, I would just have to apologize profusely because there was no way I was going to rush sex with Lina, job or not.

I was still lost in my thoughts when my door swung open. Stephanie stepped in, allowing Lina to follow behind her. Momentarily, my breath caught as my eyes scanned over her. She wore a black jumpsuit that fit her like a glove, accentuating all her curves.

Fuck, she looks so hot!

I had to quickly squeeze my legs together to keep my arousal at bay. Lina smiled, clearly aware of the effect she had on me, like always.

Thankfully, Stephanie didn't notice. "Sorry to interrupt, Melanie, but Ms. Thorne said you were expecting her. Are you available?"

"Yes. Thank you so much! I'll be taking my lunch now, so you're free to take yours as well!"

"Very well. Thank you," Stephanie said as she turned and stepped out. She closed the door behind her, leaving Lina and I to stare at each other. Lina's eyes were brimming with desire, and it felt like my tongue thickened in my mouth.

"Umm... So," I swallowed to clear my throat. "Where did you have in mind for lunch?"

"Here will do just fine," Lina replied.

Her answer surprised me. "Oh, did you want to order in? What do you have a taste for?"

"Your cum on my tongue."

"What?" I squeaked.

Lina didn't answer me. Instead, she shrugged a backpack off of her shoulders and opened it. Transfixed by her every move, I watched as she pulled out a lighter, a small bowl, and a pack of incense sticks. What was she doing?

"What... What are you up to?" I asked.

"The incense will mask your arousal, just in case someone comes in."

"*Comes in*?" I gulped. "Are you crazy? We can't have sex here!" My words came out in a rush, and my breathing hitched. I couldn't even process what she was offering.

But even as my mouth said *no*, my body said *yes*.

Undeterred by my response, Lina lit the incense, set it in the bowl, and made her way over to me. The scent of cherry blossoms wafted behind her, and all the sexual heat in my body surged to my clit as she approached.

Lina leaned in, stopping only an inch from my lips. She leveled her sultry gaze on me. "It's so cute when your mouth says no, but your body screams just the opposite!"

"I-I don't know what you're talking about," I stammered.

"Yes, you do," Lina said. She moved in closer and dragged her nose along the crook of my neck. "Mmm," she groaned. "The incense is for them, love. But nothing, and I mean *nothing*, can keep me from smelling what I do to you. Now, did you want to try that again? Maybe it will be convincing the second time."

Lina's lips hovered only a whisper away from my ear, and the shivers she was causing made it extremely difficult to think. My lace bra rubbed against my nipples with every breath, and I was getting wetter by the second.

"I can't focus enough to lie right now and I'm way too horny to deny you," I panted. "Are you going to fuck me on the desk?"

"Oh, that sounds fun. But, no. It would suck if you got fired."

"Then, what's your plan?"

Pushing my chair back, Lina sat on my desk in front of me. She closed the gap between us and kissed me. Her hands trailed a blazing path down my body, stopping at my skirt before she slowly started to hike it up toward my hips.

"Pull up your skirt, scoot up to the edge of the chair, and spread your legs for me," she ordered.

Suddenly, her texts made more sense. My mouth opened and closed, but I couldn't find my voice. Lina slid off the desk and dropped down onto her knees, smiling up at me. I still couldn't speak, but my body didn't care that my brain had momentarily malfunctioned. It moved on its own.

When I pulled up my skirt, baring myself to her, Rose smirked and licked her lips. I scooted to the edge of the chair, lowered it slightly to make it easier for her, and leaned back.

The moan was out of my mouth as soon as her tongue slid up my slit.

"Shh... You don't want to get caught, do you?" she teased.

"That's not my fault," I breathed. "What did you expect me to do when you ran your ton... Oooh, fuck!"

Lina pushed her tongue inside of me, cutting off my words and causing my eyes to roll back. I bit my lip in an effort to stifle my sounds, but then she sucked my clit into her mouth, making it even harder.

"Mmm... You're making it difficult to stay quiet."

"Can't help it," she said as she slid her fingers inside of me. "I love the way you scream when I touch you."

I gripped the desk so hard that my knuckles went stark white. Somehow, I managed to keep my scream in. I leaned back farther in my chair, so she delved deeper. All the while, thoughts of tearing off my clothes and letting her fuck me on top of the desk soared through my mind.

Lina spread her fingers inside of me before twirling her tongue on my clit again. I was so fucking full. The scream I'd only barely managed to swallow down before burst from my lips when she unexpectedly slipped a vibrator deep into my pussy and turned it on.

Covering my mouth with both hands, I attempted to quiet the scream, but when Michelle came through my door moments later, I knew I'd failed. Quickly, Lina turned off the vibrator, concealing her presence, but she didn't stop. From under the desk, she continued to lick and stroke me.

"Melanie, are you OK?" Michelle asked, concerned. "I thought I heard you scream." Her eyes scanned the room.

"Yes!" I squeaked. My voice caught, so I cleared my throat. Without looking, I felt Lina smile against my clit. "I'm fine. I-I-I thought I saw a spider on my desk, but it was just dust."

"Oh, no judgment here." Michelle chuckled. "I would've screamed and been out the door, dust or not."

I smiled back at her, hoping she wouldn't notice the way my chest heaved. Lina still hadn't stopped probing. She added a third finger inside of me. I was so close, but cumming while my boss stood ten feet in front of me wasn't an option. The thought kept my climax at bay, but only just.

"Are you sure you're OK? You seem a little... I don't know. Flustered, maybe? Did one of the authors give you a hard time?"

"No, no. I promise I'm fine," I assured her. "I was just startled, that's all. All the authors I'm working with are great."

"OK, well let me know if you need to talk," Michelle said. Seemingly convinced, she finally stepped out of my office.

As soon as the door closed, Lina turned the vibrator back on. She moved everything in and out of me in tandem. I couldn't risk Michelle coming back, so I had to bite my palm to keep quiet. Enjoying her little game, Lina flicked her tongue against my clit as she increased the pace of her strokes.

That did it. I crashed over the edge so forcefully, I broke the skin of my palm from biting down so hard. But it was worth it. Lina drank every drop my body gave her, savoring my taste until I became too sensitive and pushed my chair back.

"Trying to run away from me?"

"Never, but I don't think there's anything left for you to lick up."

"As a member of the clean plate club, it would be disrespectful to not finish my meal. Don't you think?" Lina joked.

I couldn't help but smile as I rolled my eyes. It was the middle of my work day. We were in my office. Yet, tucked under my desk, Lina grinned at me with my cum still coating her lips. And I hadn't done a thing to stop her while Michelle had stood well within earshot as she devoured me.

This woman had me firmly under her spell.

"Mhm... Now that you've eaten, can I pull my skirt down so I can order us actual food?"

"I'd rather you take the skirt off, but go ahead." She smirked. "Also, you don't need to order anything. I brought you food."

"Oh! What did you bring?"

Lina stood and kissed me. The taste of my cum on her lips sent lust funneling through my veins. Then, she reached for her backpack and withdrew two *Tupperware* containers, popping them open.

Hunger doused all the lustful heat. The scent of shrimp alfredo mingled with the incense, making my stomach growl embarrassingly loud. I was mortified, but Lina simply smiled and twirled her fork in the pasta before raising it to my mouth.

"Your tongue didn't break me, you know. I can feed myself."

"Don't say things like that to me, Mel. You know I'll take it as a challenge." She winked. "Plus, I want to feed you. Now, open wide."

Simultaneously, my mouth and legs opened. Even though she hadn't meant for her words to be sexual, my body didn't care.

Lina chuckled as she slid the fork in my mouth. The taste of the sauce and shrimp swirling on my tongue drew a small moan from me. It was no louder than a whisper, but of course, she heard it.

"Was that for my food, or is your pussy still hungry, too?" she asked as she dragged the stem of the fork down between my breasts.

"Both," I whimpered.

Lina continued the fork's descent until Michelle entered my office once more. Luckily, I wasn't far enough from the desk for her to see anything. Still, Lina had the forethought to pull my chair up to the desk with her foot, just in case.

Thank God I never took my shirt off.

"Oh! I'm sorry, Melanie," Michelle offered when she saw that I wasn't alone. "I didn't realize you had company. I was just going to ask if you wanted to have lunch with me." Walking over to Lina, she extended her arm. "Hello, my name is Michelle."

Thinking fast, Lina used the food container she held as an excuse not to shake Michelle's hand.

Trust me, you don't want her to shake your hand right now. I wouldn't be able to live that down.

"Rose Thorne," Lina replied. "Nice to meet you."

"Nice to me— Wait. Rose Thorne, as in *the* erotica author, Rose Thorne?"

"The one and the same." Lina gave her a charming smile.

"Wow, Mel. I didn't know you were dating *Rose Thorne*. Good for you!"

"Oh, that's because we—"

"We just started dating recently. She probably wanted to make sure I was sticking around before sharing the news," Lina cut me off.

It took everything in my body to keep my jaw from dropping. She just said we were *dating*, and I wasn't dreaming.

Stop freaking out. She said it to save you some embarrassment. Just keep it cool.

"I do hope you stick around. Speaking of which, you're currently independently published, right?"

Only Michelle could turn a friendly meeting into a business discussion. I looked from her to Lina. Lina's expression was polite, but it wasn't her usual panty-wetting smile. It didn't reach her eyes.

That made me happier than I cared to admit. I'd seen her smile at Xavier and Elijah the same way she smiled at me, which was to be expected. Michelle was an extremely attractive woman with an amazing body, crystal blue eyes, and a killer smile.

All that, and Lina only gave her a simple grin. That line of thought was extremely dangerous, but I couldn't stop myself, even if I wanted to. Lina had just *claimed me*, and even though we weren't in a relationship, she wasn't flirting with Michelle in front of me.

Apparently, I'd become so absorbed in my thoughts that I'd missed the conversation completely. Both Lina and Michelle were looking at me as if waiting for an answer to a question I hadn't heard.

"Um... If I say yes, would that be the right answer?"

Michelle laughed, and Lina gave me the sultry smile that always made me wet. I squeezed my thighs together tighter and moved my focus to Michelle. From the corner of my eye, I could see Lina was still smirking.

If I kept looking at her head-on, she would be able to smell my arousal soon, and since Michelle was still in the room, she'd be able to, too.

"I asked Rose if you two would be up for a double date?" Michelle repeated.

"I didn't know you were dating anyone? I'm sorry, that came out harsh" I said trying to backtrack.

"No need," Michelle grinned. "You're not the only one with secrets." She winked.

I glanced over to Lina. "So, yes was the right answer, then?"

"You know, I have another small book tour starting tomorrow, but once I get back, I'm down if you are."

Logic told me this was a bad idea, but my heart told logic to shut the fuck up. I found myself nodding.

"Wonderful. It's settled, then. Melanie, I'll coordinate with you, and we'll set a date." Michelle seemed pleased. "I'll let you two get back to your lunch." Turning, she opened the door. "Oh, and Melanie... If you wanted to take off early, I wouldn't hold it against you." She winked before closing my office door behind her.

Lina laughed. "Oh, I like her. She's funny. Since she's the boss, does that mean I get to finish what I started?"

Shaking my head, I bit my lip and smiled. "You've already finished. I came, remember?"

Lina skirted my desk, pushed my chair back, and turned it toward her. My skirt was still bunched up around my waist, and even though she hadn't touched me yet, my body was already growing wet for her again.

Leaning in, Lina ran her nose along my neck once more. "Mel, when have you ever just cum once when I've touched you?"

As I thought her question over, I realized I'd never enjoyed only one orgasm when she fucked me, but several, and each one was better than the last. I almost nodded until I remembered her games under the desk when Michelle first came in.

Tapping my finger on my bottom lip, I pretended to think it over. "Hmm... I vaguely remember one, maybe two in the past," I said with a small shrug.

"Vaguely? Two? You *must* be joking."

"Mmm... I don't know." I shrugged again. "Ever think that only two of them were worth remembering?"

I really needed to learn that if I was going to play these games with her, I had to consider my surroundings first. In the blink of an eye, Lina had me on top of my desk with my skirt halfway up my stomach and my shirt unbuttoned.

"Lina, Lina, Lina! I was kidding. Y-you know I was kidding," I sputtered, attempting to get ahold of her hands and stop her. "Did you forget where we are right now?"

"Nope," she answered as she placed one hand on my chest and shoved me backward.

Her other hand slid between my lips faster than I could stop her. As soon as her fingers slipped inside of me, my body arched for her, driving them deeper.

"Lina, please!" I whimpered. "I'm sorry. W-why don't I take Michelle up on her offer and leave early?" I asked as I gripped both her wrists.

"We can do that, but let my wrists go first."

"Will you take your fingers out of me?"

Lina didn't answer me. Instead, she smiled and rolled her thumb over my clit. My grip loosened, and she thrust her fingers deeper. My moan came out fast and loud.

"We're not leaving until I hear you scream. You're not strong enough to keep me from doing what I want. If I were you, I'd put my hand somewhere else... Unless you want your whole office to know my name."

Lina gave me no time to react. Breaking my grip on both of her wrists, she pushed me down and pumped her fingers. The only thing I could do was clamp my hands over my mouth and ride out the pleasure-filled assault.

After I screamed into my hands on the cusp of a world-shattering orgasm, Lina withdrew her fingers from my body and licked them clean.

"Now, we can go."

XI

Rose

Although I loved doing book tours, I was overly excited that this one was only three days. I mean, book tours are absolutely wonderful. Wherever I went, I got to meet fellow smut-obsessed weirdos, take hot chicks back to my hotel room, and add magnets to my travel collection on my fridge.

There was always an adventure to look forward to, but this time as I signed a book for a chick with curly hair, all I could see was Mel. The thought of bending her over the table in front of me ran through me so quickly, it made my head spin.

How was it possible I'd just seen and fucked her yesterday, and yet, all my thoughts kept straying back to her. The last person I'd missed like that was Hazel, but don't you dare tell her that. I'd never hear the end of it.

The curly-haired woman was trying to flirt with me, too, but it wasn't landing. She was really cute, don't get me wrong, but I was too distracted by memories of Mel cumming on my face in her office. Those images gave me an exquisite idea. I wanted to put it into motion right that moment, but I still had a line waiting out the door.

I have to be a professional now and a sexual deviant later.

I made it through both the signing and the reading without rushing either, and I was quite proud of myself for being so damn committed. Several women tried flirting with me during the event, and I had to gently turn down each and every one of them.

One chick actually cornered me in the bathroom and damn near threw herself at me. That was new. What shocked me more was the fact that my wild side didn't even react to it.

As soon as I got back to my hotel room, I tossed all my stuff down, grabbed a quick shower, and started putting my plan into motion. I called both a sex shop and the *Walmart* located near Mel's place and placed an order at each.

Then, I found a task rabbit who would be willing to pick up and deliver. After those jobs were done, I set my work phone up on my tripod and faced it toward the bed. This idea was either going to be amazing or it was going to be a disaster. It really all depended on how Mel was feeling.

If she was thinking about me in the same way I was thinking about her, then she would most definitely be into it. If I wasn't on her mind, then this might be a little awkward.

Honestly, I was almost one hundred percent sure she'd be into it. Mel might've started out shy, but the more time we spent together, the bolder she became. Watching her try new things and realize how much she craved them was slowly becoming another addiction.

Not long after I set up my phone, I got a text from the task rabbit, letting me know they were on their way to Mel's condo. My excitement for what was about to happen next sent heat pumping through my veins.

After I stripped down, I started recording on my work phone and climbed onto the bed. My fingers were already trailing down my body as I dialed Mel's number with my free hand.

She picked up quickly, just like I knew she would, and I'll admit, it brought a smile to my face.

"Hey, Mel."

"Hi, Lina."

"Whatcha doing?" I asked.

"Laying in bed," she answered.

I hit the button to switch the voice call to video, and she accepted. When she saw me, her eyes filled with excitement and wonder.

Perfect.

XII

Melanie

I know I just saw you yesterday, but is it bad that I miss you already?" I asked.

My question was met with deafening silence. I dropped the phone. My heart literally felt like it was going to crack open in my chest. I didn't know what to say to fix this, and I couldn't find my voice, but Lina stopped my erratic heartbeat with four simple words.

"I miss you, too."

Hearing her voice, I snatched up my phone so quickly, I almost threw it across the room. "W-what?"

Rose chuckled. "Gonna make me repeat it? Really?"

"I couldn't hear you over my pounding heart," I told her. "Say it one more time, please?"

"I miss you too, Mel."

"Wow," I breathed. "Can I stop time and just enjoy this moment?"

"You could, but then you wouldn't get my surprise."

"Surprise?"

"Mhm, should be showing up right about... Now!"

A knock sounded at my door as soon as she finished her sentence. The smile on those full lips of hers had me curious, so I jogged down the stairs. A woman holding two gift bags was waiting on my stoop. One small one and one large one. Immediately after I opened my door, she handed both of them to me, swiftly said goodnight, and walked away, leaving me dumbfounded.

"Aren't you gonna open up my surprise?" Lina asked.

"What are you up to?"

"Head back upstairs, open the bags, and you'll find out," she ordered.

I rolled my eyes but did what she said. Placing the phone down, I opened the bags. A gasp left my lips as my eyes roved over the items. The bigger bag held a tripod, a very long and thick red dildo, and a small black bullet.

The small one held a black-lace bra and red-lace crotchless panties. I laid the contents of both bags out on the bed, then grabbed my phone.

"Um, w-what is all this?"

"My surprise!"

"Yeah, OK. I got that, but why did you send me this stuff?"

"I would think that would be obvious, Mel. I want you to fuck yourself for me."

My jaw hit the floor. I could've guessed she wanted that, but hearing her say it was just too shocking. Lina laughed, clearly enjoying my reaction to her words.

"Y-you want me to..."

"Fuck yourself for me. Yes. Yes, I do!"

"I-I..."

"Come on, Mel. I know the thought of me watching you cum has you wet right now. Why you playin' hard to get?"

She was right, like always. I was soaked, thinking about her watching me please myself. But I was still nervous I would look ridiculous. I wanted to be confident, yet this whole thing freaked me out.

"Mel, your face is so easy to read," Lina said. "You're gonna look amazing. Think of it this way: You'll get to perform the ultimate tease. I can't touch you, so I'll just have to settle for watching instead," She bit her bottom lip.

That got me moving. I placed the phone down so I could take the tripod out of its package. Once that was done, I set it up in front of my bed and attached my phone to it. Lina smiled the entire time, which helped me somewhat keep my nerves in check.

"OK. I've never done this before, as I'm sure you've guessed. So, you'll have to walk me through it."

"It'd be my pleasure," she said with a wolfish grin. "Get on the bed and strip for me, then put on the bra and panties."

I did as she instructed, climbing onto the bed and crawling to the middle, making sure to wiggle my ass as I went. Lina's sharp intake of breath put a big smile on my face. Once I was situated, I stood up on the bed and turned toward the camera.

Lina watched me with rapt attention, and the look burning in her eyes made my confidence rise. I pulled off my shirt, freeing my breasts, and draped it over the camera.

"Yo! What the fuck? That's not what I said," she complained.

I giggled at her disappointment. I knew from experience that making her work for what she wanted made things more exciting for her. Stripping off the rest of my clothes, I slipped on the bra and panties before removing my shirt from the phone.

"You're being such a lil' brat right n..." Her words trailed off.

Lina swallowed hard as the camera focused, allowing her to see me fully. The hunger in her eyes had me wishing desperately she was there with me. Enjoying the way her eyes tracked my every movement, I slowly slid my hands down my body.

"What do I do next?" I asked.

"W-what? Oh, um... Shit. Hold on, let me collect my thoughts."

I couldn't stop the smile spreading across my face. It always brought me so much joy to see her so flustered. Sitting back on my knees, I parted my legs so she could see the panties she'd sent me better.

Her eyes dropped straight down and landed between my legs. Already, I felt my excitement pooling out of me. My nipples were so hard, they ached. I needed her to hurry up and tell me what to do. The sexual tension was starting to overwhelm me.

"Grab the vibrator, and slowly circle it over your breasts, then I want you to drag it down your body and stop right before your clit."

Shivers raced down my back as I bit my lip and picked up the bullet. I traced it along my collarbone and down my chest, which caused goosebumps to rise along the path I created.

Once I made it down to my left nipple, I began to circle it with the bullet until it peaked, heavy with need. When that was finished, I moved over to my right. Small moans left my lips as I did my best to keep eye contact with Lina the entire time.

"Just like that," Lina praised. "Now, turn it on and rub it through your slit. Make sure to keep it away from the sweet spot."

Her lust-charged words pushed me closer and closer to the edge, and I hadn't even gotten close to my core yet. Dragging the toy down, I ran it through my pussy. The vibrations caused me to jump as I made sure to keep the toy away from the goal.

"Lina, this is torture. Can I play with my clit now?" I begged.

"This is only the beginning, love. No, you can't touch it yet. Push the toy inside you, and get it nice and wet."

I rolled my eyes but obeyed as I thrust the toy inside of me, collecting more of my juices with every stroke. My nipples were so hard, and my pleasure was building with each second. If this went on any longer, I would cum soon without ever even touching my clit.

"Keep stroking the toy inside yourself, unclasp the bra, and twist your nipples," Lina ordered.

"Fuck! You're trying to kill me..."

"No. I'm trying to *destroy* you. I want your every climax to rack throughout your body. I want even the whisper of a touch to send you over the edge. I want to ruin you for any and everyone but me."

Lina's words were so hot that I was only able to apply a small bit of pressure to my nipple before I found myself screaming her name with my release.

"See how hard you came with just my words? That's what I want. That's what I crave. I want your body to listen and to obey my every command."

"Fuck," I said between pants. "What's next?"

Lina smiled that wolfish grin of hers before she bit her lip again.

"Lift the camera up and angle it down. I don't want to miss a second of this. Then, take off the bra, pull out the dick, and lay down."

As requested, I set the toy down, adjusted the camera, removed the bra, grabbed the dildo, and laid down. Lina smiled and licked her lips like she was as hungry as I was. That climax was mind-numbing, and already, I was starving for more.

"Now, spread your legs and show me everything I want to see."

My legs parted before she even finished her sentence. She'd had control of my body since the day she first kissed me. There was no use in denying it. My body was hers to command.

"Tease your entrance with the dick and roll the toy around your clit. Don't turn either of them on."

I whimpered but did as she'd ordered. The tip of the dildo became slick quickly, and all I wanted was to slide it in.

"What do you want, Mel? Use your words," Lina taunted.

"I-I want you deep inside of me, so deep that it would be hard for me to breathe. I want you to make me cum so hard that I'm blinded by stars."

My chest heaved, but I didn't push the dildo in, waiting for her instructions. There was something I wanted even more than what I just confessed, but I was too scared to ask for it.

"That's not all you want, is it?" Lina asked. "Tell me what else."

My eyes snapped open in shock. I don't know how she always knew what I wanted, but if I didn't say it now, I never would.

"I want you to command me, to tell me what to do, to make my body yours without even a single touch," I admitted. "Make me fuck myself as if you were here with me."

Lina groaned. "Turn on the dick only, and push it inside you as far as it can go. Stroke it quickly and deeply until you feel your body start to burn."

Lost in my passion, I followed her commands. My body was a livewire, but I continued to stroke, picking up speed, even as my wrist began to cramp.

"Turn the toy on, Mel," Lina said. "Cum for me. Scream, and let the universe know my name."

That's what I needed. Immediately, I came so incredibly hard that I dropped both toys as my body shook. Stars danced across my vision, and I screamed her name at the end. She'd gotten everything she wanted, and so had I. I was exhausted, as though I'd competed in a triathlon, but I enjoyed every minute of it.

"I want you to know I recorded every second of that, but before you freak out, I also recorded myself as I came while watching you. The video is in your inbox. Rest for now, but don't forget to take a bath before too long. I don't want you too sore when I get home. I'll text you in the morning."

XIII

Rose

Those three days went fast, and I had a lot of fun. I picked up some new magnets and talked with some readers who thoroughly enjoyed my writing. Yet another great experience on the books!

My video call with Mel helped my urges calm down. Just barely, but I was able to get through the rest of the tour without seeing her face on every curly-haired woman I signed a book for.

As soon as I got home, my thoughts went wild again, but Mel wasn't the only person I had on my mind. Eli was running rampant through my thoughts, as well.

That stunt he'd pulled at his apartment refused to let my mind rest. The only thing I could focus on was highly pleasurable revenge. I'd had it planned since I left that morning, and it was going to be perfect. All I needed was him and my playroom.

I unpacked my bag, grabbed a shower, put on a red lace set, and grabbed my phone. It was pretty late, but I hoped I could catch him before he got home and changed out of his suit.

Me: Come over tonight.

Eli: Hello to you too, Thorne. Give me a few. I just left the office.

Me: Good. Come over. NOW!

Eli: So demanding.

Eli: Keep talking like that, and you'll end up with my dick in your mouth.

Me: I'll talk in whatever way I want.

Me: You don't like it? Come fuckin' do sumthin' 'bout it.

Eli: When I pull up, I want your mouth shut and your legs open.

Me: Just get here and fuck me already.

Eli: Open the fucking door.

A smile broke out across my face as I read that text. Tossing my phone down on the bed, I rushed to the front door. I'm sure my excitement radiated off of me in waves, but I couldn't care less.

Eli was dressed in a slate gray suit this time. Somehow, he looked even more fuckable than before. There was no vest, tie, or glasses, but his shirt was unbuttoned, and his hair was unbound.

My mouth ran dry as my panties became drenched. Eli stepped in, picked me up, kicked my door closed, and slammed my back against it. My legs wrapped around his waist as my hands roved over his back.

He palmed my ass while he expertly devoured my mouth. Every breath and moan I attempted to get out, he stole. I was so thoroughly distracted that I was beginning to forget about my plan.

"Hope you're thirsty," he whispered, trailing hot kisses down my neck to my breasts. "Because I'm aching to spill my cum down your throat."

That snapped me out of my lust-fueled haze. I *was* thirsty for him, but my desire would have to wait until I made him beg. Placing my hands against his chest, I pushed him back, allowing some much-needed breathing room between us.

"You're at my place, remember? You follow the rules, you get to play. You don't, and well..."

Eli snorted and rolled his eyes. As my smirk turned into a full grin, I unhooked my ankles and unwrapped my legs from his waist. He let me slide down his body until I was on my feet, looking up at him.

"I'm here. You're right. But I only have so much restraint, Thorne. I'll play this lil' game of yours. For now," he said, gripping my chin and placing a soft kiss on my lips.

I giggled at his choice of words. If he thought he was being restrained now, I couldn't wait to see how he'd feel when I was through with him. Stepping past him, I made my way over to the basement stairs.

Eli followed close behind and slapped my ass. His arms wrapped around my body, and he nibbled my ear. I needed him downstairs for my plan to work, but the way his fingers danced over my panties made it hard as hell to focus.

"What are you up to, Thorne?"

"Maybe if you didn't ask so many fucking questions, you'd find out," I retorted.

Eli wrapped his fingers in my dreads and snatched my head back before biting my neck. A moan raced out of my throat as my nails found purchase in his arms.

"Fuck! There's no fucking up *here*, remember?"

Eli circled his tongue on my skin. "I remember," he whispered as he turned our connected bodies toward the kitchen. "But *you* forgot while I fucked you senseless on top of that island."

As I stared at the black marble, images of Eli's return raced through my mind — every flick of his tongue, twist of my nipples, and stroke of his dick deep inside of me.

I was so incredibly wet that my desire was dripping down my thigh. If I didn't focus and gain control over *both* of the lustful beasts raging inside of us, I'd end up undone on the tip of his dick on my island again. That wouldn't do.

Eli trailed his hand down my chest, but this time, I grabbed his wrist and stopped him. I tugged on his arm, and we finally made it downstairs. I'd tied long silk scarves to the headboard and my wingback chair was stationed in front of the bed.

"Strip for me, and climb onto the bed," I commanded.

Eli smiled and began to undress. The muscles in his back were tantalizing, and I had a hard time keeping my hands to myself. As I watched his shirt fall off his body, I noticed his shoulders were broader, and his arms were bigger, too.

When he turned, my breath caught in my throat. His six-pack had been upgraded to an eight-pack. I was very close to losing my mind at the sight of it, but I held onto one thought.

Just get him tied to the bed, then you can lose it.

To keep my head level, I kept repeating that over and over, but even then, I felt my control slipping as his pants slid down his thighs.

But leave it to Eli to snap me back into focus.

"I guess you were thirstier than I thought, on the count of that drool coming out of the corner of your mouth," he teased as he climbed onto the bed and leaned back against the headboard.

"Cute," I answered, tying his wrists to the wood. "You do look delicious. Obviously, you've been working out with Zey. That's why you're being so cocky, right? Think you can keep it up?"

"Cocky? Never," he joked, tugging on the scarves around his wrists. "You know your *need* to feel my dick pounding deep inside of you is practically screaming at me, right?"

Shivers raced down my back, and I had to bite my bottom lip to hold the whimper in. Keeping focus was still damn near impossible, but it was a little easier now that he was restrained.

I grabbed a rose-shaped vibrator with an attached thrusting bullet from my closet and came back into the playroom. Eli studied me with an eyebrow raised as I pulled off my panties and sat down in the chair.

"Did you plan a lil' show for me, Thorne?"

I tossed my panties at his chest and watched his eyes roll back as my scent overwhelmed his senses. A wolfish grin raced across his lips and caused a matching one to spread across mine.

"This the game you wanna play?" he asked.

I put my feet up on the ottoman and spread my legs. His eyes dropped down, straight to my glistening pussy. Eli began to struggle against the ties, and I heard a small rip.

"Aht, Aht, Ah. Don't do that. If you rip those scarves, then the game ends, and we both know you don't want that to happen."

Immediately, he relaxed and huffed out an annoyed sigh. I ignored him and turned on the toy. The vibrator's buzz filled the room.

I placed the rose on my clit and circled the bullet around my entrance as he and I maintained eye contact. The rise and fall of his chest picked up as I pushed the bullet inside of me. The thrusting of the toy drew a sweet moan from my lips.

"Oh, fuck," he whispered.

When I turned up the vibration, I finally lost my mind. My moans grew louder, and Eli began to struggle against the ties again. I should have chastised him, but I was too lost to my pleasure. Leaning my head back, I spread my legs wider, fully enjoying the satisfaction the toy provided.

"Fuck, Thorne. Untie me," he pleaded.

Eli's demand fell on deaf ears as I pushed the bullet deeper. The sound of more ripping reached me, but my focus was on the bliss only seconds away. My body convulsed, and I cried out as my climax soared through me.

"Un-fucking-tie me," he growled.

"Not yet," I shook my head. "I still have a game to play."

Eli watched me as I set the toy on the nightstand and climbed onto the bed. His length stood tall and strong, and I was eager to quench my thirst. But he wasn't primed enough yet.

I wrapped my lips around him and took every inch of him all the way down to the hilt. It took my throat a second to adjust to his girth, and tears sprang to my eyes, but hearing his soft moan was so worth it.

Popping his dick out of my mouth, I smiled up at him. His eyelids were heavy, and I could tell he wanted to force my head back down.

"I'm going to rip your lil' scarves in about five seconds if you don't let me loose," he warned.

So, I climbed into his lap with my back facing his front. "If you do that, you know I'll stop," I smirked, sliding myself down onto him, achingly slowly. The way he filled me was mind-numbing.

"Oh my God! You feel so fucking good inside me," I whispered as I rotated my hips.

"Imagine how much better it will feel when you free me," he groaned through gritted teeth.

"You haven't asked nicely yet."

"Shit, that's what you've been waiting for?"

I used his knees for leverage, raised up to the tip, and slammed back down onto him.

"Yes!"

"FUCK. Thorne, *please* un-fucking-tie me. *Now!*"

"No," I shook my head as I slammed down on him again. "Gotta make sure you mean it first.

Eli let out a wry laugh and bent his knees slightly. I glanced back at him, trying to figure out his game. He just smiled.

"Oh, I meant it," he said, ripping the scarves and freeing himself. "But I warned you I could only deal with so much restraint. You wanted to play? Let's *play*."

Wrapping his arms around my waist, Eli lifted me off of his dick before tossing me down beside him. I didn't get a moment to compose myself before he forced my head into the sheets and slammed deeply into me from behind.

The sheets muffled my scream, but I knew he heard it by the way his pounding picked up. His pace was extreme, but I matched it stroke for stroke.

Eli grabbed my hair and pulled me onto my knees. "Hands on the bed, sweetheart," he insisted. "I want full access to those tits," he whispered in my ear.

That sent fire through my veins. I put my hands on the bed as he'd requested, and his quickly found my breasts. His already erratic pace kicked up another notch as he twisted my nipples and laid his chest against my back.

The sound of his name on my lips drowned out his grunts. I felt the precipice of my pleasure getting closer and closer. Leaning all of my weight on one hand, I moved my free hand down between my legs.

Eli gripped my wrist before I could reach my clit and yanked it behind my back.

"You don't get to cum until you earn it."

I was so lust-drunk, I almost fucked up and said please, but I was able to catch myself and hold it in at the last second. I was so close, all I had to do was stay quiet a little longer.

Eli began to laugh as he kissed my neck. "You're so cute, Thorne. You really think I don't know what you're trying to do?" He pulled out of me, leaving only the tip inside as his hand found my core. "You *will* beg for me like the lil' cum-hungry girl you are, or we *will* stop."

"Oh... I am so going to kill you and Ze—" He cut me off by slamming into me and rolling his fingers. My legs shook so badly, it was a huge struggle to keep myself up, but I managed it. Eli removed his hand and pulled out to the tip again.

"You know you want to beg for me, Thorne. It's just six lil' letters, and then I'll fuck you into paradise."

Those whispered words were so close to my ear that they uncorked my mouth so quickly, it made my head spin.

"Ooh, fuck. Please! *Please*," I begged.

"Shit my bad. I meant *nine* letters. Let's try that again, huh?"

I knew what the asshole meant, and even though my pride wanted to tell him to go fuck himself, I was enjoying the way he was fucking me far too much to be defiant.

I gave in. "Eli, please!"

He slammed into me one last time as he rolled my clit and sent my soul into orgasm heaven. My heart pounded, and I couldn't catch my breath, but that didn't phase Eli in the slightest. Rolling me over, he looked down at me with a huge smile on his face.

"I like the game we played, but I think my version was better. Don't you agree?"

"Mmm... Ask me again when I can think straight," I told him.

Eli laughed and leaned down to kiss me.

"Don't sleep yet, Thorne," he whispered. "I still owe you for that demanding tone earlier."

"Uh-huh. I told you, I'll talk in whatever way I *fucking* want."

"You also told me to 'do sumthin' 'bout it.'"

"And?"

"I'm going to."

XIV
Melanie

I knew I agreed to the double date with Michelle when Lina came back from her book tour, but now that the night was here, I slightly regretted it.

Lina had openly claimed we were dating in front of Michelle, which I was secretly still doing an internal happy dance about, but now, I had to figure out what that really meant.

Could I do the things people did when they were dating? Would that be allowed for tonight, or was that crossing the boundaries? Could we kiss in public? Hold hands? Could I call her baby?

So many damn questions raced through my head that they were starting to drive me crazy. Then, Shelly came over and shut my spiraling down.

"Do what you want," she said simply as she rubbed curling gel through my hair.

"But what if—"

"No buts. If you want to kiss her, or hold her hand, or call her baby, then do it. Do you really think she's gonna stop you? She already *claimed* you, and it would be weird if y'all weren't caked up since you're supposed to be dating."

"I guess you're right," I reluctantly agreed.

"I'm always right," she answered. "Now, what are we wearing tonight?" Shelly shot me an amused grin, ready to stuff me into whatever she'd brought in the garment bag she'd draped across the back of my couch. But this time, I was prepared. She was gonna love the dress I picked out.

"Keep that lil' devilish smile to yourself. I actually have something," I informed her.

"Ooh, well let's see it, then," she prompted.

Following me into the closet, Shelly waited for me to produce the dress. I'd bought it the day I agreed to the dinner date, just so I wouldn't be frazzled, and at that moment, I was so grateful I did.

I pulled it off of the hanger and hung it in front of my body for her to see. It was an A-line, deep-red dress with a V-neck halter and flared bottom. Shelly studied the dress and then began to clap.

"I'm so proud of you. My baby's all grown up."

"Oh, shut the fuck up! You're so annoying!"

"Maybe, but you met me this way and still signed up for our friendship, so suffer in silence."

With a quick roll of my eyes, I dropped my robe and slipped into the dress. The strapless pull-up bra I'd put on had my tits raised up to the sky, looking fantastic.

Shelly adjusted the front over my breasts until everything fit well. Once she was satisfied it was perfect, she stepped back and took it all in.

"Ooh, you might not make it to your dinner, Lane," she teased. "After one look at you, she's gonna tear you out of that dress."

That's what I was hoping for!

"You really think so?" I asked.

"Yeah. If I liked you like that, you wouldn't make it out the door of your apartment, let alone to the restaurant."

Just as we left the closet, Lina walked into my house and froze in the entryway. She looked breathtaking like always, wearing black crepe wide-legged pants, a burgundy crushed-velvet blazer, and a black-lace bralette.

"You really need to stop dressing like that if you want to make it out the door," Lina said as her eyes tracked down my body.

Knowingly, Shelly turned and smirked at me.

Yeah, yeah. You told me so.

"You know, it's kinda rude that you're going on a double date, but you never asked me if I wanted to go on one," Shelly whined.

I laughed. "You'd have to be dating someone to garner an invite. Is there something I should know?"

"Nah. But you ain't have to shut me down like that. I thought we were friends." She put on a show of wiping away fake tears.

Lina laughed at her while I pulled on my heels.

"So, do we know where we're going?" Lina asked, "I don't remember if you told me or not."

"I think Michelle may have sent me the address while I was in the shower, but I don't remember where my phone is."

On cue, Shelly handed it to me, kissed my cheek, and then whispered in my ear. "Remember. Do whatever you want, and have fun."

I nodded once, and Shelly headed straight for the door. Lina opened it for her and tapped her own cheek. Laughing, Shelly raised up on her toes and kissed Lina's face.

"Happy?" Shelly asked.

"I just wanted to be included since you were giving out kisses and all," Lina said with a slick grin.

"Mhm. Sure, whatever you say." Shelly winked at me. "I'll talk to you guys later."

Shelly closed the door behind her as she left, and I checked my text messages to see if Michelle had sent me the information about the restaurant, after all.

She had, and I couldn't help the laugh that flew past my lips when I realized where we were heading.

"I wanna laugh," Lina whispered in my ear. "What's so funny?"

When she'd first started doing that, it used to make me jump, but now, I was used to it. I could tell Lina noticed the change because she pouted.

"Not my fault you've done it so much, I got used to it." I kissed the pout away and smiled at her reassuringly. "I laughed because we're going to *Casper's Secret*."

"Oh! That is funny. Well," she said as she backed me against the wall. "Since I already know the way and how long it'll take to get there, we can be late, can't we?"

The heat of her gaze, coupled with the close proximity of her lips to my neck, turned my brain to mush. Desire began to pool between my legs.

She placed a whisper of a kiss on my neck and let out a chuckle.

"You know I can smell you, Mel. Your body is already screaming 'yes.' Just say the word."

I wanted to. I really did, and if it was just the two of us going to dinner, I would've. But because Michelle would be waiting for me, I regretfully couldn't.

"You can have your dessert after dinner, not before. Now, let's get going." My words came out more confidently than I'd thought they would.

"Fine," Lina sighed.

When we pulled up to the restaurant, I sent Michelle a quick text to see if she was already here or if we should just wait in the car. Secretly, I was hoping for the latter if I was being honest with myself.

I didn't want to keep Michelle and her date waiting, but if they weren't here yet, I had several ideas about how to pass the time. I was about to suggest a few of them to Lina when my phone vibrated with a text telling me they were inside.

"Damn it!"

"What's wrong?" Lina asked, drawing my focus from my now-dashed naughty thoughts.

"Huh? Oh... Uh, nothing. They're here, so we can go inside."

"Cool."

Lina climbed out and came around to open my door for me. She held out her hand to help me get out of the car. After the door was shut, she kept ahold of it. I tried my best not to show how happy that made me.

We walked into the restaurant, and just like before, all the staff lit up when they saw Lina. They were equally happy to see me, too, which was surprising. It could've been them just doing their job, but it made me feel welcomed all the same.

The hostess led us to our table where Michelle and her date were already seated. The location was cool, but Lina's table from our first date had been far better.

I thought Michelle's date was supposed to be someone. Woooow, Melanie. Shelly would've been so proud of you for that thought.

He and Michelle stood up to greet us while I was busy internally berating myself. That was such a Shelly thing to think, and it wasn't really nice. Hoping it didn't show on my face, I shook his hand when he offered it.

Michelle's date introduced himself as Blaine Santiago, and the way he said it made me feel like I was supposed to know who he was. I didn't, but that wasn't saying much. If someone wasn't in the book, anime, or video game world, I wouldn't know them.

Blaine was nice-looking. Tall with broad shoulders. He'd styled his black hair in a messy quiff with a low fade, and his beard was trimmed. His chocolate-brown eyes continued to stray below my neckline, which was uncomfortable, but I didn't want to bring attention to it and ruin the night.

Once we were all seated, the waitress came back to take our drink order. Neither Lina nor I drank alcohol, so when we both ordered a Shirley Temple, Blaine gave us a questioning look.

"Isn't that a kid's drink?" he asked.

"It's a drink kids happen to like, but I don't remember it ever being labeled as a 'kids only' drink," Lina shot back.

"I guess you're right. I just didn't expect two grown women to choose that instead of a cocktail, or at the very least, a mocktail."

"I think it's cute that you both ordered the same drink," Michelle chimed in. "It's another thing you two have in common."

"Mmm. So, Rose, was it? Are you some type of writer, or do you work for Michelle as an editor, too?"

It was an innocent enough question, but his tone rubbed me the wrong way, almost as if being an editor wasn't an accomplishment. I didn't know enough about him to understand if his phrasing was terrible or if he was just an asshole. I decided to reserve my judgment for now.

"I am a writer, yes, but I'm actually a published author. And no, I don't have the patience Mel has for editing. I just like to put all the words on the page and then let my editor check to make sure all my bridges connect. Editors are magical beings, and I would be hopeless without them."

I couldn't keep myself from smiling. Even if Blaine hadn't meant to downplay us as editors, Lina had placed us right back on the pedestal.

The waitress came back with our drinks and asked if we wanted some appetizers.

Lina knew what I wanted, so she ordered our entrees and asked for the side Caesar salads to come out early with the rest of the appetizers.

"Do you two have any individuality at all?" Blaine pressed when the waitress walked away.

"Excuse me?" I snapped.

Even if I'd wanted to, I wouldn't have been able to keep the annoyance out of my voice. All I could think was: *Did he really just say that out loud?* Likewise, when I turned to Lina, she wore her cruel smile, and I knew she was just one more word away from laying into him.

Even Michelle was staring at him like he was crazy, but I guess he was oblivious to how outrageous his question was because he doubled down. "Well, you two ordered the same drink, the same salad, and the same entree. I'm just wondering if you chicks have the same brain, is all."

"Do you enjoy the taste of pleather?" Lina asked as she sat back and crossed her arms.

"I don't understand what you mean," Blaine responded.

"The more you talk, the further those fake-ass shoes slide into your mouth," she explained. "So, I'm just tryna figure out if you like the taste, is all."

Michelle, who had taken a sip of her drink, ended up choking on it. At first, I was afraid she was offended on Blaine's behalf, but then I noticed the smile she hid behind her glass.

Blaine scoffed. "You're unnecessarily rude, aren't you?"

Bro, you got a whole lotta nerve.

"Naw, I just match energies," Lina remarked, taking a sip of her own drink.

"And this is attractive to you?"

The question was directed at me, but given that his eyes were focused on my breasts again, it was hard to tell. I'd had enough. His comments had already annoyed me, but the ogling was really getting on my nerves.

Lina noticed where he directed his gaze, too. With a straight face, she said, "If you so much as look at her for a second longer, I will gleefully remove your eyes with my spoon and force-feed them to you."

The look of shock on Michelle's face probably mirrored my own. I expected Lina to be annoyed, but I was not ready for her to threaten Blaine with bodily harm, especially while wearing such a beautiful smile.

"Did you just threaten me?" he asked. "Do you know who I am?"

Blaine was beginning to raise his voice, and the other tables were taking notice. Guests started to watch us. I guess he thought that if he brought attention to us, it would cause Lina to back down and possibly even apologize. She wasn't deterred one bit, though.

"I don't make threats. Only promises," Lina added as she twirled her spoon. "Wanna see just how well I keep them?" Her smile widened.

"The owner is a personal friend, you snide little bitch. I could have you thrown out and banned from this restaurant with the snap of my fingers," Blaine tried, but his bluff missed its mark.

"If you're going to tell lies, you probably shouldn't do it when the person you're lying about is in the room," Casper said, approaching Blaine from behind and grabbing his shoulder.

Diners at the surrounding tables began to whisper again. Blaine went as white as a sheet. Things were about to get extremely interesting, and I had a front-row seat to the show.

Lina raised a brow. "Hey, Cas."

"Hey, Rose," he said. "Hey, Melanie. Hi, Miss..."

Extending his hand to Michelle and taking hers in his own, Casper kissed her knuckles. He hadn't taken his eyes off of her, and her eyes hadn't moved off of him, either.

"Michelle," she told him.

"Lovely."

"Is he single?" I whispered to Lina.

"Not for long," she said loudly.

Michelle blushed, and Casper smiled before turning his focus back to Lina.

"Why didn't you tell me you were coming?" he asked. "I would've had them set your table up."

Lina shrugged. "I needed a bigger table so that I could treat both these ladies properly. Are you expediting or cooking tonight?"

"Expo."

"Oh, then you should join us. Michelle needs a dinner date with balls," Lina said, pointedly staring directly at Blaine.

He didn't even say anything in his defense, just stood up with a huff and left the restaurant.

Unfazed, Casper took a seat and focused all of his attention on Michelle. "So, how'd you end up with a chump like him?" He asked the very question I wanted to.

"This was only our second date, and he wasn't anything like that on the first one."

"Oh, good. I thought I was gonna have to judge you on your poor choice in men for a minute there," Casper joked.

"You were gonna judge my choices based off of him?" Michelle scoffed. "How would you feel if I judged you based on the last girl you slept with?"

Without missing a beat, Casper replied, "I don't know yet. Ask me tomorrow morning when you wake up with your head on my pillow."

Oh. My. God! Do all of Lina's friends talk like this?

Lina wrapped her fingers around my chin and turned my face toward her. Her conspiratorial smile made me slightly anxious about what she could be possibly planning. Leaning in, she brushed her lips against my ear and whispered, "You've been watching them kinda hard, don't you think? It's making me a lil' jealous, and you know how I get when that happens."

"Well, you haven't given me anything interesting to focus on," I whispered back, unable to stop myself from playing along with her games.

Lina bit her lip. "How 'bout now? Is this interesting?" she asked, trailing her fingers along my thigh under my dress, heading toward my core.

My eyes darted around the dining room, just to see if people were watching. Thankfully, no one noticed, not even Michelle and Casper, who had yet to stop flirting.

Lina pulled my panties to the side, and I had to bite down hard on my lip to keep quiet.

"Don't be quiet now," she taunted as her fingers traced my slit. "Am I being interesting enough?"

"Yes. Yes," I panted, barely remembering to whisper despite the crowd.

Lina pushed two fingers inside of me, causing me to grip the table and close my legs to try and stop her. She chuckled in my ear and tapped my thigh with her thumb.

"Let me in, Mel. You know you want to," she teased.

"If I let you in, you're gonna make me scream in the middle of this restaurant."

"No, I won't. I promise!"

"And you always keep your promises, right?" I asked as I obliged, opening my legs.

"You know I do," she answered as she rolled her thumb over my clit. "Now, be my good lil' brat, and tell me what you want."

"Make me cum," I sighed.

She stroked her fingers in and out of me, and I held my breath so I could keep in every moan that wanted to fly free from my lips. Somehow, no one around us saw what she was doing to me, and that was a blessing, but when my orgasm hit, a quiet, strangled moan left my lips.

Michelle and Casper glanced over with concerned faces, and I scrambled to think of a passable excuse to explain the sound.

"Bit my cheek by accident," I said lamely, shooting Lina a dirty look.

She just smiled and sucked on her cum-slick fingers. Michelle and Casper nodded and went back to their conversation.

"You broke your promise, Lina!"

"No, I didn't. You didn't scream. You moaned. But when we get home, you'll be screaming for me all night," she said with a wink.

Check, please!

XV

Melanie

I was usually most hyped for Friday because it meant I was only one step away from the weekend. I'd rather have dealt with the most "Mondayest Monday" than *this* Friday, though.

Yes, I know. That's not a real word, but it truly conveys just how much I didn't want to deal with this bullshit. If you haven't figured it out yet, it was the day of the arraignment hearing, which meant I had to see King's stupid face.

It was a given that I had to be present since I was the one pressing charges, but still, being in the same room as him and not being able to grind my heel into his balls was pure torture.

A part of me wondered if I could get away with it, considering the circumstances, but logic slapped that thought out of my mind. Even if the judge was a female, she'd still have to punish me for inappropriate conduct, and that was something I had no interest in.

I won't lie and say I wasn't a little nervous to see him again, but I was grateful Elijah, Lina, and Xavier were there with me. Yes, I said Xavier, too. He was strictly on Lina duty.

I wouldn't even kid myself into thinking I was strong enough to keep her from attacking King if he so much as looked at me wrong (which we all knew he probably would).

Elijah, though capable of keeping her in check, had to be in attorney-mode and wouldn't have been able to stop Lina, either. So, that left Xavier. When I'd texted him about it, I was unsure how he'd react, but he came through, quickly agreeing and saying it was a really good idea for him to come.

I'd just finished putting my hair into a bun when I heard my front door open. Leaning my head out of the bathroom, I caught Lina closing it behind her.

She was wearing black slacks, a red blouse with a chain draped over each shoulder, and black boots. Her hair was also styled in a bun, which was so cute and instantly brought the word *twinsies* to mind.

Lina caught me staring and smiled before making her way over to me. She lifted my chin and kissed me gently. I hadn't known that was what I'd needed, but all the nervous energy plaguing me vanished at her touch.

"Ready to go tell his bitch-ass to drop the soap?" she asked.

A half giggle, half snort left my lips. It was a mortifying sound, but Lina didn't seem to care because she focused on petting Kuro. If she wasn't going to bring it up, then neither was I.

"I guess, I'm as ready as I'll ever be," I told her.

"Alrighty, then we better get going or else Eli will nag my ear off. You look way too hot for court, by the way. I'm tempted to be late, nagging be damned."

I knew I was staring again, but I couldn't help it. I don't know who she was looking at, but she couldn't have meant me. Stepping back into the bathroom, I checked myself out in the mirror.

My red blouse was extremely plain. My slacks weren't even form-fitting, and she'd seen me in these boots several times before. *Hot* was *not* the word I would've chosen to describe my outfit. Maybe plain. Wholesome. Boring.

Lina stepped into the bathroom and crowded me against the sink. The heat in her eyes had all the moisture in my body pooling in one place.

"Stop."

Her command was simple but powerful. My internal self-deprecation obeyed immediately.

"H-how did you know?"

She pressed her lips under my ear, grabbed my hips, and pulled my body flush with hers. I'd thought she was joking when she said she wanted to be late, but now, I wasn't so sure.

"You're so damn predictable, Mel. Every time I give you a compliment, there's a look in your eyes that screams you don't think I mean it. I thought you'd gotten over it, but I guess I was wrong."

"I'm sorry. I-I'm just not used to getting them."

Lina met my gaze in the mirror and smirked at me.

"I didn't say that to make you apologize. It just means I have to keep giving you compliments until you *do* get used to them."

Twenty-five percent of me took that comment at face value. The other seventy-five percent was spiraling over what that could mean.

Are you going to be around long enough for that? How long will you allow me to be in your life? Will you get bored with me? Will you replace me if I don't get used to it? Could this mean a future relation—

A swift slap to my ass brought me back to the bathroom. I looked up to see Lina smirking at me again. She shook her head and walked back into the living room.

"Come on. We have to go. If we stay any longer, you're gonna drive yourself crazy thinking about what I just said. Later, Kuro."

She was right. It wasn't the time. I needed to deal with this King bullshit first, then I could spiral later.

We left the house, drove to the courthouse, and met up with Elijah and Xavier. Elijah told us it could take a while before our case was called, so we'd have to wait, unfortunately.

The two men wore suits that fit them sinfully well. The more I saw them, the more obvious it became why Lina had chosen them as her... Huh. I'd never considered what we were called. Of course, she calls us fuckables, but if an outsider wanted to label us, what word would they choose?

Group? Team? *No, that one sounds stupid.* Orgy? *I think that one only works if we're all fucking at once.* Harem?

Harem fit the best, I guess. Why was I even thinking about this in the first place? Oh, yeah. The two men in front of me cut quite the sexy picture. The woman in this courthouse, and even a few of the men, couldn't walk past without sneaking a lust-fueled glance in their direction.

On a base level, I understood how they all felt. Xavier was so tall and well built, with his red and black hair up in a man-bun, while Elijah had his honey-blonde dreads in a ponytail and square wire-framed glasses on. His build and height didn't match Xavier's, but in the battle of sex appeal, they were evenly matched. I couldn't help but think that if I updated my glasses, Lina would think I looked sexy in them, too.

Don't ask me why I had that thought. I just did, so I thought I'd share it with you. Moving on. The funniest thing about the whole situation was that even as all the onlookers drooled over the guys, neither of them could stop sneaking glances at Lina, not even noticing the stares.

There was only one available chair outside the courtroom, and Lina let me have it, opting to lean against the wall next to me. She tilted her head down so it seemed like she was scrolling on her phone, but her eyes kept darting around as if she was ready for anything.

The way she behaved made me wonder what had to happen to a person for them to always be in 'go mode.' Then, I began to question whether it had something to do with her past, which she'd still managed not to tell me about. As soon as all this King BS was over, I'd try my hand at getting her to open up to me again.

My favorite smile crept across her lips, causing me to look away. My blush was blaring hotly on my light skin. In the future, I really needed to try *not* to get caught if I was going to keep staring at her like that.

A man's voice interrupted my thoughts. "Is the idea of seeing me again making you blush like that?"

There were several individuals I disliked for one reason or another, but I'd never experienced hatred before. Hearing such a ludicrous comment come out of his disgusting mouth filled me with so much repulsion that I felt like I was drowning.

The scent of cherry blossoms and teakwood hit my nose and drew me back to the courtroom. Lina squatted in front of me, reminding me to breathe. I guess my internal drowning looked like a full-blown panic attack externally.

Seeing him again did put me in a slight state of panic, considering what happened the last time we were alone. But her scent grounded me, and I felt the tidal wave of negativity recede.

"What the fuck did I ever see in you?" he pressed. "Oh, wait. I remember. I saw an easy score. Are you really having a fucking mental breakdown right now? Nothing even happened. Quit being such a dramatic whiny lil' bi—"

I swear, I saw the anger rolling off of Lina in waves. She had been trying to keep her cool, and it had seemed like she was going to be successful, but all her calm flew out the window the minute he started to call me a bitch.

Already, she was standing and heading toward King before I could even think to grab her wrist and stop her. Thankfully, Xavier had far better reflexes than me. Quickly, he positioned himself between the two of them.

My initial focus had been on Lina, but then I noticed Xavier's expression. When we first met, he'd worn such an easy smile.

Even this morning when Lina and I had arrived, that same look was on his face.

It was a smile that made you comfortable and probably got him laid almost a hundred percent of the time, but there wasn't even a small trace of it now. There was, however, an extremely angry vein running up his neck and a deep scowl.

Maybe it had been a bad idea to have Xavier come, after all. If they both lost it, things could get really bad. Honestly, I didn't care about myself or my situation. I just didn't want either of them to end up in trouble over this *trash lord*.

Shaking off my anxiety, I finally looked at King. I could tell by the smirk on his face he was quite impressed with himself. I, on the other hand, was not.

King was wearing an overly-large, muted-green suit, plastered with the *Gucci* symbol. No way was that tacky suit authentic, but his choice in attire was not even a minor concern. Taking him down a fucking peg was what mattered right then.

"Me, the bitch? Nah, I don't think so," I stated. "Wouldn't getting knocked out by a girl who's a hundred pounds lighter than you make you the bitch?"

The look of disgust that saturated King's expression was supposed to intimidate me, I guess, but it didn't. Instead, the smiles on both Lina's and Xavier's faces held my focus. Thankfully, my dig had successfully cooled their anger.

Actually, I take that back. It had successfully cooled Xavier's anger. The smile on Lina's face promised violence. She was still trying to step around Xavier to get to King.

Effortlessly, Xavier spun her, placing her back against his chest.

OK, bringing him was a great idea. There's no way I'd be strong enough to do that.

He leaned down close to her ear, and I felt a vicious stab of jealousy over such a simple yet intimate act. That was until I heard what he was actually saying.

"Remember who you're here for, Red. Not to entertain this piece of shit but to support the cute girl that makes your cold heart melt."

Immediately, her gaze found mine, and I don't know if my eyes were just playing tricks on me, but it looked like she might actually have blushed.

I didn't make that up, right? She blushed because of what he just said, right? Am I tripping?

"I have no idea what you're going on about. My heart is still completely frozen solid." She huffed as her eyes darted away from me and back to the scene before her.

The hope blossoming in my chest was almost snuffed out, but then Xavier *and* Elijah started laughing. My head ping-ponged between them, trying to figure out what the hell was so funny.

"Red, I really don't know who you think you're foolin'. Anyone with eyes can see that's bullshit. You're just blind to it... I guess."

Well, she isn't the only one because I have no idea what the hell you two see. Someone wanna give me the cheat code to unlock that special sight, please?

"You idiots do know I'm still here, right?" King grumbled, clearly annoyed that he wasn't getting the attention he craved.

Honestly, I think we'd all completely forgotten him. I for sure did. I'd been too absorbed with what Xavier had said and Lina's reaction. Finally, Elijah spoke up and completely obliterated whatever pride King still had.

"We do, but your presence is like that of a toddler who's begging for attention." He cocked his head to the side. "Shall I go grab you a snack from the nearest vending machine? Or perhaps you need your hand held on the way to the bathroom."

Lina, Xavier, and I all laughed. King's face turned as red as a lobster, and that just made us laugh harder. Elijah's analogy was as accurate as it was hilarious, and it was exactly what we needed to calm down.

Lina even came back to stand next to my chair and returned to her people-watching, dismissing him entirely. Rejected, King looked like a tea kettle ready to blow its top. The amount of pure vitriol about to come out of his mouth wasn't going to land after the embarrassment he'd just suffered, but that didn't mean he wasn't going to try anyway.

He opened his mouth to speak, and I prepared for whatever would come out of it, but the words never came.

"Tiberius! Get over here. Now!"

A man surrounded by a gaggle of people stood just past the entrance, dressed in a suit that must have cost a fortune. Unlike King, this man didn't just buy his off the rack. It was custom-tailored, like Xavier's and Elijah's.

The stranger had a salt-and-pepper beard and a shaved head. He wasn't a bad-looking guy, but something about him was vaguely familiar. I didn't know who he was yelling at, but whoever it was, they were in serious trouble.

King turned away from us and started toward the man.

"Your name is Tiberius?" I asked. "Seriously?" I couldn't keep the shock or snark out of my voice. That was just too surprising. King — Oh, excuse me, *Tiberius* — stopped and turned back to sneer at me.

"For your information, you uncultured cunt, King is synonymous with Tiberius."

Uncultured cunt? Who the fuck talks like that? I didn't even think you knew words that big.

"Yeah, but no one in their right mind would want to be named Tiberius. It doesn't really inspire ass-kissing. Ass-kicking, maybe," Rose taunted, smiling cruelly.

Since *Tiberius* had stopped to confront us, he forced the stranger and his posse to make their way to us, too. This was obviously a problem for the man because he slapped Tiberius upside the head when he reached him.

Not one person from the posse reacted to the assault. Hell, not one person in the busy-ass hallway reacted, and four of the people milling around were cops.

Who the hell is this guy?

The stranger directed his gaze at Lina. "I'll have you know the name Tiberius inspires an abundance of *ass-kissing*. You're about to experience a preview of it very soon, young lady."

The cruelty of Lina's smile paled in comparison to the man's, but it was his lecherous glare that made my stomach churn. Lina kicked off the wall, ready to tell the jerk off, but Elijah stepped in front of her and addressed the dick first.

"Have your underhanded business practices finally caught up to you, Harper?" Elijah asked.

"How dare you speak to my father so casually," Tiberius bellowed. "Who the f—

Harper backhanded Tiberius so hard, I heard the crack of it echo throughout the hallway.

"Quiet, Tiberius," he barked. "The day I need the likes of a pathetic-wannabe-playboy to come to my defense against *anyone* is the day I end it all."

Tiberius's lip began to bleed, but he kept his mouth shut. Yet again, no one reacted to Harper's behavior, and that wasn't even the most shocking part about this whole nonsensical situation. The word *father* kept repeating in my mind.

That's his father?

"I wasn't aware you could spawn," Elijah said, raising a brow.

As Harper turned away from his son and faced Elijah, the cruel smile was back in place.

"Yes, well. He's quite the failure, I agree. His mother is no prize either, but one must make certain sacrifices when they impregnate the heiress of an influential family."

"You mean, she slept with you... On purpose?"

"She wasn't forced if that's what you're implying. Although, that could have been arranged if need be."

My jaw was on the floor. There was no way in hell he'd just said that out loud without consequence. But he had. *Wow*. An older man from the posse stepped up, and all I could think was. *Finally, someone's gonna tell this guy he can't say or do things like this.*

"Sir," he began, addressing Harper. "Although he would never be successful in making that allegation stick, it would be best not to say things like that to Mr. Whitfield, seeing as he is an officer of the court."

That's it? That's all you have to say to him after such a display of blatant disrespect?

Undeterred, Harper waved a dismissing hand at the older man, who then stepped back. And just like that, my hope for any form of reprimand was snuffed out.

So, this is what it looks like when you're rich enough to get away with murder.

"There's no need to worry. He wouldn't be successful, like you said, Wilson. Moreover, young Whitfield here is up for a promotion, I hear. I'm sure he wouldn't want to jeopardize that by slinging around baseless allegations."

"If that was your attempt at a veiled threat, you failed," Elijah informed Harper. "Interesting how you heard about my promotion when I rooted out all the attorneys in your pocket from the prosecutor's office. Who shared the great news, I wonder?"

Elijah's spine was far stronger than mine. I felt like I was watching a severe battle of wills. If it was me against Harper, I'd probably lose. But then a worrying thought struck me. In all battles, there is a winner and a *loser*. So, who'd win here? I hoped, for Elijah's sake, it would be him.

"You're clever, boy, but not *that* clever. I think I'll keep my source to myself, thank you very much."

"I ain't your boy, Harper," Elijah snarled. He'd barely displayed any emotion through this whole debacle, but by the look on Harper's face, this was the reaction he'd wanted most.

"*Ain't?* Well now, it seems even dressed in a mediocre suit, the hoodlum is still there, *ain't* he?"

Outside of a small, angry vein that throbbed on his forehead, Elijah gave no other reaction to Harper's words.

"Since you're unfortunately not here for yourself, I'll assume you're here for him, but I don't think it will matter. Judge Patterson is presiding, and we both know how much she vehemently hates you."

The expression on Harper's face could only be described as satanic. Think of the most cruel smile you've ever seen, and still, you wouldn't even get close to the smile I saw.

"Ah. Well, we'll just have to wait and see, now won't we?"

The conversation was obviously over because Harper and his clique walked away. As they left, Lina grabbed Elijah's wrist and tugged, turning him to face her. The look in her eyes screamed there would be retribution if he didn't immediately explain what had just happened.

Elijah sighed and gently removed her hand before filling us in.

"Yes, yes. I know, Thorne. You don't like being shut down like that, especially in public. I'd say sorry, but I'm not. That man is Tiberius Richard Harper. He's the CEO of TRH Realty and the dirtiest and wealthiest man in this country.

"He is *not* one you want as an enemy. I know you're not afraid of anyone, and that's great, but the truth is that man can ruin your life with a single text. Although you don't care, I know for a fact there are three people in this courthouse who do."

"If he's that terrible of a person, then why are you confident he won't win the case?"

"Because, as I said to him, Judge Patterson hates Harper. Almost all of the members of the city council are in Harper's pocket, and Judge Patterson is running for mayor."

"OK, so what you're saying is she's gonna make Tiberius an example because of her hatred for his father?"

"Exactly. All we have to do is wait for the case to be called, then Tiberius will be served his comeuppance."

Hearing that put us all at ease. At least one of the Harpers wasn't going to get away scot-free, or so we thought.

About an hour and a half later, the case was finally called. The Harpers and their legal team were already in the courtroom when we entered. Both men wore disgusting smiles on their faces, which was mostly annoying as hell but also concerning.

Lina randomly stopped next to them and looked Tiberius up and down.

"So, if he's Tiberius Richard Harper Sr., that means you're Richie's lil' dick, right?" she asked, waving her pinkie at him.

Xavier and I laughed, and Elijah rolled his eyes, but he still had a huge smile on his face. Tiberius's jaw hit the floor.

"You are *by far* the most classless woman I've ever had the misfortune of meeting," Harper remarked, "but I still find myself intrigued. Who are you, and how are you involved with my son's situation?"

"Ro—"

"Don't pretend you actually care to know, Harper. Last I heard, women weren't your *type*." Elijah rushed out, cutting her off. She shot him another annoyed look, which he ignored. Harper studied their interaction with starved interest.

"Is this, perhaps, Mrs. Whitfield, then?" he asked. "I hadn't heard anything about you settling down, but you've displayed a fascinating amount of possession and protection every time she's attempted to interact with me."

Xavier, Lina, and I all looked at Elijah, waiting for his response. Would he shut Harper down, or would he confirm it just to keep Harper away from her? It would be interesting if he chose the latter because, knowing Lina, she probably wouldn't play along.

"I will neither confirm nor deny your speculation, seeing as that's none of your business."

Harper seemed as though he planned to respond, but the bailiff interrupted him by announcing the judge.

"All rise for Judge Robert Byers."

"Son of a bitch," Elijah growled.

I looked to Elijah, hoping I'd heard wrong. Seconds later, a male judge entered the courtroom and sat behind the bench. Elijah was pissed, and that worried me even more.

"I thought you said the judge was going to be a female?" I asked.

"I did! Now, I get why he's here. That son of bitch must have paid someone off to switch the judges," Elijah whispered.

"Is this judge in his pocket, too?"

Elijah grimaced. "There has been speculation he's in a plethora of pockets, but nothing has been confirmed or proven. I'm sorry to say this, Melanie, but at this time, we'll just have to hope for the best. There's nothing else we can do."

I nodded my head in understanding. There was no point in being upset with him. He could only control so much, and he was doing all of this as a favor. We just had to hope for the best, like he'd said.

Elijah spoke to the judge and laid out all the charges. Tiberius was facing aggravated domestic assault, B&E, and attempted sexual assault. When the judge asked Tiberius for a response, he pled not guilty. Naturally.

"I'll start by saying this. The charges before you are quite serious, Mr. Harper. Are you sure you want to waive your right to a jury trial?" the judge pressed.

Wilson, obviously the head lawyer since he'd been standing next to Tiberius as the charges were read while all the other lawyers sat in the gallery, replied, "We are sure, you're Honor. We do not feel the state has enough to prosecute those charges. Although we were not given the chance, I believe Mr. Whitfield and I can come to a decision that would be beneficial to both parties involved."

Elijah looked surprised. "Your Honor, the state isn't offering a plea deal in this case."

"Ah, but you should be. As I said, the state does not have nearly enough evidence to support the charges before the court. If it so pleases the court, I would like to add to the record that this is simply a ploy for Mr. Whitfield to besmirch the Harper name."

"Listen here yo—"

"Enough," the judge interrupted. "You two need to save this song and dance for someone interested. Mr. Wilson, keep your allegations to yourself unless you plan on filing a suit. For now, Mr. Harper, you will be taken into custody to await your preliminary hearing, which is set for three weeks from today. Bail is set at fifty thousand dollars. Bailiff, please take Mr. Harper into custody." The judge slammed his gavel down.

With that one bang, everything changed. That morning, I'd stepped into the courtroom thinking I'd be able to put this behind me. Now, I was so unsure about the situation, and it didn't feel like Elijah was sure, either.

As ordered, the bailiff stepped up to handcuff Tiberius, who stared daggers into my soul the whole time.

"I hope you don't think this is over, *Mel*. You're going to regret ever filing charges against me. I'll make sure of it," he hissed.

The bailiff began to pull him away, but Lina wasn't going to let him have the last word.

"Oh, yeah, lil' dick? You gonna go beg Daddy to make us as miserable as your ass is about to be? We all know you have no power."

Tiberius tried to respond, but before he could, the bailiff, who was clearly over him, tugged him through the back door. I could still hear him screaming as he was dragged away.

"I find myself wanting to know more and more about this woman who clearly doesn't know when to remain seen and un-heard," Harper, unmoved by his son's plight, remarked with an-other cruel smile as he stopped beside us.

"Yo, I don't know what fucking century you think you're living in *Baldy*, but I'll happily bring a relic like you into the twenty-first," Lina bit out, barely containing her fury.

Elijah stepped between her and Harper again, focusing his at-tention on Wilson.

"I hope you know that my opening statement will win me this case before you even have a chance to provide yours."

This time, Wilson spoke. "Based on the lack of evidence, we are suggesting you offer us a deal. Drop the charges down to domestic assault, and we'd be willing to agree to a TRO."

"Domestic assault only includes a ninety-day sentence and a five-hundred-dollar fine. In layman's terms, you want a slap on the wrist." Elijah scoffed. "You think I'd go for that?"

It was taking everything in him to keep his cool, and it didn't help that Harper stood behind Wilson with an *I told you so* grin on his face again.

"I know you will accept them, Mr. Whitfield, because you have no choice. You don't have enough to support your charges, and it's better for Ms. Thompson than having the case thrown out com-pletely. Wouldn't you agree?" Wilson eyed me before he started for the courtroom doors.

This couldn't be happening. They wanted Tiberius to get away with practically no punishment at all, and all I'd get out of it was a stupid piece of paper telling him he had to stay away from me. Was this really my life right now?

Lina was livid, Xavier was quiet, and Elijah was pissed, too. His demeanor had changed. He didn't seem as confident as he had before the hearing began. Now that the legal talk was over, Harper seized his opportunity to put us in 'our place' one last time.

"I've told you repeatedly I'm not a good opponent for you. You and I, my boy, aren't even playing the same game."

Slamming his briefcase shut, Elijah sucked in a deep breath before he glared at Harper.

"Games are for kids. Speaking of which, shouldn't your concern be with your child? If things do happen to go your way. Ninety-three days is still a lot of time. Something undesirable could happen while he's locked up."

"Mr. Whitfield, th—" A female lawyer stepped up, outraged.

"Don't stop him now, Leanne. That one actually sounded like a genuine threat. Perhaps, you'll be an interesting opponent after all. Please, feel free to use any incarcerated friends you may have at your disposal. My son could use some roughing up," Harper said as he left the courtroom, legal team in tow.

My mind was reeling over all the events of the day, but I was also secretly hoping Elijah did have some unsavory friends in jail because if not, Tiberius's short stint was probably going to be a breeze.

His earlier threat came back to mind.

I hope you don't think this is over, Mel. *You're going to regret ever filing charges against me. I'll make sure of it.*

I wasn't necessarily worried about his threat coming to fruition because, as Lina had said, he had no real power. My concern lay with his father. If Harper decided to get involved, that could spell actual trouble for me.

I could hope and hope Harper would never waste the time, the effort, or the money it would take to support Tiberius's revenge plot, but there was just no way for me to know.

XVI

Melanie

When I woke up the next morning, I felt like there was a malignant cloud floating over me. I had no idea where it came from, and I couldn't figure out how to shake it.

My schedule was short that day. I only had two classes, and then I was supposed to be meeting a new author in the evening, so calling in sick didn't really seem worth it.

Climbing out of bed, I started my morning routine. The shower steam woke me right up and had me ready to take on the day. I'd hoped it would help the cloud dissipate, but it didn't, unfortunately.

Even after I'd gotten dressed, had my breakfast with Kuro, and put my bag together, I still couldn't shake the negative feeling. It was really starting to annoy me, but there was nothing I could do about it, and I needed to get going.

As soon as I opened my door, the most horrendous scent hit my nose, making my eyes water. My welcome mat and front door were covered in a variety of condiments. As if that wasn't enough, there was a distinct scent of urine mixed in with them.

What the fuck is this? Did some new kids move into the subdivision or something?

It was going to be such a pain to clean this shit up, but there was no way I could just leave it. I took several pictures of the mess, reported it to my front office, and emailed my professor that I was going to be late.

After that was all done, I went back inside, changed my clothes, and put on rubber gloves. There was no saving the mat, so I threw it away. It took what felt like forever before the smell of bleach was the only scent left.

When I finally made it to campus, my first class was already over, so I went to the library to kill time until the next one.

I was deeply enthralled by the book I was reading until something hot flowed down my back. I jumped up, causing the chair to fall back. Behind me were two girls I'd never seen before.

One of them held a cardboard cup in her hand, and I guessed I was now wearing her midday coffee.

I should have just kept those crappy clothes on.

"Oh my God! I'm so sorry," the coffee holder rushed out. "My friend bumped into me, and my cup spilled a little."

A little? Really? I'm pretty sure I'm wearing the entire fucking cup.

"I'm sorry, too. I'm happy to pay for the dry cleaning," the other girl added.

"Uh, that's OK. You don't have to."

"No, no. I insist! What's your Cash App? I'll send you some money real quick," the friend said, snatching my phone out of my hand."

"Here, let me at least try to stanch the stain," the other girl chimed in, turning me around and patting my back with a napkin.

Well, aren't you two pushy?

"Wow, you have a lot of apps! Sorry, I can't find your Cash App."

You shouldn't have taken my phone in the first place, dummy!

Slightly annoyed, I gave her my Cash App tag, and she sent me a hundred bucks. My shirt was old anyway, so I wasn't going to get it dry-cleaned. Still, having a free Benjamin for my troubles went a long way in calming me down. I still didn't understand why she took my phone when she could've just told me what her tag was, but I didn't have time to think about it. I needed to get to class.

"Thanks. Just be careful. If that coffee happened to be fresh, you could have burned someone," I said.

As I collected my stuff and began to walk away, the first girl's muted voice sounded behind me. "The bitch is just lucky there's no cafe in here, and we had to walk. Otherwise, she *would've* been burned."

Quickly, I spun around to confront them, but they were gone. I scanned the room but found no sight of them. As I left, I tried to convince myself I really didn't hear that, but I failed.

This day was just getting worse and worse, and I was about ready for it to be over. Hopefully, I could get through my last class and my meeting without any more incidents.

I sent a quick text to Shelly to explain what had happened, and when I got there, she was outside of the classroom with an extra shirt. It was always good to be friends with a person who liked to change her outfit every other hour.

"So, who were these chicks again?" Shelly asked as I changed in the stall.

"I have no idea," I admitted. "I've never seen them before, and I didn't think to ask for their names."

"Hmm. But you said she sent you money through Cash App, right?"

"Yeah, but it's just a screen name, not a real one, so there's no way to track her through it."

"Wow, that's really crazy. You're having such a bizarre-ass day."

"Tell me about it," I complained as I threw my coffee-drenched shirt away.

When we walked into class, all the front-row seats were taken, so we had to make our way to the middle row. We'd made it halfway to the available seats when I stumbled.

"Aye, watch where the fuck you're going. These are new shoes!"

I glared at the guy who'd tripped me, fully prepared to go off on him, but Shelly popped him upside his head with her notebook before I could.

"Move your damn foot when you see people walking by and you won't get your lame-ass shoes stepped on," she snapped.

Shelly passed him and helped me up. The guy kept giving us dirty looks. Shelly gave them back to him each time. Class ended, and the guy gave us one more look before he left.

"What the fuck was his fucking problem?" Shelly asked.

"I don't know, and honestly, I don't care," I said as I packed up my stuff. "I gotta get home and change so I can make it to my meeting on time. I love you, and I'll text you later."

"Kk. Bye!"

How could one day suck so terribly?

Lina had been texting me all day, but I was so busy dealing with all the bullshit that I hadn't been able to reply. When I made it to my parking spot, I stopped and looked through my text messages.

Then, I turned my attention to my car. The first thing I noticed was the word *Rat* scratched onto the hood. The crack in my windshield was the next thing I saw. Staring in horror, I noticed my tires had been slashed, too. I screamed. I knew I looked like a complete lunatic, but I was just so fed up with the day that I couldn't hold it in anymore. The word "rat" pieced everything together for me.

Tiberius was making good on his fucking threat. This wasn't what I had expected. All of it made me feel like I was back in high school.

Don't get me wrong, my day was absolutely terrible. Still, I had an important meeting to get to, so spiraling would have to wait. As I tried to rein myself in, I hoped he was currently getting fucked with no lube in his jail cell, but just because I wished for it didn't mean it was happening. His father had probably already bonded him out by now.

This shit is ridiculous. Hopefully, it will be over once I leave the school.

Thanks to my dad's *AAA* membership, I was at least able to have my car towed to a *Belle Tire*, but I had to leave it overnight, so I called a *Lyft* to take me home. When I got back to my house, I took the fastest shower I'd ever taken in my life.

I pulled my hair into a neat ponytail, fed Kuro, grabbed my work bag, and waited for another *Lyft* to take me to the office. Even after everything I'd had to deal with, I was still going to be thirty minutes early for my meeting.

Things are finally looking up. Thank God!

The *Lyft* dropped me off at the entrance, and I hustled over to the elevators. I was still early, but I didn't want to risk anything. My thinking was the sooner I could get to my office, the less likely some other type of disaster would strike.

The elevator reached my floor without incident, but as soon as the doors opened, Steph rushed inside and ran right into me.

"Oh my God! Melanie, where have you been? I've been calling and texting you for over an hour!"

"What are you talking about?" I asked, checking my phone screen. There were no notifications. "I don't have any texts or calls from you! And why are you freaking out? What's the emergency?"

"The author you were meeting today has been here waiting for you for over ninety minutes! She wanted to call Michelle, but I've managed to talk her out of it!"

"Wait, wait? WHAT?"

I rushed past her as she attempted to explain the situation to me, but I didn't even make it a foot into the office before I saw the author I was supposed to meet leaving my office in a huff.

"I'm so s—" I tried.

"I really don't appreciate being kept waiting, Ms. Thompson! Especially when you're the one who moved up our meeting time!"

"But I—"

"Save your excuses. I'm not interested in hearing them. Michelle will be hearing from me in the morning."

"Wait! Ma'am, please!"

I didn't think there was a way to slam a glass door, but somehow, she managed to do it, leaving Stephanie and me standing in the middle of the office, dumbfounded. I whirled around on Stephanie, who held her hands up defensively.

"Did you think I was going to hit you? Can you please tell me what's going on before I completely lose my mind?" I said as we walked back into my office.

My co-workers were all watching the spectacle. I hoped that if we confined the crazy to the four walls of my office, then they would go back to work. Stephanie rushed over to my computer and flipped the screen to me to show the meeting had in fact been moved up.

"I didn't do that!"

Stephanie's face was full of concern as I stared at the meeting slot in my schedule. The time was there in black and white, but my brain still couldn't process it. I know Stephanie didn't change it because she only had the access to view, not edit. So the only one who could've changed it was... me.

"You said you'd been calling and texting me this whole time, right?" I asked as I showed her our empty text thread. "I don't have anything from you. No calls. No texts. Nothing."

Stephanie stared at my phone for a moment before she left the office. She came back a second later with her phone and showed me a text thread. It was my number alright, and it was full of texts.

You hear about people catching their significant others red-handed by cloning a number and setting a trap, but I'd thought you had to have the phone's sim card to do that. Obviously not. The coffee-spill craziness from earlier made sense now. Those bitches had not only wanted to burn me, but they must have done something to clone my cell.

Apparently, Fake Me and Stephanie had been talking the entire day up until the new time of the meeting. Then, Fake Me went silent. I called the number from her phone, and it just rang and rang before the call disconnected.

"What the fuck?"

"What are we going to tell Michelle?" Stephanie asked, hesitantly.

"Oh my God! Michelle! When does she come back from her trip?"

"This Friday."

"OK, OK. We need to see if we can fix this somehow, and we need to make sure it's resolved before she gets back."

"Sure, but what do we do about the phone issue?"

Shit! That's a great fucking question.

I dialed the number again from her phone. This time, my phone began to ring. I wasn't really sure what that meant for the *Clone-A-Phone* game, but I needed to get in touch with the author first.

After I changed all of my work passwords, reported the cloning to my phone company, and emailed the author that I had been hacked and hadn't changed the meeting time, I was exhausted.

Thankfully, the author agreed to another meeting, but she wasn't going to be available until Friday. Meeting her Friday ran the risk of Michelle finding out about today's mess, but that was a risk I was going to have to take.

Friday was what was convenient for her, so that is when we would meet. I wasn't going to push my luck, especially on the cusp of what had just happened. When it was all said and done, Stephanie dropped me off at home, and I drowned myself in strawberry shortcake ice cream.

The one upside to all of this bullshit was that I was off tomorrow. So, I was going to decompress tonight, and then I was going to be a hermit for the full day. He couldn't fuck with me if I didn't leave the house... Right?

XVII

Rose

There was quite a surprise waiting for me when I woke up this morning. Inn had a bouquet of black roses delivered to my house with a note telling me to come over.

That got me excited as I pondered the possibilities of what he had in mind. We were going to fuck, obviously, but how was he going to fuck me this time? That was the question, and it was one I needed the answer to.

For a moment, I considered the possibility of him only wanting to have a writing session, but I dismissed it. He wasn't a tease like me, so there was no way he'd do something like that.

I rolled out of bed and went to the bathroom to grab a shower. Once I was clean, I pulled on a black-lace lingerie set and a skin-tight red maxi dress. Even if he did want to tease me, there was no way in hell he could resist me in this.

When I pulled up to his house and got out of the car, Inn was already determinedly making his way to me.

Are you gonna fuck me out here in front of all of your neighbors? I could be into that.

Inn scooped me up in his arms and ran us back into his house before slamming the door shut.

"Luna, are you crazy?"

"What the fuck did I do?" I asked, extremely confused.

I'm sure I read that note right.

"You can't wear something like that during the day! You'll have every man in this neighborhood beating down my door to get to you."

A huge shit-eating grin spread across my face. He shouldn't have told me that. Now, I just wanted to tease and torture him.

"Aw. What's wrong, Inn? Don't want to share me?"

I backed up toward the door and opened it just a crack. Moving quickly, Inn slammed it shut and pinned me against it.

"Not interested in sharing you with anyone, actually," he assured me. "When you're here, you'll scream my name and my name only."

"Is that so?" I asked, biting my lip. "Am I gonna be screaming soon?"

Inn slowly trailed his hand up my body, causing my breathing to quicken. His fingers danced over my collarbone before he whisked his hand away and walked toward his office.

"Maybe later."

No doubt, my jaw made an audible thud as it hit the floor. His flippant response left me legitimately gobsmacked.

What the fuck was up his butt? He didn't turn around once before disappearing into his office, forcing me to follow after him.

"So, if I'm not here to scream your name, why did you want me to come over?"

"To hang out? What reason were you thinking?" he asked, raising a brow.

"Is this some type of joke?"

"I'm not sure what you mean," he said before turning back around to his computer.

"I-I... What the hell? I thought we were going to fuck!"

Inn actually ignored me and continued to type. I was dressed like sex on a stick, and he actually returned to his computer! Oh, no. No, no. I was about two seconds from blowing up on him.

Stomping over to his chair, I spun him to face me. The innocent expression he wore, as if I was the one who was tripping, sent me into full-blown anger.

"OK. Do you not see what I'm wearing right now?" I pressed.

His eyes burned a path down my body. When they moved back up to my breasts and the amount of cleavage the outfit showed, they lingered.

"A flattering yet extremely revealing dress?" he asked hesitantly.

"W-what? It's... It's..."

Inn stared at me as I babbled. I knew I sounded like a complete idiot, but my brain couldn't process what was happening. Determined to make my point, I stepped back, slipped my dress off, and tossed it at his face.

He pulled the fabric off of his head, dislodging his glasses, and stared right at my lace-clad breasts. He swallowed once — hard. Then, he got up and held my dress out to me.

"You should put this back on. I don't want you to catch a cold."

Once again, my jaw hit the floor. This motherfucker was serious! This whole thing was infuriating, and I'd had enough of his games. Snatching my dress from him, I turned on my heel and headed for the exit.

"Where are you going?"

"To find one of those other men you were talking about earlier. I don't want to 'hang out.' I want to cum."

"Is that all?" he whispered from behind me.

When had he caught up to me? I didn't even hear him.

Inn spun me around and forced me up against the wall. He lifted my chin as he leaned down. Our lips were a breath away, but he didn't kiss me as I'd expected.

"How'd I do?"

"Huh?"

"I'm writing a new character, and he has an aloof attitude. Did I pull it off?"

I'm going to kill him.

I pushed him back and attempted to kick him, but Inn caught my ankle before it connected. That was completely unexpected, too. I didn't think he had reflexes like that. He tightened his grip on my ankle and lifted my leg until my foot was level with my head.

Thank God I'm flexible, or this would fucking hurt.

Inn traced my seam through my panties, sending shivers racing up my spine. The position he held me in was interesting, and I was all for it, but if he didn't hurry up and fuck me, I really was going to kill him.

"I wonder how tightly your pussy would squeeze my dick like this..."

"Don't talk like that unless you're actually about that life."

Inn laughed and kissed his way from my calf to the bend of my knee. He kept his hand firmly planted between my legs, stroking my lips and sending tiny trills of pleasure through my body.

"You really think I'm not about it?" he asked.

A ripping sound reached my ears as Inn pressed his thumb through the thin fabric. As soon as it rubbed my clit, a gentle moan flew from my lips. He pushed three more fingers through, widening the hole he'd created until my panties were crotch-less. Then, he dragged his fingers down.

"Hey! These were my favorite pair!"

"I like them better this way," he teased. "I can get to what I want faster when they're like this."

The three fingers entered me so quickly that the one knee I held myself up with buckled.

"You're not losing feeling in your legs already, are you?" He taunted, stroking them inside of me. "That was quick."

He must've been joking if he thought *this* was going to tire *my* legs out. Proving a point, I leaned all of my weight on the wall to support myself and smiled up at him.

"This is fucking child's play, and you know it. Is that the best you've got? Should I call Eli or Zey to give you some pointers?"

I was playing a dangerous game. On one hand, Inn could take that the completely wrong way and tell me to leave. Or, he could take the challenge for what it was and completely wreck me. I desperately hoped for the latter.

"You're going to regret saying that."

Like lightning, he dropped my leg, ripped my panties off, and tossed me over his shoulder.

"Am I really? You sure you're not just talking tough?"

Ignoring me, Inn walked us to his bedroom and tossed me onto his mattress. We'd never made it there during my last visit, so I took a minute to take it all in. The first things I noticed were the mirrors on the ceiling above the bed.

They were fascinating but not nearly as fascinating as the two long straps attached to the headboard with cuffs connected to the ends.

"Are you working on more than one character? I didn't know you were into bondage," I said as I raised one of the cuffs.

"Why're you asking? Would you like that type of character, Luna?"

"Hmm," I said as I tapped my finger against my mouth. "It depends."

"On?"

"How well he fucks me."

"Makes sense. Well, let's see if I can live up to this imaginary character."

Inn crawled onto the bed and attached the cuffs to both of my wrists. Then, he kissed down my body and undid the front clasp of my bra with his teeth.

You're full of all types of surprises today.

Palming my breasts, he pushed them together and rolled his tongue around my nipples before nibbling them. Momentarily forgetting the cuffs, I tried to pull his shirt off, desperate to feel his skin against mine, but there wasn't enough slack in the straps to reach.

That was annoying, and I guess it showed on my face because Inn started to chuckle. He kissed a heated trail down my stomach until his hot breath was an inch from my pussy.

We stared at each other for a moment before he ran his tongue through my slit. My eyes rolled back, and it felt like electricity was running through my veins. All I wanted to do was force his head deeper between my thighs.

Now, I get why you cuffed me first. Smart play on your part.

"Am I living up to your imagined character yet?"

"You should be using your tongue to make me cum instead of asking silly questions," I told him.

"Oh, you mean like this?"

Slowly, Inn began to devour me, spelling his name out with his tongue. I arched my back to give him even more access, and he slid deeper inside of me.

"Oooh... Yes! Just like that."

His hands snaked up my body and found my nipples, aching and desperate for his touch. As soon as he twisted them, I came. The high of my climax was wonderful but short-lived as Inn pulled away from me and climbed off the bed.

"Luna, from now on when I ask you a question, I expect an answer. Understand?"

Ooh, I'm really going to like this new character.

I nodded and bit my lip. My plan was to play along as much as possible and keep my brattiness at bay. I wanted to see just how much fun this persona could be.

Inn pulled his shirt off and placed his glasses on the dresser. Watching his muscles bunch as he unbuttoned his pants caused my mouth to water. When his dick finally sprang free, all of the moisture in my body pooled at my center.

He was beautiful when clothed and devastating when naked. It was damn near impossible to focus on just one part of him. My eyes pinged from the deviant smile curving his lips to his lickable abs and finally landed on his full, thick length.

"Luna?" he asked.

"Huh," I answered, startled.

"Are you drooling?" He smiled at me.

Was I?

Dazed, I ran my hand across my mouth, but my fingers came back dry. Inn's smile widened. I couldn't believe I had fallen for that.

Bastard.

Grabbing my ankles, Inn pulled me down until I was lying flat on the bed. Then, he forced my legs up until I was fully open to him.

"Hold onto your ankles for me, and don't let go or I'll stop."

"What are you planning to do?" I asked as I followed his instructions.

Inn shook his head. "I don't remember saying you could ask questions."

Oh, fuck!

The brat in me wanted to react to that, but I ignored the impulse. This was getting far too interesting, and I didn't want to ruin it.

"Are you ready to answer my questions now?" he prompted.

"Yes!"

Inn climbed on the bed and rolled his tip around my clit. A small gasp left my lips and I had to retighten my grip on my ankles, almost forgetting what he told me.

He slid into me slowly, only giving me a few inches. It was absolute torture because no amount of wiggling would drive him in deeper, so I had to wait. His fingers danced around my nipples, adding to my torment.

"How tightly will your pussy grip my dick in this position?"

"So tight, you'll have no choice but to bust inside of me," I answered without hesitation.

"Oh, yeah? You think you'll make me cum first?"

"Yeah. I know I will!"

Inn leaned over me and reached into his nightstand to grab something. When he was done, he sat back and waved a bottle of lube and a dildo attached to a cock ring at me.

Fuck me!

"That's the plan. Still think you'll make me come first?"

I hadn't meant to say that out loud, but fuck it, who cared? My focus was on the dildo. I watched as he slid the ring over his shaft and lubed both dicks up. If he'd have asked me if I was drooling again, the answer would've been yes!

"Do you want this, Luna?" he asked, stroking the dildo.

"Yes! Yes, I want it!"

"Then, beg me for it."

When had he learned to talk like this? Has he been speaking with Zey and Eli?

"Lunnaaaa," he sang. "I'm waiting."

"Inn! Please... *Please*, fuck me with both of them. Fill me up. Fill me up completely," I rushed out, practically panting.

Simultaneously, he slid both the dicks inside of my entrances, making me cry out. I was so incredibly full that I forgot how to breathe. I stopped for so long that my blood rushed in my ears.

Inn appeared above me, looking like a blessing from the god of sex himself. He grinned down at me, framed by my open legs. That smile was absolutely devious, and I just wanted to kiss every inch of it.

"Ready for more questions?"

"Y-yes."

"You said I needed to take some pointers from Zey or Eli, right?"

"I-I'm sorry. I shouldn't have sa—"

But Inn cut me off, placing his finger over my lips.

"Don't apologize now. Just answer the question, Luna," he said, sliding in deeper.

"Ooh, God! Yes! Yes! I said that. I said that!"

He nodded, accepting my answer before he pulled out of me.

"Please... Please, don't. I-I... need..."

"Don't worry, I'm not going to stop. Just want to make sure I have your full attention."

All that was left inside of me were the tips of both dicks, and I was seconds from losing my mind.

"Still think I need pointers?" he asked, slamming into me.

"No! Fuck! You don't. You don't!" I screamed.

He grabbed my thighs and picked up his pace. I made the mistake of opening my eyes. In the mirror above our heads, I could see him stroking in and out of me.

That almost skyrocketed me over the edge, but Inn stopped moving just in time. He looked up at the mirror and smiled at my reflection.

"Do you like seeing how I beat this pussy up?" he asked, slamming into me once again

I opened and closed my mouth, but no sound came out. I was so damn shocked, I'd forgotten how to speak and ended up just nodding my head.

"Has either one of *them* fucked you like *this*?" Another slam.

I shook my head as I screamed once more, almost losing my grip on my ankles.

"Whose pussy is this?" Slam.

"Yours," I managed to choke out.

"What's my fucking name?" Slam.

"Ooh, my God! Quinn!"

"Can I cum inside?" Slam.

"Yes! Fuck! Cum inside me!"

"Beg for what you want." Slam.

"Jesus! Quinn, please! Please, cum inside me."

"Well, hurry the fuck up and cum so I can bust inside you like you want," he ordered as he grasped my breasts and twisted my nipples.

The climax that tore through me felt like an out-of-body experience, and every second of it was *fucking amazing*. I liked the old Inn, but this new side of him definitely needed to come out and play more often.

"So, uh, what was that about you making me cum first?" Inn teased.

"I got no idea what you're talking about," I said as I waved the cuff straps.

He chuckled as he unlocked them. Immediately, I rubbed my legs, trying to fight the soreness. Inn slid out of me slowly, crawled off of the bed, and disappeared into the bathroom.

"Did you like the new character, Luna?" he called out to me. "Did he fuck you well enough?"

"Yes," I mumbled as I started to nod off. "I *really* liked him.

XVIII

Melanie

You know when you experience something so horrible that you wish someone would pinch you so you could wake up? Good. Glad I'm not alone.

The headache-and-ice cream hangover was causing my head to pound, but I still couldn't believe yesterday actually happened.

My plans to be a hermit were still in effect up until Lina sent me a text asking if I wanted to go with her to the tattoo shop. That changed things. I literally leaped from my bed and rushed down the steps to get dressed.

She was just the distraction I needed. Plus, it was awesome she was allowing me to share in the experience. I wasn't sure if any of the others had done that with her before, but I was just going to pretend they hadn't and I was the first.

Lina came to pick me up an hour later, and we were off to the shop. We pulled up to a building with a red and black sign that read: Sextink. The owner's sense of humor was interesting, to say the least.

The place was bigger than I was expecting, but it was really cool. The atmosphere inside made it feel like we were walking into a vampire den.

The walls were painted a deep red and trimmed in black. They were covered in beautiful art to showcase all the artists' talents. There were three tattooing stations set up to the left and right of the entrance and a piercing station against the back wall. The chairs were all black leather and tufted, adding to the Victorian vibe, and hurricane lamp replicas shined all over the place.

For such a big building, it was kind of intimate. I could see why Lina got her tattoos here. It was just her type of place.

But then a tall, devilishly handsome man emerged from a room toward the back of the shop and made his way over to us.

Nevermind. Scratch my earlier thoughts. He's most definitely the reason you come here.

The stranger had caramel skin, a full but trimmed beard, a devious smile, and eyes only for Lina. His long dreads were bound by a red scarf, and he sported a pair of round wire-framed glasses that reminded me of *Harry Potter.*

Any other time I've seen someone wearing a pair of glasses like that, they looked like a nerd. Not this guy. He had so much damn charismatic magnetism leaking from him that I'd bet he really could do something magical.

The man came toward us so fast, it looked like he planned to scoop her up in his arms and kiss her, but Lina took a step back right before he reached us. He stopped short with a questioning look, brow raised, before he turned his head to me.

Now that he was closer, I could see how his long eyelashes cascaded over his pretty scarlet-brown eyes. His beard wrapped around full, kissable lips, and everywhere, tattoos peeked out of his long-sleeve shirt.

The man's eyes tracked down my body and back up again before settling on mine. The scrutiny made me uncomfortable, but I wasn't going to look away first. For some reason, I felt like that was the game we were playing, and I didn't want to lose.

"This isn't fair. You've never brought another fuckable here before," he said. "I like having you all to myself when you come to get new ink." The man held his hand out to me, completely shocking me.

"Hi, name's Zyriel," the man offered. "I know it's a choking hazard, so I'll pronounce it for you. Sai-ri-elle."

I shook his hand. "Uh... Hello. I'm Melanie. My name isn't a choking hazard. I guess you're one of us, too?" I asked.

Zyriel smiled and shook his head. "I was, but I'm not her favorite anymore," he answered, aiming a pout at Lina.

She ignored the comment, sidestepped him, and headed for the hallway. Zyriel let go of my hand and followed after her. I guess his curiosity about me had been satisfied. Not wanting to stand there awkwardly like an idiot, I trailed behind them.

They both slipped into the room Zyriel had stepped out of earlier. My guess was that the room was his private studio. I hesitated in the doorway before following them inside, taking the room in.

The room was styled like the rest of the shop with the same red walls, but unlike the main room, the art in here was placed more aesthetically. It was still a showcase, but it was subtle and didn't overwhelm my eyes.

Lina was already seated in the main chair, and Zyriel was sitting on a stool, setting up his station. There were two throne-like chairs in the corner to my left that I assumed were for guests.

The one closest to the door was full of art supplies, and I wasn't going to move them or mess anything up. Second throne it was! Once I was seated, I noticed Zyriel was watching me. I wasn't really sure what his damage was, but I was kind of over the staring.

"Can I help you with something, dude?"

"Actually! Yeah, you can. Like I said, you're the first one she's brought."

You did say that. And I've been trying to control my heart rate ever since.

"So, what makes you so special that Star brought you here? Tell me all the secrets. Maybe one of them will help me get back on her good side."

OK. I'll be the first to admit I wasn't expecting that. I couldn't answer that question, even if I wanted to. I have no idea what makes me so special.

"Is there some new policy I don't know about that says I can't bring someone into the shop with me?"

"Nope, I'm just curious," he replied.

"More like you're being annoying."

"Oh, so I can't talk to her? I can't make new friends? Is she off limits?" Zyriel asked with a grin.

How fascinating that he'd asked me how to get on her good side when he seemed more interested in annoying her. Their interaction reminded me of the way Lina behaved with Xavier and Elijah. It gave off the 'old friends' vibe as if they'd known each other for years and years.

A small voice inside of me was trying to convince me I needed to be jealous of how close they were, but I ignored it. He was her past, and I was her present. There was no point in focusing on anything outside of that fact.

Zyriel snapped his fingers. "Oh! I just remembered that I picked up a new knife for you recently. Wanna see it now?"

"That's a dumb question. Of course, I do!"

He pulled out a black butterfly knife, covered in beautiful red roses. Yeah, if he wasn't still pining after Lina, I was a millionaire. If she was bothered by it at all though, she didn't show it as she studied the knife.

Was it crazy to think she looked hot holding a deadly weapon?

Probably.

Was I thinking that, anyway?

Yes!

Just then, a gorgeous woman stepped into the room and stared directly at Lina. She had beautiful ivory skin that was covered in vibrant tattoos. Long red hair flowed down her back and freckles peppered her cheeks and nose.

The woman was tall and stacked. My eyes roved over her body, taking in her full hips, slim waist, and huge tits. The more I looked at her, the more inadequate I began to feel.

Is she a customer or an artist? Please be one of those two options!

"I didn't know you were coming in today, Rose, the woman said with seductive smile."

Of course, she's another fuckable? Jesus, how many of these people am I going to meet today?

"You weren't supposed to, and yet, here you are," Zyriel interjected, clearly annoyed with her.

"Shut the fuck up, Zyriel. No one fuckin' asked you," the woman snapped.

"And no one wants to fucking see you, Lilly. Fuck off," Lina retorted.

OK. So, she's another one from the past. Thank God!

Lilly batted her eyes. "Aww, don't be like that. I know you miss me."

"Not even in your wildest dreams," Lina said, rolling her own.

Lilly shifted her focus from Lina to me. Honestly, I'd remained quiet just so that wouldn't happen. Unlike Xavier, Elijah, or even Zyriel, she didn't seem all that friendly.

Now I could be completely wrong and just judging her solely on her looks, but based on the bombastic stink eye she gave me, I was almost seventy-five percent sure she was a bitch.

"Who's the fuckin' tagalong? And when'd you start letting your hoe of the week come into the shop during the day?"

Alright. Now, I'm one hundred percent sure.

"You're sooo gonna regret saying that. She's not with me, idiot," Zyriel said before he broke out in a fit of laughter.

Lilly's head snapped over to Zyriel and back to me so quickly, she probably had whiplash. She looked me up and down, and I could tell she wasn't impressed with what she saw.

Lina twirled the knife between her fingers as she watched Lilly. The look in her eyes was intense. Was it lust? No. That wasn't likely. Lilly was extremely attractive, but since she wasn't supposed to know Lina was here, I could safely assume there was bad blood between them.

Ignoring the look Lina shot her way, Lilly gave me all of her attention. Leisurely, she leaned against the doorjamb and tapped her index finger against her lips.

"She's cute, Rose. Plain-looking and young for your tastes, but cute, I guess. Where did she pick you up, kid? Bookstore? College library? Local Coffee Shop?"

Bitch, who's the fucking kid? You're like one, maybe two years older than me, tops.

"Lilliana, you're testing my patience. I advise you to quit while you're ahead," Lina growled.

Lilly's eyes quickly cut to Lina before zeroing in on me again. I don't know what the growl did to her, but it caused my chest to tighten. I'd seen Lina be all kinds of aggressive before, but this was on a whole 'nother level.

A part of me was a little worried, but a bigger part of me was extremely turned on. Maybe I'm a little soft in the head for feeling that way, but it's the way I felt.

Lilly pushed off of the wall and stalked toward me. "I'm gonna go with the coffee shop. Look, kid. You seem sweet and all, but sweet isn't gonna cut it. Rose needs aggression, and you look as innocent as a kitten. You should just g—"

Lina tossed the knife, embedding it in the wall inches from Lilly's head. The room literally froze. Even Zyriel stopped messing with his inks. Lilly's eyes were the size of the moon, and I didn't blame her.

Oh, shit!

Lilly was only one step from having a knife sticking out of her head. All I kept thinking was. *Is this real life? Did that just really happen?* Both our heads snapped over to Lina as she sat back in the chair.

"You'll only get one warning, Lilly. Lay even one hand on her, and I'll take *both* of yours."

"What the fuck! You... You could have... Are you outta your fuckin' mind?"

"Lilly! Just go. I've seen her throw knives before. She doesn't miss. Take the warning for what it is," Zyriel barked.

"Don't fuckin' call me that. You know I—"

"Yeah, yeah. Only she can call you that. Whatever, I don't fucking care. Just go bitch somewhere else."

OK. Lilly is a nickname, and only Lina can use it. Noted.

Lilly huffed and stomped out of the room. I couldn't keep my eyes from straying up to the weapon. Who knew Lina could even throw knives? And why did she and Lilly have such bad blood between them?

Yet again, I found myself with an abundance of questions I was bursting at the seams to ask, but I reined the impulse in. I wasn't an idiot. That would've been the absolute worst time to ask Lina anything.

"Did you tell her I was going to be here, Sai?" she asked, turning on him.

"Don't even give me that look. I didn't tell her shit. But you know I close the shop when you come in. She's not a complete idiot."

"Mhm. Tell me again why you haven't fired her yet?"

"*I* didn't sleep with her. You did. Actually, I warned you off of her, but can't nobody tell you anything, right?"

"What's your point?"

"My point is that other than annoying you, she's actually an asset to my shop. So, no walking papers for her. Sorry, not sorry."

"You're so fucking annoying. Whatever. Let's just get on with this."

"Always so bossy." He chuckled. "We startin' on the owl tatt, right?"

"Yeah."

I guess they were over the situation since they'd moved on to discussing the tattoo. Still, the urge to ask what had just happened was bubbling up, and I was trying my best to swallow it down. But Lina suddenly pulling her shirt and bra off helped me forget every single question I had.

Now, I had a new question. What the fuck was going on this time? Seeing her in any form of undress always severely distracted me, and I know we already established that she and Zyriel had a past.

It still irritated me when I noticed the lust burning in his eyes as her breasts swayed before she laid down on her stomach. My annoyance wasn't justified by any means, but it was still there.

The only thing that kept it in check was the fact that I was her present. So, I focused on that and shut my mouth as he applied a stencil to her back.

I'd never been to a tattoo shop before, but I'd seen the process when I'd watched Ink Master. So, I knew he had to touch her to place the stencil on her skin, but the way he did it drove me fucking crazy.

His hands went from her shoulder blades all the way down to just above her ass. It was just a little too much touching for me, and I felt a bit overwhelmed, so I asked where the restroom was.

Zyriel spared me a quick glance to tell me it was back down the hallway toward the front of the shop before going back to feeling up Lina.

Yep, yep. Gotta get outta here. If I react the way I want to, I'll look like a lunatic.

Lina and Zyriel started talking about the tattoo as I left the room. I found the bathroom quickly, rushed in, and splashed water on my face. I didn't know what the fuck was wrong with me.

I'd met the other boys, and even though there was some touching then too, it didn't burn me up like this time. Maybe, it was because Lina was shirtless. I mean, yeah. That's probably what it was, but I still couldn't be mad about it because she could strip in front of whoever she wanted to.

But why did she have to do it without any fucking care in the world?

Oh my God! This line of thought was irrational at the highest level, but I couldn't stop myself. Hence, the face bath in the sink. Cold water cooled my heated skin, allowing me to think straight again.

After I dried my face, I left the bathroom and was going to make my way back to Lina and Zyriel, but voices from the front of the shop stopped me in my tracks.

"Who the fuck is that lil' bitch?"

Lilly stood behind one of the stations with another woman who was equally gorgeous and covered in tattoos. She could either be a customer or a fellow coworker. I wasn't sure.

Who she was didn't really matter. *What* Lilly was bitching about did. I inched as close to the edge of the wall as I could so I could hear them, but they couldn't see me. Was I really going to eavesdrop on their conversation?

I sure as hell was.

Look, I know this isn't high school, and I'm a full-ass adult, but at the moment, I didn't care about any of that. Overhearing them shit-talking had piqued my curiosity, which compelled me to stay and listen.

The other woman wore a conspiring smile as she pulled her long, lilac-dyed hair into a high ponytail.

"Why are you pissed? I thought you and Rose were still fucking?"

That's fucking news to me!

Lilly chewed her nail but paused when she heard the question. She glanced around, and I quickly stepped back, hoping she hadn't caught me. My heart pounded, and I thought maybe it was best to go back to Zyriel's room.

"We are," she answered. "I was just with her last night. The fuck you askin' me that for? I told you about it already."

Ah. So she's one of those. Cool.

Now that I knew just how much of a pathetic liar she was, I wasn't as curious about what they were discussing anymore. I was legitimately going to walk away, but my feet wouldn't budge.

"Mhm. Sure. Whatever you say, Lil."

"The fuck is your problem?" Lilly barked. "Do you need some fuckin' proof or somethin'?"

"Oh! Now that you mention it, that would be great. Shouldn't be hard to get a pic, right?"

"Oh... Uh... Um... Sure. I-I'll take a pic when I see her tonight."

"Ooh. You didn't tell me you were seeing her so soon. Don't send me nothin' lame either. Make sure you make it sexy!"

Alright. Now, I was over this whole conversation. But since Lilly was so convinced I was just some innocent kitten, I felt it was my duty to prove her wrong.

"It's gonna be really tricky for you to take a picture when she'll be cumming down my throat. If you *do* decide to stop over tonight, I'll probably be screaming, so make sure you knock loud. K?"

Both their jaws hit the floor. I turned away and slowly walked back to Zyriel's room. Internally, I was losing my shit.

Did I really just say that out loud? To her face? Oh my God!

"Are you OK?"

The question pulled me out of my thoughts. I looked up to see both Lina and Zyriel staring at me with concerned faces.

"Huh? Oh, yeah. I'm good. I-I was just looking at all the art out front. I was thinking of getting some ink myself. Possibly."

"Oh. OK, cool. Thought you got lost somehow. Well, we can talk about that after I finish laying down the outline for Star first. Cool?"

"O-of course," I said before sitting back down.

Zyriel took my lie at face value because he didn't know me, but Lina did, and she hadn't stopped studying me since I'd walked into the room.

I wasn't going to break under the scrutiny. If it meant I had to actually get a tattoo done in order to avoid talking about my extended bathroom break, then that's just what I was going to do.

An hour later, I finally relaxed and sat back in the chair. I was convinced Lilly was going to burst into the room at any moment and attempt to take my head off, but she never did.

At some point, I must have fallen asleep because I was awakened by a shirt-wearing Lina stroking my cheek.

"So, what type of ink were you thinking about?" Zyriel asked as he pulled out a sketchbook.

Oh, fuck! I'd forgotten about that!

XIX

Melanie

When I walked into my office this morning, Michelle was already sitting in front of my desk, waiting for me. My stomach dropped as soon as I saw her. This wasn't going to be good. I just knew it.

"Am I fired?" I asked, unable to stop myself.

"What? No, of course not, but I do need you to help me understand what's going on. I got quite the earful this morning about what happened on Wednesday, and none of it sounded like you."

Michelle pulled out the chair next to her, and I slumped into it. I told her the truth about the Tiberius situation, and she sat and listened patiently.

When I finished, she got up from the chair and began to pace back and forth. That was concerning, but I wasn't going to ask any questions, just in case she happened to change her mind and wanted to fire me, after all.

Her pacing was nerve-wracking, and I couldn't keep myself from fidgeting. I was so damn nervous about what she was going to say. Finally, she took mercy on me and stopped.

She walked back to the chair, sat down, and looked into my eyes.

"I'm still not firing you, so you can stop looking so defeated, Melanie. The story I was told this morning is very different from what you just said, but I don't know her, and unlike some of your coworkers, you've never been a problem child." Michelle sighed. "With that being said, I have to figure some things out and see what the fallout will be."

"And what does that mean for me?"

She shook her head. "You're going to take some time off. You have more than enough days saved up since you never take any. So for the next week, you won't be here. No work. No coming up to visit. Just rest and recuperation. While you're off, I'll see what I can find out and the dust can settle."

That was fair, I guess, but it was still frustrating because I didn't do anything wrong. Scratch that. I let an idiot into my life. That's where I fucked up, and now I was paying for it.

A lot of people would be geeked over the fact that they got to take a week off with pay, and if my life didn't suck ass right then, I would've been happy, too. I just couldn't muster up that joyful feeling.

The only small positive about this bullshit was that I'd already finished all of my other projects. So, my being off for a week wouldn't affect anyone, but I still wasn't happy about it.

I was grateful to Michelle, though, because this was her business, and she had to protect it and put it first. I was glad that she was also protecting me, too.

"I'm pretty sure I know the answer to this, but I'll ask, anyway. Do I need to make arrangements to have your projects reassigned?"

"No," I told her. "I finished everything last week to make sure I was prepared for the new project."

Michelle nodded, then leaned forward and grabbed my hand.

"I know this doesn't seem fair, but until your situation is over, it's what's best for the company and for you. You understand that, right?"

I nodded my head and offered her a small smile. I didn't fully agree, but I understood. I could've been cleaning out my office, but I wasn't, so I was going to focus on the small wins.

After the meeting with Michelle was over, I let Stephanie know about my time off. By necessity, she would become a shared assistant for the other junior editors until my return. She wasn't crazy about the idea, but the alternative of having no job for a week wasn't ideal, either.

The drive back home was depressing, and even though my day had literally just started, I was exhausted. So after my shower, I climbed into bed and crashed, desperately hoping this was all a terrible dream.

XX

Melanie

Calling this *time off* was bullshit, considering the circumstances, but I guessed I should be grateful Michelle believed me. Still, I was so over this. The fact that this Tiberius nonsense had reached me at work had me angrier than I had ever been in my life.

Obviously, I'd completely underestimated his level of commitment to revenge, and even more than that, his desperation. The little bastard was smart, sending other people to harass me so I couldn't prove beyond a doubt he was behind it.

The day was almost a bust until Lina called me. As usual, that lifted my spirits. I nearly cracked the screen accepting the call when I saw her face dance across it.

"Why you laughing?" she asked.

"No reason. I just did something extremely embarrassing that I am not gonna tell you about, so don't ask me."

"Ooh, but now I'm so curious..."

I doubled down. "I don't care. I'm not sharing, so move on."

"So bossy," Lina laughed.

"You like it, and you know it."

"Mmm... That's true. Whatchu doin', love?"

"Nothing much, just lying in bed," I replied as I snuggled into my covers.

"Gasp! Without me?" she joked.

"I mean, you're more than welcome to join me. I'll open the door for you," I said as I got up and made my way downstairs.

"Oh! Say no more. I'm getting in the car now."

"Are you sure?" I smirked. "I only had one more thing to say."

"Yeah? And what's that?"

"When you get here, my legs will be open, too."

"Fuck! I—"

Before she could finish her sentence, I hung up the phone. That was a bold-ass move, and I regretted it slightly, but then I pushed that thought away because Lina loved boldness.

It would be fine. Or, it wouldn't be. No way to know until she showed up. After I unlocked the door, I took a quick shower, just to freshen up, and slipped into a black silk dress.

It was nothing like I'd ever worn before, but since meeting Lina, my sense of fashion had thoroughly improved. The dress was form-fitting and had high slits on both sides. As if that wasn't scandalous enough, it had a very deep V-neckline that went down almost to my navel. If she was pissed at me for hanging up, this would distract her, at least temporarily.

Satisfied, I went back up to my bedroom, sat on the bed, and waited. About ten minutes later, my front door crashed open.

Oh, shit! Maybe she really is pissed.

"MELANIE!"

I jumped out of bed and slowly made it over to the top of the steps. Downstairs, Lina was searching for me. She kicked the door closed and stepped into the house.

My heart was beating out of my chest, but when her eyes found me at the top of the steps, it felt like it exploded. A powerful and lust-filled heat radiated off of her, and even from ten feet away, it overwhelmed me.

"Y-yes?" I whispered before clearing my throat. "What?"

Lina's shocked expression about my attitude almost shook my resolve until that damn grin spread across her face. She bit her bottom lip and took the dress in. As her hungry eyes roved over my body, it felt like a whisper of her hands was walking over my skin.

Goosebumps popped up everywhere she looked. It was like she couldn't pick just one place. But then her eyes met mine, and my whole dominant facade began to crack.

Leaning back against the door, she crossed her arms. That same lustful heat was still there, but there was also a blistering calm. I didn't know what she was planning, but my entire body and soul were excited for it.

"Come here," she commanded.

On absolute instinct, I moved down the first two steps before I stopped myself. The smile on her face widened, and she raised an eyebrow at me. I swallowed so hard, I'm sure it was audible.

"If you want me, come get me," I challenged.

Her jaw dropped, and it took everything in me to keep mine from doing the same. This was taking bold to a whole 'nother level, but I was going to embrace it and ride it as far as I could.

Lina pushed away from the door and stalked toward me. I thought for a moment I'd won. That she was actually going to come to me. But then she stopped at the bottom of the steps.

Damn it! Always such a fucking tease.

Since this was the game we were playing, I wouldn't let her count me out just yet. Instead, I climbed back up those two steps, making sure to exaggerate the sway of my hips, and leaned over the railing.

Her eyes landed on my cleavage, just as I'd planned. What I didn't plan for was what she did next. Lina unzipped her jacket, revealing her glorious, bare breasts. My tongue grew so thick in my mouth that it was almost impossible to swallow.

Lina tossed her jacket onto the couch and stared up at me with her hands on her hips. Hard as it was, I managed to tear my gaze away from her chest and look her in the eyes.

She was still smiling, thinking I'd succumb to her soon, and as horny as I was... She was probably right. That didn't mean I wasn't going to at least try to make her work for it, though.

Reaching down, I hiked my dress up until the slit fell over my hip. Lina's eyes flicked to the opening, and I got so excited that I forgot to hide my smile.

"You really think you're gonna win this, huh?" she asked.

"Well... I am a lil' competitive," I said as I shrugged. "Who knows? I just might."

Lina pulled a chair out from the dining room table, faced it toward the steps, and sat down. She put an elbow on her knee, leaned forward, and rested her head in her hand.

"So cute that you think you will. Did you get the harness I ordered?"

That question sent my mind to so many lustful places, I temporarily forgot how to speak. Lina cleared her throat and brought me back to her question. "Yes! Oh... Um... I mean. What would happen if I did?"

Lina chuckled, leaned back in the chair, crossed her arms obscuring my view of her breasts, and crossed her legs. Somehow, even topless, she gave off the impression of a fierce businesswoman negotiating a deal. She was like a shark, and in her eyes, I was the tasty dolphin. In the past, she would've eaten me alive, but now, I was going to make her fight for her meal.

Holding my ground, I moved over to the top of the steps and sat down with my legs open, making sure to pull up my dress so she could get an eye-full. She closed her eyes for a moment but gave no further reaction.

"Where is it? And where's that dick I sent you?"

"Why do I have to answer your questions when you ignored mine?"

Lina sighed and simply stared at me. I could hear my clock ticking on the wall. It was so fucking quiet. If she didn't say or do something soon, I was going to forfeit.

"Mel," Lina prompted.

"Yes?"

"Ten seconds."

Ten seconds. That's all she said. No explanations. Nothing. Just those two words. She continued to stare at me. I had no fucking idea what that meant. Lina lifted both her hands and spread her fingers. Trying to understand was making me spiral.

"Ten," she began to count.

Ten seconds to grab the harness?

"Nine."

Nine seconds to get the dildo?

"Eight."

Eight seconds to grab them both?

"Seven."

Seven seconds to go to her?

"Six"

Six seconds to do what?

"Five."

My nerves were fried. I was no closer to figuring out what she meant when she lowered her fourth finger. Unable to take it anymore, I hustled down the stairs. The counting ceased when I stopped in front of her. She'd only had three fingers left.

Lina reached out and traced the V of my dress. Just that whisper of her touch made my knees weak and pulled a moan from my lips.

"Answer my questions, Mel," she instructed.

Lina rolled her fingers around my nipples. The urge to keep her doing that was the only thing I could focus on. The game was over, and I'd lost, but at least now I could reap the benefits of submitting.

"Left side nightstand. Second drawer. They're both in there."

Her hands had returned to the slits in the dress, and my breathing was starting to pick up. I could hear the blood rushing through me as her fingers dipped beneath the fabric and traveled across my hips.

I was so incredibly wet that her fingers would slide in easily. She was inching closer and closer, but then, her exploration stopped. I don't remember at what point I'd closed my eyes, but they immediately snapped open.

"Do you know what happens when bad girls try my patience?" she asked.

There was only one correct answer, but I really wanted her fingers inside of me, and since I was going to be teased anyway, I might as well tease her back. Could it make my punishment worse? Probably, but that really just meant more fun.

"Hmm... You spank them until their ass is redder than a cherry?"

She smiled but didn't respond. She did, however, stand up and slip my dress down my body. The cool air and the heat of her gaze stirred up a severe need to be as close to her as possible.

"Turn around," she demanded.

That was unexpected. It threw me off so much that I hesitated, and she spun me around herself. Her hands were so hot, but she hadn't actually touched me again. It was like there was a bubble between my body and hers.

This was driving me insane. I wanted her to touch me. I *needed* her to touch me. I was past the point of resistance. If she wanted me to beg for *anything*, I would drop to my knees right then and plead as much she wanted.

She clapped her hands, startling me. All my thoughts scattered as the bubble finally popped. I hadn't even realized I was holding my breath, but it rushed out of me so quickly, I wound up light-headed.

"You didn't hear anything I just said, did you?"

Did she say something? When did she say something?

"I-I... I didn't. What did you say?"

"I told you to put your arms behind your back."

"Why?"

She wrapped her fingers in my hair, and when she tugged, I nearly lost my composure. I couldn't even begin to explain what the anticipation was doing to me. There was only so much teasing I could take.

Stepping back, I pushed my body against hers. Lina sucked in a breath through her teeth, bringing a smile to my face. It quickly disappeared when she pulled my head back and bit my neck.

"Oh, fuck!"

"Put. Your. Arms. Behind. Your. Back."

All of my plans to resist disappeared. I was ready to completely submit. I just hoped she was ready to ravage me, too. I put my arms behind my back as she'd demanded.

There was some shuffling behind me, and then I heard the snap of a belt. That got my heart racing.

Is she going to spank me with it? Would that be fun, or would it be a disaster?

I braced myself for the sting. Lina chuckled. Unsure if I was allowed to turn around or not, I settled for glancing over my shoulder at her.

Her smile was huge, and it was highly distracting, but I still wanted to know why she'd laughed.

"I am going to spank you, Mel. *Repeatedly*," she informed me as she fastened the belt around my wrists." "But not with a belt. You're *going* to do *everything* I say, but I'm not your mother."

"Oh. I heard that some people have a *mommy fetish* from Shelly. Do you want me to call you *mommy*, Lina?"

She chuckled and buckled the belt. It was tight enough to restrict but not to harm. Then, she picked me up, carried me upstairs to my bedroom, and tossed me onto the bed.

It was a bit of a struggle, but I managed to get myself up into a seated position. Apparently, while I'd had a face full of my covers, she'd pulled off the rest of her clothes and rummaged through my nightstand.

After she found her prize, she strapped up and stood in front of the bed. My mouth began to water, already knowing what she was going to demand. I was off the bed and on my knees before she had a chance to say anything.

"Oh! Are you trying to be a good girl now?"

"Maybe," I said before I parted my lips for her.

She took no time at all to slide the dildo deep into my mouth. I gagged a few times until my throat could adjust, but once it did, I took the opportunity to give her a show.

I pulled back until just the tip of it was between my lips. Making sure to keep eye contact with her, I rolled my tongue around it several times before taking the whole thing back down my throat.

Lina bit her lip as she watched me, but when I swallowed it deeper, she clamped down so hard that I was sure her lip would bleed. She grabbed my hair, yanked the dildo from my mouth, and helped me onto the bed.

She pushed me onto my knees and forced my head into my pillows. From behind me, I felt the tip teasing my slit and rolling through my lips. It was pure fucking torture, but I did sign up for it.

When I felt it right at my entrance, I got so excited because I thought finally she was going to fuck me. In almost all of our interactions, she'd never immediately done what I wanted. Don't ask me why I thought this time would be any different.

The tip still probed my pussy, but instead of entering me, she spanked me. Hard. Before I could think to keep it in, a scream was out of my mouth. That was the hardest she'd ever spanked me, and it took me an extra second to adjust to the impact.

Lina didn't give any longer than that to get used to the sting before she started to tease my entrance with the tip again, and that was all I could focus on.

Once more, I thought she was going to slide in, but she spanked me again, just as hard as the first time. It was the most jarring experience of my life. There was pain, but even more than that, there was pleasure. My only gripe was that the pleasure was just as short-lived as the fucking sting.

Five more times, she teased me and then spanked me. After the last slap, I realized it corresponded with the seven seconds it took me to make it down the steps to her.

Thank God it didn't take me the full ten! My ass is hot!

"Now that part of your punishment has been rendered, do you have anything to say, Mel?"

The tip rested barely inside of me. She pulled my hair, lifting my head off of the pillows so I could talk. I wanted to be a brat, but the dick's pressure was too exciting, so I gave in.

"I'm so—" *Oh, God!*

Lina slid into me then, so fast and deep that I stopped breathing. I don't know how, but I'd forgotten how long and thick this dildo was. Somehow I did, and my body had to quickly remember.

"My bad, I slipped," she said. "What were you trying to say?"

I didn't believe that for a fucking minute, but I also didn't think I would gain anything by calling her out on it.

"I was telling you I was so—"

My words became a strained gargle as she slammed into me again, somehow reaching even deeper than the first time. I got the gist of this twisted fucking game she was playing.

Was I mad about it?

Fuck, no! Each of those strokes were amazing, and all I had to do was hold out for five more, then I'd get my prize. She was going to fuck me as wildly as I wanted, whether that was her plan or not.

"Not sure what language that was supposed to be," she pressed, "but it sure as hell wasn't English. Try again."

Now that I understood the rules, I took my time saying sorry, but I was only able to get the S out before she was deep inside of me again. I kept thinking that there were only four more strokes, and then the game would end.

Then, a distressing thought crossed my mind, and that took up all my focus.

What if at the end of those strokes, she stops completely? She loves to edge me, and this would be the equivalent of blue balls for a woman. That's like fucking catnip to her.

My thoughts continued to turn while she slid out of me, leaving only the tip again. As soon as I heard her start to speak, I screamed out "I'm sorry" before she could even finish the question.

"Damn. You figured me out."

Oh. My. God. I'm so glad I guessed right. Evil woman. These teasing games are starting to get so damn brutal. But, fuck! I can't lie and say I'm not addicted to them.

There were two ways to play this. If I responded in my usual meek manner, she could end this whole thing because she wanted me to be more confident when I was with her.

On the other hand, I could be bratty and piss her off enough that she'd want to stop, as well. There was risk in either choice, but one thing was for certain. Pissed or not, Lina responded better to confidence than she did to meekness.

"It was easy to figure out. You are *extremely* predictable, after all."

The room was pregnant with so much silence that I started freaking out, thinking that I chose wrong. I planned to look back to see if she was upset but ended up with my head forced into the pillows again. I was grateful that I'd managed to turn my face to the side or I'd probably be suffocating.

Honestly, I would willingly give up any and all the fucking air in the world because the way she was pounding into me was stealing the rest of the breath I managed to suck in. Her strokes reached deeper and deeper, and I was seconds from that mind-blowing climax I'd been craving since the beginning.

"Let's see just how fucking predictable I really am."

She gave me no time to even ponder what she'd meant by that because she rolled me on my side, placed one of my legs over her shoulder, and increased her pace.

"Fuck! Oh my God! Yes! Yes! Please, don't fucking stop!"

"You like this huh?"

"Yes! I love it," I cried out, barely able to catch my breath.

"And if I wanted to stop?"

Hearing the word stop temporarily turned me into a whole new person. My eyes found hers, and the deviant smile on her face made me snap.

"You better not fucking stop!" I ordered.

That damn smile widened as she rotated her hips and hit even more delicious spots. She pulled back, leaving only the tip again, and glared down at me.

I glared back. There was no way in hell I was backing down. Not when I was so close.

"What do you want?"

This was our newest game. She'd started it the same night she sent me the dildo. I knew the point of it was to build my confidence, and in several respects, it worked. But it was still jarring when she made me play along.

Not tonight, though. Tonight, I was too hungry for everything I knew she could and would do to me. So this time, as I glared back at her, I wouldn't just tell her what I wanted. I would command it.

"I want you to fuck me. Fuck me until I can't string a sentence together."

"It'd be my pleasure," she answered as she slammed into me.

Lina rolled her thumb over my clit and pulled the belt strap, making me arch my back more so she could go even deeper. My climax finally came, and it was glorious. All my nerves fired, and I felt bliss throughout every part of my body.

She undid the belt, freed my hands, rolled me onto my back, and spread my legs. Then, she grabbed my wrists and lined herself up with my entrance once more.

"Do your best to keep your legs open, Mel. We wouldn't want me to stop now, would we?"

The question must have been rhetorical because she filled me up before I had a chance to answer it. Her pace was devastating, and it was fucking amazing. Every time she hit a spot that made my legs jump and even look like they were gonna close, I snapped them open.

If I had any say in the matter, we weren't ever going to stop until my body couldn't take anymore, and even then, I'd still want to go again.

Lina raised an eyebrow and smiled when I caught myself and forced my legs back open again.

Letting one of my wrists go, she walked her fingers up my body. When she reached my nipple, I thought she would just twist it, but she just rolled it between them, leaving me desperate for more.

"What do you want, Mel?"

"Twist it," I commanded without even the slightest hesitation.

As soon as she did, a fierce orgasm rolled through my body, and I whispered her name like a prayer. After countless more climaxes, Lina finally pulled out of me.

I might have fallen asleep for a moment because a random thud startled me. When I looked up, Lina was strapless and lying between my legs.

"Did you enjoy yourself?"

"Yes. I had an amazing time," I croaked out, hoarse.

"You know we're not done yet, right?"

"A-Aren't we?"

In answer, she ran her tongue through my slit, making me shiver.

"You can still string sentences together."

"Oh, I guess that's true."

"Mhm. Gotta change that," she replied before she sucked my clit into her mouth.

XXI

Melanie

I was incredibly sore when I woke up, but that soreness and stiffness was so fucking worth it. Lina had fucked me so well, I couldn't even string coherent thoughts together by the end of it.

The head she woke me up with helped ease some of the tension, but it still didn't help beat down the lingering desire to be fucked again. My body was so fucking tired, but I couldn't keep my thoughts from straying back to last night.

I was curious to see if Lina'd left a mark in the shape of her handprint on my ass. As I climbed out of bed, she came back up the stairs with a box in her hands. She placed it on the comforter and slid it toward me.

"Is that for me?" I asked.

"Mhm. It was on your mat when I came over last night. I'd have told you about it then, but I was extremely distracted."

"Oh, yeah?" I said, dragging my nail down the middle of the box to cut the tape. "What distracted you?"

Lina rolled her eyes. "A sassy lil' red-head that wanted to test my gangsta until she came on my dick."

I had only just started pulling tissue paper out of the box when I screamed and scrambled off of the bed. Startled, Lina jumped and looked at me like I'd lost my mind. Then, she glanced down at the overturned box on the floor.

Peeking out from inside of it was a bloodied dead rat. The message it represented was clear. My stomach soured. I could deal with the juvenile bullshit, and I hadn't lost my job, so I could get over that, too. But this was different. Could I cope with a threat to my life?

Lina flicked her gaze from the box, to me, and back to the box again. The room felt like it was closing in on me. I knew it wasn't because I lived in a fucking loft, but my mind didn't care.

"What the fuck is going on?" she pressed.

I couldn't answer her question. I couldn't even breathe. I tried to pull in air, but my lungs remained empty. My vision clouded, and I knew I was going to pass out at any moment.

My eyes hadn't left the gruesome carcass in the middle of the floor since I'd screamed. Lina had been talking to me the entire time, but I couldn't hear her questions over the pounding of my heart.

She grabbed my chin and forced me to look up at her. Even though I couldn't move my head, my eyes still attempted to stray over to the package. Seeing this, Lina turned us until the box was behind me.

I still couldn't hear what she was saying, but my vision began to clear, and I was able to suck in oxygen again. Wrapping me in her arms, Lina hugged me close to her chest.

I cried for what felt like an hour before I was finally able to calm down enough to speak. After I explained everything to her, she didn't say a word, which was concerning. I didn't know if she was pissed, or scared for me, or just fed up with our whole situationship.

That last one didn't really seem plausible, but I couldn't stop those stupid thoughts if I wanted to.

After a while, Lina brought me downstairs and sat me on the couch before walking away. I assumed she went to clean up the rat, which I felt bad for because it wasn't her mess to clean, but I was grateful that I wouldn't have to do it. I waited for her to return, listening to her move around upstairs. There was a lot more rummaging going on than I'd expected. I was slightly curious about what she was doing, but I was far too tired to turn around to look.

It felt like another hour passed before Lina came back to the couch. I looked over at her and saw two suitcases and Kuro's carrier waiting by the door. I opened my mouth to ask about them, but Lina beat me to it.

"You're moving in with me until this bullshit is over. There won't be any ifs, ands, or buts about it. Let's go."

"I-I need to collect some things first."

"Everything you could need has been packed or will be bought if necessary."

I hesitated. "Kuro will need supplies."

"We'll stop by the store on the way home," she assured me.

Home. Why does one fucking word put me so much at ease?

I couldn't think of anything else to say, so I just nodded, and we left.

On the way, we stopped at the store to pick up some supplies. When we made it back to her place, Lina went to move my stuff in and let Kuro out. I knew I should probably set up his things, but I just couldn't find the motivation.

This week had been a lot, but today was too much. Today was the metaphorical straw that broke the camel's back. I couldn't believe he would go this far. How was this my reality? This was the type of shit you'd read about in books or watch on TV.

My mind was overstimulated, and I needed to just chill for a second. My first reaction was to go to Lina for comfort, but with her being so mad, I didn't know if talking to her was the best thing to do right now.

Deciding against it, I chose to go and sit in one of my favorite places in her library: the reading nook. It was as if that spot was made just for me. Whenever I pulled out a book and climbed into it, I felt like everything was right with the world.

That was the feeling I needed, to be able to zen out. Maybe Lina would be ready to talk later, but for now, I was gonna sit there and vibe until she was.

XXII

Rose

You know how when you find out shitty information, you're supposed to take a moment to collect your thoughts so you don't end up starting a fight? Yeah, well... Shit.

I didn't have the patience for that. So when I found Mel in the library, instead of broaching the topic gently, I went off.

"Why the hell wouldn't you tell me about this?" I demanded.

Mel was sitting in my reading nook, staring out the window. She jumped at my tone. That made me feel bad... Slightly. I hadn't meant to bark out my question, but I was still pissed she'd hid this from me.

Beneath the surface, a second emotion I was trying to ignore fueled my rage, but the anger is where I wanted to keep my focus. Still, behind anger, there's only one powerful emotion. I could deny it all I fucking wanted, but the truth of the matter was. I was... *scared*.

The shit that had happened so far had been all petty, childish bullshit with no real teeth. Of course, that was until the *rat* and her trouble at work. Something serious could've happened, and that's what had me pissed.

Why did Mel think she had to deal with this alone?

"There was no reason to involve you," she answered weakly.

The fuck did she just say?

"I'm not sure I understand, so before I lose my shit, run that by me again."

Mel sighed and looked over at me. The exhaustion in her eyes stoked the flames of my anger and helped me ignore the fear. She shouldn't have to deal with this bullshit. Of course, no one should, but I only cared about her. Yes, yes. I admitted it. We can analyze that later.

"What would be the point of telling you, Lina?" she asked. "Honestly? What could you have done?"

I opened my mouth to respond but snapped it shut. If I *was* going to do something about it, there was no way in hell I was going to tell her. She mistook my silence for agreement and turned back to the window.

"Regardless of what I could or couldn't do, you could've told me."

"Again, to that, I say what would be the point? You want me to share with you, but you don't want to share with me."

Alright, the fear had been bitch-slapped right out of the fucking way. Pure anger surged, becoming quite comfortable in the seat of my emotions. We were not going to be turning this into *another* fucking conversation about those damn nightmares.

"Mel, that has nothing to do with this."

"But doesn't it, though? You want me to talk to you about something that is causing some level of trauma in my life, but you won't tell me about yours. How is it different, Lina?"

"Because you didn't even exist in my universe when the 'trauma' you wanna know about so badly happened to me. But I sure as hell *have* existed in yours *before* this shit happened. So yeah, that makes it different to me, but maybe I'm wrong."

OK, OK. I knew that was harsh. I wasn't trying to take her head off, but the comparison just set me off, and I couldn't hold it in. I didn't wait for her response before I stalked off.

If I'd stayed, I would've said something even worse, and that would've gotten us nowhere. So, I took that damn moment. I headed down to the media room, booted up my *PlayStation*, picked a game, and started killing things.

I'd been playing for at least an hour when Mel came down. By then, I was over my anger, but I was still annoyed by what she'd said, so I ignored her. It wasn't the most mature decision, but it's what I did. Sue me.

Anyway, I kept my focus on the game while Mel lingered in the doorway. I wanted to tell her to just come sit down, but my stubbornness wouldn't let me. She came into the room on her own a moment later and stood directly in front of the TV.

"Your mother isn't a glassmaker, Mel. Move," I instructed as I rolled my eyes and leaned over to try to see around her.

She didn't move, though. Instead, she dropped the button-up she was wearing, and I, in turn, dropped my controller. Beneath, she wore a red lace lingerie set that instantly made my mouth water.

If this was her version of an apology, it was one of the best ones I'd ever received in my life. Still, I wasn't going to roll over for her, just like that. That's really not a part of my nature. I shook my head to clear it, snatched the controller, and *attempted* to go back to playing.

Mel had yet to move, so I leaned over again and started killing what I *could* see. The benefit of having a seventy-five-inch TV is that she could only block so much of it with her petite frame.

This was going to be a game of wills, and Mel knew that. If she wanted my attention, she had to take it. I wouldn't just give it to her. Not tonight. A part of me was curious about what she would do, but another part just wanted her to take her power back.

Right then, getting me to heel and give her my attention was the best way for her to do it. I'd deal with the Tiberius situation later. For now, though, the ball was in her court.

Bending down, Mel grabbed something out of the pocket of the shirt. Apparently, she'd come prepared to get my attention, no matter what. I was dying to see what she had planned.

She walked up to the coffee table, shoved all the remotes onto the floor, and sat down on top of it. I was annoyed that she didn't give a fuck about my remotes, but compared to the need to know what she was going to do next, that feeling was minor.

Since she wasn't in front of the TV, I went back to the game, but I won't lie and say that more of my focus wasn't on her. I snuck glances at her through the corner of my eye and got killed for it.

I cursed and saw her smile in my peripheral vision. She knew I'd been momentarily distracted, and she knew why, too. Mel looked over her shoulder at the TV, and I used that moment to take in her magnificent body.

Unfortunately, she turned back toward me, so I had to quickly return my gaze to the screen. A stronger enemy needed my attention, so I wound up absorbed in the game. That was until I heard the clasp of her bra click.

Mel's breasts were free, and they looked delicious. Instantly, my tongue was thick and my throat was dry, in desperate need of a taste. The controller vibrated in my hands, letting me know I'd died again.

"Son of bitch!" I complained.

"Did I distract you?" she asked coyly. "I'm sorry. I didn't mean to. I just got a lil' hot, that's all."

OK. If this is the game you wanna play, by all means, let's play.

"Nope, all good," I lied. "Just hit the wrong button. I've seen your tits before, so they ain't all that distracting anymore."

"Is that so?"

"Yep."

"Good to know," she said, spreading her legs. "So then, this isn't distracting either since you've seen it before, right?"

"Nope," I squeaked out before clearing my throat.

Mel's panties were crotchless, and her beautiful glistening pussy was staring at me, ready to eat. My mouth had been dry before, but now it was flooding with water.

Well-fucking-played. I was not expecting that at all.

It took me way too long to tear my eyes away from her pussy, and even then, I couldn't stop myself from sneaking glances every few seconds. I could feel the heat of her gaze watching me, and yet, I still couldn't resist looking at her.

After what felt like an eternity, I finally mustered up the strength to look back at the TV. This game between us was heating up, but I hated to lose, so I was going to hold out for as long as I fucking could.

Somehow, I think I forgot that Mel is quite competitive and not above playing dirty. Because seconds later, when I heard how wet she was as she ran her fingers through her pussy, I almost tossed the damn controller and ravaged her.

She was drenched, and it took every fiber of my being to ignore the sounds.

"Lina," she moaned. "I was wrong earlier, and I'm sorry." Another small moan. "I bet you want to punish me." Another breathy moan.

If only you knew how badly I want to.

"I'll be good for you," she whispered as she drove her fingers deeper inside. "You can do anything you want to me."

Fuck! Don't give me that type of permission.

I gripped the controller so tightly that my knuckles whitened. It was the only thing I could do to not lose my control. Mel was half-naked, writhing, and literally ripe for the taking, but I hadn't heard it yet, so I still had to hold out.

Suddenly, she stood up and pulled off her panties. Even crotchless, I'm sure they were soaked. She laid them gently across my forearm before sitting back down on the coffee table.

Her scent hit my nose like a bullet train, and I almost lost my shit. My eyes rolled as her smell permeated my senses. I had to take a deep breath through my mouth in order to regain my composure.

I thought that would be her last trick, that she was going to give in. I was so wrong. I'd completely forgotten about the item she'd taken out of the shirt pocket. When I heard the familiar buzz of a vibrator, I dropped the controller once again. My eyes locked on her in seconds. The smile she wore was dazzling.

The bullet was already moving in and out of her, making the same little wet noises as before, only so much fucking louder. What started out as a game for me was now torture. I wanted to fuck her. I needed to fuck. *Savagely*. And I was running out of the desire to resist with each shaky breath she took.

Mel rode the toy, and her free hand played with her nipples. My eyes took it all in. I was seconds from giving up and having my way with her when she finally whispered the words I'd been waiting for.

"Lina, please fuck me."

Four works even better than three.

Instantly, I placed my hand on her heaving chest and shoved her down onto the table. Mel looked at me through her shaking legs. The view was magnificent, but there was so much else I wanted to see, too.

I pulled the toy from her hand and turned it off before raising it up to my lips. Just as I was about to lick it clean, Mel snatched my arm and pulled it to her mouth.

She rolled her tongue around the tip, making sure to lap up all of her pre-cum. I was enthralled by the show, but then she moved down to my fingers.

Jolts of pure electricity raced through my veins after every flick of her tongue. Someone apparently thought we were still playing the game. Perhaps, she was thinking she somehow had the upper hand since she'd riled me up.

If that was the case, then I needed to relieve her of that silly little delusion. Several things happened in quick succession then, so let me break them down for you.

First, I wrapped my free hand around her throat and forced her back down on the table, then I snatched the hand holding the toy, wrenching it from her grip, and pressed it against her clit.

"Look at me, Mel," I ordered. "I got a few questions, and I want clear answers," I told her as I loosened my grip on her neck so she could speak.

She leaned up onto her elbows and glared at me as her chest heaved. It was a sight to behold.

"You gonna take all day? Ask your questions."

Ever the defiant one, huh? Let's see if you can keep the act up this time.

"You said I could do anything to you, right?"

"That's what I said."

"Are you sure you want to give me that type of permission?"

"How many times do I—"

I tightened my grip around her throat and cut her off. Her defiance was delicious, but I wanted her to fully understand what I meant by my question.

"Let me be clear. This lil' attitude you're giving is cute, and I'm going to fully fuck it right out of you. But I need you to hear me. Once you give me this permission, there's no taking it back. Understand?"

Mel sat up, leaned forward so I could see her eyes clearly, and gently squeezed my hand, making me tighten my grip on her throat once more. That sent shivers down my back. My wild side screamed that I needed to just accept that as the permission, and the blistering look in Mel's eyes almost had me right there.

She was so turned on that she was breathing raggedly, and her cum-flavored breath tickled my nose. I wanted to suck every drop of it off of her tongue. Was I torturing myself with this situation? Fuck, yes! But I had to hear the words, in whatever form they came in. I just had to make sure she was sure.

"Lina?"

I'd been so absorbed in my thoughts of tasting her and our joined hands on her neck that I hadn't realized she'd spoken up.

"Uh... What?"

"You know it's obvious, right?" she asked as she giggled.

"What is?"

"How much you want to fuck me. Since you want to hear my words so badly, hear me when I say this. I want you to fuck me in every single way your sexually depraved mind can imagine."

She leaned in even closer until her lips were just a whisper away from mine.

"And I better not be able to walk out of this room when we're done, either."

It was impossible to explain what her words did to me. Ideas of what I was going to do flooded my mind so quickly that I froze. Then, I heard her giggle, and that woke me up.

The game was on.

I broke out of her grip, released her neck, stood up, and walked out of the room. I knew her curiosity would compel her to follow me, so I walked right into the playroom.

"Lina?"

Her voice was filled with so much uncertainty that it brought a huge grin to my face.

Where'd all that defiance go?

"Lina..."

Her plea went unanswered, and I went through the dresser in the closet in search of the supplies I needed. In the mirror, I could see her reflection fidgeting as she stood in the doorway.

My smile widened as I finalized my selection. Mel moved closer to try to see what I'd gathered, but I shut the drawer and left the closet before she could.

Her soft footfalls trailed behind me as her lust and wonder filled the room. She was needy, but not nearly needy enough. We had to change that. I laid out the items on the bed before turning to face her.

Mel opened her mouth to speak, but I pressed my index finger to my lips. Her mouth closed. She huffed out a breath and crossed her arms, clearly annoyed.

The defiance was back.

Perfect.

"Get on the bed and lie on your back. Don't speak," I commanded, cutting her off as she opened her mouth again.

Mel rolled her eyes and climbed onto the mattress, laying flat like I'd requested.

"Knees up."

Her head popped up, and she raised a brow. I could practically taste the heat of her burning questions. She'd have a hell of a lot more as we continued, but I was going to ignore every single one. After a moment of hesitation, she pulled up her legs until her knees were raised.

Two of the items I'd grabbed from the drawer were a set of special cuffs. They'd gone unused for a while because I hadn't found anyone to rile me up enough.

But this level of defiant obedience was such a heady combination that it would be disrespectful not to use them on her. The cuffs were constructed of large loops, smaller loops, and a chain that ran between, connecting them.

Mel, propped up on her elbows, was watching me, trying to figure out what I was doing

Always so damn curious.

I wrapped one larger cuff around her knee, secured it, and then repeated the process on the other. The heated gaze she'd given me earlier wasn't even in the same league as the one she was giving me now.

It was adorable how she was so excited when she had no idea what I was about to do to her. But she'd be begging for more when I was done.

"Give me your arms."

"What are you go—"

I raised an eyebrow at her this time, and she swallowed down the rest of her question. She sat up and held her arms out toward me. After I attached the smaller cuffs to both her elbows, I placed a hand on her chest and gently pushed her back down.

As soon as her feet left the bed, her mouth flew open. What I wouldn't have given to be able to read her mind right then. I'm sure an abundance of possibilities raced through it, but none of them would come close to reality.

"Have you figured it out yet, Mel?" I asked as I trailed my fingers through her swollen slit.

She shivered and moaned, looking at me again through her open legs. Her eyes were half-closed as she enjoyed the pleasure I provided. My fingers were drenched when I pulled them away from her lips.

Mel whimpered and tried to scoot toward me, desperate for my touch, but my fingers were already in my mouth, so her efforts were pointless. As soon as the taste of her cum hit my tongue, I felt at peace. This is what I craved: complete submission. And in this position, I could do any and everything I wanted to.

She watched with starved interest as my tongue glided over my fingers, lapping up her desire. If she bit her lip any harder, she'd leave behind permanent teeth marks.

"You're gonna fuck me. What's there to figure out? Although, you're taking your sweet-ass time doing it," she grumbled as she laid her head back down.

If there was one word to describe the smile on my face, it would've been euphoric. Seeing her tied up with her pussy on full display was just so captivating, and she still had the nerve to give me lip.

As I rolled her taste around in my mouth, her earlier words began dancing around in my mind on a loop.

I better not be able to walk out of this room when we're done, either.

"When I'm done, you won't even be able to crawl out of this fucking room."

"Big claim from someone who's barely even touched me," she remarked.

I hadn't meant to say that out loud, but my God, I was so glad I did. Mel was still grumbling, but she gasped when I thrust two fingers inside of her. She was about to be taught a hard lesson in patience.

"Don't you know good girls who listen and wait get whatever they want?" I asked as I drove my fingers deeper.

Her walls tightened around me, and I slid in another half-inch before pulling my fingers out. Mel would give herself vertigo if she kept moving her head that fast. She was aggravated enough that she actually growled at me.

"I'm not as good as you think. It's more fun to be your *lil' brat*," she answered with a devious smile of her own. "Now, hurry up and fuck me," she demanded as she wriggled her body.

"So demanding..." I taunted.

Stepping back, I began to strip. Mel licked her lips as each piece of clothing fell off of my body, but she became even more interested as I secured the harness around my hips.

After I had my dick in place, I stepped back up to the bed, gripped her thighs, and pulled her toward the edge of the mattress. Her skin was blazing to the touch when I grabbed her. She was literally hot and ready.

I grabbed the tip and rubbed it through her lips, reveling in how wet she was for me. Other people were addicted to chocolate, or drugs, or alcohol, or even sex.

But this.

Having an exquisite woman tied up, breathless, and frenzied for my touch...

This was my addiction.

My ambrosia.

And I was about to have my fill of it until I overdosed.

Mel wiggled, trying to force me inside of her. It was a valiant effort on her part, but she was unsuccessful. She wouldn't feel anything until I wanted her to. I popped her pussy with the dick, just to see her reaction.

The look on her face was a mixture of surprise and longing. I wondered if that was the look I gave Zey when he did it to me, but based on her expression, she liked it. Good to know.

Horny lil' masochist.

I decided she'd been teased enough (at least for now) and slowly inched the tip inside of her. Mel sighed contently, thinking I was finally going to give her the relief she craved. After all this time, she still hadn't learned to never let her guard down around me.

The last two items I'd grabbed from the drawer were two vibrators. I grabbed one, turned it on, and pressed it to her clit. She screamed as shivers raced throughout her body.

"Mel."

"Yes?" she breathed.

I pulled the vibrator off of her clit and slid another inch inside her. She writhed and whimpered, unable to keep up her defiant act any longer.

"Lina. Lina, *please*. I'll say whatever you want. I'll do whatever you want. Just stop torturing me. I can't take it anymore."

I gave her two more inches, heeding her pleas. She arched her back, trying to force me in further, but it wasn't going to be that easy. I was only a third of the way in, and this was the longest dick I'd used on her. It was a process, and I was going to take my time so I didn't hurt her.

She wasn't the only one that needed to learn patience. I did, too, but I was quickly losing the last bit of it. I wanted to fill her up completely, but the goal was to render her legs useless, not break her.

"Have you ever tried anal?" I asked as I placed the toy back on her clit.

"Oh my God! No, but if it's what you want, do it! Fuck my ass. Touch me everywhere. I don't fucking care. Just hur... Oh. Oh, God. Yes. Yes! Fuck!"

Watching her climax while she was tied up like this, begging me to fuck her ass, had my wild half battling for control. I barely reigned it in, knowing that if I let it take over, I would fuck her in the ass with no adjustment period, and that's a terrible way to have anal for the first time.

"No, no, no. Please, *please* don't," Mel cried as I pulled out of her.

"Don't worry, my lil' greedy one. I'll fill you up again. But I need something first," I said as I slid the anal trainer inside her pussy, using her cum to lube it up.

"What? What do you want? Just tell me! I'll do it."

So fucking eager. I love it.

"Tell me what you want. And be specific."

"I want every inch of your dick inside me. All the way to the hilt. I want your hands on my breasts, twisting my nipples until they're sore. I want you to choke me until stars dance across my vision.

"I want you to fuck me until the only name I remember is yours. I want yo... Oh, yes. Yes, just like that."

I'd started sliding into her again while she told me everything her dirty little mind could think of. She was up to six inches now, and I was so excited to see if she could actually take the full twelve. But first...

Her ass had been begging to be filled, and I wasn't one to disappoint. As soon as the tip of the trainer touched the puckered skin of her hole, she tensed up. I put the vibrator back on her clit, and she immediately relaxed.

"This will feel strange, but you can't clench or it will hurt. You have to relax. I'll go slow, I promise. I'm not going to hurt you."

When I pushed the trainer tip in, she tensed for a second and then relaxed. I went slowly as I'd promised, overly grateful I was using the smallest trainer instead of the medium one like I'd originally wanted to.

The way she took the trainer, she would level up to the medium size quickly. But for now, the small one worked just fine. Once it was all in, I grabbed the remote for it and looked up at her.

"Are you ready, Mel?"

"Y-yes..." she stammered.

Mel shook so damn hard when I turned the trainer on, she looked like she was having a seizure. My dick almost fell out of her completely, but I placed a hand on her chest and held her down again.

Watching her twitch and jump was becoming my new favorite movie. She was completely focused on the trainer until I slid the rest of the dick inside her. Her eyes grew huge, and it looked like she'd stopped breathing, but she took every single inch, all the way to the hilt.

My strokes started out slow but picked up in speed the louder she screamed and begged. I kissed, licked, and bit every span of skin I could reach from that position. She was going to be dressed in hickies when I was done, and anyone who saw her after today would know she'd been claimed and fucked well.

I leaned back and pounded into her ruthlessly as I twisted her nipples. Her screams raised up another octave as she begged me to fuck her harder. I gave her everything she wanted, even when she started speaking gibberish.

All of a sudden, her head popped up, and she had a look of pure panic on her face. I knew what was coming, but clearly, no one had ever made her squirt before. That was a crime. Secretly, I was glad I was going to get to enjoy her first experience with her.

"Lina, Lina, Lina. I-I. Wait!"

"Shh...it's OK. Just let go."

"No, no. I-I... I have to."

"Do you trust me?" I asked as I placed the vibrator on her clit once more.

"Yes. Yes!"

"Then, cum for me."

I ramped up the vibration and pulled out of her completely. It was like I'd uncorked her because when she came, she turned into a fucking sprinkler and soaked me, herself, the bed, and the floor.

A full minute must've passed before her body finally ran out of cum. I turned the trainer off and slowly removed it, then I laid her down gently. Cumming that hard could cause her to cramp if she shook too hard for too long. Once her body calmed, I glanced down at the puddle we'd created.

I should've put a wet sheet down, but fuck it, that was so worth the mess.

"Did I just wet the bed... as a fucking adult?"

Laughter bubbled up and flew past my lips before I could stop it. I undid the cuffs. I knew she was confused, so I shouldn't have laughed, but that damn question was so fucking innocent, I just couldn't help it.

"So, I guessed right. You've never squirted before?"

Yet again, her eyes were wide and full of wonder. She was experiencing so many firsts with me, and it was pretty magical. OK, that made me sound like a love-sick dolt, but it's how I felt, and we're going to move past it.

The hickies I'd left behind started to darken, and I realized I'd been a little frenzied when I was biting her. She had them on her neck, chest, breasts, stomach, and thighs. I was a little disappointed that there weren't any on her ass, but I could work on that another time.

"W-was that what that was? It felt like I..."

"Had to go to the bathroom," I said, finishing for her.

She nodded her head frantically.

"Trust me. Although that's what it felt like, you didn't piss yourself. You came. Hard. Now let's get you cleaned up," I said, holding my hand out to her.

"Um... Yeah... Small problem with that."

"Oh! And what's that?" I teased with the full force of my wolfish grin.

"You know exactly why, you freak!"

"Of course, I do, but I want to hear you say it."

"Ugh! Because I can't fucking move!"

Of course, you can't. I win!

XXIII

Rose

Now that I'd had my moment and fucked Mel senseless, I could get back to my anger. The nerve of this motherfucker to think he could fuck with her and not suffer any consequence!

The preliminary hearing was next week, and after hearing the plea deal bullshit that they wanted, I knew it wouldn't matter if we were granted the TRO. Tiberius was going to continue to fuck with her until it ruined her life.

This had to stop, but obviously, the situation was too much for the legal system to handle, especially since the motherfuckers could buy off whoever the fuck they wanted. The answer was simple then: I just had to go *outside* of the law. I'd done it before, so I had no issue with a repeat performance.

Honestly, I never thought I would go down this path again, and I most definitely didn't think I would be doing it for someone else. But for Mel, there was no hesitation. I wouldn't walk down that path; I'd *sprint* down it.

That bright smile on her sweet face. That light-hearted giggle that warmed my heart. (Thanks, Zey, for pointing it out). The way her eyes brightened whenever I was in her presence. I could lose those things if Tiberius had his way, and that wasn't something I could accept.

Yesterday morning really brought it home for me. When she saw the rat and the light dimmed in her eyes, I wanted to wrap my hands around his neck and squeeze until his lungs were empty.

What made me angrier was the fact that she had thought she had to hide it from me. I'd already suspected something was wrong, but I hadn't expected this. People deal with shit differently. I understand that, but hiding something like this should have never been the answer.

There was just no way I was going to let that bitch-ass motherfucker steal everything I had learned to crave with every fiber of my being. If that meant I had to permanently torch my invitation past the pearly gates, so be it.

My mind was set. All I needed was to make a phone call. Gently, I pulled my arm out from under Mel's sleeping form, climbed out of bed, and quietly closed the bedroom door behind me.

The last thing I needed was for her to know anything. Not that I gave a fuck about Mel judging my morality — no one could judge me harder than I judged myself — but on the slim chance I was caught, she needed to have plausible deniability.

I waited a few minutes just to make sure she didn't wake up before I headed for the library.

Even though I could protect myself, my brother still insisted on me installing a panic room for emergencies. To end his incessant bitching, I finally relented and let him draw up some plans. Once we agreed on a design, I handed it over to my contractor, and they built one into the library.

Everyone thought my choice of location was a little off, but I figured that I spent most of my time at my desk when I was alone, so that was the perfect place to put it. After I walked into the library, I pulled a book back on a shelf to the right of the entryway.

The bookcase clicked and swung out toward me. I stepped into the panic room and slid it back into place, just in case Mel came looking for me. Inside, there were monitors set up so that I could see every room in the house.

I set the channel to the bedroom to keep an eye on Mel. Thankfully, she was still fast asleep, so that was one less thing to worry about. To the left of the monitors, there was a huge safe containing various important documents and valuables. It held a couple of burner phones, too. I grabbed one, turned it on, and called the one number saved in it. The line trilled for so long that I thought he wouldn't answer, but then it connected.

"I miss you," I said before abruptly hanging up.

Since I never thought I'd be calling this number again, I had agreed to use 'I miss you' as the code for when I needed to schedule a meet. I was slightly annoyed with that decision, but there was nothing I could do about it now.

After a few minutes, the phone vibrated with a text notification.

> Unknown: Miss you, too. Want to see me?

> Me: Yes. Soon.

> Unknown: Now?

You would just love that, wouldn't you?

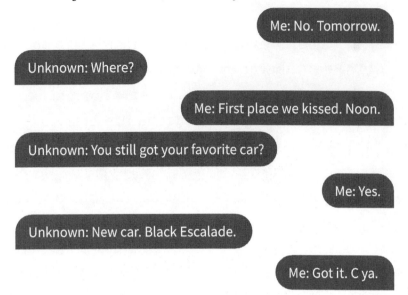

Me: No. Tomorrow.

Unknown: Where?

Me: First place we kissed. Noon.

Unknown: You still got your favorite car?

Me: Yes.

Unknown: New car. Black Escalade.

Me: Got it. C ya.

Immediately, I erascd all of the messages, removed the SIM card, turned the phone off, and broke it. There was almost a zero percent chance anyone would be able to trace this back to me, but arrogance could get you caught up. I took no chances.

When I glanced back at the monitors, Mel was sitting up in bed, probably looking for me. So, I closed everything up and took a seat at my desk. A few minutes later, Mel wandered in, looking sublime in nothing but my old t-shirt. She found me exactly where I'd wanted her to.

"Why are you in here?" Mel asked with a sleepy voice.

"I just had to take care of something," I told her.

"Had? So, that means you're done, right?"

"For now."

"Then, come back to bed with me."

"Sure, love. I'll be there in a few minutes," I promised.

Mel nodded and left. I leaned back in my chair and stared up at the ceiling. As I pondered my plans, I came to a startling realization. I was about to have a man killed for a girl I'd been sleeping with. Not my girlfriend. Not my wife. Just a fuckable.

And yet, I felt that even if this somehow came back to bite me, it would still be worth it. I didn't know when Mel had come to mean so much to me, but she did, so perhaps it was time to tell her about my past.

At the very least, it was something to consider, but that would have to wait until after I made my deal with the devil.

When I woke up, it was a quarter to eleven. That was an accident, but it couldn't be helped. Mel looked too good in my t-shirt, and it's not like I wasn't gonna fuck her again.

The right side of the bed was cold, letting me know Mel had been awake for a while. She was probably in the library. That was her favorite place in the house — after the playroom, of course.

Getting to the meeting would take a thirty-minute drive, so I needed to hustle. I jumped out of bed, grabbed a shower, got dressed, and headed for the library. Mel was snuggled up asleep in the reading nook with a book on her chest.

If that wasn't the sweetest fucking image I'd ever seen, I didn't know what was. As I snapped a quick picture of her, I considered that maybe it would be best not to wake her, but then I realized she would worry if she didn't know where I was.

To let her wake up to an empty house just didn't feel fair. So, I stroked her cheek gently, and she began to stir. When her eyes opened and found me, a beautiful smile spread across her face.

That smile was the reason I didn't mind buying a permanent residence in Hell. Just seeing her so happy to see me reaffirmed that I was making the right decision.

"I have some errands to run and will be back this evening, OK?"

"Do you want some company?" Mel asked.

"No, love. You stay and rest." I leaned down and kissed her. "Get your energy up for when I come home."

She stretched her back like a cat and snuggled farther into the nook.

"I can do that."

Mel was already falling asleep as I headed out. She was safe and content, and that's just the way I wanted her.

The meeting place I'd selected was the library in the city I'd grown up in. I hadn't been there in years, and now that I was finally coming back, I wouldn't even be able to check out any books. Tragic.

When I pulled up, a black Escalade was idling in the back of the lot. I parked next to it, climbed out, opened the back door, and slid inside. The driver was unremarkable, mostly because I was more focused on the gun the passenger pointed at my head.

Well, this is gonna be interesting.

The passenger looked like a fucking kid, which irked me even more because the little pissant had the nerve to aim a Glock at me. When I made it out of this, I was gonna bend him over my knee and spank him.

"You Moon?" the kid asked.

"You holding a gun?" I responded.

"What?"

"Oh, I thought we were asking dumb-ass questions."

The driver laughed and pulled out of the parking lot while the boy sucked his teeth and lowered the gun.

"Why are we leaving? She didn't answer the question," the boy whined.

"Yes, she did," the driver told him. "In the exact way he said she would. You just don't listen."

"Man, whatever," the boy replied, pouting and finally turning around in his seat.

"We have a bit of a drive, Ms. Moon. If you get hungry, there are snacks in the cooler next to you."

I side-eyed the cooler, not really interested in it. More of my focus fell on the kid because he turned back around and glared at me. We played a round of chicken, staring at each other until he blinked.

Again, he sucked his teeth, and I just laughed at him and closed my eyes. Now that I knew I wasn't in immediate danger, I decided I was going to sleep. I was tired enough that I knew it would be nightmare-free.

I know what you're thinking. They could've killed me while I slept. True. But then again, they could've killed me when I was awake, too. At least if I was passed out, I wouldn't feel it, right?

"Blake," the kid said. "I think she passed out. Is she crazy? I was just pointing a gun at her."

The driver chuckled. "Obviously, she's comfortable, DJ. So, shut it and let her rest."

They were still talking, but as I drifted off, their voices faded out.

I slept deeply. When I finally woke up, it felt like I'd only been out for a few minutes, but DJ was in my face with his hand on my shoulder.

I was still a bit groggy and briefly forgot where I was, so when my eyes focused on him, I went straight into fight mode. I grabbed his arm and twisted it.

"Ow, lady! That fucking hurts!" he howled.

"Ms. Moon, I'm sorry to wake you, but we're here," the driver said, ignoring the kid.

After my brain registered what was happening, I let DJ's arm go. "My bad."

"*My bad!* Bitch, you could've broken my arm."

"What are you, twelve?" I asked him. "If I wanted to break your damn arm, I would have. Quit whining, and get the fuck outta my face."

Blake laughed, stepped out of the car, walked over, and opened my door for me. DJ gave me the stink eye the entire time, then stuck his tongue out at me before I followed suit.

If I had died because this lil' fucker had sneezed, I'd have haunted him for the rest of his damn life.

The neighborhood we were in was pretty run down, but the house before me looked completely abandoned. Maybe I shouldn't have fallen asleep earlier. I had no fucking idea where I was.

The driver slid back into the SUV, and the Escalade pulled off without so much as a goodbye. I started to wonder if perhaps I *was* going to die today. It was a chilling thought, but there was nothing I could do about it, so I walked up the path to the front door.

Two men sat on the porch, and they were both watching me intently as I came closer and closer to the stoop.

"You ain't from 'round here, sweetie," one of them said. "Best be gettin' back to where you came from... 'Less you lookin' for a good time." He leaned on the railing to block my path

Honestly, I was starting to get annoyed. I just wanted to talk to Rian and get this shit over with. After having a gun pointed at me, I wasn't in the mood to pretend to be nice.

I attempted to step around the man, but he stopped me by grabbing my wrist.

I frowned at him. "Let me ask you a question."

"What you wanna know, Sweet Cheeks?"

"Is that the hand you jerk off with?"

"Why you askin'? You wanna jerk me off, baby?"

"Not on your life, but I don't want you to lose the only hand that's willing to touch you. I suggest you remove it from my wrist."

"The fuck you say to me?"

"You hard of hearing or just dumb?" I asked him. "Should I say it slower for you?"

"Why you lil' b—"

"Roscoe, you heard the lady. She may look fragile, but she's got sharp edges. If you aren't that attached to your life, by all means, keep ahold of her wrist," Dre interrupted, flashing him a cruel smile.

There were positives and negatives to Dre being here. The positive was that he knew who I was and would get these idiots away from me before I had to start hacking limbs off.

On the other hand, the negative was that he and I had a past, one I was hoping he would've let go of by now.

There he stood behind the screen, looking just as devastatingly beautiful as he had when we first met: Tall and broad-chested. Kissable, full lips. Sun-burnished tan skin and a smile that used to turn me to mush. His hair was longer now, and it covered half of his face, hiding a jagged scar he'd had since before we met.

I told him the scar never bothered me, so he used to wear his hair pulled back when we were hanging out, but I guess that was over. That made me a little sad, honestly, but there was nothing I could do about it.

One ice-blue eye looked me up and down with so much heat, I knew my hope that he'd moved on was misguided.

"Who the fuck is this bitch?" Roscoe asked, confused.

"This *woman*, you imbecilic waste of oxygen, is Moon, and she's very dear to our boss's heart. Call her a bitch again, and I'll spoon-feed you yours."

Roscoe released my wrist so fast, you would have thought it had burned him. He and the other goon scurried to the opposite side of the porch, putting as much distance as possible between us and them.

"*She's* the boss's Moon?"

Dre ignored the question and held the door open for me. I winked at Roscoe before stepping into the house. Inside was a stark contrast to the outside. The walls were painted a calm beige, and complimentary furniture had been aesthetically placed.

There were rugs of varying sizes and textures covering most of the floor, and the whole place gave off a warm vibe. As soon as the front door was locked, Dre grabbed my wrist and pushed me up against it.

He tried to lean down, but I put my hands on his chest and pushed him away. Using his momentum, I caught his ankle with my foot and tripped him. He had a smile on his face that annoyed the hell out of me.

Dre laid on top of the rugs, looking up at me as I sat on his chest and glared down at him. His hair had gotten jostled in the fall, and I could see both his beautiful eyes now. He lifted his hand and attempted to stroke my cheek, but I grabbed his wrist to stop him.

"Don't."

"It's been at least eight years, right? And yet, you still won't let me touch you."

"Whose fault is that?"

He rolled his eyes and grumbled. "Just because I broke your silly fucking rules."

I moved my grip from his wrist up to his thumb and bent it back. He hissed and tried to pull his hand out of my grasp, but I tightened it and forced his thumb back even farther until he stopped struggling.

"One, silly or not, they are *my* rules, and if you want to touch *my* body, you follow them. Two, rule-breaking wasn't the issue. I rebuffed you for months because I knew you would be a problem.

"But you convinced me you would be cool, so I finally said yes. We slept together *once*, and you thought you owned me after. Which, if you're uncertain, *that's* a fucking issue."

"How was it so wrong that I didn't want my woman to sleep around?"

Almost a decade had passed since we last saw each other, and he still didn't get it. I was *a* woman he wanted to sleep with, not *his* woman. Why was that so fucking hard to understand?

I wasn't going to do this with him again. I didn't have the time or the patience. He wanted to see if there was still something between us. I had no idea how he held out hope for that, but his delusion wasn't something I could dissolve. That was his problem.

I came here for Rian. Dre could hope and dream all he wanted as long as he took me to Rian while he did it.

Letting his arm go, I climbed off of him and stood up. "Where is he?" I asked.

"You only ever had eyes for him," Dre responded.

"Now, we both know that's not true. I had eyes for you first, but if you wanna be a lil' bitch about it, who was the one that introduced us, huh?"

"I introduced you to my tattoo artist. I assumed you would get some new ink, not fuck him!" He bit out.

"Not my problem that you made the wrong assumption. We were never exclusive, Dre."

"So, you had to go for my boss, too! Just to prove a fucking point?"

"First off, it wasn't to prove a goddamned thing to you. I can do whatever the fuck I want with my body. And two... Well, actually I don't have a two. You're just a fucking dumbass."

Dre rolled over, stood up, and walked toward the back of the house. He made no indication I should follow him, but I did anyway, hoping we were getting to the point.

He stopped in front of a door with his back to me and his hand on the handle. I was literal seconds from pushing him out of the way when he started to whisper.

"Did you have to choose him over me?"

I stepped to his side and placed my hand over his.

"For the last time, I would have enjoyed you both. *You're* the one that changed the game. Get over it," I said before I twisted the handle and opened the door.

Dre remained outside in the hall, staring at me, looking completely defeated. My heart had been hardened against him for years, so even though he wanted that pathetic look to mean something to me, it meant nothing. That was mostly his fault because of how he acted when I shared my time with Rian and Sai, but worse was his reaction when I fucked up and told him about my past. He's the reason I haven't told another man about it. There was no way to come back from it, so he just needed to move on.

And to think that there was an extremely minuscule part of me that thought a roll in the sheets with him would've been fun since I was seeing him again. But the conversation we just had shut that shit down real quick. The only thing sleeping with him now would bring me was a fucking headache.

Yeah. No thanks. He and I were done. I closed the door in his face. No second chances. If that didn't wake him up to that reality, then nothing would.

A loud snore sounded from behind me and pulled my attention off of the Dre nonsense.

When I turned, I found Rian on the couch. Our years apart had done him well. Even asleep, he was gorgeous. His long dreads fanned out across the couch arm, and he had his own arms crossed over his chest.

One of his hands was buried in the cushion, and I knew without seeing it that he was holding a gun. He was more skittish than I was when he was woken up, and I didn't feel like getting shot.

Quietly, I made my way behind the arm his head rested on so I was completely out of range. He'd yet to stir, so I leaned down until I was just above his face.

"Rian," I whispered and kissed his forehead.

"Dre, if you just kissed me, I will kill you," he said sleepily.

"When did you start letting Dre kiss you?" I asked. "I didn't know you swung both ways."

His eyes snapped open and quickly found my face. He jumped up so fast, our foreheads nearly collided, but thankfully, I moved out of the way at the last second.

"It was so late when you called last night that I thought I may have dreamed it."

"Well, do you still think you're dreaming?" I questioned as I sat down on the coffee table in front of the couch.

Rian grabbed my hand and placed a small kiss on my knuckles. His eyes roved over my face, taking me in. I understood the feeling. Seeing those scarlet-brown eyes track over my body sent shivers down my spine.

Not what I'm here for. Not what I'm here for. Not what I'm here for.

Even as I repeated the words in my head, I couldn't stop myself from enjoying the bounty that was his caramel skin, the feel of the rough texture of his hand on mine, and the little jolts he caused when his thumb stroked my knuckles.

"Have you missed me, Moon?"

"Nope," I said evenly as I pulled my hand from his grasp.

"That's not what you said last night," he responded as he sat back and draped his long arms over the back of the sofa.

The movement caused his shirt to ride up and gave me the perfect view of his *V*, as well as what looked like tattooed vines on his tight stomach. Hard as it was, I managed to tear my gaze away from them and look him in the eyes.

He wore a roguish smile, letting me know he'd sat in that position on purpose. Rian was always the shameless flirt, but I couldn't take the bait. We had more important matters to discuss.

I scoffed. "Keep your shirt on. No one wants to see that."

"So, this really wasn't a social call?"

Standing, I walked over to his desk, sat behind it, and put my feet up. His eyes never left my body until my feet settled. He raised an eyebrow at me, waiting for my answer.

"No. It really wasn't."

"Well, that's fucking boring," he sighed.

"Can we get on with it, please? Boring or not, I have a job I need done, and I don't want to be here any longer than necessary."

Rian jumped up, stormed over to me, slammed his palms down, and leaned over the desk.

"Need to get away from me that badly?"

We stared at each other for what felt like an eternity. There was lust burning in those auburn pools of his, but what burned brighter than the lust was the anger.

I wasn't going to bring it up, and he for damn sure shouldn't be bringing up the past, but I could only control myself. So, I opted to ignore the lust and anger, choosing to steer us back toward the task at hand.

"So, back to the job I need done," I pressed.

"*After* you answer the question."

"Rian, can we just not and say we did?"

He sat in the chair in front of his desk, put his feet on top of it, and crossed his arms, mirroring my posture.

"You want my help? You'll answer my questions. Those are my terms. You don't like them? I'll happily watch that ass walk out my door."

My God! How did I get myself into this shit? Oh, yeah! Because of a curly-haired redhead's smile and a body that wouldn't quit. I hadn't expected it to be this difficult, but I should have.

Obviously, I was going to have to work for this, which was aggravating. But what the fuck could I do? He was right. I needed him. Apparently, that meant I had to play this fucking twenty-questions game.

"Is that really the question you wanted to ask?"

Rian slid his feet off of the desk, leaned over it, and tented his fingers in front of his face. Silence impregnated the room as we stared at each other. I'd opened the door slightly, and I knew he would crash right through it, but it was the only way I could think to get through this interrogation quickly.

"Why did you leave?"

"You told me to go."

"THE HELL I DID!"

"Don't yell at me," I hissed. "You said, and I quote, *This isn't the life you want to live*, end quote."

"Quit with the bullshit. You don't get to twist the situation and think I'm just going to accept it. I told you that in the beginning before we even got involved. You disappeared three years later. So, I'll repeat. Why did you leave?"

"I left! What do you want me to fucking say?"

"You know what I want to hear. Quit being such a pussy, and answer the damn question!"

"Because I had to beat you to it," I whispered.

Rian stood up so fast, the chair sounded like a whip when it fell over. He snatched a lamp off of the desk and threw it across the room. A commotion outside the door went off seconds after the lamp crashed to the floor.

It sounded like there was a scuffle outside the door, as if someone was trying to get in.

"What the hell is that bitch doing to our boss?" DJ yelled before it went silent again.

My eyes went from the shattered lamp to the heavily breathing figure in front of me. This reunion was bringing up too many emotions, and I didn't want to deal with them, as per usual. So, I changed the subject.

"You know that lil' fucker pointed a gun at my head?"

"He did WHAT?" Rian snapped, turning back to face me. "Wait, wait. No, we're not doing that," he shook his head. "I'll deal with him later. Right now, my focus is on you and the bullshit you're trying to feed me."

"If it's bullshit, why the fuck are we talking about it, then?"

"Because," he bit out slowly, "I'm going to get my answer, no matter how fucking uncomfortable it makes you."

This was one of the key ways Rian and Zey were different. Zey wanted to know about me just as much as Rian did, but he had the patience to wait for me to be ready to share. Rian never did.

Now, was I ignoring the fact that it'd been literal *years* and his patience level was even lower than it used to be. Yes. Yes, I was. I didn't want to have this conversation. Ever. If there was a road I could take to avoid this, I was going to drive down it until my wheels fell off. Avoidance brings me peace.

OK, that's complete and utter bullshit, but it sounded poetic in my head.

"I got bored," I said pathetically as a last-ditch effort.

"Get. Out."

"Xadrian, wait. I—"

"No! I'm not playing this game with you," he barked. "You've always been so damn smart. There's no way you didn't know."

I couldn't hear this. I couldn't. But there was no way I could cover my ears as if I were a child, so I got up and headed for the door, ready to bolt. Rian cut me off, backing me into the desk once more.

He gripped my chin tightly, forcing me to meet his gaze. I dug my nails into his hand, but he didn't flinch. He also made sure to turn his body enough to prevent me from kneeing him.

There was no more running. He was going to make me face our history and blockade my road to avoidance until he was satisfied with my answers.

"Admit you knew."

"Please, don't."

"We're done with the games. I want to hear you say it. Admit you knew I'd fallen for you."

"My God. Yes! OK! I knew. IT'S THE VERY REASON I LEFT IN THE FIRST GODDAMN PLACE."

The amount of shock in his eyes was astonishing. He released my chin and stepped back, searching my face as he tried to process what I'd just confessed. After all these years, he had his answer, and I wanted him to choke on it.

Although I knew it wasn't fair, I gave no fucks. Being forced to talk about this gave me invisible hives. He wanted to know so badly, and now he knew, but I wanted some satisfaction of my own.

Rian's guard was down, so I balled my fist and swung. Unfortunately, I wasn't in a good enough position. There wasn't as much power behind the punch as I'd wanted, but the blood that dripped out of the corner of his mouth was gratifying, at least.

Rian licked his lip and spat. "That was fucking cheap," he complained. "Make you feel better? If you thought it would get me to stop asking questions, you musta forgot who I am."

With a shake of my head, I shuffled past him. Obviously, this was just going to be a waste of time, so I needed to reevaluate. Maybe

I could get Dre to put me in touch with some contacts. That was probably a bad idea, but I didn't have much of a choice.

My mind zipped between so many options that I stopped paying attention to my surroundings. Rookie mistake. Before I got too far, Rian swept my legs out from under me.

I was able to get my arms beneath me fast enough to keep myself from hitting my head, but that's all I managed. Rian was already turning me over and pinning me to the ground. He sat over my waist to keep me from kicking and loomed above me.

"Where the fuck you think you're goin'?"

"Did you not just tell me to leave?" I asked, struggling against him.

"I never got my answer."

"The fuck you mean, you never got it? I just literally screamed it at you!"

"My original question was why did you leave, but now I'm rephrasing. Why would you leave if you knew I loved you? Don't make me force it out of you, Moon. You know I will," he whispered as he lowered his mouth to mine.

"I left before you could leave me," I managed to rush out before our lips touched.

He reared his head back as if I'd slapped him, and I wish I'd been able to. It would've been better than letting him kiss me. I don't know what would've happened if I hadn't stopped him.

Rian wasn't the only one with repressed feelings. At this point, if I could just get him to focus on now and not the past, I could get out of here. Seeing Dre and then dealing with all of this chaos with Rian was causing my hackles to rise. I was going to get real mean if he pushed me any further, and I wasn't going to care how my words or actions affected him.

Rian rolled over and stared up at the ceiling.

This felt extremely familiar, but unlike with Zey, I wasn't looking to fuck after we talked. Well, at least my sane half wasn't. My wild half was all for the fucking idea, as per usual.

"What type of ass-backward sense does that make? You know what? I'm gonna get a fucking headache if I keep asking, so I'm tabling this discussion for now." He grimaced. "What do you *need*, Moon*?*"

Thank fuck, we can finally get to something that matters.

"Have you heard of TRH Reality?" I asked.

"Yeah. The CEO sent some *representatives* to try to get people in the neighborhood to sell so he could turn these lots into condos. It was fun to shut down. Why?"

"His useless and pathetic waste of life and air of a son has been causing fucking problems that I need resolved."

"Are we looking for an *R* or *I* resolution? Or, do we have another *E* situation?"

Even though I was positive we weren't being listened to, Rian was always going to be cautious, and I didn't blame him. Remaining vigilant was what kept him off the radar.

If the letter code was hard to follow, worry not. I'll tell you what they mean. Just make sure you keep it to yourself. *R* meant relocation. *I* meant intimidation. And *E* meant eradication. Wet work. What I came here for.

"I'll take door *E* for two hundred, Alex," I responded.

Rian turned his head to look up at me and raised a brow. "What did this guy do to you, again?"

"He's causing problems. I need you to solve them. That's all you need to know. There's also a time limit: three days. What do you want in exchange?"

"I only want one thing."

If you told me he was going to ask for an absurd dollar amount for killing someone, I'd have agreed with you, but after the conversation we'd just had, the only thing on his mind was me.

"I'm not fucking you."

Rian chuckled. "That's too bad, but I'll live."

"Wait. Then, what do you want?"

"One night."

"You just sa—"

"I know what I said, and I meant. I'm not asking you to fuck. I want to spend time with you for one night. If we end up fucking, that's a bonus I won't say no to," he said with a slick smile. "Those are the terms. Agree or leave. Your choice."

This felt like a big trap, but I was too close to the goal to back out now. So, I nodded my head once and made the deal. Rian nodded back before he stood up and walked over to his desk.

He pulled open a drawer, removed a burner phone from it, and tossed it to me.

"Two days. I'll call so you can finalize. Until then, keep the phone off, just in case."

"What about the payment?"

"Don't you worry your pretty little head about that. You'll know when I'm ready to collect."

"Whatever," I said, rolling my eyes. "Can I *go* now?"

"See, that smart-ass attitude is what gets you into trouble. I should make you stay, but I don't feel like dealing with Dre's whining."

"The question was rhetorical. You can't make me stay anywhere."

"Wanna bet?"

We stared at each other. Unresolved feelings, burning lust, and boiling anger swirled around us, filling the room. I wasn't planning on making a habit of putting hits out on people, but if I needed to revisit this dark path, I was going to need to find a new hitman.

I was never going to see Rian again. Scratch that. After this damned 'one-night' hangout thing he wanted, I was never going to see him again. He smiled and started to laugh, then made his way to the door.

"I really have missed you, Moon."

I gave no response as he opened it and let me out of the room. We walked back to the living room and found all three of the guys waiting for us. Blake sat on the couch, drinking some strong-ass coffee, by the smell of it.

Dre had been leaning against the front door with his eyes closed, but they cracked open and zeroed in on me as soon as I stepped into the room. DJ sat in the middle of the floor, holding an ice pack to his bleeding jaw.

Rian moved like a demon. He was on top of DJ before anyone could react. DJ tried to scramble away, but it was too late. Rian already had a grip on his shirt and was holding him up by the arm.

"Did you really aim a fucking gun at her head?" Rian barked.

"You said we needed to make sure she was the right chick..." DJ answered.

"I TOLD YOU TO ASK A FUCKING QUESTION, NOT POINT A FUCKING GUN AT HER!"

"Why is everybody yelling at me over some random bitch?"

In my mind, the scene played out in quick succession. DJ called me a bitch once again, and Rian moved to slam him against the ground because he had a terrible temper. Dre watched, wishing he was the one slamming the kid, and Blake continued to drink his coffee, unperturbed.

I had literal seconds to stop this disaster before it started. The word had just left DJ's lips, and Rian was already moving into position.

"XADRIAN, STOP!" I commanded.

The way he moved made me think I'd been too late, but he halted, leaving DJ just barely floating above the ground. Rian regained control of himself and set DJ on his feet. He released his shirt and walked away from the child.

"You live today because *she* made it so. She won't be here tomorrow. Tread lightly," Rian warned.

DJ rushed toward me, and Dre bolted after him. I wasn't sure what the fuck was about to happen, but I wasn't about to be taken out by a fucking kid, either. So, I shifted into a fighting stance, ready to defend myself. Then, DJ did something I'm sure none of us expected.

He beelined behind me and used me as a shield against Rian and Dre. Clearly, he was terrified of them both but he also had the unfortunate trait of not knowing when to shut the fuck up.

Dre and Rian continued to head toward us, but they stopped when I put my hand up.

"I get that you all have to be tough guys and can't show any other emotion outside of rage, but beating on a lil' kid is kinda beneath you, don't you think?"

"Um... I'm twenty-one, ma'am."

"You should really learn how to read the room and just shut the fuck up," I told him and popped him upside the back of his head.

Blake laughed and sat his coffee cup down. Rian rolled his eyes and went to sit on the couch next to Blake, while Dre stayed where he was and stared daggers at DJ.

"Alright, well, I'm bored. Who's taking me back to my car?" I asked.

"I will."

"Me."

"You can't leave."

Blake, Dre, and DJ all spoke at once, making me dizzy. That was a lot of responses for one simple question. Rian said nothing, just sat on the couch with his head leaned back and his eyes closed.

Obviously, I was going to have to referee this nonsense myself. Great. The bastard was looking way too comfortable after all the commotion this day had brought on.

"Thank you. Fuck, no. The fuck you mean I can't leave? Have you lost your fuckin' mind?"

I spoke to each man in turn before grabbing a pillow from a nearby chair and launching it at Rian's head. The loud thud was awesome, but the look of annoyance on his face was even better.

"See, that's why you need to stay. If I did that, he'd have shot me," DJ said as he hid further behind me.

"That's because I'm awesome, and one day, you'll be aweso me... Maybe."

DJ still clung to me as I tried to make my way to the front door, but Dre stepped in front of me and blocked my path. There was no way in hell I was getting into a car willingly with him, and he knew that.

If that's what he wanted, then he'd have to drag me out. The problem with that is he wasn't above dragging me out, kicking *and* screaming. The fucking psycho would actually enjoy it. He already had an aggravating smile on his face, so I'm sure he was thinking about it.

"Dre, Blake will take her back," Rian ordered.

Anger radiated off of Dre, but he said nothing and stepped out of my way. I shot him a satisfied smirk over my shoulder as I headed for the door. Was I being a complete brat about this? I sure as hell was. Served him right for thinking I was going with him.

DJ finally let go of me and scurried over to the car as soon as we were outside. He climbed into the back and waited for me to slide in next to him. Nope. Wasn't interested in that option at all.

Pointedly, I shut the back door, walked over to the passenger side, and slid into the front seat.

"Why didn't you sit back here with me?" he pouted.

"Because I didn't want to be bothered."

"Oh, OK," he said, sounding disappointed. "Well, how do you know the boss and the dickhead?"

I had to stop myself from laughing. Before, he wanted to shoot me in the head, but now that I was someone who could keep Rian and Dre from hitting him, he wanted to be friends.

This whole damn thing was so fucking draining, and I wasn't in the mood to entertain anymore. So, I made myself comfortable and went back to sleep. DJ woke me up again when we arrived but made sure to keep his distance this time.

"Don't even think about it," I said as DJ got out of the car, looking like he was going to follow me to mine.

"But..."

"No buts. You're going home with them, not me. I've got no interest in adopting lil' wannabe badasses. If you don't want to get hit, learn to keep your mouth shut."

DJ moped. I ignored him and climbed into my car. The whole day had been a whirlwind, and I was ready to go home and kiss a certain curly-haired redhead's smile.

That very smile floated through my mind as I drove off.

XXIV

Rose

It'd been two days to the exact minute, and I hadn't heard from Rian yet. Don't ask me why I was so nervous. I knew he would get it done, but being the control freak that I was, I needed to know what was going on — like yesterday.

I'd sat behind my desk in the library all day, pretending to work just in case Mel came in. My mind tortured me with the possibility of something going wrong, and I had to stop myself from calling to check in with him over fifty times.

The nervous energy flowing through me wasn't helping, so I put the burner down and logged into my laptop. There was a document that I didn't recognize. It took me by surprise until I realized it was Mel's book.

Now, listen. Should I have read it without permission? Nope, not a word. But think of it this way: She pulled it up on my computer and left the document open, so subconsciously, she wanted me to read it.

OK, yeah. You're not buying what I'm selling, but you know I had to read it, so you might as well get your yelling over with because that was exactly what happened.

I scrolled all the way to the top of the doc and started reading. She really needed to have more confidence in herself because her book was very good. She'd made a few rookie mistakes, but that was the nature of the game.

Suddenly, the burner vibrated, breaking my concentration. I was tempted to keep reading and ignore the call, but the need to know about the Tiberius situation outweighed my desire to finish the story.

After I emailed a copy of the book to myself, (Look, I said I wasn't gonna read it right then, not that I wasn't gonna finish it when I could.) I went back to the part where she'd left off and snuck into my safe room.

"Hello?"

"There's an Uber waiting for you outside."

Click.

"Really, mutha fucka? You just gonna spring that on me?" I hissed at the phone.

Before leaving, I searched the house for Mel, trying to conjure up a believable excuse as to why I was heading out, but I couldn't find her anywhere. That was odd. So, I went back to my office, grabbed my phone, and planned to give her a call. Only then did I see a string of texts she'd sent me over an hour ago.

> Mel: I came by to tell you I was heading out with Shelly and would be back later, but you were so engrossed in your work, I didn't want to disturb you.

Damn, how absorbed was I in her book? I could've gotten caught.

> **Mel:** Missing you already.

> **Mel:** You didn't read that. ACT LIKE YOU DIDN'T READ THAT!!

> **Mel:** Hiya. This is Shelly, and I have confiscated Lane's phone so she doesn't have a heart attack. I am also kidnapping her since she won't be able to face you for at least 24 hours after sending a text like that. TTYL.

The biggest smile spread across my face as I finished scrolling through the texts. She was so fucking adorable, and she'd given me the perfect excuse to go missing for a few hours. So, I grabbed my keys and locked up the house, then stepped outside and slid into the backseat of the *Uber*.

Blake was texting someone, probably letting Rian know I had gotten into the car.

"Why say an Uber was here when it was just you?" I asked. "Actually, fuck that question completely. How the hell does he know where I live?"

Blake chuckled as he pulled out of the driveway and headed for the front gate. "Ms. Moon, you've known the boss longer than I have. If there's information he wants, he'll get it, no matter the means."

He was right, of course, but I still didn't like it. That was something I would make known to Rian as soon as we got to wherever the fuck we were going. Something Blake said did bring up another question, though. I didn't remember meeting him back when I used to hang out with Dre and Rian.

"So, how long have you known the boys?"

Blake studied me in the rearview mirror before focusing back on the road.

Yeah, yeah. I know. Asking questions is dangerous, but I was curious.

We'd left my neighborhood and were already merging onto the freeway before he finally decided to answer my question.

"I've known them for about six years now," he told me.

"Ah, so you came around after I'd already left, then."

"That explains so fucking much," he muttered.

"What do you me... Nope, actually, forget I asked. I'm not the least bit curious about how they were after I left. At all."

Blake glanced back at me once more and smiled. "Whatever you say, miss," he said, then turned on the radio.

Don't talk like you can read my thoughts.

Ninety minutes later, we pulled up to a fucking huge-ass abandoned high school campus. It must have been a private school at one point. The building was way too expansive to have been a public school.

Blake pulled behind what seemed like a rec building before he stopped and shut the car off. When he came around to open my door for me, a loud thumping sounded from the rear.

My head snapped over to Blake. He was grimacing at the trunk. "That isn't..."

"No. That's DJ. He figured out we were going to see you today and wanted to come. Boss didn't want him to, but I found him sneaking around, so I gagged him, tied him up, and tossed him in there."

"Oh, cool. I was gonna be a lil' pissed if I had to share a ride with the undesirable one. Pop the trunk."

"Uh... Miss?"

"Just do it," I ordered. "He's not gonna stop thrashing if we don't do something."

Blake looked at me as if I'd grown a second head, but he still popped the trunk as I'd requested. I lifted the lid to see DJ, trying to undo the ropes around his wrists and ankles. He was yelling, but the gag muffled the sound.

As soon as he recognized me, he calmed down... for all of two seconds before he tried talking again. I put my finger up to my lips, and he stopped.

"Talking to me with your mouth gagged like that is pointless. I can't hear you. Sit here quietly. If you're good, I might let you ride in the back with me when we're done here. Got it?"

Eagerly, he nodded and laid back down. This time, he watched calmly as Blake shut the trunk.

"I know this is a moot point, but it would be really nice if I could keep you around," Blake joked. "You wrangle them up so effortlessly."

"I get that it would make your life easier, but no thank you," I said, patting his back. "I've no interest in signing up for that level of headache."

We headed toward the building's double doors, but before we made it, Dre burst out of them. He made a beeline for Blake, spouting some bullshit about how unfair it was that Blake got to know where I lived, but he didn't.

Dre threw a punch that Blake quickly rendered useless by catching his wrist and twisting his arm behind his back.

"See what I mean? Headache," I repeated as I walked backward toward the doors. "Hey, idiot! Quit fuckin' around. I didn't want any of you to have my address, so I'm the only one who gets to be pissed about this whole thing."

Dre stopped struggling, and Blake released his arm. After Blake fixed his tie, he winked at me. I could hear his thoughts as if they were my own.

See what I mean? Idiot wrangler.

I couldn't help but chuckle before letting the doors close behind me.

The room was dimly lit so that no one could see in from the outside. All the doors and windows were covered over. In the center sat a huge pool filled with brackish water. A wooden chair with attached chains sat in front of the pool, and a row of bleachers had been pulled out against the back wall.

It was aggravating that my eyes did this against my will, but they quickly found Rian, stretched out across the middle row. My anger at him for knowing my address renewed, and I headed straight for him.

Rian sat up, descended the bleachers, and started toward me, too. I knew he would expect me to slap him, so I changed up my mode of attack. Once he was within kicking distance, I spun around and aimed a roundhouse kick at his head.

The bastard dodged at the last second, so I was only able to clip his chin. He gave me a predatory smile as he took a step toward me.

"You're angrier that I ruined your plans by springing the Uber thing on you than you are about me knowing your address."

"I don't know what you're talking about," I denied.

"Oh, sure. You were gonna try and force me into accepting that tonight was going to be the end of our deal. I know your sneaky lil' tricks almost as well as I know my own. You won't get rid of me so easily."

"Children, can we put the 'I want to fuck you but don't want to admit it' energy away for now, please? We have business to handle," Blake said as he clapped his hands, pulling our focus off of each other.

"He's right. I'll deal with you later," I said, stepping back and searching for Lil' Dick.

Rian grinned. "Looking forward to it."

He kept up that predatory smile, and I chose to ignore everything it was doing to me. The smug bastard was right, though. I'd expected him to figure out where I lived as soon as I'd agreed to the *one-night* arrangement.

I'd planned for tonight to be that night, but because he'd surprised me, I had to rush out of the house wearing only leggings and a T-shirt. I had the perfect outfit picked out, too. It would've driven him crazy if he'd let me go home wearing it without spending time with him first.

Unnecessarily intelligent bastard.

Dre glared as he strutted past us both and headed for the locker room. A moment later, he returned with a man whose wrists and ankles were cuffed to a belly chain.

The man had a bag over his head, and judging by the muffled screams coming from underneath, he was probably gagged. With Blake's help, Dre sat him in the chair and secured the chains around him since Tiberius had begun to thrash.

Once he was secured, he resumed the muffled screaming with renewed vigor. It was beginning to give me a fucking headache. I walked over to the chair and placed my foot between his legs.

After I applied a little pressure to his nuts, he instantly calmed down. I nodded to Dre, and he pulled the hood off of Tiberius's head. Tiberius blinked his eyes a few times before focusing on me.

We were apparently back to the screaming and thrashing portion of events. Why did people do that? As if it was going to change anything about their situation? That was an aspect of human nature I truly didn't understand.

"Shut the fuck up before I make bloodied-wine out of your worthless grapes," I warned him.

His head snapped back as if I'd slapped him, which I was really considering doing, but I fought the urge. Now that he was calm once more, I removed the gag.

First came the threats.

Yet again, something I never understood. What's the point of threatening the people who are holding you captive, especially when no one knows where you are? They can't help.

Tiberius continued to bitch and moan, and my headache was starting to slowly come back.

"Oh, for the love of everything that is right with this world, will you shut the fuck up? No one knows you're here, no one's *gonna* know you're here, and when your pathetic soul leaves your useless body tonight, no one will even shed a single tear."

"Heh. Hey, that rhymed. Cool."

"When my soul leaves my body..." he started. "Have you lost your fucking mind? You can't kill me!"

"Why can't I?"

"Because — Because... Because," he sputtered, searching for an excuse.

I waved my hand at him, urging him to spit out whatever he was trying to say, wondering if he had an even remotely valid reason as to why I couldn't kill him.

"Because... You can't just kill people!"

"I'm not killing *people*. I'm killing *you*," I said evenly.

"But you can't do that!"

"I feel like he's completely missing the point here," I said as I glanced back at Rian, who just shrugged and shook his head.

"Alright. I'll give you one more try because I'm now getting extremely bored with this conversation. Why can't I?"

"Don't you know who my father is?"

I laughed. "You know I do, and that isn't a reason for me not to kill you, so let's get on with it, shall we?"

The blood drained from Tiberius's face. "Wait, wait, wait! I have money! Name your price," he whined.

I was wondering when we were going to get to the bargaining portion of this encounter.

"You mean to say you *had* money, right?" Rian asked.

"Had?" Tiberius questioned, confused.

"Oh, yes!" Rian answered. "Who do you think paid the hacker to leave a paper trail that will make sure no one looks for you? And then, there are my fees for getting rid of your body and the cleanup that will be required. Killing someone correctly is quite an expensive business. Thanks for footing the bill."

"Hacker? The one that hacked into..." I cut myself off before I said Mel's name.

So far, I'd been able to keep Rian from finding out about her, and I wanted to keep it that way for as long as I could. Although, the hacker being involved made things a bit tricky. If Rian happened to ask about previous jobs, then he already knew.

Rian smirked. "Yes, it's the same hacker that hacked your lil' *girlfriend's* phone. Funny how you forgot to mention her."

Well, fuck. You just gotta be so fucking nosy about every fucking little thing, don't you?

"I didn't forget to mention her at all. My personal life isn't your business anymore."

"What lil' girlfriend?" Dre asked.

"That's none of your fucking business either," I snapped.

There was no way I was going to dispute the 'girlfriend' thing out loud. That would just bring up more questions. For all intents and purposes, that was all they needed to know, and it would keep them at bay for now.

I know what you're thinking: That was just a lame excuse, and I didn't deny it because I liked people knowing she was mine. Well, I have absolutely no idea where you came up with that, and you're crazy.

Moving on. Tiberius had grown quiet while Rian and I discussed his insistent need to know my business. Maybe he had finally come to terms with his new reality. When I focused my attention back on him, I realized at some point, he'd started crying.

"Are you really crying right now?" I asked.

"How the fuck am I supposed to react? You're gonna kill me over a commonwealth whore that wouldn't recognize what confidence was if it slapped her."

This time, his head snapped back because I actually punched him square in the face. His nose exploded and sprayed me with blood. I'd hit him so hard that Blake and Dre had to catch the chair to keep him from falling into the pool too early.

"Damn it, Moon," Rian snapped. There's blood on your clothes now. Couldn't you keep control of your temper, just this once?"

"His nose looked like it was itching, so I thought I'd help out."

"So, you scratched it with your fucking fist?" Rian barked.

"Yep, now wake him up."

Dre pulled a bottle out of his pocket and waved it under Tiberius's nose, immediately reviving him. With his nose still leaking, Tiberius looked around, probably hoping that the moments before I'd knocked him out were just a nightmare.

"Yeah, no. This isn't a dream, but don't worry, it will be over in a moment."

"Please," he begged. "You don't have to kill me. I'll leave and never come back. I promise."

"Oof," I said, placing my foot back on the chair. "Of all the times to make such a poor choice in words. Oh, well. I'll be holding you to that promise," I said as I kicked the chair over.

Splash! His screams became gurgles as he sunk deep into the pool. I watched the raging water until it settled. The bubbles shrank, becoming smaller and smaller until they disappeared altogether.

Finished, I looked down to see the damage his blood had done to my clothes. My shirt took the brunt of it, but unfortunately, there were some drops on my pants, too.

"Well, this won't do," I grumbled.

After discarding my top, I kicked off my shoes and slid out of my pants. Dre's eyes, full of unbridled heat, trailed down my body. Blake got a good look before clearing his throat and averting his gaze.

Guess it was good I decided to wear panties today.

Rian pulled off his drop-tail style shirt and handed it over. "Was that the outfit you were planning to wear for me?"

With Rian shirtless, I saw all of those rippling muscles, covered in battle scars that made my tongue grow thick. I realized the vines were accompanied by red roses and the tattoo seemed to continue past the waistband of his pants.

Trying to ignore the fact that those tats even existed, I spun away from him. I slipped on the shirt, and his scent hit me like a ton of bricks. Seizing the moment, my mind decided it would be fun to assault me with all the memories of how I used to wear his shirts after we fucked. I had to get a hold of myself. If I let my body react to him, he wasn't going to let me go.

So, I focused back on my anger, and it helped me control my desires. The shirt ended up looking like a dress on me.

Apparently, I'd gotten so lost in his scent that I'd stopped paying attention because Rian leaned down next to my ear and chuckled.

"Looks like someone missed the way I smell. You can keep it if you want. Or, I could drive you home and leave my scent all over your body and your sheets."

I swung my fist, but the fucker dodged and laughed. He backed away with my ruined clothes in his hand, then tossed them into a barrel I assumed he'd use to burn both mine and Tiberius's things.

"And there's no way I can convince you to end our deal tonight, right?"

"Not in the slightest," he told me.

"Ugh. Fuck, alright. Blake, take me home, please," I grumbled as I headed for the double doors.

"Of course."

"I'll be seeing you soon, Moon."

"Fuck you!" I yelled.

"Just tell me when."

There was no need to turn around. I could hear the smile in his voice, and I knew if I looked back, it would be brimming with deviance. I just kept repeating a mantra in my head.

Just one more night, and then I'll never see him again.

XXV

Melanie

It should have been a happy day. Tiberius was supposed to be suffering the consequences of his actions, but because he had a rich father who didn't believe his family had to follow the same rules and laws, he was going to get off with a slap on the wrist.

The whole thing was so fucking aggravating, especially with what I'd had to endure last week. Now, he was going to be able to harass me or send others to harass me for the rest of my life? How did that make sense to anybody?

Lina sat next to me as we waited for them to call the case. Elijah and Xavier stood nearby, talking. I was so grateful to have them all as a support system, but I still felt terrible about involving them in my mess.

Now that I knew Tiberius was bold enough to send people after me, it was only a matter of time before he started going after them, too. That thought kept me up all night, and I was so fucking exhausted.

I still didn't have any concrete proof that he was behind the craziness last week, so I was really stuck between a rock and a hard place. If I said anything to the cops now, his father would find out somehow, and that would just spell more trouble.

I'd have to wait until I was completely sure, but waiting came with its own set of problems, too. He'd already fucked with my car, my home, my classes, and my job.

There really was no telling what he would do next. Monday through Thursday had been eerily quiet. I figured he might have backed off because of the hearing, but what would happen tomorrow or the next day?

Before, I wasn't an anxious person, but this situation sure as hell turned me into one.

Lina squeezed my hand, pulling me from my depressing thoughts. I looked up to see she was watching me.

I really don't want anything to make her life harder. Maybe we shouldn't see each other anymore?

As soon as I finished that thought, my chest tightened. I would make the sacrifice if I had to, but the mere possibility of not having her in my life caused my heart an unimaginable amount of pain.

Lina leaned over and kissed my forehead. Her signature scent, a mixture of cherry blossoms and teakwood, grounded me like always. I would miss her terribly if I had to end things, but I could do it if it meant her life wouldn't be ruined.

"Lina, I think that maybe we s—"

"Why don't we wait 'til after the hearing before you start freaking out," she said, cutting me off.

"But..."

She shook her head and gave me my favorite smile. I still had so much apprehension about what was going to happen, but when she looked at me like that, I couldn't feel as anxious about it. Lina was right. I could freak out after. For now, I would just focus on the fact that I didn't have to go through this alone.

Harper and his legal team came into the courtroom a couple of minutes before the case was called. Tiberius wasn't with him, but I didn't think anything of it.

His bitch-ass was probably going to make some type of grand-fucking-entrance. Lina, Xavier, and I were seated in the gallery while Elijah was talking to Wilson.

The rest of the gallery continued to fill up. Still, there was no sign of Tiberius. Elijah stomped back over to us, fuming. That was majorly concerning for me because all I could think was: *How could today get any worse?*

"Is everything alright?" I asked timidly.

"As you can see, the Satan's spawn is not here, and Wilson keeps fucking stonewalling me. He's telling me they have no idea where he could be, which I know is fucking bullshit, and I'm trying to figure out what cards they're gonna play."

What cards *could* they play at this moment? According to the bullshit plea deal they wanted us to accept, he was going to get away with everything already. What would Tiberius gain from not showing up?

More and more questions rolled through my mind until the bailiff called for us to rise as the judge walked in.

As soon as he was seated, his eyes went straight to the empty defendant's chair before zeroing in on Wilson.

"Is there a reason that chair is empty, Mr. Wilson?"

"Your Honor."

"I know who I am. That wasn't my question. I'd like an answer."

Wilson tried to look back at Harper for what I assumed was a believable lie, but the judge didn't appreciate that one bit.

"Don't look to the gallery for the answer. You're Mr. Harper's lawyer, correct?"

"Yes, Your Honor."

"Then, answer the question."

"I regret to say that I do not have the answer to your question," the lawyer admitted.

"Is that why you were looking to Mr. Harper Sr.?" The judge asked.

"Yes. That was my intention."

"Well, let's see if we can discover the truth from him, then. Mr. Harper, any idea as to the location of your son?"

Harper sucked his teeth before he stood to address the judge. I was just as curious about his answer as everyone else.

"I, unfortunately, do not have the answer to your question, either."

"So, let me see if I understand this correctly. Neither the lawyer nor the father knows where the defendant currently is. Is that right?"

"Yes, Your Honor," they answered simultaneously.

The judge glanced at his watch for a moment before staring back at the two men.

"Well, I have quite the busy docket today and no more time to waste. With that being said, I will be signing a warrant for his arrest, and this case will be recalled. I suggest you find him before law enforcement does."

The judge banged his gavel, and the courtroom emptied out. I sat frozen, unsure of where the fuck to go or how to process this.

What did this mean? Were Harper and Wilson being honest? What about the harassment? Would it stop? Would it get worse?

I couldn't decide if this was a good or bad thing. There just wasn't enough information to figure it out on my own. My favorite scent filled my nose again, and I looked up to see Lina smiling at me.

"Come on. Let's go celebrate," she said, holding out her hand.

"But where is he? What does this mean?"

"It means his bitch-ass is on the run, and you get to go back to your life."

"Just because he's on the run doesn't necessarily mean he will stop," I said. "He might just sic his little minions on me again."

"Alright, let's say for argument's sake that you're right and he wanted to continue harassing you. He'd need to be able to communicate with them, but that would mean he would have to use his phone, and that can be tracked, sooo that wouldn't work."

"Fair point, but he could've memorized their numbers, so he could use another phone."

"You really think that bonehead is gonna remember all those numbers? If his father isn't in on it, then he's going to be running from the police and his father's goons. That's a lotta heat to escape. He won't have time to think about you."

"But what if h—"

"Melanie, stop it!" Lina barked. "I understand that last week was rough, and I'm not discounting that at all, trust me. But you can not live like this. If you keep asking yourself *what if, what if, what if,* you'll go crazy.

"You live with me behind a locked gate. Michelle already said you can go back to work after next week, and I will go to every single class with you if you want me to. Just stop and focus on the here and now... Please."

"You would willingly go to every class with me?" I asked, smiling.

"Yes, you lil' brat. I would. Can we go celebrate now?"

"Yes!"

Lina pulled me up from the chair and walked beside me toward the courtroom doors. Elijah and Xavier were waiting for us outside, but Harper and Elijah seemed to be having a heated discussion. As we approached, Harper stomped off.

Lina's gaze flicked from Harper's retreating form to Elijah and then to Xavier.

"What did Dick want?" she asked.

"He said he doesn't know where his son is, which I still don't believe. I told him this disappearance would open up a whole can of worms for him, legally."

"I'm sure you enjoyed throwing that in his face," Lina said with a devilish grin.

"I might have. So, are you ladies ready to go celebrate?"

"Yes, we are, and you're treating," Lina informed him.

"Of course, I am," he said, rolling his eyes. His expression shifted into a small smile. "Let's go."

We all left the courthouse, went to a nice diner, and had a great lunch. Even though the Tiberius situation was still fresh in my mind, it wasn't at the forefront of my thoughts.

Like Lina had said, if he did want to risk getting caught by fucking with me while on the run, he shouldn't have run in the first place. I had no way to tell the future, so letting him occupy my mind wasn't healthy. It wasn't the life I wanted to live.

So, fuck him, I decided. He could literally go to Hell. I refused to live looking over my shoulder. If he did decide to waste his time and come after me, I would deal with that bullshit when it happened.

For now, I needed to start working on my plans for Lina's upcoming birthday. I only had a couple of weeks. There were so many moving pieces to my plan, and I would need some help, so I guess it was finally time to schedule a meet up with the *wife*.

XXVI

Melanie

No one can really prepare you for how you will react to a situation. Even when you have no right to feel any particular way about it, it doesn't change the fact that you *do* feel a certain way when it happens.

So, when I opened the front door to Zyriel dressed in all black, looking like he was created just for the purpose of bringing a woman orgasmic bliss, I was... annoyed.

That's the best word that I could come up with to describe how I felt. Well, annoyed and surprised, I guess. I distinctly remembered him saying he *used* to be a fuckable. So, what the fuck was he doing here?

"Uh... Hey, Zyriel. Um, don't take this the wrong way, but what the hell are you doing here?"

Woooow, that was subtle.

He shook his head. "The curse of being a twin: Everyone always mixes you up for your brother."

Twins? Brother? What the fuck is going on?

"Ook. Then, what's your n—"

"Xadrian, what the fuck are you doing here?" Lina asked. Her voice was tense.

Guess that answers that.

Xadrian looked over my head and honed in on Lina, wearing a dubious smile. His eyes held the lust everyone always had whenever they looked at her, but underneath it was something that seemed like pain.

Wonder what that's about?

"I'm here to complete our..." He grew quiet as he looked from Lina, to me, and then back to her again. "Business."

"And you thought... You know what? Fine, whatever. Stay there. Mel, can I talk to you for a second, please?"

I nodded. Xadrian stepped inside and sat down at the island. He shot me a gentle smile that I didn't trust one bit. Lina grabbed my hand and headed for her bedroom.

The warmth of her grip helped suppress my annoyance, but I had an abundance of questions. She knew I was going to explode as soon as we crossed over the threshold because she spun around and kissed me with so much heat, I saw stars.

Damn it! I know what game you're playing, and fuck me if it isn't working.

Lina broke the kiss and placed her forehead against mine, our sexually charged breaths mixing.

"I know you have questions, but I won't be able to answer them right now. As he said, we have business to settle up, and that business is going to keep me away until tomorrow morning."

That was a surprise I wasn't expecting. Once again, I felt emotions I shouldn't have been feeling. I was used to sharing her with the other fuckables, but I had no interest in sharing her with that Xadrian guy.

I planned to say just that, but Lina put her finger against my lips and stopped me from being an idiot.

"I'm sorry. I'll make it up to you when I get back," she promised.

"How will you make it up to me?"

"In whatever way you want. But for now, why don't you call Shelly over and have a girls' night? You guys can talk shit about me for leaving you alone. I gotta get dressed, or he's gonna come looking for me."

I rolled my eyes at her. I liked the idea of having Shelly over, but talking shit wasn't gonna be my focus. Worrying about what the two of them were doing all night was.

Lina gave me one more small kiss and then went into her closet. I grabbed my phone from the nightstand and sent a text to Shelly.

Me: Can you come over tonight? I'm in panic mode.

Shell: Did you make a mistake and tell Rose you love her while you guys fucked?

Me: What? No! I would've died if I did that.

Shell: At least you'd get to cum before you died!

Me: OMFG!!

Me: Can

Me: You

Me: Come

Me: Over?

Shell: Sure! What time?

Me: Now!!!!

Shell: Kk. Be there soon.

Now that that was settled, I put my phone back onto the nightstand and went to find Lina in the closet. She wasn't there. I thought I may have missed her, but seconds later, the sound of running water came from the bathroom.

I found Lina bent over the sink, washing her face. Her black jeans had her ass looking incredible. I felt the urge to peel them right back off of her. When she stood up straight and turned toward me, my breath caught in my throat.

She was wearing a blood-red corset that pushed her breasts up and had my mouth watering for a taste of them. A surge of jealousy filled my chest. She'd never worn anything like that for me.

Really, Melanie! Everything she wears makes you want to strip her out of it. Don't start getting jealous for stupid reasons.

The little voice in my head was right. I'd looked through her closet before. The woman didn't believe in plain clothes. Everything she had was tight and alluring. I was still a little jealous, though.

Lina pulled on a black leather jacket and black high tops, sprayed my favorite mixture of essential oils on her chest, and walked toward me. She used her fingers to lift my chin (I didn't even know my jaw had dropped) and dragged her thumb over my bottom lip.

"You're making it extremely difficult to leave when you smell like that, Mel," she whispered.

Then, don't leave.

Every single fiber of my being wanted to say that out loud, but it would've been a waste of breath. She was leaving, and I couldn't stop her if I wanted to, but I could torture her for it.

"Whose fucking fault do you think that is? You look like *this*," I said, waving my hands toward her outfit. "You smell like that and expect my body not to react?" I playfully snapped. "Maybe I won't have Shelly come over, after all. Maybe I'll go downstairs and play with all your toys. Fuck myself into a blissful oblivion," I taunted, turning and heading back into the bedroom.

The surprise in Lina's eyes made my little stunt worth it. Served her right for leaving me. I almost made it out of the bedroom door before she snatched my wrist and forced me up against the wall.

"Now, why would you want to have all that fun without me?" she asked, dragging her fingers down my chest.

You started this game. I'm simply just playing along.

"Who's the one leaving?" I responded.

"Well, me, but..."

I raised up on my toes and ran my tongue over her bottom lip. "No *buts*," I whispered. "Didn't you say he'd get restless and come look for you? Better get going."

I'd stunned her once again (Go me!) and left her staring at the wall as I made my way to the library. Xadrian was still seated at the island, leaning over it with his head in his hand. He wore a huge smile, letting me know he'd probably gotten at least an earful of our conversation.

I stuck my tongue out at him and walked into the library. Behind me, I heard a deep chuckle, but I refused to look back and acknowledge him. I was already seated at her desk when Lina rushed in.

"You do know there's a camera in the playroom, right?"

I glanced at her over the laptop and grinned. "Oh, yeah. You're right about that," I mused, then looked back down at the screen dismissively. "Guess I'll just have to cover it. Have a good night, Lina."

She stood at the threshold, her mouth opening and closing. I hid my victorious smirk behind the screen. I'm sure she wanted to say something, or more than likely do something, but Xadrian appeared next to her and tugged her arm.

"Come along now, Moon. You've been outplayed by this lil' minx. While I'm fully enjoying the show, we need to head out. Accept the loss and say goodnight."

Pure retribution blazed in her eyes, but she allowed Xadrian to lead her away from the library. I slumped in the chair as soon as I heard the front door close.

Torturing her was awesome, but now that I was alone, all the worrying came flooding right back. Shelly really needed to hurry the hell up and get here.

When the bell rang, I practically sprinted to the front door and snatched it open. Shelly's hands were full as she rushed in and placed all the items she carried on the island.

By the smell of things, there was a fresh pizza buried underneath all of the bags. The scent made my stomach growl.

Treacherous body! How could you think of food at a time like this?

"What's with all the snacks?" I asked as I rifled through the bags.

"Well, you said you were in crisis mode, and I didn't know what to bring, so I brought it all, including ingredients for your whipped cream."

"Why the whipped cream?"

"For sending nudes to Rose. To make her regret doing whatever she did, of course. Oh, by the way, what *did* she do? I'm trying to figure out how upset I should be with her."

A serene smile crept over my lips. Leave it to Shelly to burst in like the whirlwind she was and take some of my worries away.

The nudes suggestion would have been a hell no in the past, but tonight, it was the best idea ever.

"OK. Since I have to make the whipped cream, I'll fill you in, and you can decide after you have all the facts."

"Fair," Shelly agreed before taking a bite of a slice of pizza.

I gave her the full download as we ate half the box of pizza and I made whipped cream. She sat quietly and didn't interrupt me once, as I'd expected her to, which had me even more worried.

When the whipped cream was finished, she dipped her finger into the bowl, scooped out a huge dollop, and sucked it into her mouth. Her eyes rolled back with pleasure, and she let loose a small moan.

"You know I could just give you the recipe, right?" I asked.

"Don't want it. I won't make it like you do. Now, tell me more about this Xadrian guy."

"Outside of him possibly being a past fuckable and the fact that he's a twin, I don't know anything about him."

"Hmm," she pondered, tapping her finger against her lips. "You said there are three current guy fuckables right now, right? Is it possible he is the one you haven't met yet? Also, the fact that she's been with a set of twins is *legendary*."

"Can you focus on the crisis at hand and not her sex life, please? No, he can't be one of the guys because the third guy's name is Quinn, not Xadrian."

"Oh, well shit. I wish we had some insider knowledge."

"Oh my God! Shell, you're a genius," I exclaimed as I kissed her cheek.

"Of course, I'm a genius... But what did I do?"

"Insider knowledge! I actually know someone who would have that."

Hazel picked up on the third ring and requested to turn the call from voice to video. I hesitated because she was wilder than Lina, and I had no doubt she would answer the phone fully nude if the mood struck her.

Hoping she was at least wearing a bra, I hit the accept button and braced myself. She popped up on the screen, clothed (thank God) and smiling.

"Hey, Mel! To what do I owe this pleasure?"

"You let her call you Mel?" Shelly whispered.

"She's the type of personality you can't really tell anything," I whispered back. "I think of her as an extension of Lina, so it doesn't really bother me."

"Oh, OK. And who is she?"

"I'm the wife," Hazel answered, interrupting us.

"She's her WHAT?"

OK. The first time Hazel said that, I didn't like it one bit, but seeing the look of shock and confusion on Shelly's face was hilarious. I was slowly starting to like the joke.

"She's just trying to freak you out," I told her. "Hazel is Lina's version of you."

"Oooh, the hot best friend. Got it, got it. Well, she is really hot."

"Aw, thank you. So are you, Blondie! I'm sure you and I could have a ton of fun," Hazel said with a wink.

I don't think I'd ever seen Shelly blush. Her mouth was just as fucking reckless as Lina's and Hazel's, so it was really surprising to see her stunned to silence.

Still, I needed to get things back on topic. "Although I would love for you to keep teasing her since she's always teasing me, that's not the reason I called."

"And for what reason, pray tell, did you call me, sweet Mel?"

"What do you know about a man named Xadrian?"

At the mention of his name, Hazel sat up and stared at me for a few moments. I hadn't thought she was capable of making such a serious expression, but I guess I was wrong. Now, I wasn't just anxious. I was getting scared. Who was this guy, and why was his name so concerning?

"What do you know about Xadrian?"

"Nothing, other than the fact that he's a twin and he just came and took Lina away to finish some *business*, or whatever."

"You know he's a twin?"

"Uh... yeah. I called him Zyriel when I opened the door, and he said I'd mixed him up."

"How do you know about Sai?"

Alright, I was doing my best to keep calm since I needed information from her, but I was getting really ticked off. She kept asking me questions and had yet to answer mine.

"I met him when Lina went to start the new tattoo on her back."

"She took you to the tattoo shop?"

"Yes! Will you answer my question now?"

"In a minute." *Click.*

After all those questions and not one answer, she just randomly hangs up on me? I liked Hazel well enough, but right then I wanted to punch her.

Shelly dipped her finger in the whipped cream and scooped out another dollop.

I popped her hand. "If you keep eating that, we won't have any left for the pictures."

"Were we actually gonna do that?" she gasped.

Nodding my head, I dipped my finger into the whipped cream and dabbed some onto the tip of her nose. "Yep."

"Oh, this is gonna be epic."

XXVII

Rose

To say I was pissed was a fucking understatement. Rian knew how much I hated random pop-ups. And as if his unannounced visit wasn't bad enough, Mel had answered the door.

Mel. Oh my God, Mel.

I was really starting to come to terms with the fact that she was going to be my undoing. Where was the shy girl who'd run all the way home after I simply said hi to her? Who was this teasing, defiant, and challenging woman who consistently drove me crazy?

All I wanted to do was go back home and fuck her brains out, but wishes are for kids, I guess.

"When we get to our destination, I expect you to be present. I know you're thinking about how to speed up our time together so you can rush back and fuck her into oblivion, as she said, but I'm not gonna let you leave until tomorrow morning."

I was two seconds away from laying into him when I heard Hazel's ringtone.

"Yo," I answered.

"Why are you with the evil twin?" she asked.

I was so surprised, I actually looked around in the car as if Hazel was in it, watching me. Rian raised his brow at me, but I ignored him.

"How do you know who I'm with, Hazel?"

"Because your girlfriend and her version of me just called and asked me about him. Oh, and you forgot to tell me she met Sai. What else haven't you told me?"

A shit ton.

"Mel called you and asked you about him? What the fuck for?"

I was whispering, but the smirk on Rian's face told me he was listening to the entire conversation. I really wanted to slap him. He drove faster than I did, though, and I wasn't in the mood to crash.

"Why do you think she asked?" Hazel said. "Because she's jealous, dumbass!"

"Hey, there's no need for name-calling."

"Then, don't be dumb! I thought you only kept in touch with the good twin."

Trying to figure out a passable excuse as to why I was hanging out with Rian was going to take more brain power than I was willing to expend, so I just gave her a simple answer.

"There was a situation I needed him to handle. He handled it, and now I'm paying up. Yes, he wanted me for the night in exchange. No, I will *not* be sleeping with him. Yes, this is the last time I'll be seeing him. No, I don't have any unresolved feelings. Does that answer all your questions?"

Rian chuckled after hearing my last statement. Slapping him was becoming more and more appealing by the second, consequences be damned.

"I'm going to hang up now," I said, focusing my attention back on the call.

"What do I tell Mel?" Hazel prodded.

"Whatever you want."

"Fine. You didn't deny it when I called her your girlfriend, by the way."

I rolled my eyes and hung up the phone. Why was everyone I knew trying to drive me crazy today? Like, seriously, what the fuck?

Rian was still smiling, and I couldn't take it anymore. I reached over to backhand him, but he caught my hand and pulled it toward his mouth, attempting to kiss my palm.

I tried to pull my hand away, but he tightened his grip, and I had no choice but to accept the kiss. We will *not* talk about what the sensation did to me, so don't even ask about it.

"Let. Go," I growled.

"I did that once. I don't think I'll be doing it again."

I couldn't hear things like that, especially when his lips were on my skin. Fighting not to react to his words was a battle that I failed. He finally released my hand as shivers raced up my arm.

"Why do you have to be so fucking a..." Mel's text tone sounded from my phone. I glanced down. "OH MY GOD!" I'd expected to see her bitching about whatever Hazel had said, but instead, I was getting a barrage of nudes.

As if that wasn't enough torture, she was covered in whipped cream. One of the pictures made me reevaluate my sanity. She'd covered one of my twelve-inch dicks in whipped cream too, and she was licking her way to the top. The very next picture showed her deep-throating the damn thing, and I was immensely impressed with how much she was able to take. If I gripped my phone any harder, I was going to crack the screen.

"Take me home," I demanded.

"No."

"Rian! Take me back!"

"Moon! No! If it was an emergency, she would've called. Obviously, that lil' minx is doing something to rile you up, and I commend her for it, but I am not taking you back until after we're done." Rian rolled my window down. "If you keep it up, I'll toss your fucking phone out of the goddamn window." He gestured outside of the car.

I glared at him but remained quiet. After a moment, he rolled my window back up. My phone continued to chime, but I placed it in my lap and attempted to ignore it. Rian began to laugh after the fifth text, and I punched his arm.

"Don't wanna look at your texts anymore?" he asked.

"Are you gonna take me back?"

He sighed and flipped on his turn signal.

"If you don't want me to ask you stupid questions, then don't ask me any, either."

He chuckled again and pulled into the driveway of a huge modern house. The sun had just set, and the way the light hit the front windows looked magical.

The windows stretched from the floor to the ceiling, but they were tinted, so I couldn't see through them. Not that it would matter since the house was set back deep enough on the property that nobody would be able to snoop. They'd have to survive the three-mile walk from the front gate first.

The circular gravel driveway led up to wide, dark wooden steps. A standalone hammock sat on the porch, filled with pillows and blankets. I had an itch to climb into it but refrained.

"Whose house is this? You steal it?"

I'd meant it as a joke, but I guess it didn't land because he just shook his head and started toward the door. He pulled keys out of his pocket and shook them like a smartass.

Just cos' you got the keys doesn't mean you didn't steal it, but I'll keep that to myself.

Rian unlocked the door and stepped inside. I shot one more glance at the hammock before following him in. The interior was so damn startling that I momentarily thought I had walked into my house.

Rian was in the kitchen pouring himself a glass of water. He'd pulled off his jacket and laid it across an island that looked disturbingly like my own. Without the jacket, I could see he was wearing a black tank top that showed off his muscular and scarred arms.

My heartbeat pounded in my ears. I backed up against the door and searched for the knob but couldn't find one. Spinning around, I stared at the door, confirming what I already knew.

There was no handle, only a keypad with a fingerprint scanner. I had no way out.

This was one of the reasons I couldn't be around him. He knew I hated to be trapped and had done exactly that in the past, coming up with some bullshit explanation that I needed to learn to take control of that fear.

Fuck that shit. Don't fucking lock me up. Then, whether or not I have the fear wouldn't fucking matter.

I'd screamed that at him the last time he'd trapped me in a room with him, and he'd promised to never do it again.

"Liar," I said. My voice broke.

"The fuck are you talking about, Moon?"

"You said you'd never lock me up again," I whispered "Open this door, Rian."

"Just calm down," he said, stepping around the island.

"Don't you come near me! Open this fucking door! Open it right fucking now!"

Panic was setting in. I knew exactly where I was, but my mind didn't give a fuck. Images of the locked door from my nightmares floated in front of my eyes.

At some point while I was pounding my fists against the door, I'd begun screaming because he was yelling at me to stop and calm down. I couldn't do that, even if I wanted to.

The panic had a bruising grip on my heart, and it didn't seem like it was ready to release it anytime soon. Even when he pulled me against his chest and wrapped an arm around my waist, pinning my arms to my sides, I still continued to thrash against him.

I even resorted to trying to headbutt him, but I'd forgotten about our height difference. I only managed to hit his chest.

Fuck you for being so goddamn tall.

"Jesus, Moon. Stop fighting me, and give me your hand!"

"No! Let me the fuck go! I want to go!"

He grabbed my left wrist, and although I refused to cooperate, he managed to place my thumb over the fingerprint sensor. As soon as the lock clicked and the door opened, I calmed down.

Rian pulled the door wide open and backed away from me.

"I'm so, so sorry. This was supposed to be a surprise, and I got caught up in being around you again. I'm a fucking idiot, Moon. You know that, but I promise that wasn't how this was supposed to go. If you want me to take you back, I will. We can forget the deal."

The image of that damned door finally cleared, and the sight of the sky's sherbet hues helped me regain control of my breathing. I hated what Rian had done, but I also heard the pain in his voice. He really hadn't meant to upset me.

Even though he shouldn't have forgotten about my trigger, a bigger portion of this was my own damn fault. I'd only told him a small fraction of my past and that was only because I needed his help solving a problem, and then the whole Dre blowup situation happened so I never told Rian anything more than what I felt was necessary to share.

Not that I thought I would ever be in a situation like this again, but it was probably time to start trusting people enough to tell them about my traumas so I could avoid scenarios like this.

But that was a lot to wrap my head around. Figuring it out had to wait. For now, I owed Rian a little payback for his lack of explanation before my meltdown. So, I closed the door and turned to glare at him.

The uncertainty in his eyes made me second-guess my next move, but only for a second.

"You'll... You'll stay?"

"On one condition," I answered, then kicked him in the stomach.

When he doubled over, I swung my fist across his jaw. Riled, Rian rushed me and pinned me against the door. His scarlet eyes burned like wildfire, focusing on my lips.

He was going to kiss me this time. I knew it, and I wasn't going to even try to stop it. But I *sure* as hell was going to make him regret it.

He closed the distance between us, pressing his mouth to mine. The kiss was gentle for about two seconds before he deepened it.

Damn. I'd forgotten how amazing of a kisser you are.

Rian's tongue swept across my lip, begging for entrance, and I granted it. As soon as the tip of it passed my teeth, I bit down as hard as I could. The metallic taste of blood was strong, but it didn't deter him one bit.

He growled against my lips, slid his tongue deeper into my mouth, and pulled my hair. A breathy moan slipped out of me without permission, and although it was gentle, he heard it. That was all he needed.

Rian's hands cupped my ass as he picked me up and walked us deeper into the house. My legs wrapped tightly around his waist, and we'd yet to come up for air, but as we approached what I expected was his bedroom, Mel popped into my thoughts.

I can't even begin to explain why seeing her face made me hesitate. That's a lie. I know it, and you know it, too. But I'm not up for discussing it right now. Still, her image did clear the sex-crazed haze consuming me, and that was extremely helpful.

Rian felt my energy shift and pulled away. His eyes searched my face for a moment before he sighed and leaned his forehead against mine.

"I guess you meant it when you said you weren't gonna fuck me, huh?" he whispered.

"I meant it."

"Ugh, fuck! I really wish you didn't, but I will respect your decision."

Kissing me once more, he set me back on my feet, then stroked my cheek with his thumb. I imagined the look on his face was the same as the one he'd worn when he found out I'd left all those years ago.

"Take a look around," he said. "This was meant to be *our* home, after all." Rian shook his head and disappeared into a room at the end of the hall.

I stood frozen where he'd left me. I'd already figured that out when he pressed my thumb against the sensor, but hearing it out loud was stupefying. The gray wood floors, the black furniture, and the gold accents... The marble island, countertops, and kitchen backsplash...

It was everything I'd talked about when he asked me what I would have wanted in my future house. It was everything I had in my current home. The realization helped me get moving.

If the front of the house was as I'd described it, then that meant the rest of the house had to be, as well. Halfway down the hallway, there was a set of double doors. I went straight to them and pushed them open.

The library was stunning and actually bigger than my own. The shelves were mostly empty, but a few of them were filled with several of the series that I'd read and enjoyed while we'd spent time together. All of the spines were worn, and I never left my books like that, so I knew he'd read the books repeatedly in an attempt to hold onto a connection to me.

This was going to be a long-ass night.

Seeing everything in this damn house was stirring up too many fucking emotions. It was mind-numbing. I was still looking at the books when he came in and tossed something at my head.

"Please, put that on," he insisted. "I know you wore that outfit to be cruel, but I was hoping I'd get to sleep with you at least one last time." Rian leaned against the threshold of the library.

"Isn't seeing me in your shirt gonna be torture, too?"

"Yes... but it will cover up your tits, and that's what I need right now. Please?"

It was a fair request, even if it came with an ulterior motive. His scent was all over the shirt, and he probably hoped it would rev me up again. He wasn't wrong, but I'd already made my decision. I wouldn't sleep with him.

Nothing was going to change that, but I could give him the small reprieve he asked for. Rian pointed to the nearest bathroom, and I went to change.

When I came out, I couldn't find him at first. He wasn't in the kitchen, the living room, or the library. I stared at what I assumed was the bedroom door as I twisted the hem of the T-shirt in my fist. He'd said he respected my decision, but he didn't say he accepted it.

You're not going to make this easy for me, I see.

I pushed the door open, revealing, as I'd guessed, the master bedroom. It was just how I'd described it to him: dark gray walls, a black metal king bed, a throne-style reading chair in the corner, black rugs scattered around the space, smaller shelves for books sporadically placed against the wall, and tall, black French patio doors that led to the backyard.

The balcony was open, and I could hear the sound of running water. It beckoned to me, and I found myself stepping through the doors. Rian was lying on a huge bean bag covered with pillows and blankets staring out into the backyard.

My gaze shifted toward the sound of running water. It was coming from a waterfall connected to an inground pool. The backyard was huge, but what drew my focus was the weeping willow tree in the far back.

That was one of my favorite types of trees, and I'd only mentioned it once. At the time, we'd been discussing something inconsequential, and he asked if I liked trees. That was my answer.

I could see Rian watching me out of the corner of my eye. He raised what looked like a remote, and an abundance of outdoor lights wrapped around the willow sprang to life.

Then, Rian grabbed my hand and pulled me down to the bean bag. I couldn't take my eyes off of the tree, but when he rubbed my cheek, it felt wet. I dragged my own fingers along my face.

Why the fuck am I crying?

"W-why..." My voice broke again. "Why did you do all this?"

He sighed, laid back on the bean bag, and patted the spot next to him. I crawled over and laid beside him. Even with the lights from the backyard and the tree, I could still see thousands of stars in the sky.

"You already know the answer to that question, Moon."

"But why do you love me? I-I'm not worthy of it. It's wasted on me. Why not give your love to som—"

Rian cut me off with a kiss, but this one was different. It was dripping with passion, not sexually fueled.

"I get that what happened to you makes you feel and think that way, and I guess I'll never get the chance to change that, but I chose to give my love to you, and that won't ever change."

"But I d—"

"I know you don't love me back. I can see that I've lost to that lil' minx already. And maybe that's my fault. I kept hoping you would come back. When you didn't, I should have sought you out sooner.

"But it's OK. I think she was meant for your love, so I'll just have to get over it... One day. Tonight, I just want to hold you one last time before you disappear out of my life again."

Questions stirred in my head. Did I love Mel? Was she meant for me? Was I meant for her? Was I good enough for her? I could go down the rabbit hole if I let my mind wander, but I pushed the thoughts back.

Outside of the little stunt he'd pulled with the lock, Rian had been as respectful as he could be. I would give him the courtesy of focusing on the here and now for the rest of the night.

We stayed like that well into the evening, talking about how life had been for each other during our time apart. We swapped one-night-stand stories and tales of our craziest hook-ups.

My stories were greater in number, but he outdid me in the wild nights category. When the temperature dipped too low, we moved inside, and he finished the tour. The gym, the media room, and the playroom were all there.

There wasn't a detail he'd missed when this house was built. It was still jarring to see, but I was slowly getting used to it. We ended up in the gym for a while. He wanted to check my technique, so we spared for a bit before heading to the media room and playing some video games.

I lost the first few times, then came back with a vengeance and kicked his ass. We laughed and joked, and there was peace. The anger and some of the hurt he'd carried for almost a decade started to ease.

This is how I should have left things. I thought this was going to be hard, and I didn't want to deal, so I ran away. I was wrong. This was actually easy, and although I was still going to leave once the night was over, it would be a mutual separation this time.

Rian flicked through a streaming service, searching for something to watch and settling on a random movie. He didn't ask, but I knew it was what he wanted, so I crawled over and cuddled up to him.

Maybe about halfway in, he started to snore. I giggled. I could do anything I wanted to him, and he still decided to let his guard down around me. With a smile on my face, I decided to put my evil plans away and finished watching the movie in his arms.

XXVIII

Rose

Rian must have gotten up early because when I woke up, I was alone in the middle of the bed, tangled in the blankets. My head popped right up when the scent of breakfast reached my nose.

Moments later, he walked in, holding a tray, and placed it on the bed in front of me. It was full of pancakes, bacon, and scrambled eggs. My stomach growled, and my mouth began to water.

Everything was so damn dramatic yesterday that I didn't even realize I hadn't eaten. I was starving. Rian had already cut up the pancakes and drowned them in syrup, just how I liked them.

I went to town as he climbed onto the mattress beside me. As I ate, my eyes kept straying to those tattooed roses.

I swallowed. "You just had to come in here shirtless, didn't you?"

"I don't know what you're implying. I don't sleep in clothes. You know that. Be happy I decided to put on pants before I brought you breakfast."

Fair point.

"I'll take you home after you finish eating," he said. "Our deal is complete."

I'd been waiting to hear those words since the start of this whole thing, but now that he'd finally said them, I was a little sad.

Back when we used to hang out, Rian tested the limits of my patience on a daily basis. Still, I wouldn't lie and say I didn't care about him or that I wouldn't miss him. But our auras held the same kind of darkness, and he needed someone who would bring light into his life. Neither of us could offer that to the other.

According to him, Mel was supposedly the person who could do that for me. I wasn't too sure. There was a lot of darkness swirling inside of me, and I wouldn't be able to forgive myself if I dimmed her brilliant light just to lighten my load. Still, something he'd said last night had been bugging me. I probably shouldn't have brought it up because I knew it was going to cause a lot of unwanted feelings to resurface, but I had to know the truth.

"You know, don't you?" I whispered.

He silently stared at the ceiling for so long that I was beginning to think he hadn't heard me. Then, he finally answered. "Yeah."

"See, this is why that dumb-ass shouldn't fucking drink," I sighed. "Can't keep a damn secret worth his life."

"He wouldn't be my right hand if that were true. Plus, you know the only way two people can keep a secret is if one of them is dead."

"So then, I'm justified for killing him since he spilled the beans?"

Rian chuckled, turned his head, and looked up at me. "Give Dre a break, Moon. He took your Houdini act harder than I did. He had nothing to occupy himself, and I had an underground empire to run.

"I found out the hard way that your leaving cut him deep. He was being an even bigger asshole than usual one day, and I made a joke, said that he was the reason you left us. So, he told me who Enzo really was as retaliation. Screamed that you left us because you thought we'd turn on you and hurt you like that piece of shit did."

"That's not even remotely true," I said. "Even in all his dumb-assery, I knew Dre wouldn't hurt me like that. Didn't think you would either."

"Then, why didn't you tell me? Why did you lie and say it happened to your cousin? Why not be honest and admit it that day I locked you in a room with me and you went crazy? I would have never forgotten that if you told me. Not that I'm making excuses for what I did yesterday, but I don't get why you never trusted me enough."

"I didn't want you to know how broken and worthless I was. I didn't want you to leave me. It's easier for me to choose to be alone rather than to be *left* alone." Tears spilled down my cheeks, and Rian moved the tray off of my lap, pulling me into his arms.

"I never would've left you. You should've trusted me."

"I couldn't take that chance. I'm sorry."

"I know, Moon. I know."

After I finished my breakfast and dressed, Rian stayed true to his word. Without complaint, he took me home. For a while, we sat in my driveway in silence. This was it. Once I left his car, I was never going to see him again.

It just felt so damn final, but this was how I'd wanted it, right? I guessed it was time to rip the fucking *Band-Aid* off. Plus, I owed a certain lil' brat an abundance of punishment, which I was itching to dole out.

When I was halfway up the driveway, Rian called my name. He tossed something at me, and after I caught it, I saw it was the house keys. He had already pulled onto the road when I waved the ring at him.

One last time, he stopped and rolled the passenger window down.

"Are these..."

"Yes."

"I can't t—"

"It's yours, Moon. Do whatever the fuck you want with it. Live in it. Sell it. Burn it. I don't fucking care. I won't be back. It was never a home to me... not until last night. It won't be a home anymore with you gone."

Then, Rian drove off before I even had a chance to respond, leaving me speechless in my driveway. I studied the keys in my hand, unsure of what I was going to do about them. That was something I would have to think about later. At the moment I didn't have time to dwell on it.

Right now, the only thing taking up residence in my thoughts was Mel and the way I'd have her screaming my name so fucking much, she'd think it was her own. So, I walked into the house and quickly checked on the cats, then went off in search of Mel.

The house was silent, which was extremely disappointing. How dare she get me riled up like that and not be here so I could exact my revenge? It just made me even more eager to get my hands on her, but unfortunately, I had to wait.

It was OK, though, because it meant I had more time to prepare for her impending punishment. I opened the refrigerator, hoping there would still be some whipped cream. She'd left me a big bowl.

Perfect.

The look in Mel's eyes before I went with Rian last night had been crystal clear. She'd loved what I was wearing, but she'd hated that I wasn't wearing it for her. So today, I was going to wear something special.

Searching for the perfect clothes, I leafed through my lingerie collection. When my fingers found a bright red velvet and lace corset, the outfit began to come together.

I took a quick shower and rubbed my body down with her favorite scents. Then, I put on the corset, a red lace set of panties, black-lace thigh-high stockings, and my black lace robe.

With my outfit perfected, I only needed one more thing to put my plan in motion: Mel needed to come home.

An hour later, I was sitting in a chair in the library. The front door opened, followed by the sound of overlapping voices. I tossed my book aside as soon as they came in. It was time.

Finally.

Excitement overwhelmed me. It was so overpowering that I could literally taste it. Abandoning my chair, I walked out of the library, leaned against the wall, and crossed my arms. Shelly and Mel were in the kitchen, chatting it up. Mel had her back to me, and since Shelly was facing me, she saw me first.

"Oh, shit!"

"What?" Mel asked.

Shelly pointed a finger in my direction, and Mel turned around. She gasped as soon as her eyes found me.

"Say goodbye to Shelly, Mel," I instructed.

"Goodbye to Shelly, Mel," she repeated absentmindedly.

Mel's eyes trailed up and down my body, taking in my outfit. Unconsciously, she bit her bottom lip, then started walking toward me. Obviously, she not only didn't realize that she'd repeated what I'd said verbatim, but she'd forgotten that Shelly was still here.

"Alright, well..." Shelly started making her way toward the door. "I can see that my existence doesn't matter to her anymore, so I'll take my leave. You look extremely hot, by the way." She winked. "You kids have fun."

Mel didn't even notice. She didn't stop until she was directly in front of me. Then, she pulled my head down and kissed me. I hadn't even realized I'd missed her kiss so much, but as our lips touched, I realized it was the very thing I needed to breathe.

A gentle moan left her lips, causing me to momentarily lose focus. That was the sound I craved, and I needed more of it. Swiftly, I picked her up, pressed her back against the wall, and deepened our kiss. She gave me more of those beautiful sounds before she pulled back.

"I guess you liked the pictures, huh?" she asked me with a smirk.

Thank you for reminding me.

"You two had a bunch of fun with that little photo shoot, didn't you?" I challenged.

"We sure did!" Mel's expression was mischievous. "We didn't want you to miss me too much while you were finishing your *business.*"

"Mhm... Don't you worry. You never strayed far from my thoughts the entire time I was away. Want me to show you just what I was thinking about?" I whispered against her lips.

"Yes," she panted.

Setting Mel back on her feet, I turned her toward the steps and spanked her ass.

"Get downstairs. Now. You know how I want you."

Quickly, Mel nodded and hustled down the stairs, pulling off her clothes as she went. Although that was a sight to behold, I was a little worried she might trip, so I rushed over to the landing to check on her.

Thankfully, only her discarded clothes were left behind. With my near heart attack averted, I was able to return to my plan. I grabbed the whipped cream, my phone, and a tripod, then headed downstairs.

Mel was ready for me, obediently laying in the middle of the bed with her legs spread open. I placed the tripod and whipped cream down on the dresser near the door so I could grab a picture of her. She noticed what I was doing and spread her lips with her fingers.

I think I took at least twenty or thirty shots of that one pose because it was perfect, just how I loved to see her, and she fucking knew it. Then, she surprised me by lifting one of her breasts and pulling her nipple into her mouth.

Fifty pictures later, I finally set my phone on the tripod and grabbed the Bluetooth remote. Mel watched me, gaze smoldering, as I disappeared into the closet.

I'd already tested some of her limits after that little fight we'd had, but I wanted to see if I could push her past them. I was so overwhelmingly curious about just how much she would let me do to her.

A small part of me assumed she would let me do anything to her, which I'll be honest, truly excited me. But I wouldn't make the choice for her. The permission she'd given me that other night wouldn't extend to this.

After grabbing an array of toys, I dug my spreader out from the bottom drawer and headed back into the room. Mel had apparently grown impatient while I was gathering my supplies because she'd retrieved the bowl of whipped cream and brought it over to the nightstand herself.

She'd also taken the liberty of dotting her body with little piles of whip. Most of the piles were small, but the ones on her nipples and pussy were quite generous.

"I'm guessing you want me to take my time in certain areas, huh?" I teased.

"Maybe," she replied, licking her fingers clean.

"Now, what if it was my plan to cover you in whip myself? You could've ruined it."

"I see it as helping you get to the end goal quicker," she said, grinning at me.

"Mhm," I hummed as I slowly started to lick the dollops of whipped cream off of her body.

Gentle moans spurred me on as I swept my tongue along the path down to her breasts and gave each nipple some well-deserved attention. The combined flavor of the cream and her skin was exquisite as it danced across my tastebuds.

Abandoning her breasts, I forged a new trail down her stomach, which caused her breathing to pick up, so I slowed down, making her whine and whimper. At one point, Mel became so desperate that she tried to push my head down, but I grabbed her wrists and pulled her hands away.

"Impatient, love?"

"Immensely," she breathed.

"Think you've waited long enough?"

"Yes!"

But I drew out her torture, dragging my tongue down until I reached the space right above her lips. I watched her squirm as she tried to hike her hips up. The tip of my tongue dipped into the whip before I drew back slightly.

"Please," she whispered.

So quick to beg, now aren't we?

I dove in then, devouring both her and the whipped cream all at once. Mel cried out and attempted to pull her wrists free. I let them go, and she wrapped her fingers in my dreads. She began to quiver as she rode my tongue to paradise.

Mel would get one free orgasm, so I hoped she enjoyed it because every one to follow, she would have to work for. Her release exploded over my tongue a second later, and I drank every drop of her nectar until I was lust-drunk.

When she came back down, Mel sat up and pulled my lips to hers. Her tongue scoured my mouth for every drop of her cum, stealing only the breath I had in my lungs. That high feeling was coming back, and it was heady.

Her fingers danced up and down the corset's bodice, likely in search of the loops to undo it. If I didn't regain focus, all of my planning would be for naught, and I couldn't let that happen.

She'd yet to be thoroughly tortured, and the lil' brat was still cocky about the photos. I wanted to test her boundaries. So, I backed up and smiled down at her heaving chest, her red cheeks, her kiss-bruised lips, and her glistening pussy.

Mel's body was my canvas and my toys were my tools. To-gether, I would create a magnificent masterpiece to behold. I was eager to get started, but first, we needed to change up the position.

After I moved the tripod farther away from the bed, I opened a photo app and set it up so that it would take repeating shots. Next, I hit the button on the Bluetooth remote, allowing it to start taking pictures, ensuring I wouldn't miss anything.

Once that was finished, I shifted Mel up into a seated position and fastened the spreader to her ankles. She watched curiously as I worked, but she didn't ask one single question.

Someone's finally learned.

After I'd secured her ankles, I helped her climb off the bed and stand. I made sure she was mostly in focus on the camera so I'd catch every one of her reactions to what I was about to do to her.

"Mel, are you ready to try something new today?" I asked as I grabbed the nipple teaser off of the bed.

"Yes," she practically shouted.

"Are you sure? I don't want to overwhelm you. You might not be ready for this level of pleasure."

I just couldn't help myself when it came to teasing her. She was so easily riled that I had to fuck with her whenever possible. The glare she gave me in response only made me want to toy with her more, but I restrained myself.

"I can take anything you give me," she answered defiantly.

"Big talk for someone so small."

She scowled. "Yeah, but I can back it up. Just make sure that whatever you plan to do to me is worth my time."

Oh my God! I've created a lil' sex-crazed monster! I fucking love it!

"If you couldn't already tell, this is a nipple teaser." She nodded her head in understanding. "And it comes with a vibration and warming setting that I will let you control, but only when I tell you to. Got it?"

Mel offered me another vigorous nod before opening her hand to accept the teaser. I handed it to her, then leaned down to roll my tongue over her nipple. A small gasp flew from her lips, and she sucked in her teeth when I put the clamp on.

A range of emotions flashed across her face as she adjusted to the sensation. I repeated the process, securing the second clamp on her other breast, then I pushed the button to activate the warming setting. In seconds, her expression shifted from unsure to blissful.

"Oooh. This feels nice," she said.

"What's about to happen next is gonna feel even better," I promised.

"Well, stop taking all day and get to the next part already!"

Shaking my head, I angled her away from me and bent her over. Then, I cuffed her wrists and attached the chain to the middle of the spreader. I'd worried just a bit that the cord for the nipple teaser wasn't going to be long enough with her in this position, but thankfully, it was.

For a moment, I stepped back and simply enjoyed the sight of her like that.

"Are you going to keep staring at my ass, or are you going to put something in it?" she taunted, staring back at me through her open legs.

Oooh, see now, you're just testing my gangsta again.

Before I'd even realized I'd moved, I had the anal trainer lubed up and slowly entering her ass. This time, she didn't even tense once. Within seconds, the trainer was fully inserted.

"Hit the lowest setting for the vibrator," I ordered.

Obeying my command, Mel turned on the teaser. At the same time, I activated the trainer. Instantly, she moaned and her knees buckled beneath her. I grabbed her hips and kept her from collapsing.

"You know what'll happen if you fall, so I won't even give you the warning," I said before letting go and returning to the closet.

My panties were already soaked, and I could feel my desire dripping down my legs. This was about to be *a-fucking-maz-ing.* I stripped out of my panties and abandoned the robe, then strapped up.

Even though she'd wanted to tease me by deepthroating my twelve-inch while I was gone, she wasn't going to be taking that today. Instead, I was going to use my ten-inch on her because what I lost in length, I gained in girth and texture. This one was ribbed to hit every single needy spot inside of her body.

Mel had her eyes closed when I came back, probably enjoying the vibrating sensation racing through her, but the moment I stepped into the room, her lids snapped open. Even from upside down, I could see the hunger burning in her gaze.

Wordlessly, I positioned myself, lined up with her pussy, and teased her entrance with the tip. She tried to force me in, but I grabbed her hips and kept her still. I teased her a bit more before I started to slowly inch inside of her.

"L-lina... Oh, fuck! Yes. Yes!"

At about halfway in, I grabbed the paddle off of the bed and used it to rub small circles on her ass. Mel's legs had begun to shake, but she found her inner strength and forced them to still.

"Ready for your punishment, Mel?" I taunted.

"Oh my God! Yes. Fucking punish me, please," she pleaded.

I spanked each cheek once with the paddle. The trainer was starting to slide out of her ass, so I pushed it back in before turning up the vibration. Then, I pushed the rest of the dick in, too, until I was buried all the way up to the hilt.

"Oh my God. You're so fucking deep!"

"If you can still talk, I'm not deep enough," I said, withdrawing back out to the tip.

Maybe I should have used the twelve-inch on her.

It was too late to turn back now. She was primed, and I wouldn't waste time switching out straps. So, I spanked her ass with the paddle and slammed into her all at once.

The screams she gave me were euphoric. The louder she cried out, the harder I pounded into her and spanked her. Her ass was bright red, and yet she begged me for more, telling me to paddle her harder and fuck her faster.

I felt like we were both possessed because I gave her everything she screamed for and then some. The smell of sweat and sex was heavy in the air, and it was a musk I wanted to bottle up and smell for the rest of my life.

"Fuck, yes! Fuck me like that! Fuck me just like that. Oh. My. Fucking. God. Please, please... Don't fucking stop!"

By that point, I was so lost in our ecstasy that if she *had* wanted me to stop, I wouldn't have been able to. Fucking her had become a way of life for me, and I was severely addicted to it.

"You wanna cum, Mel?" I asked, bending at the knees slightly so I could savagely hit her G-spot.

"Yes! Fuck! I wanna cum! Make me fucking cum! Make me squirt! Please, *please*!"

Dropping the paddle, I grabbed her hip with one hand and reached down with the other.

"Hit the button and drench me, baby," I ordered as I yanked the trainer out of her ass.

Immediately, Mel turned up the vibration on her nipples and came so hard, she damn near pushed my dick out. I had to drop the trainer so that I could use both hands to catch her because she couldn't hold herself up anymore.

"Give me a second to get the cuffs off of you."

After I was completely out of her, I unlatched her bonds and unhooked the spreader. We were both drenched, and she was blissfully exhausted. I turned the teaser off and gently removed the clamps from her nipples.

Mel stared up at me with a delirious smile on her beautiful face as she sat down on the floor, surrounded by a puddle of our making.

"So, what did we learn today?" I asked as I walked to the bathroom to run the shower.

"I learned that I need to have more impromptu photo shoots with Shelly if this is the result," she giggled.

What was this girl doing to me? The very thought of her continued defiance had me excited and wanting to fuck her all over again. When I came back into the room with a warm cloth, Mel was leaning against the bed, asleep.

Damn. Guess round two will have to wait.

XXIX

Melanie

Hazel was on her way to my house so we could plan out Lina's birthday dinner. Don't jump the gun: I was still living with Lina, but we'd agreed to meet at my house to keep Lina in the dark.

It had been a couple of weeks since the preliminary trial, and I hadn't had any trouble at school or work. Just in case, I was still keeping my guard up, but so far, it had been quiet, and I prayed it would stay that way. Tiberius's absence gave me more time for Lina.

A knock at my door filled me with equal parts anxiety and excitement. I don't know why I was so damn nervous to meet Hazel. She was always nice to me, so it wasn't like this meeting was going to be disastrous.

Maybe it was because I was getting a closer look into Lina's life, and that's what really had me nervous? I wasn't sure, but I wouldn't figure anything out until I let her in.

After I opened the door, Hazel rushed right inside and gave me a kiss. On the lips! It wasn't a passionate kiss, by any means. Just a small peck, but it shocked the hell out of me.

I don't know how to react to this.

I didn't get a chance to say anything as she gripped my chin and turned my face this way and that.

"Wow! The video chat didn't do your eyes justice, Mel. They're absolutely gorgeous!"

"Um... thank... you? You do realize you just full-on kissed me on the mouth, right?"

"Mhm," she said simply before walking past me. "Yeah, that's how I greet my girlfriends."

And your husband is cool with that?

"OK... And how many girlfriends do you have?"

Hazel leaned against the back of the couch and crossed her arms. It looked like she was actually counting, which made me think she and her husband might be some type of hybrid swingers.

"Well originally, it was just Rosey, but since I have you now, I guess it's two," she answered with a dazzling smile.

Both of you make me so damn dizzy. But does this mean I've been accepted?

"So, what do you have planned, and how can I help?" Hazel asked.

It was good that we were getting down to business because if we didn't, I was going to ponder over her *acceptance* all day. Instead, I broke down my plan for her, step by step.

We would have dinner here because if everyone went to Lina's house, she'd see all the cars in the driveway, but at my house, since the complex had a huge parking lot, she wouldn't be able to tell anything was off. I was going to ask if Casper could cater it since she loved his food. And then, there was the guestlist and decorations to consider.

Naturally, all the fuckables were invited, and the besties, too, of course. I was grateful my table could seat ten people. If it couldn't, seating arrangements were going to be interesting.

At first, I'd thought I would create a group chat to make it easier, but then I remembered just how much I hate those, so I decided against it. I ended up sending the invites out individually.

That was a nerve-wracking experience. Elijah and Xavier immediately each sent back excited replies. Quinn asked who I was, but quickly accepted my invitation once I said I was a fellow fuckable.

Myra and Wynter both had a few more questions than the boys, and that made me extremely nervous. I couldn't respond back right away. Hazel grabbed my chin, forcing me to look up at her.

"Chicks are far different from dicks, and you know that. You have to assert your dominance. You can't back down with either of them, especially Wyn. She'll eat you alive," she advised.

Myra was quick to shut down, accepting the invitation when I told her that if she wanted me to answer her questions, she had to ask them in person. Wynter was trickier, though. I didn't want to piss her off, but I didn't wanna be a punk, either.

I stared at the text thread for so long that Hazel had to snap her fingers in my face to get my attention back.

"Give. Me. Your. Phone," she ordered.

"W-why?" I asked, handing it over.

"Because your confidence meter isn't filled all the way up yet. So, I'll take over for you... This time. But you have to face Wyn on party night."

Hazel's fingers danced over my screen for a few minutes before she handed the phone back to me. When I read over the text messages, I was shocked by what she'd said.

> Me: Hi. My name is Melanie, and I am throwing a birthday party for Lina. I would like it if you came.

> Wynter: You have the wrong number. I don't know a "Lina."

> Me: Sorry. Uh, Lina's the nickname I use for her. It's Rose's birthday party.

> Wynter: Where tf you come up with "Lina" for a nickname?

> Me: Her first name is Rosalina.

> Wynter: How do you know her first name?

> Me (Hazel): Girrrl! You got too many questions. I ain't on fuckin' trial. Is you coming or nah?

> Wynter: I never said I wasn't coming.

> Me (Hazel): 'Ight then. We'll see you there. Info is on the pic I sent earlier. Bye.

"Oh my God! You made me sound so rude! What if she thinks I'm a bitch now?" I asked, hurriedly.

"Sweet, Mel. Any woman fucking Rosey besides herself is already a bitch in her mind. You have to match energies with Wyn. If she plays nice on party night, then you play nice. If she gets feisty, then you get feisty. Simple as that."

I frowned. "What makes you think I can be feisty?"

Hazel closed in on me and smiled. It amazed me that we were the same height when her personality made her seem like she was seven feet tall. She twirled her finger in a circular motion and then tapped my nose, making me blink.

"Because the Rosey I know doesn't do weak, love. If you couldn't hold your own, she would've dropped you months ago. For all intents and purposes, you live with her now. Stake your claim. You've earned it."

Hazel's words rolled around in my thoughts before they sunk in. She was right. I knew that if I was weak, Lina wouldn't be interested in me. Hearing her confirm that filled up my confidence meter even more.

"So! Got off the phone with Cas, and he, of course, agreed to cater. That takes care of the food and the guest list, and I'm bringing the cake. How did you wanna decorate? Balloons? Streamers? Strippers?"

"Strippers? Was I supposed to get strippers? I don't know any strippers. Do you know any strippers?" I balked.

"Oh, my lord. You are so fucking precious," Hazel said, laughing and shaking her head. "No, I don't know any strippers... unless we count you and Rosey."

My eyes went wide. "I'm not a stripper! I've never stripped in my life!"

"Oh, yeah?" she said, backing me into the couch again. "Then, how does Rosey get to taste her favorite treat, Mel?"

Hazel's fingers trailed down my chest as she spoke, and even though she wasn't Lina, my heart rate quickened.

I completely understand why you two are besties. Y'all give off that same fuck me *energy in everything you do.*

"Point taken," I breathed.

"You're so easy to rile up, Mel. It's like catnip for us both. But I'll leave you alone... For now. Don't stress. I'll come early and set up with you and Shelly. We already know the color theme since both of you weirdos are obsessed with black and red."

"What's wrong with black and red?"

"Nothing, nothing. But blue is nice, too," she grumbled.

We teased each other as we ordered all of the decorations. The whole experience was crazy to me. I'd never planned anything for anyone before, and now, I was not only throwing a party for a woman I'd fallen deeply in love with, but I was getting to plan it with her bestie.

Did this mean that we could be besties one day, too? Was it foolish or naive to hope for that? Don't get me wrong, I would never replace Shelly. She was my absolute ride-or-die. Still, it would be really cool if Hazel and I became friends.

"OK, now that everything's settled, can we call Rosey and have her come over? I'm only allowed to have threesomes with women when I'm away from the hubby."

"Excuse me," I squeaked.

Hazel broke out into a fit of giggles so contagious that I couldn't keep myself from joining in.

"Even if Rosey decides for some stupid reason not to keep you, I will. You're so much fun to mess with."

"Glad I amuse you."

I guess that answers the friends *question. And although I'm grateful that you like me, I really, really hope Lina does keep me around.*

XXX

Melanie

I was so overwhelmingly stressed out, and the party hadn't even started yet. Thankfully, Shelly came over this morning and helped me decorate. We hung black and red streamers over the stair railing and taped them halfway up the windows (since that's as far as we could reach).

Hazel had picked out a black velvet runner that looked amazing on my dark wood table. She'd also brought some blood-red chargers to put under the plates. She arrived while I was setting the table and slapped me on my ass, making me jump.

"Hi, beautiful! Are you excited for tonight?" Hazel asked.

"Yes, I am." Then, I shook my head. "Don't you know how to greet people normally?"

"Normal is overrated and no fucking fun. Plus, you know you like it."

"How come I wasn't greeted like that?" Shelly whined.

Hazel licked her lips and smiled. I was not getting into that conversation, so I went back to setting the table and did my best to ignore them.

"Turn around and show me what I'm working with, then," Hazel instructed.

Out of the corner of my eye, I saw Shelly spin around and wiggle. Hazel rubbed her hands together, then slapped Shelly's ass. The sound alone sent shivers racing down my back.

She didn't slap my ass like that! Oh my God! I've been around these two too long. I'm starting to think like them.

"Ooh, that was good," Shelly purred.

"Of course, it was. Ima master ass-slapper!

I rolled my eyes. "Oh my God! Will you two pervs focus? Is sex really the only thing on y'alls' minds?"

"Yes," they answered simultaneously.

"OK, that was a dumb question. Let me rephrase," I said. "Can you two please put your dirty minds on a shelf somewhere and finish helping me?"

Hazel and Shelly exchanged a slick smile before looking back at me. The way they stared screamed trouble, but I wasn't having any of it.

"I don't care what your twisted minds are plotting. If it's not party related, then I..."

They began to walk toward me, and that made me extremely nervous. I tried to back away, but I forgot I was in front of the table. I knew my eyes widened because their smiles became mischievous as they closed in on me.

The two of them began to vigorously tickle me, coming at me from both sides. I screamed, laughing, and tried to bat them away with the napkins in my hand. Then, Quinn walked in, drawing their attention.

"Uh?" he said, frowning in confusion. "I don't usually just burst into someone's home like this, but I heard screaming..."

"Oooh. I've seen your pics, but you're so much hotter in person," Hazel remarked, still running her fingers up and down my side.

Quinn only seemed more confused. "Thanks for the compliment... I think? Who are you?"

"Wouldn't you like to know," she answered before returning her focus to the tickle torture.

"Yeah, that's why I asked," he grumbled.

Elijah and Xavier strolled in a few minutes later, and all the boys talked with each other. I really wanted to be a part of that conversation rather than being tickled to death. Instead, I had to settle for observing while I struggled to escape their clutches.

Had Quinn met the other boys before? If so, how? Had Lina been there, too? So many questions would go unanswered if I couldn't get Shelly and Hazel off of me.

Xavier must've seen the crisis on my face because he walked over, literally picked me up, and carried me away from the tickle demons.

"You looked like you needed a rescue," he said with a smirk.

"I really did. Thank you. It's kinda amazing how much you can see from all the way up here."

He chuckled. "Height does have its advantages. Speaking of which, is there anything you need us to hang up for you since all three of you are vertically challenged?"

"Hey!" Hazel and Shelly simultaneously whined.

"If you weren't holding me up, I'd kick you for that," I threatened.

"And here I thought you were too sweet." He smiled. "Glad to know I was wrong," he added as he put me down.

That has a double meaning. I just know it!

There was no time to wonder about his remarks, though. I still had way too much to do. First, I needed to fuss at the tickle demons. So, I grabbed the napkins I'd dropped, unrolled them, and started whipping them at Hazel and Shelly. They were all giggles as they ran around the table, dodging them.

Done with that task, I shifted back into party-mode. I had the boys finish hanging up the streamers. With their help, the height was much better, but I wasn't gonna admit it to them.

After I popped each of the girls a few times, I went back to setting the table. Slowly, everything came together. Black and red rose petals were scattered down the middle under black electronic candles. Black dinner plates sat on top of the red chargers. In the center of each plate, I placed a long-stem red rose.

As I was admiring our work, Shelly smiled at me and said, "Lane, this really looks great! You did such a good job."

"Yeah! No thanks to you two sex-demons," I grumbled.

"Whatever. You're too damn tense, trying to make this party perfect for your girl—"

Rushing over, I covered her mouth with my hand. Had she absolutely lost her fucking mind? Shelly knew Lina wasn't my girlfriend, but for her to try and tease me about it in front of the fuckables wasn't cool. What if her jokes offended them?

"Are you crazy? You can't say that out loud," I whispered fiercely.

Shelly licked my palm, forcing me to snatch it off of her mouth. "I can't say it out loud, or I shouldn't *say* it at all?" she whispered back.

Wait, wait. Which one did I say?

Shelly snatched my left wrist at the same time that Hazel grabbed my right. Once again teaming up against me, they drug me into my closet.

"You boys can talk amongst yourselves while we get dressed. We'll be back in a jiffy," Shelly announced.

"Did you want us to blow up these balloons?" Xavier asked. He waved the unopened package in the air.

Hazel stopped at the door of the closet and smirked. "That depends. How well do you blow?"

Xavier chuckled and winked before he ripped open the package and dumped out the balloons.

How the hell am I gonna make it through tonight when they all talk like this?

When the girls and I came out of the closet, my living room, kitchen, and dining room were filled with a sea of black and red balloons. The space had really come together, and it looked, well... perfect.

Everything was set. While we were getting dressed, Casper came over and set up all the food. Wynter and Myra were here, too, and they were fucking stunning.

Myra wore a black sleeveless halter top and a matching black miniskirt, while Wynter was in a long, skin-tight red dress with a waist-high slit on each side that showed her beautiful tattooed skin.

I really need to get some tattoos.

As I looked around at the other fuckables, I realized that they were all stunning. Xavier was immaculate in his black slacks and red silk shirt with the sleeves rolled up, also showing off his ink. Elijah wore a black three-piece suit with a red tie. Quinn, though a bit more casual than the rest, wore a red polo shirt and black jeans. It was a simple outfit, but he wore it well. Shelly kept with the theme, too, wearing a cute red maxi dress that fit her curves to a tee. Hazel, the only outlier, wore a blue corset and a long blue skirt to match her hair. She was gonna be true to herself, and she was perfect the way she was.

"So, who's the trick in blue?" Wynter asked.

We're getting started early, I see.

"This trick in blue is Rosey's wife, " Hazel answered cooly.

"Her what?" Five voices all asked at once.

Shelly and I shared a giggle as they looked at each other, trying to figure out if what she'd said was true. Wynter seemed the most shocked, which she deserved since she was being rude.

"You must be joking," Wynter said, glaring at Hazel.

"Oh, but Wyn," Hazel countered as she glared back, "What if I'm not?"

Lina would be here any minute. We didn't have time for a female pissing contest. It had been funny at first, but I was already over it.

Breaking the tension, I clapped my hands to gather everyone's attention.

"Hazel is the best friend, not the wife," I clarified. "But if you still wanna compare your fuckable resumes, she'd beat you since she was the first. Can we get ready for the special guest now, please?"

"And you are?" Wynter pressed.

Does everything you say have to be in that tone?

Smirking, Hazel glanced over at me and a raised brow. She didn't even have to give me that look. I already heard her voice repeating in my head.

Match energies.

So, I took her advice. "There you go, asking too many questions again. I'm the host of this party and the most recent fuckable. K? K. Moving on."

If I have any say in it, I'll be the last one, too.

Hazel beamed with pride, and she did a silent clap. She was clearly impressed, and from the look on Wynter's face, so was she.

I didn't understand why Wynter would be impressed with me, but I was just going to take it and run with it.

"OK. Should we hide or something? I've never really thrown one of these be..."

Just then, Lina walked in and froze in the doorway. She looked around the room before her eyes landed on me. My favorite smile spread across those beautiful lips of hers as she closed the door behind her.

"Looks like you've been a lil' busy, huh Mel?"

"Son of a..."

"Surprise!" Hazel yelled, cutting me off. Then, she tipped her head toward me. "Tell her you're surprised, or she'll somehow blame herself that you weren't."

"Wow, it's like you've known her all your life," Shelly said with a smile.

Damn, am I really that predictable?

Lina greeted everyone, giving out small hugs and a peck on the cheek as she went, but when she made it to me, she gripped my chin and kissed me squarely on the lips.

"I was thoroughly surprised. You guys all look hot," she said to the room. "And you look absolutely gorgeous."

She kissed me on the lips! She didn't kiss them like that. What does that mean? No, no. Focus, Melanie. We still have dinner to get through.

Not lingering on that kiss was the hardest fucking thing I'd ever had to do in my life, and her compliment didn't really help, either.

I thought the little black dress I was wearing was cute, but hearing that compliment filled me with joy.

Lina, of course, looked amazing like always, wearing black skinny jeans and a red button-up with black roses woven on it.

I hadn't even realized I'd stopped moving and talking until Shelly whispered in my ear.

"Remember the party, Lane?"

"Right! Um... The food is already here, so if you're ready to eat, I can make you a plate. Lina, you're the guest of honor, so you're at the head of the table, and everyone else can feel free to sit wherever."

"Where are you going to sit?" Lina asked.

On your lap.

"Um... I-I... I didn't put much thought into it."

"Then, that means you and Hazel will sit by me tonight."

"Oh, OK. Whatever you want. You're the birthday girl, after all."

Internally, I was freaking out. On one hand, I was ecstatic that she wanted me to sit by her, but on the other, I was worried I'd be stepping on someone's toes. They'd all been around longer, so should I really be the one by her side?

I shifted my eyes around, just to see if anyone had any visual objections. To my surprise, no one did, not even Wynter. Xavier and Quinn had turned themselves into waiters, creating a small assembly line and fixing plates for everyone.

"Ooh, I do love being served by gorgeous men," Lina said as she sat down.

"We know you do." Xavier winked.

"Got any evening plans, Luna? I'd love to serve you *more*," Quinn added as he suggestively sucked salad dressing off of his finger.

"If tonight turns into an orgy, I can't participate, but Ima watch every damn second," Hazel said before digging into her food.

Shelly, Myra, and I shared the same expression of shock, but Wynter, Lina, and the boys all laughed.

"For the record, orgies were not included on tonight's menu," I announced.

The entire table laughed again, this time including myself. All the stress I'd felt in the weeks building up to this was gone. It was like we were old friends, and there was no tension at all. It was comfortable.

"Since we're all a bunch of perverts and regular conversation is boring, Rose, I have a question for you," Shelly said, smirking.

Lina chuckled. "I can't imagine anything you ask is gonna be crazier than what Hazel says on the daily, so ask away."

"What's your wildest sex story?"

I choked on my drink and shot a glare at her. What the hell type of question was that, and at a dinner no less?

"Lachelle!" I admonished.

"Melanie!" she countered. "Don't first name me. You wanna know, too."

"And so do I. So please, Rosey, do tell," Hazel said with a smirk.

"What the fuck you mean?" Lina asked Hazel. "I'm positive I told you after it happened."

"Mmm... That's possible, but you have a lot of sex, and what I consider your wildest and what you consider your wildest could be two completely different stories."

"Fair point. Well, the wildest story involves three people only you and Mel know about," Lina said.

Hazel sat and thought for a moment before her face lit up and a gorgeous smile spread across her lips. "You mean drug night?"

"I mean drug night."

"Um, the rest of the table has no idea what you two are talking about. Share the secrets," Shelly eagerly prompted.

I nodded my head in agreement because I was so confused as to who she was talking about. Two, I guessed, would be the twins, but who the hell was the third person?

"So one night, I went up to my tattoo shop to update the tattoo on my forearm, and the tattoo artist's brother came up to the shop to visit at the same time."

"Wait! Tattoo shop? Does this story involve the twins?" Shelly asked.

Lina smiled as confirmation and continued with her story.

"This chick, Lilly, b—"

"I really hate that bitch," I mumbled under my breath.

"Many do. Anyway, she brought me something to drink and told me she would catch me later because we had plans that night. Then, she left, and it was just me and the boys chillin'.

"About thirty minutes later, I started feeling extremely hot and bothered. Now, we all know I'm always horny, but this was something different. I couldn't focus on anything *but* fucking.

Turns out, Lilly had spiked my drink with some goat weed type of bullshit, and that shit had me sexually intoxicated. You can guess what happened next."

"So, you had both of the twins at the same time?" Shelly asked, hanging onto every word.

"I did. *Repeatedly*," Lina said, smirking.

"Oh my God. I just need one day in your sex life. Just one. I honestly don't think I could handle more," Shelly whined.

The table erupted with laughter once again, and everyone else started sharing their stories, which were almost as wild as Lina's. Myra invited us all to her upcoming fall gallery event, and we all enjoyed the dinner. After the meal, we sang "Happy Birthday," cut the cake, then sat around and chilled.

It truly was a perfect night, and now that the dinner was almost over, my mind was focused on the other birthday surprise I'd planned for the next day. I just needed to get all of my pieces together first.

As soon as everyone left, Lina cornered me and tried to *thank* me for the birthday dinner. I dodged every kiss and touch I could, but she didn't make it easy.

I'd thought not lingering on the kiss had been hard. Turns out, I was wrong. Not fucking her, or at the very least, not letting her fuck me was the hardest thing I've ever done.

When she kissed my neck, I almost broke, but I held the moan in and danced away from her, giving her the excuse that I needed to clean up.

"Why are you running from me, Mel?" she asked. "Do you want me to chase you? I don't mind the chase if you don't mind being tied to my bed and ravaged when I catch you."

Why does she have to say things like that to me? She knows it drives me fucking crazy and makes me weak.

Once everything was cleaned off, she attacked me.

Lina picked me up and sat me on the table, scattering the rose petals and candles. I couldn't even catch her hands before they were hiking up my dress and baring me to her hungry gaze.

"You didn't even wrap my present for me," she teased. "Just the way I love it."

"D-don't please. I have something planned for tomorrow, and I want you to wait."

Lina actually pouted, which was fucking adorable, but she nodded her head and pulled my dress back down. With our hormones temporarily in check, we chilled on the couch, watching movies, and then we went to bed.

I'd already told Hazel, Myra, and Wynter my plan, and they had not only agreed to it but were extremely excited for it. Hazel had dropped off the girls earlier so that Lina wouldn't see their cars and we could keep up the charade.

She also picked up a bottle of the goat weed solution that Lina had talked about at dinner. Unlike Lilly, I wasn't going to spike any drinks. Everyone could take it willingly if they wanted to.

I just wanted to see if we could heighten our experience, and I wanted to bring as much pleasure to Lina as I could. Everything was set. The girls and I raided Lina's toy chest and pulled out anal vibrators, dildos, clit vibrators, and the nipple teaser.

Everyone already had their outfits on and looked amazing. Wynter wore a crotchless, lilac lace bodysuit, while Myra had on a blue-lace bra and panty set.

Apparently, the three of them had gotten together and decided I should be the only one to wear red. I didn't agree to it at first, but they insisted, so I caved. While Hazel was at the store, she picked up a red set that had no material to cover any of the important parts, but that was just the way Lina liked it, so I knew exactly why Hazel bought it.

While we were in the kitchen dipping strawberries into chocolate, there was a knock at the door. We were all confused because Lina wouldn't need to knock. I was the only one that hadn't changed yet, so I went to answer.

Lilly was the very last person I expected to see standing there. She looked me up and down before trying to step into the house, but I put my hand up to stop her.

"You shouldn't be here, Lilly."

"First off, don't fucking call me that. And second, what are you, the lil' guard dog? Go yap somewhere else. I'm here to see Rose," Lilly said as she slapped my hand away.

Lilly attempted to push her way through the door again, but this time, Wynter stepped in and blocked her. I guess she didn't care that she was only wearing lingerie because she stood right in the entry, so anyone passing by could see her.

Lilly took in Wynter's body. The two of them shared some similar features, and I promise I wasn't being a bitch when I say this, but Wynter was clearly the upgrade.

"Who the fuck are you?" Lilly repeated.

"The guard dog," Wynter said, cocking her head to the side. "She's the owner of the house." She gestured to me. "And you heard what she said. You shouldn't be here. Get lost, bitch."

"Hey, *Lilly*. I just got off the phone with the security office, and your name has been removed from the approved visitor list. They are on their way to escort you out," Hazel called from the couch as she waved her phone in the air.

"Bye-bye," Wynter taunted before she slammed the door in Lilly's face.

What just happened? I thought Wynter didn't even like me. Not only did she say I was the owner of Lina's house, but she also backed me up. I'd already known I didn't want this woman as an enemy, but I never even dreamed we could possibly be friends.

"Why did you say I was the owner?" I asked, unable to stop myself.

"You live here, don't you?"

"Well... yes. I mean..."

"Melanie, it's clear that you and Ro are going to be together. In a room full of people she's slept with, she only had eyes for you. I'm not going to get in the way of that. I'm just glad I get to hit one more time before she realizes she loves you back and drops the rest of us."

"Wow, Wyn. You're more sensitive than I gave you credit for," Hazel interjected.

"Yeah, yeah. Bite me, Blue."

"How hard?" Hazel taunted.

Wynter smiled back, shook her head, and went back to helping Myra with the strawberries. Hazel stood up from the couch and gave me a hug and kiss.

"You girls have lots of fun *and* orgasms," she said with a grin. "And send me a copy of the footage. I need more inspiration. Talk to you later." She waved at us as she walked out of the door.

Myra came over then and held out a strawberry for me to eat. I bit it and smiled at her. I guess they were both nicer than I'd originally thought.

"You ready?" she asked.

"Yeah, I just need her to get home already."

XXXI

Rose

I wasn't really sure what I was expecting when I walked into the house today, but what I got blew my mind. As soon as I opened the door, there were rose petals spread everywhere.

There was a path of tealight candles leading toward the stairs, and that's exactly where my feet took me. I followed the trail down, right to the playroom.

When I stepped inside, what I saw damn near stopped my fucking heart. Mel, My, and Wyn were all on their knees, surrounded by rose petals. My eyes tried to take everything in, but they continuously landed back on Mel.

The outfit she wore screamed Hazel, but I loved every inch of it. My fingers itched to get her out of it, but I didn't want to ruin Mel's plans. Instead, I took out my phone and snapped a quick pic, then put it down on the dresser.

"All three of my lil' brats on their knees for me. What am I going to do with you?" I asked.

"Whatever you want," Wyn answered as she dragged a finger down Mel's thigh.

Please, let this not be a dream. I will literally never wake up if it is.

"Whatever I want?"

"Any and everything you want," My added, dragging a finger down Mel's other thigh.

"Your wish is our command," Mel said, crawling toward me.

Oh my God! Am I really seeing this right now?

She crawled all the way to my feet, stopped, and looked up at me with a huge smile on her face.

"What do you want to do to us, Lina?" Mel prompted.

"Everything," I whispered.

"Then, do it," she replied.

Placing my hands under her arms, I picked her up and pressed my lips to hers. She wrapped her legs around my waist and deepened the kiss. Someone pulled my hair, making me moan and tearing Mel and me apart.

"You're moving too fast, Ro. We have plans," Wyn informed me before crashing her lips to mine, replacing Mel's

Wyn's kiss was just as intoxicating. I felt like I was losing my mind, but I was extremely curious about these supposed *plans*. Breaking our kiss, I glanced over to see Mel and My kissing while she was still in my arms. That was one hell of a sight I wasn't prepared for, and it was a-fucking-mazing.

"Is this a part of the plan, because if it is, I need more of it!"

They separated and gave me dreamy smiles. My walked over to the nightstand, picked up a cup and a chocolate-covered strawberry, then brought them over to me. She offered me the strawberry first, which I bit haphazardly because Wyn had started kissing Mel's neck.

"Pay attention, Ro," My instructed, holding the cup out to me. "This has goat weed in it, and we would really love it if you drank this."

"I'm guessing you three already did?"

"Maybe," Mel answered with a giggle.

"Well, I sure don't wanna be left out."

Unwrapping her legs from my waist, Mel slid down my body. My handed me the cup, and I quickly downed the contents. After My took the cup, Mel placed her hands on my waist and walked me backward, pushing me into my chair.

"You have to wait until it kicks in before you get to touch," she ordered.

"But... but... It's my birthday, and I don't want to wait," I complained.

Mel leaned in and whispered against my lips, "Be good and wait. We'll make it worth your while."

Nodding, I leaned back into the chair. Myra and Wynter went over to the dresser while Mel sat on the ottoman, facing me. She spread her legs wide open, and I noticed her panties were crotchless. The sight had me jumping out of the chair.

"No, no," Mel said, wagging a finger at me. "You have to wait."

Reluctantly, I sat back down and grumbled. Seeing that much of her body and being unable to touch it was actually pissing me off. Still, I tried to hold on to my patience for her.

Heat slowly began to build up in my body, so I started pulling off my clothes to cool down. It wasn't helping. The heat was here to stay, but I quickly forgot about it when My dropped to her knees in front of Mel.

Wyn sat on the bed behind Mel and attached the teaser's clamps to her nipples. My house could have been burning down around me, and I wouldn't have given one fuck. Nothing was going to distract me from the show.

Wyn turned the teaser on, which made Mel whimper, but she started to moan when Myra moved in, too. My legs bounced because I was so damn anxious, and the fact that I couldn't see everything was going to drive me insane.

"Mel, it's kicked in, and I'm losing my patience."

"Can you wait a lil' longer for me... *Please?*" she breathed.

Oh my God. What is that *voice?*

"Can I at least move the chair so I can see? I'm missing out."

She nodded, and I immediately dragged the chair to the left of them. I could see everything now. Myra was tongue-deep between Mel's legs, and I was extremely jealous. Wyn reached down and spread Mel's lips for My, and I was at a loss for words.

Mel leaned her head back against Wyn's shoulder as she weaved her fingers into My's hair and began to grind against her face. Mel's chest rose and fell quickly. She was so damn close, and the fact that I wasn't giving her that climax myself was pure fucking torture.

When Mel came, the fine thread that was my patience completely snapped, and I pulled My away by her hair and kissed her, lapping up every drop of Mel's cum from her tongue.

Mel's taste went straight to my head. I was desperate for more. After breaking my kiss with My, I dipped my head down between Mel's legs and drank straight from the source.

It wasn't enough. The lust-filled beast inside of me wasn't satisfied, With the goat weed in my system, I couldn't wait any longer. I was *too* hot. I was *too* horny. I was *too* desperate.

"All of you strip and lay on the bed," I commanded.

"Aww, but we still have strawberries to eat," Mel said with a smile.

"I'm about to fuck y'all until your pussies are numb. I don't give a damn about no fuckin' strawberries. Now strip, or I'll tear you out of your clothes."

All three stripped and laid on the bed as I'd asked, Mel in the middle. That sight took me a moment to register. I was really about to fuck three beautiful women all at once for my birthday, and I knew it was all because of her.

So many feelings were running through me. It was overwhelming, but the one emotion I needed to focus on right now was lust. All of them were ready, and I was just standing there in shock.

When I went to the closet to strap up, there was an array of toys already laid out. The girls had clearly been busy. That was just fine because they'd chosen my favorite things.

I used my shirt to carry everything back into the room and placed them on the foot of the bed next to My. Then, I handed a vibrating plug to both My and Wyn. They already knew what to do, so I didn't waste any time telling them.

Mel watched as My and Wyn sucked on the toy before pushing it into their bodies. I repeated what I did to them back on punishment day and gave them each other's remote.

"Do I get one of those, too?" Mel asked.

"Next time. This is your last day of training. Now suck," I said, holding out the trainer to her lips.

She opened her mouth and vigorously licked all around the toy. Once it was wet enough, I slowly slid it into her ass and handed her the remote.

Why wasn't I blessed with more hands?

Now that all the preparations were made, I could get onto the real fun. I lined up my dick with Mel's entrance and then took an additional dick in each hand and lined them up with Wyn's and My's.

Then I told them all, "Lowest setting first."

As soon as I heard the vibrators turn on, I slid into all three of them. Their collective moans shook me to my core. The sounds they made were the sweetest melody, but I needed a crescendo to complete my symphony.

Synching up my strokes inside of all three of them, I increased my pace. Their moans were harmonious and grew in tempo. Maybe I really was more predictable than I thought I was because before I got to tell them to up the setting on their toys, they all did it simultaneously.

Their moans became screams, urging me to go faster. My goal was to have them all cum at once. It was taking everything in me not to focus solely on Mel.

Her heavy-lidded gaze hadn't left mine the entire time, and I felt like that look was a siren song, luring me in so I'd only pay attention to her. I was trying to remain fair and give them all equal amounts of my attention, but then My and Wyn both reached over and opened Mel's legs wider.

It was too much to resist. I temporarily abandoned the dicks inside Wyn and My and renewed my pace with Mel. Her screams filled the room. At some point, the nipple teaser had been removed, and both My and Wyn had taken Mel's breasts in their mouths.

My name became the chorus of the song. It was like someone had pushed the repeat button, especially for Mel. She was so damn close, but it was my hand that she needed in order to crash over the edge. So, I gave it to her.

I rolled my thumb over her clit, and her body trembled in her climax. She looked like she'd forgotten how to breathe for a moment. I leaned down and kissed the breath back into her body.

As she came down from her high, I turned my attention back to My and Wyn. They'd already turned their toys all the way up. It took them mere seconds to cum. My wrists were sore, but I honestly gave no fucks. I'd ice them when this was over, but for now, I was *only* thinking about round two.

"What do you want to do next, Ro?" Wyn asked, panting.

"I want y'all to take turns riding me," I answered as I pulled out of Mel.

"Tongue and dick?" My asked while kissing Mel's shoulder.

"You know it."

"You're gonna get really wet," Mel teased.

"No. I'm going to get drenched!"

XXXII

Rose

The night before still felt like a fucking dream, but I'd lived it. The four of us had enough sex to supply a porn production company with a gold mine. My and Wyn had left only an hour ago, and Mel and I were lounging in the media room.

At some point, the three of them had passed out, and I was left alone to look over the havoc we'd wreaked. It was awesome. Aftercare times three was a fucking lot, though. Not sure if I ever want a repeat of that.

Maybe next time I'll do the last round in the shower, so I won't have to carry each of them to it, one by one. Actually, I realized I'd still have to carry them out, so it would be all for naught.

Arm workout aside, I'd had so much fun, and it was the absolute best birthday I'd ever experienced. All thanks to this sweet and amazing woman with her head on my chest.

I'd already been considering opening up to Mel for a while. Now, I was finding that the pros outweighed the cons. There was still a severe fear of what the outcome of opening up might be, but I was hopeful that it would be positive.

My heart began to pound, and I became fidgety. Mel noticed. She sat up and looked at me. The concern in her eyes helped me find my words, but I still couldn't just come out and tell her, so I came up with a compromise.

"Let's play twenty questions," I suggested.

"Huh?" she asked.

"Play twenty questions with me."

"Where did that come from?"

"I just wanted to play a round with you."

Mel grew quiet as she thought for a moment. Part of me hoped she wouldn't come right out and ask me, but if she did, I was going to get it over with and answer.

"How'd you learn how to fight?" Mel started.

I almost fell off the couch in surprise. The talent she had for asking questions completely different than the ones I'd been ready to answer was amazing.

Gathering myself, I answered, "Rian and Dre taught me."

"Who's Dre?"

"Someone you will *never* meet."

Mel frowned. "Mmk. That's not mysterious at all."

"Next question."

"Is it karate or kung fu?" she pressed.

"They're MMA fighters, so it's a mixture of fighting styles, but Rian called it CQWA."

"And that means?" She raised a brow.

"Close-Quarters-Whoop-Ass." I'd laughed when Rian first came up with the nickname for his fighting style, but it fit.

Mel started to giggle, and I couldn't keep myself from smiling.

"Who is Rian to you?"

That question was unexpected because I thought Hazel had already given her the full run-down, but I never followed up to check. Honestly, I was grateful because it delayed the big question, if only for a few more minutes.

"Like Sai, he was a fuckable from the past."

"Why don't you keep in touch with him like you do Zyriel?"

"You know how magnets have a positive and negative side?"

She nodded gently, urging me to continue.

"We are both the negative, and as fun as it would be to crash against each other, it'd be a disaster in the making."

She accepted the answer and then looked down at her lap. The atmosphere in the room changed suddenly. Mel was quiet for so long that I knew the question was coming. I was as prepared as I could ever be to answer it.

"What happened?" she asked quietly.

I was prepared for her to ask, like I said, and I planned to answer, but still, hearing her say those words froze my heart. My typical defense mechanism was to ignore the question and distract from the uncomfortable feelings the conversation would cause. But I shoved it down. I'd started this by telling her to ask me questions, so I was going to woman-up and tell her the truth.

"So, I like sex. Like, *really* like sex."

Mel nodded, patiently waiting for me to continue.

"Well... um... Ugh. So, I was molested by a family member as a kid."

"Oh my God..." Her voice betrayed her shock but also a hint of pain.

I shrugged. No point in getting upset about something that happened nineteen years ago.

"Yeah, well. He used to sit me in front of his TV in his bedroom and have me watch porn with him. But soon enough, that got old for him, and he started to touch me. I told him I didn't like it and asked him to stop.

"He didn't. He always had some justification as to why it was OK for him to do what he did, that what he was doing wasn't bad. At one point, I just accepted it and let him do what he wanted."

"C-can I ask why?"

I shook my head. "Why? That's simple. I have a younger cousin, and I figured it was better to accept it rather than let him get bored and move on to her."

"Oh, Lina. I'm so sorry."

"Why are you sorry? You didn't do anything."

"N-no. I know, but I jus—"

"I know what you meant. I just hate when people say *sorry* for something they had nothing to do with. The only one who should've been sorry was his pathetic bitch-ass.

"But you wanna know what the best part of the whole situation was? When he did finally say it, I was twenty-five years old. Sixteen years later, he finally gave me a pathetic apology," I bit out.

This is why I hated talking about this shit. The memories were bad, but the anger was worse. I still had so much of it pent up inside of me and hadn't really had an outlet for it.

"S-so, that's what the nightmares are about?" Mel asked, steering me back to the conversation. "About him?"

"Yeah, but only during his birthday month. The other one, the one you woke me up from, was about someone else."

"Wait, you were attacked more than once?!"

"Only twice."

"O-only... twice?"

"Mhm. I had a boyfriend in high school, a kid named Samuel. He was sweet and gentle at first, but he turned out to have D.I.D."

"Isn't that a mental disorder?"

"Yeah. Dissociative Identity Disorder, a.k.a. Multiple Personality Disorder."

"I've heard about it, but it's so rare. It was kind of talked about like it was a myth."

"I *wish* Enzo was a myth," I whispered.

"Who?"

"He was the other personality, the angry one," I sighed.

"Long story short, Enzo wanted to have sex. I wasn't the sex addict I am now back then and wasn't interested.

"I unfortunately thought I had a choice, but I quickly found out that I didn't. A gut punch here, snatched hair there, and I was on the ground with him on top of me. The rest you can guess."

"Lina. I-I'm so s... I-I don't know what to say." Sadness weighed down Mel's features.

"There's nothing to really say, love. It's what happened, simple as that. That was the *last* time anyone had the ability to force me to do something I didn't want. But hey, because of them, I blossomed into a badass nympho, so it's all good," I said, trying to lighten the mood.

"Please don't do that."

"Do what?"

"Minimize your pain. If you don't want to talk about this anymore, that's fine, but don't act like what happened to you isn't tragic and wrong," Mel snapped.

"*Tragic*. That's a bit much, I think. But wrong. Yeah, it was wrong. It's a part of my life, though. They're things I can't change, so I don't get caught up on them. I've moved on."

"The fuck you have."

"What did you just say?"

I didn't like how she'd said that. Her words immediately made my hackle begin to rise, and my defensive walls were going back up. The voice inside of me that wanted to share was screaming at me to calm down, but I couldn't.

"Nothing," she sighed. "Never mind."

"No, don't back down now. Speak your mind." I struggled to suppress my emotions.

"Maybe another time, I think a subject change is in order."

Still, my anger seeped out. "There won't be another time. Once this conversation ends, I'm done talking about it. So, if you got something you wanna get off your chest, do it now."

"Lina I—"

"No, Mel. It's now and only now. No more questions about it after today."

I couldn't talk about this more than once. It couldn't be some drawn-out thing. I just couldn't deal with that, so I meant what I said. Once we were done talking about this, I never wanted to be asked about it again.

"Ugh. Fine." Mel blew out a breath. "You say that you've moved on from it, and you're trying to convince me you're not scared by it. Yet, you have us sleep downstairs because you don't want us to hear you cry out from a nightmare."

"That's no—"

But Mel interrupted. "You set these rules to create the illusion that you don't want us to get too attached because you just want a sex-only situationship. That's partly true, but the real reason is because you think that if we see you like that, it would make you look weak, and that terrifies you."

"OK, that's en—"

"But it doesn't. It makes you human, Lina. Pushing people away is what makes you weak. At the end of the day, we want you to be happy because being with you makes us happy. But we also want to be let in, not shut out."

"What's the point of showing you that, huh?" I snapped. "What do you gain from seeing me in such a pathetic state?"

"Oh my God! It's not pathetic!" Mel answered, her anger rising to match my own. "It shows me that you aren't a heartless, sex-crazed, emotionless person. I want to hold you when you're scared and kiss your tears away when you cry. I want to be there to tell you everything is going to be OK when you're unsure. I want to see that softer side of you."

"Why do you wanna see that so fucking much?" I demanded.

"Because I love you!"

Hearing her speak those words should've made me happy, and on some level, they did, but the traumatized little girl inside of me, the one who had been repeatedly hurt and abandoned, couldn't accept what she was saying.

She doesn't mean it. Crying is weak. Enzo told you crying wouldn't stop him and only made you look pathetic. The real you is too much to deal with, and she'll get bored. You know the truth.

I wanted to say it back to her, but those words kept repeating in my mind. Could Mel be different? Would she stay after she scraped away all of the attitude and feigned confidence? Would she like what she saw when the walls were torn down? I couldn't risk it.

So instead, my walls solidified. "You seem to have it confused, love. I'm fuckable, not loveable."

"What the fuck did you just say?" Mel asked, glaring at me.

"Were you under the impression that this was some kinda romance novel?" I asked as I leaned back against the couch. I knew I should stop, but I couldn't help myself. "It'd take more time than I'm worth to fix me."

The look of shock on her face immediately made me regret my words and broke my heart. The words just kept coming, fueled by the fear that she wouldn't accept the *true* me. It gripped my heart too tightly, and I couldn't go back.

"I never wanted to fix you. I wanted to heal you," she whispered.

"Heal me? Lofty goal, don't you think? Don't waste your time. Just fuck me, Mel. Trust me, it's all I'm worth. What you see is what you get. What's wrong? I got your attention with my attitude. Now you don't like it anymore?"

"I never said I didn't like it. I just... just... I-I just want to love you. *All* of you," she said, her voice breaking.

"Yeah, well this is all you're getting, so be happy I shared. Are you done?"

God, why am I such a fucking bitch?

A tear rolled down Mel's cheek, and as it did, I felt a part of me die. I wanted to take it all back and tell her I loved her too, but I could see it in her eyes. It was too late. I'd hurt her too badly.

"Yeah," she sniffed. "I'm done."

Quickly, Mel wiped the tear away, stood up, and walked out of the media room. Seeing her retreating form killed me. I knew she'd meant it. I knew she loved me, and I loved her. Why couldn't I just say that out loud and trust that she wouldn't leave me?

Don't go.

After all of it, the words I needed to say to get her to stay abandoned me. She was right about everything. Having anyone see me in that state made me feel weak, powerless. Worthless. I absolutely hated to feel that way.

Now, because I was being a stubborn idiot, I'd pushed her too far, driven her away, and there was no telling if she was going to come back.

When I heard my front door slam shut, I raged and flipped my coffee table over, causing everything on top of it to crash to the floor. Yuki, Tsuki, and Kuro ran from the room in a hurry. Shaking,

I sat in the middle of the floor and screamed until my throat felt like it was bleeding.

I know what you want. What you're screaming at me. Go after her, right? I should've. But even though I was prideful, it was my fear that wouldn't let me move. So, I sat there, staring at the mess I'd made while the girl I loved walked right out of my life.

To Be Continued...

Fucking Double Chapter
Rose

L illy wanted to hang out tonight, but honestly, I was a bit weary about it. Lately, she'd been getting clingy. It wasn't the cute kind of clingy, either. It was the full-on aggravating and annoying kind, like a leech. And if I was being honest, I was at my wits end with it.

But I'd still agreed to hang out with her. First, though, I needed to see Sai to update the script tattoo on my forearm.

When I pulled up to the shop, Lilly was already outside. I'd purposely waited until we were face-to-face to tell her I was updating my tattoo because I knew it would annoy her. Since she'd been annoying me, it was only fair that I do the same.

"How many titles do you have to add this time?" she asked, crossing her arms.

"Five," I answered, walking past her and into the shop.

"Damn, girl. How the hell did you find time to write and publish five more books?"

"It's literally what I do. I write. All day, every day."

Sai was in a chair up front, waiting for me. He popped up as soon as he saw me walk in. I rolled my eyes when he smiled. I'd already been bitching to him about Lilly's clinginess, but he had no sympathy for me.

You slept with her after I told you not to. Don't come whining to me because she annoys you.

The fucker is supposed to be my friend, and yet, he liked to throw my error in judgment in my face rather than let me gripe about it.

Dick.

Sai came over and tried to kiss me, but I dodged him. The only response he got for his feigned wounded look was me sticking my tongue out at him. If he wasn't going to humor my bullshit, then he would get no kisses.

Lilly trailed behind us as we headed back to his studio. While we walked, I couldn't help but notice what she was wearing. Her black leggings hugged her body beautifully and her black tank with a deep V-neck collar displayed her breasts.

I shook my head. Even if I truly wanted to get rid of her, she wasn't going to make it easy. I swear, I could be such a guy sometimes. My head was annoyed with her, but my hormones said: *Fuck all that being annoyed shit. I'm horny.*

As Sai applied the stencil, I was temporarily distracted, focused on watching him. Lilly lingered in the studio's doorway, and my eyes continued to stray over to her. Suddenly, she jumped like she'd been zapped and quickly left the room. I didn't know what the fuck was up with her, but I didn't pay it too much mind.

A few minutes later, Rian walked in, completely shocking me because he didn't usually visit the shop. Even with all the badass energy he gave off, he was afraid of needles, so he'd yet to get any tattoos.

Either way, I already knew what he would look like since Sai had two full sleeves, a chest panel, and tattoos on his upper back. Still, I really wanted to figure out how we could get Rian past his fear. He needed some ink on that caramel skin of his.

Most people could almost forget they were twins until they were in the same room. Then, it was a mind-fuck trying to tell them apart. I never had that issue, and it wasn't because Rian refused to wear his glasses, even when he needed them. It was because I'd been sleeping with both of them for over a year and could tell them apart, intimately.

Seeing them together like that gave me some great inspiration for a spicy scene, and it got me wondering why I'd never tried to sleep with them both simultaneously.

Rian headed straight for me, gripped my chin, and gave me a heated kiss. He swallowed my moan before breaking away and pulling back.

"That's not fair, Star! How come he gets to kiss you when I don't?"

"Did you not just see what happened? He didn't ask for a kiss. He took it," I said, rolling my eyes.

"Fair point," Sai agreed, pulling my hair and crashing his mouth against mine.

His kiss was just as heated, but he took it a step further, sucking my bottom lip into his mouth and biting it. Now, I was really wondering how the hell I'd never slept with them both at the same time.

I needed to start trying to figure out how to make that happen in the near future. Sai placed one more small peck on my lips before he went back to applying the rest of the stencil.

Lilly walked back in a moment later and offered me a drink. I didn't give it a second thought, thanked her, and drank it. (Never, ever take drinks from crazy chicks.) She waited until the cup was empty, kissed my cheek, and told me she would come over later.

At first, I thought that was just too easy. I'd expected way more whining about her having to wait until I was done. But then, she left the studio and never returned. I was stunned.

A half-hour later, Sai was finishing up the second title when a surge of heat flooded my veins. All I had on was a pair of shorts, a tank top, and a sports bra, but I felt like I was wearing two winter jackets. I was so fucking hot!

"Oh my God!"

"What's wrong?" Sai asked as he finished the last line.

My heart pounded in my heaving chest. The heat was driving me crazy, but what was wilder than the heat was the fact that I was *drenched*. Don't get me wrong, I was in a room alone with two gorgeous men I fully enjoyed fucking, but I'd never been wet like that before, especially unprovoked.

Rian smelled my desire first. His eyes burned like fresh embers as he sat up in the waiting chair. Sai stopped tattooing, probably because he could smell me, too. I had no earthly idea what the fuck was going on, and I couldn't figure out how to stop it.

"What are you thinking about, Moon?"

"Nothing!" I swore. "I wasn't having any lewd thoughts. At least not right now, but thirty minutes ago, I was!"

"And what were you thinking about thirty minutes ago, Star?" Sai pressed as he put his tattoo gun down on the tray.

"I'm not saying. If I do, whatever the fuck is happening to me might get worse," I panted. The heat continued to build.

I gripped the top of my shirt and pulled it away from my chest so I could fan myself with my free hand while Sai cleaned up my arm and wrapped the new ink. Every usual desire I had to be touched was quadrupled, and I couldn't focus my thoughts on anything other than being fucked.

Rian, still sitting across the room, stared at me curiously. The eight steps it would take to get to him were too much, so I spun around and savagely kissed Sai instead.

"What the fuck?" I heard Rian ask, but I paid him no mind. I was too focused on the added heat of Sai's hands as they pulled me from the tattoo chair and into his lap. I was completely frantic, kissing a path from his lips to his neck. When I bit him, the growl that reached my ears fueled my lust-filled frenzy.

"Really, Zyriel?" Rian asked. "She's clearly on something."

Sai turned his head to address Rian and ended up giving me more access to his neck. I happily bit him again, drawing a groan from him before he snatched my dreads and tugged me away.

"First, have you ever known her take anything stronger than a Tylenol? And even that's rare. Second, what the fuck do you want me to do? She's practically tearing me out of my clothes right now," Sai exclaimed as I unbuttoned his shirt.

"What the fuck did that chick give her?" Rian demanded.

"The hell if I know, but if it makes people crazy like this, I kinda want some."

Out of the corner of my eye, I saw Rian leave the room, and that made me sad. The sadness was temporary, though, because Sai distracted me by rolling his tongue in circles on my neck.

Every one of my nerves were so fucking sensitive. The small swipes had me so deliriously close to the edge that I couldn't fucking breathe. His tongue left my skin, making me whimper, desperate for the contact again.

Seconds later, I opened my eyes to see Rian with his hand on Sai's shoulder. He'd pulled us apart to show Sai the small bottle in his hand. I didn't give a fuck about whatever the hell the bottle was. I needed hands on me. Everywhere. In every place.

"Fuck me."

"Wait, Moon. I think that chick spiked your drink with a mood enhancer," Rian explained, trying to show me the bottle again.

I snatched the bottle from him, threw it toward the garbage can by the entrance to the studio, and aced the shot. Rian's gaze flicked from the garbage can back to me. The look in his eyes screamed that he was conflicted, as though he wanted to fuck me but wasn't sure if he should.

The decision was easy. Since he was having such a hard time making it, I was going to do it for him. He always had a pocket knife on him, and today was no exception.

I grabbed it from his pants, flipped it open, pulled his shirt away from his body, and sliced through it with one swing. Rian stepped back, fearing that I would nick his neck, but my aim was precise. His shirt fell open. He was mark-less.

"Girl what the f—"

"Fuck. Me," I repeated, cutting him off. "I want you to fuck me. I need you to fuck me. Right here. Right now. Both of you. *Please*."

Sai and Rian shared a look with each other as if they *still* couldn't come to terms with what I was asking. They were taking far too fucking long to come to a consensus, and I was out of my mind with lust.

So, I slid off of Sai's lap, dropped to my knees in front of Rian, made quick work of undoing his pants, and sucked him into my mouth. Even if his mind was still unsure, his body wasn't.

His dick hardened as I took him deeper down my throat. His fingers tangled in my dreads a moment later as he worked it in and out of my mouth. Finally, I had a small piece of what I craved.

But the intoxicating fire burning through me was an inferno, and giving him head was like that last drop of water that falls from an upturned canteen in the middle of the desert.

It satisfied nothing, and I was starting to get desperate. After another long suck, I removed Rian from my mouth and looked back at Sai. He was naked and finally ready to give me what I needed.

"I don't know how I feel about seeing you naked," Rian griped at his brother.

"Seeing you ain't on the top of my list either, but she's clearly not gonna stop until we fuck her. So, when in Rome, I guess." Sai shrugged.

Their words were meaningless to me. I had a hand wrapped around both boys, and that's what held my focus. Switching back and forth from Rian to Sai, I pumped them down my throat until I was dizzy.

I guess Rian decided to join in because he picked me up and carried me out of the studio. The shop was closed and empty (not that I would've given a fuck if it wasn't) but I don't think seeing two men with their dicks out was good for business.

Sai had a daybed in the back where he crashed if he'd had a long session and didn't feel like driving home. Rian tossed me onto the bed, and Sai moved in, pulling my shirt and bra off.

As soon as my breasts were free, Sai grabbed them, pressed them together, and sucked my nipples into his mouth. My moan filled the room. Finally, I felt the pleasure I was yearning for.

Then, Rian pulled my shorts off and ran his fingers through my slit. I was so fucking sensitive that I came right after his thumb brushed against my clit. Tremors rocked me so hard, I'm sure it looked like I was seizing.

"Did you really just cum? I barely touched you," Rian inquired.

"Yes! Now, do it again," I begged.

"Well," Sai said as he laid down on the bed and hooked his finger. "If you want it so bad, come get it."

He didn't have to tell me twice! Eagerly, I climbed on top of him, grabbed his dick, lined it up, and impaled myself. Every single thick inch of him was sublime, and I was in paradise.

I started wildly riding him and granted myself another magnificent orgasm. The bliss raced through my entire body, but I was still hungry for more. Before I even got a chance to turn and look for Rian, I felt his dick probing my ass.

About damn time!

I leaned forward, reached back, and pulled my cheeks apart for him. He slid in roughly, and I loved it. I was so unbelievably full. It was pure bliss. Then, Rian started up a merciless pace while Sai bit and sucked my nipples.

I would deal with Lilly later, but I was so fucking happy right then. I would eagerly drink whatever she gave me again if it meant I was going to be fucked like this.

Rian and Sai gave me four more orgasms before the heat began to recede, but they obviously weren't finished with me. Sai pushed me back so he could sit up. They were both stroking inside of me, and I was getting closer and closer to heaven every second.

"If you keep this up, Moon, we're going to bust inside of you."

"Do it! Cum. Both of you. Fill me up and spill every drop of your cum inside of me. I want it! I want every fucking bit of it!"

Each boy kissed opposite sides of my neck, then bit me at the same time. I wasn't expecting the shock of being bitten, but I reveled in it. That last climax was absolutely mind-numbing.

I laid on top of Sai's chest with Rian pressed against my back. Our hearts pounded in our chests as their warmth leaked out of me. That was wilder than I'd ever imagined, and my wild half wanted to go again.

There was no way... at least not yet. But after some rest, a massage, and a warm bath, I was most definitely down for round two!

"Are you better now, Star?"

"Only a little. Give me about an hour, and I'll be ready for more."

"You can't be serious!" Rian whispered as he kissed my shoulder.

"You know I am! Take me home, boys. We have so much more fucking to do!"

Acknowledgments

Oh, who to thank? There are so many!

Thank you to my ARC readers from book one! You guys really helped me stay strong and keep going because even after the book was published, I still didn't feel like I was good enough! You proved me wrong.

Thank you to my word wizard and bestie, Sam! You are the reason this book is an extra level of amazing! You polished her up beautifully!

Thank you to my besties: Evie, Sarah, Alexandria, Shelly, Chassie, Natoshia, Jessica, Cyn, Amna, Stephanie, Tanya, Jen, Desi, and so many more! You guys made sure I never stopped and always felt worthy enough to be called a published author.

Thank you to my mother, father, grandparents, aunts, uncles, and cousins who supported me and purchased my book! I know some of you won't read it because it may traumatize you, but I am just happy you wanted to support me!

Thank you to myself for letting people fill up my confidence meter and continuing to write, even when I thought it would be better to stop.

Thank you to all of the readers who took a chance on my book and supported me, whether it was through helping me maintain a 1,000 page read goal every month on KDP, by purchasing the eBook from Amazon, or by purchasing a physical copy from me!

Each and every one of you is the reason why I keep going everyday, and I just wanted to say... Well... Thank you!

Also by

New to Kitty? Make sure to check out the book that started it all! Pick up *Lust Drunk Nights,* the first book in The Kiss & Tell Trilogy, today! Find out how Rose meets Mel and see how both of their lives are changed for the better.

Scan Here To Grab Your Copy Today!

About the author

Kitty N. Pawell is a wild creative that hails from Detroit, Michigan. She was a girl with a simple dream, to become a published author. That dream has now been achieved. Kitty enjoys writing, reading, and binging anime shows, as well as devouring manga. If there isn't a pen in her hand, she's in her craft room creating something pretty awesome. Her inspiration for her books comes from real life experiences and wild dreams, so expect great things from her in the future.

Website: kittyscreativeemporium.com

Social media handles: @kittynpawell